PAUL
FRITZE

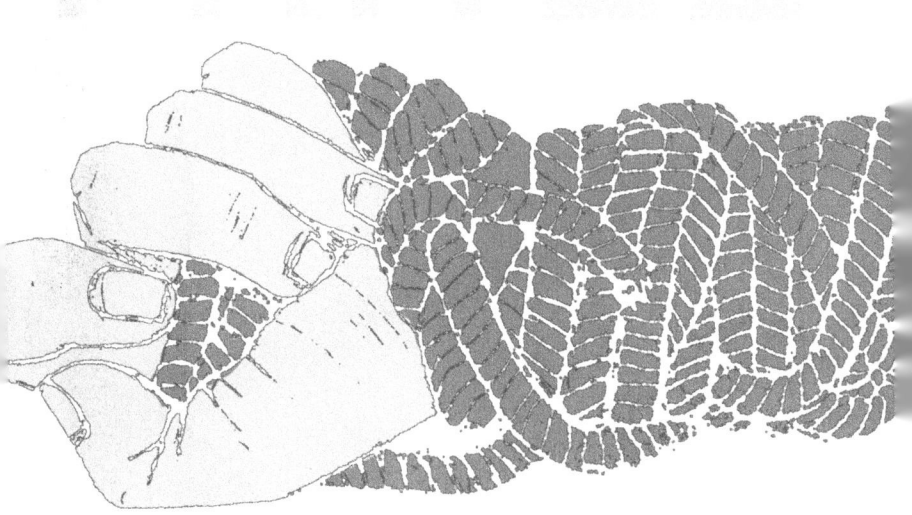

FALSE
GUILT

FALSE GUILT

Peter Fritze

Copyright © 2015 Peter Fritze

This book is a work of fiction. Names, characters, places, and incidents either are products of the author's imagination or are used fictitiously. Any resemblance to actual events or locales or persons, living or dead, is entirely coincidental.

All rights reserved, including the right to reproduce the book or portions thereof in any form whatsoever.

This book uses Canadian spelling.
Parental guidance is advised.

ISBN 978-0-9937025-4-9 (book)

ISBN 978-0-9937025-6-3 (ebook)

TORONTO, CANADA

May 7, 1998

1

"Tell me this," the man across from Paul Tews said. "What the *hell* is wrong with my son?"

Fifteen minutes earlier, moving a tray along a railing in front of a Greek fast-food place, Paul had heard his name. He'd been flattered that the President of Pan Canadian Securities asked to join him for lunch. Now he understood why. His question was a fair one.

The man's eyes, sunken in a drawn and pallid face and washed out like the dying edge of a watercolour, bore into Paul. Overhead light reflected off his scalp. He wore a tailored dark suit, the jacket square over a stiff shirt and impeccably knotted tie. Other patrons of the Royal Bank Plaza food court teemed around their metal table and chairs.

"I mean, Paul, I bet you know Art better than me. How many years did you live with him and those other undergrad friends on Robert Street?"

Paul's food started tasting like cardboard. "Art found the place in second year in '92. Asked Louis, Mark and Lee to join him. They had an extra room that I took in third year."

"Art wanted Kate in that room, didn't he? Except she must have felt uncomfortable. Even by today's standards. Being with four guys."

A smile crept across Paul's face. "She was two years older than everyone else and at least ten years older emotionally. We were very immature. Except maybe Art."

"Art? Mature? I wouldn't know. I only see my son when he wants money."

Paul was surprised. "Very controlled and confident. Really good at what he does."

"He was born lucky. I mean, good family, despite the divorce. Got his mother's looks. And some gifts from both sides." An unkind summary, Paul thought. "And now he ends up like this." Art's father glanced at the crowd, sighed, then looked back at Paul with a hopeful smile. "So you're at Collins, Shaw for the summer. When did you start?"

"Monday."

"Ah, only your fourth day. Too early to say if you like it."

Paul laughed. "What I know is that I'm completely lost. There's an unbelievable amount to learn."

"Doesn't surprise me, you in law school. We only met a few times but you struck me as very insightful and motivated. Your father must be proud."

"He died when I was eighteen. Pretty sure my mother is, though."

"And when do you finish?"

"One more year," Paul said, starting to relax. "April '99, there's going to be one hell of a party."

Art's father laughed. "Collins, Shaw is a good firm. We used to do a lot of work with them but we hired in-house. I mean, Bay Street lawyers are just getting too expensive, if you don't mind me saying."

"I don't," Paul said. "I don't even know if I want to work downtown."

Sighing once more and pushing his half-eaten plate of food away, Art's father said, "Paul, I'm a tough guy. I've stared down every problem I've faced. But I don't know what to do with Art. Do you have any ideas? What I *do* with him?"

Though only twenty-five, Paul recognized a powerful man beaten down. "I think Art will be fine," he said. "He usually makes life work for him."

Art's father leaned in. "I know about the cocaine. I mean, I've paid for it, haven't I?"

Paul pushed a hand through his wavy brown hair and tugged at an ear. "In part, anyway."

"That bad?"

"It got worse when he went to L.A." Paul wondered how much Art's father knew about his son's experiences there.

"And when did it start?"

Paul shrugged. "I don't know too many details."

"Paul, please."

Sucking in a breath, Paul said, "Another guy at Robert Street introduced him. About the time I got there."

Art's father took a few seconds to absorb the news. "When he was in L.A.," he said, "the requests for money came faster and faster. For a long time, I sent him whatever he wanted. Then I made a few calls and figured things out. After that, I stuck to a monthly allowance, even if he complained, and then, when he came back last November, I cut him off and told him to get a job. *And* I told him if he keeps using cocaine I'll write him out of my will."

Paul's face flushed and he looked away. "If it makes you feel any better, I know he tried reducing it recently." He shot a hesitant glance across the table. "Anyway, he's a brilliant guy. I meant it when I said he'll get things working for him."

"I don't see *him* going to law school," Art's father said, snorting. "And he's a failed actor as far as I can tell. I mean, right now, he pours people coffee for a living."

Paul was at a loss. The lunchtime din suffused the pause in their conversation. Finally, Art's father said, "Sometimes, Paul, sometimes I ask myself which one of us will die first."

Another fair question, Paul thought.

2

Like a painting blackened by decades of soot, the nineteenth-century prosperity at Queen and Bathurst Streets had become obscured. At a colonnaded red brick building on the northwest corner, the inscription "The Canadian Bank of Commerce" was streaked with grime, and the front steps were littered with cigarette butts from lonely souls waiting every evening for a folding cot inside. Across Bathurst, dented aluminum siding covered the first floor of a hundred-year-old warehouse. And diagonally across Queen, the owners of a heavy metal club, Hammer, had painted the brown and yellow brick building purple.

On Wolsley Court, the first parallel street north of Queen, drug dealing was pervasive and prices for beaten-down houses were low. Italian families who'd made Wolsley their home a generation back were selling to immigrants from Hong Kong. The Chens had arrived in Toronto five years earlier, and three years later, they had scraped together a down payment for one of the smallest houses. Anxious for income to offset mortgage payments, they rented Paul the basement apartment, setting aside misgivings about his gender when they heard he was a law student.

The previous owners had constructed the apartment by renovating the basement and building steep stairs from the back alleyway. The bathroom and bedroom were separated from the kitchenette and squashed living area by a flimsy centre wall. Before Paul moved in, Mr. Chen had refreshed the rooms with a thin layer of robin's egg-blue paint.

In the kitchenette, Paul washed dishes, reliving his first Thursday at Collins, Shaw. Across the room, light snuck through the grated ground level window and lay in bars across a tired couch. Post-grunge played through the tinny speakers of a stereo on the floor next to a worn swivel chair. On a coffee table, legal texts were stacked in order of size.

The drumming of shower water came to a hard stop. A few minutes later, as Paul doused suds over the last dish in the sink, a plate encrusted with spaghetti sauce, Art walked past him into the living area. He wore the same jeans he'd arrived in but had stolen one of Paul's shirts. It strained across his broad shoulders and was halfway buttoned up. He rubbed his thick auburn hair with a towel then flopped onto the couch, kicking up his bare feet and letting the sodden towel fall into a heap on the ground.

Paul had found Art unannounced in the alleyway behind Wolsley, ragged from his shift at the coffee shop. He wondered how the others would react when he arrived with Art in tow. Would they really suggest Paul should have told Art he couldn't have a bite to eat, a shower and their company that evening?

"Fucking landlords," Art said. His hands moved about, unable to find rest.

Paul had already heard the complaint. "How late is your rent, exactly?"

"Three months."

Paul looked up at Art, still working the plate. "You've only been there for five." Odd how embarrassed he felt for Art, he thought.

"They're not supposed to do that, I read somewhere. You're a lawyer, man. You should know about that."

"I'm not a lawyer yet and I have no interest in residential tenancy law. Pay him." An embarrassment that made him irritable.

"What, when he locked me out?"

"For Christ's sake, pay him."

"I don't have the money."

"You're the one that always says 'Life is what you make it.' So make the rent."

"I will," Art said, shrugging. His eyes darted around the room. "Can I stay till Monday? That'll give me time to ask my old man for some money."

"One night. Mr. Chen will complain."

"What a great bunch of friends."

Wiping the plate dry with a kitchen towel and laying it on the counter, Paul tried to stare Art down. "You're joking, right?"

"Kate kicked me out last night. Now you."

"I said you could stay the night."

"I can't believe Kate did that. And didn't lend me any money either. Her problem is jealousy."

Shaking his head, Paul spread the towel over the oven handle. He walked into the living area and fell into the swivel chair. Art sat up, and knees bouncing, he leaned forward and turned off the stereo.

"I was listening to that," Paul said.

Art batted a hand at the stereo. "That stuff's shit. In L.A., it's all rap and hip-hop."

"Look around you. Does this look remotely like L.A.?"

"Kate has *serious* jealousy issues. She can be such a bitch."

"Art, you *make* her jealous. You're always putting yourself out there, right in front of her."

"Haven't done that in a long time. And she does the same to me."

"That's crap. You still do it and I've never seen her do it."

"I don't know why you're defending her," Art said, casting a surly glare. His knees bounced harder. "Anyway, you'd think she'd let me stay at her place till Monday. Ragged me the whole time last evening. *One* night I asked to stay and she couldn't do that. Jealous bitch."

"Pay the landlord."

"How much do you think a barista makes?" Art asked. "And technically, my old man cut me off. It won't be easy to get the cash from him."

"I heard."

"What?"

A black phone on the floor rang. Paul leaned over and picked up the receiver. Louis sounded excited. "The Salty Dog?" Paul said. "What script? … Okay. Art's coming, too. … Yes, he is. I'll explain later. Around eight thirty? … Yes, okay." He returned the receiver.

"What are you going to explain?" Art asked.

Paul ignored the question. "Let's go," he said.

"I have an errand to run."

"Can't it wait?"

"Relax. It won't take long. Can I borrow a jacket or something?"

A few minutes later, Paul followed Art up the steps to the alleyway. The early May air was cold and damp. Both shivered under windbreakers and pushed hands into pants pockets. A hundred yards down, two men interrupted a huddled conversation. Inhaling from cigarettes, they eyed Paul and Art walking away.

It was eight fifteen and thick clouds hung low in the fading light. At Queen, Art crossed in front of a blaring streetcar and into a sea of skins waiting for Hammer's Thursday show. Paul barely kept pace, throwing a wave of appreciation at the streetcar driver.

They crossed and headed south on Bathurst. Art, his back straight, chest out and angular jaw set hard below his aquiline nose, said nothing. Matching strides alongside, Paul felt inadequate, though at six feet he was only two inches shorter. A cute blonde, maybe nineteen, snug in black leather, walked toward them. She offered Art an oblique smile but he didn't notice.

At Richmond Street, Art pointed west, returned his hand to his pocket and took the north side. Paul hung close, almost in a jog. A modern commercial building emerged on the right, across from a 1970s low-rise school surrounded by an asphalt play yard. A few feet beyond the building, Art stopped under a budding ash and looked across the street.

He focussed on a two-storey Victorian. Rotten gabling hung along the bottom of the roof and hunks of peeling white paint revealed red brick underneath. Art took his hands out of his pockets and rubbed them together. "Come on," he said and bolted across the street.

"Who lives here?" Paul asked, catching up on the other side and feeling uneasy.

"A friend," Art said with a quarter-turn of his head.

They darted around a half-open wrought iron gate. Art pressed the front door buzzer then turned around and surveyed Richmond. Paul hung back. Inside the house, a man and woman shouted at each other. Nobody showed. After a few seconds, Art rapped on the door.

Feet thumped inside the house over squeaky hardwood. The door opened a crack, revealing half an unshaven face beneath thick, tousled black hair.

"What are you doing here?" the man asked Art. "You know to call first."

Art eyed him. "I need your help, Tony," he said. "You know what I mean."

"Do you know how much you owe me?" the man asked, exposing more of his face. "And who the fuck is this?"

Paul's tension leapt, and looking between Art and the man, he stepped back another foot.

"He's okay," Art said. "He's a friend."

"Do I really need to be here?" Paul asked Art.

"I don't care if he's Gandhi," the man said. "You don't bring people here."

After shoving a hand in a pocket, Art withdrew a clenched fist. He let it hang at his thigh for several seconds then curled it open. Folded bills lay thick in his palm. "I got paid today, Tony."

The man opened the door enough to show all his face. His lips pressed together as he assessed the contents in Art's hand. "That's nowhere close to ten thousand."

Art exhaled hard. "Seriously, Tony. It's a down payment." The man stood still, looking unconvinced. "Tony, I *need* some blow."

"Fuck, Art, I thought you were done with this," Paul said, turning away. "I'm going. Meet us at The Salty Dog."

"You do that," the man said to Paul, who'd already cleared the gate. With a sigh, the man relaxed his lips. "Come inside, movie star," he added. "Let's see what you got there."

3

The Salty Dog had been their favourite pub since second-year university. On Queen west of Bathurst, its tables and chairs had been kicked around, the beer was cheap and students without pretensions were welcome.

Paul snapped open the front door and edged in behind a group of cackling girls. He raised himself on his toes and scouted for his friends. At a table in the back left corner, Louis's moustache worked hard in animated conversation. His shock of straw-blond hair and stocky build added ten years to his twenty-five.

Paul thrust his way through gusts of perfume and a sea of patrons at the bar to the table. Slipping off his chair at the near end, Louis shook Paul's hand. Lee and Mark, seated along a long wall, smiled, while Cyril, slumped in the corner at the other end, nodded. Paul took off his windbreaker and sat across from Mark. "Whose idea was this?" he asked.

"This guy's," Louis said, throwing a thumb at Mark. "He's got some big secret to tell us. But *I*, I have something much more interesting." In front of him was a bound document. "My script is done. The follow-up to *A Cannibal's Eyes* and *Rot-A-Tot-Tot*. Cyril helped, too."

"I don't know about a secret," Mark said. Scanning the pub, he removed his glasses from his broad face and cleaned them below the table with a corner of his shirt.

Cyril, scrawny with a narrow, stubbly face and matted dark hair, leaned out the pub corner to avoid an elbow. "I told you," he said to Louis, "that script's not ready yet."

"It's just for Paul's comments," Louis said. "He got his short story in the *Acta Victoriana*, didn't he?"

Paul reached for the script. "*Robert Street Rage*. Oh, you didn't, did you, Louis?"

A huge grin lifted Louis's moustache. "I did. Just a working title, though. I'm also thinking of *Robert Street Rampage*. Or maybe just *Robert Street*. With the right graphics, that's got horror written all over it."

"Where's Art?" Lee asked. He tensed and squeezed a bicep, assessing the impact of diligent weightlifting on his small frame.

"He's coming—I think," Paul said. He flipped open the first few pages of the script and found a summary. "And I see you're using real names."

"Until I think of something better," Louis said.

"*Eight students—two women and six men—share a large Victorian mansion in a small New Hampshire college town.*

Kate: Kind, caring, amorous.

Grace: Beautiful, elegant, canny.

Louis: Intelligent, creative, a visionary.

Art: Handsome, artistic, a bon vivant.

Cyril: Thoughtful, innovative, loyal.

Mark: Brawny, tough, savvy.

Lee: A spark plug, whip smart, good-hearted.

Paul: Fetching, gifted, reliable.

They're as close as a family, supporting each other at every turn. And they need to be, because, one by one, they're being cut down by a serial killer who's on the loose.

And in the family."

"Guess who did it," Louis said to Paul.

"Obviously Art."

Louis's grin redoubled. "You got it."

"And Grace is—?"

"The Foxy Lady, of course," Cyril said. "I'm surprised you had to ask."

"I figured as much," Paul said.

A young woman with a stiff smile arrived to take their order.

"Read it, Paul," Louis said, his voice booming over the pub's din. "It's goddamn brilliant." He turned to look at the server. "We've been waiting for you."

"Sorry, it's been really busy," she said, reaching into her apron for a pen and pad.

"We all like Asian girls like you, but especially him," Louis added, this time throwing a thumb at Lee. "He's *very* interested in giving you his order."

After one look at Lee's absurdly wide grin and reddening sallow skin, the server's smile faded. "Sorry, I'm taken. What are you boys going to have?"

"Actually, I'm taken, too," Louis said, curling his moustache, "but she doesn't know that yet. So, you know—"

The server lost her smile completely and gave Louis an icy glare. "Look, like I said, it's busy."

"We'll all have a Canadian," Paul said.

The server turned and left. Cyril sat forward and leaned both elbows on the table. "The Foxy Lady, again," he said to Louis. "Are you going to grow out of your junior high crush some day? It's old and it's embarrassing."

Louis laughed. "Never. Right, Paul? Never."

Paul, feeling a cut of anguish and worried his friends would see him blush, looked away. "She's all yours, Louis."

"I'm trying to convince her to act in this film," Louis went on.

"She won't be right," Cyril said. "No character."

"Cyril, you're a great assistant producer but I've still got say over casting. She's got plenty of character. The 'still waters run deep' kind. Hell, she *is* this role."

"Yeah, yeah," Cyril said, shaking his head.

"Is Art coming or what?" Lee asked after several seconds, looking at Paul, hanging on to his absurd grin.

"I already told you. I think so," Paul replied. The server arrived with five beers. Avoiding eye contact, she set them on the table. "He's a train wreck," Paul added, taking a gulp from the closest bottle. "His landlord kicked him out. No place to stay."

"What the hell's happening to him?" Mark said. "If ever a guy had everything going for him."

Paul eyed Lee. "What do you care if Art shows?"

"He owes me money. And I need it for my business. I lent him *a lot* in L.A."

"How much?" Paul asked.

Lee looked away, his grin cratering. "Ten grand."

"Whoa," Mark said.

"Ten grand," Paul said, trying to fathom. Then he shrugged. "Get in line, I guess."

"What do you mean?" Lee asked. Everyone leaned in as Paul recounted his visit to Art's dealer. All remnants of Lee's smile vanished. "I need that money," he said. "My little data management company can make it. My parents even stopped reminding me of med school all the time."

"If you ask me, it's because things are catching up with him," Louis said after a long sip. "Sorry, but that guy can't be trusted."

"Let that one go, too, Louis," Cyril said. "He screwed Dagger Films. Very old news."

"Do you know how many other computer engineers are out there looking for money?" Lee asked, looking around the table. "What am I going to do?"

"I'm *not* letting it go," Louis said to Cyril. "I made him with *A Cannibal's Eyes*."

"It was obvious he was going to let us down on *Rot-A-Tot-Tot*," Cyril said. "Still think that's a stupid title."

"*Obvious?* He *promised* to work it. The next goddamn thing you know, he thinks he's a big deal in L.A."

"He got an agent, Louis," Mark said, "who did his best for him. What the hell? From your perspective, he's gotten what's coming to him. He's not even in the game anymore."

"His old man got him the agent," Louis said. "And if there's one thing you should have learned in law school, it's that a promise is a promise." He lifted his beer toward his lips then tipped the bottle toward the pub entrance. "Speaking of the serial killer," he added, and without averting his eyes, he gulped down the rest of his beer.

4

Art had forced his way through a crowd at the front of the The Salty Dog. He nodded at the group then walked toward them, his stride still assured but more relaxed. A nearby table of young women broke their conversation. Pushing pouty lips down straws, they watched him arrive.

Art took the remaining free seat across from Lee. Everyone paused for him to speak but instead he looked around the pub, dragging a wrist under his nose, wiping away stray mucous.

"Hey, Art," Lee finally said, smiling. "How's it going?"

"Great," Art said. "I need a beer."

Paul signalled the server. Art finally offered the table his attention. He looked at Mark, then Cyril, and smiling thinly, said, "Jock man. Little man." Both looked away and returned to their drinks.

"Look at those pupils," Louis said. "I'm surprised you can see in here."

Art glanced at Louis. "I'm doing just fine, man. Just fine."

"That's not what I'm hearing," Louis said, staring.

"What are you hearing, exactly?"

"That maybe you should be working on my second film after all."

Cyril rolled his eyes. "Oh, for Christ's sake," Paul said.

Art tilted toward Louis. "Still on that, are you, man?"

"I have a name," Louis said.

"You make life work for you, Louis. Take advantage when you can."

The server arrived with Art's beer. "Who's this for?"

"Me," Art said, catching her eye. She smiled at him before slipping to the next table.

"Sorry, but you mean ignore your obligations," Louis said, continuing his stare.

"Be serious. Nothing was in writing."

"This issue is more than two years old," Paul said.

"Let it *go*, Louis," Cyril added.

"Cheers to you, little man," Art said.

Louis's moustache kinked. "It's called trust."

Art took a long slug of beer then said, "It's called *opportunity*. And I had it."

"Your old man found it for you. And sorry, how'd that work out for you?"

"My *agent* got me that work. You're just pissed that I had parts in two major films with people you could only dream of working with."

"Bit parts. And you ended up in gay porn, as I recall."

"It was not *gay*."

"You were fucking women *and* men, Art—in the *same* movies," Louis boomed. The nearby table of women stopped talking again and exchanged looks. "For your little habit."

"Louis, enough," Paul said.

"Why don't you pay attention to your little assistant producer down there?" Art said, re-acquiring his thin smile. "If you want to know about habits."

"I'll pay attention to whatever I want," Louis said, straightening his back, his moustache quivering.

"*Enough*," Paul said.

A pear-shaped man with a tag "Your Manager - Trevor" appeared. "Everything okay, guys?" he asked. "More beers?"

"Another round," Paul said.

"Sure," the manager said, signalling the order to the bar. "Just to let you know, your voices are a bit loud, okay?"

"Sorry, Trevor," Louis said, "but I thought it was a pub."

"Just pointing it out. I'll get your beers."

Lee intercepted the break in the conversation. "I need to talk to you, Art," he said. His grin looked expectant, as if Art was bound to be solicitous after his exchange with Louis.

Paul shook his head. Lee could dig his own grave, he thought.

"I don't have any money, Lee," Art said with a short glance.

Lee kept his grin, looking around the table for understanding. "My business. I'm in the start-up phase. Tons of costs, no revenue."

Art paused as the server arrived with the second round. He raised his beer to one of the women at the next table. "Get some of that Hong Kong money from your parents," he said from the corner of his mouth before sipping.

"What do you mean? They don't have that much. Besides, they still think they're saving for med school." Lee's grin wavered. "What about your father?"

"Spent it all on the divorce," Art said, glancing around the table again.

Paul suppressed a gag.

"Let's talk about something else," Mark said.

"But he's *president* of his company," Lee said.

"It's not going to happen, Lee," Art said, wiping his nose again. "Not now. A barista doesn't make that much. Not even with tips."

"The jock man has something to say," Mark interrupted. Everyone turned to look at him. After several swallows of beer, he said, "I'm gay. There it is. I said it."

Louis coughed, then said, "Goddamn it, now I have to change my script."

Paul guessed the others would be surprised. Mark, the high school football player, bound for a U.S. scholarship until his knee was blown out by an illegal cross-block. Mark, with a forty-six-inch chest and thighs each thicker than Cyril's abdomen. Mark, the poor man's Clark Kent. When he was serious about something, his face stiffened and became stern. Everyone around the table saw it except Cyril.

"Yeah, yeah, right. Fuck off," Cyril said. Mark turned toward him, and in an instant, Cyril shrank. "Sorry."

"I'm not looking for apologies," Mark said.

"Well done, little man," Art said with a cutting laugh.

"*You* can fuck off," Cyril hissed at Art. He looked back at Mark. "Anyway, no judgment from me," he added. Various "or me's" chimed in. Mark looked at Cyril a second time, his expression still unyielding. Cyril's thin face stayed rigid until Mark nodded. The table relaxed and silence followed as beer bottles found lips.

"What took you so long?" Louis finally asked. "Sorry, but you didn't figure this out yesterday."

Mark shrugged. "For one, it's 1998. People don't shit their pants quite as much as they used to. For another, Collins, Shaw hired me back as an associate—so I made the team. Nice to see you there, by the way, Paul." They raised their bottles toward each other. "And I'm among friends."

"Kate wondered," Paul said.

Mark looked at him dubiously.

"How would you know?" Art asked.

Paul shrugged. "She mentioned it."

"I won't tell my parents," Lee said. "I can't."

"What the hell, Lee?" Mark said. "Who's talking about telling parents? It's none of their business."

"They wouldn't understand."

The server reappeared. "One more round?" she asked.

"Not for me," Louis said. He looked the server up and down then turned to the table. "My father set up a meeting tomorrow morning with some potential investors for *Rot-A-Tot-Tot*. Got to get ready for that. Need to be sharp."

"I have to go to the bathroom. Which way?" Art asked.

The server pointed to the other back corner.

"Did I tell you what *Rot-A-Tot-Tot's* about?" Louis asked Paul, his moustache shooting up in mirth.

"I suppose it's something sick like children being held captive by a crazy."

"You see, Cyril," Louis said, stabbing a finger toward him, "I *told* you it's a goddamn good title." He looked back at Paul. "Works out for them in the end—after lots of blood."

"I have to go to the bathroom, too," Mark said. As Art got up, Lee and Louis shifted to let Mark's hulking body pass.

"Took you long enough to get that production off the ground," Art said, giving Louis a sideway glance.

"Don't start again," Paul said.

"As you know, Art, there were a lot of last-minute changes," Louis said. "But this one's going to make more than *A Cannibal's Eyes.*"

Art shook his head and laughed, then headed toward the men's room with Mark following.

"Why waste your time on that prick?" Cyril asked after a few seconds. "He doesn't listen to you any more than the Foxy Lady does."

Louis chuckled. "I like getting under his skin. And I guarantee you, one day the Foxy Lady *will* listen to me. Now let's get out of here."

5

Louis, Cyril and Lee gave Paul some cash, took turns slapping him on the back and headed out of The Salty Dog. Paul waited for Mark and Art. It was nearly ten. He felt tired and needed a good night's sleep. Robert Platz, a Collins, Shaw rainmaker, had called him into his office and told him he needed to join all the other summer students on the due diligence team for a large transaction closing Tuesday. Paul paid the tab, covering Art's share and giving the server a healthy tip.

A few minutes later, Mark returned alone. His face was stern again but also red, with a film of sweat across his brow. "That guy is such an asshole," he said under his breath, pulling some bills from his wallet. "He's doing a line in there. Right on the counter. What do I owe you?"

"Don't worry about it," Paul said, pushing Mark's money away. He glanced past Mark toward the bathroom. "I should talk to him," he said with a sigh.

"You should," Mark said. "You know where this game leads better than any of us."

"It was different with my brother," Paul said. He looked at Mark and smiled. "Glad you finally told everyone. I was tired of keeping your secret."

"We'll see if anyone's attitude changes," Mark said.

Paul was going to predict no one's would, but Mark had already gathered his jacket and started walking to the front door.

A minute later, Art surfaced and they left, Paul with Louis's script squeezed under one arm. Outside, the clouds had plunged, creating a dense mist that transformed street lamps into glowing, floating cotton balls. As they walked back to Paul's apartment, Art filled their conversation with invective. When he opened the door minutes later, Paul was browbeaten. He threw the script on the coffee table and found the swivel chair. Art fell back onto the couch.

"Did you really need to do a line at the pub?" he asked. "None of my business, Art, but—"

"It's not. And don't take Mark too seriously."

"What does that mean?"

Art acquired a derisive smile. "On the way to the can at the pub, he implied I should be interested in him."

Paul wanted to remind Art of his undisguised pansexual flirtations, but he passed. "I can't—doesn't matter. I'm talking to you about your cocaine use."

"You're not my father, man."

"I thought you were taking a break from that stuff."

"Occasionally I do that so I can get it up again, if you know what I mean. Terrible side effect. But coke does have its allure."

Paul tried to catch Art's eyes but Art wouldn't have it. "The thing is I've always admired you," Paul said. "But you've got to get your shit together. I *know* what happens on this path."

Art pushed himself up from the couch, went to the kitchenette and opened the forty-year-old fridge. "You got any juice?"

"Art, *listen* to me."

Art found orange juice and poured himself a glass. "I told you, you're not my old man."

"I know that. I had lunch with him today."

"*What?*" Art said, jerking the glass and spilling juice.

"Don't get paranoid. I bumped into him in the food court and we had lunch. I had a wonderful time talking about you."

Art threw the towel from the oven handle over the spilled juice and gulped down what remained in his glass. "I don't want you talking to my old man," he said, returning to the couch and squinting at Paul. "He's a controlling bastard."

"I didn't really have a choice. He's worried. Like my parents were about David." Paul often felt a blunt edge when he mentioned David. "Like I was, too."

"Who's David?"

"My brother."

"Oh, yeah."

"And he went to rehab, Art, if you remember. And didn't make it."

"So what's the point then?"

"The point is he gave himself a chance, at least for a while. You're not even doing that." Art laid his head against the armrest of the couch and closed his eyes. Paul ran a hand through his hair, then, flicking the other, decided to discard the topic. Bed was a better idea. "I think I have a blanket you can use," he said.

"Kate's interfering in my life, too," Art said, raising his head and re-opening his eyes. "Last night, before she kicked me out, she was sending me off to this and that doctor, like you."

"People care about you, Art," Paul said, standing and stifling a yawn. "Kate's a good person. You should listen to her."

Art nodded slowly. "She's very fond of you, man."

Antagonism wafted toward Paul. "She was at Robert Street all the time."

"Seems like the two of you are—special to each other," Art continued, sitting up. "I have the serious impression that you got involved while I was gone."

Paul stumbled over Art's incisiveness. Or had Kate told Art, and Art was baiting him? "Like I said, don't get paranoid. She'll always be your girl. Even if you treated her like shit when you bolted for L.A."

Art stood. "I'd appreciate knowing. It's only fair—since you know so much about me."

"Settle down, Art."

"Don't fucking tell me to settle down." Art's eyes narrowed and his lips hardened. "I think you did."

"Did what?"

"Have a go with her."

"Go ask *her*."

"I don't need to." Art halved the distance between them. "Are you serious, man?"

"What are you *talking* about?" Paul said. "You were gone for two years."

Art moved in, imposing his height, and bumped against Paul. "I see. Some fucking friend you are."

Crowded against the swivel chair, resentment swelling through him, Paul pushed Art's chest. "See, this is the type of bullshit with your coke use."

Art pressed back, causing Paul to stumble over the chair. "Everyone lecturing me on my behaviour," he said. "You and Kate—*that's* bullshit."

"You weren't even fucking *here*," Paul said, trying to straighten up, "and it was only three months."

Art thrust an arm around Paul's neck and pulled him down into a headlock. But Paul knew Art excelled in drama, not schoolyard brawls. He gored one of Art's wrist with his fingernails and Art screeched, loosening his grip. Paul pulled his head free and flung Art toward the centre wall. Art crashed against it, leaving a crater in the drywall.

He lunged back at Paul with unexpected speed. They fell to the ground, bumping against the coffee table, legal texts flying. For more than thirty seconds, they rolled in each other's clutches. Finally, gasping, Paul gained the advantage, forcing Art onto his back, pinning each arm with a knee. He cocked his right fist, preparing to smash Art's perfectly proportioned features. *Can I do this?* he asked himself.

"Stop!" Mr. Chen yelled. He stood in the entryway to the living area, a key in his hand. "You guys are crazy."

Paul looked up. Peering from behind Mr. Chen, amazed and scared, was his eight-year-old daughter. Paul felt his gush of testosterone abate.

Mr. Chen pounced into the room and examined the wall. He jabbed a finger at Paul. "You fix the wall. You fix it. With *your* money."

Paul stood up, still gasping, and pushed sweat on his brow through his hair. Art lay heaving on the ground. "Get out of here," Paul hissed. "Honestly, I used to care. Now I just want you dead."

6

Paul tossed and turned. Every time sleep crept into his body, it was stonewalled by replays of his altercation with Art, the crunch of the drywall and the look in the eyes of Mr. Chen's daughter. Then the phone rang.

In the darkness, Paul stumbled to the swivel chair in the living room and picked up the receiver. Words flew at him. Paul switched to the couch and kicked up his feet, knowing Kate would be a while.

"I'm not angry with *you,* Paul, though I could be. You know, telling Art about our fling—I hadn't done that yet. Actually, I wasn't planning to at all. But the truth is I'm *glad* you told him. It was good for him to hear. Though I don't understand why you had to fight."

"He started it. I'm completely pissed off. I was this close to punching his pretty face till he stopped breathing."

"I *know*. He can do that to you. I'm just glad *he* was jealous for once. If that's what it was."

"Seemed like it. You two are crazy."

"I *know* I've been affected by that—that *boy*—but I'm not the crazy one. By the way, are you hurt?"

"No."

"He seems to be fine, too. I just told him to go to sleep on the couch. Nice of you to send him over here."

"I didn't. I kicked him out. Honestly, he chose you."

"Tonight he did, anyway. What was I going to do, tell him he couldn't stay two nights in a row?"

"Kate, I'm tired."

"You know, I had my three years with him, and then he left, and now, when he needs me, he shows up. How long did it take me to feel *normal* again? Almost the entire two years he was in L.A. Now he's back and still taunting me with other women. Wednesday night, I just let him have it. Then I kicked him out. I'm really tired of him."

"I've had it with him."

"*Damn* tired of him, Paul."

"Everyone is. His father cut him off in November."

"He told me. Anyway, I'm glad you told him about our fling. I can't stand it when he makes me jealous. But we have to do something. *Something*. If only to get rid of him. Any ideas?"

"Look, I'm afraid what will happen if I see him again. He's back using coke. I tried to tell him about David tonight. He didn't give a shit."

"I told him to go see the doctor."

"Rehab, Kate. He needs rehab. Then the two of you can be together or apart or whatever you want."

"*Apart*, Paul. Please don't get sanctimonious."

"Fuck sanctimony. I just want to go to sleep."

"Frankly, I don't want to ever see him again."

"So read him the riot act. You're the one person he might listen to."

"It'll just make me angry. But, you know, if we did it together—"

"I have other plans. Count me out."

"Paul, listen. We'll get together tomorrow night. A Friday night, like we used to in undergrad. And when he gets here, we'll tell him together to get professional help. Louis, Mark, Lee, Cyril, you, me—everyone."

"We did a version of that tonight and it didn't work. The thing is, Art amazed us once, but he doesn't anymore."

"No. I'm going to insist. I've been good to every one of you. I need this. For me."

Paul sighed. "If I agree, can I go to sleep? I have a lot on my plate."

"For me, Paul."

"Fine. For you, Kate. But only if we get together late. Good night."

Paul tossed and turned for another hour, brooding how he would deal with Art the next time he saw him. Then, as he had so many recent nights, he settled on the smell and softness of the Foxy Lady's skin, and sleep eventually came.

7

Underslept and irritable, Paul was sardined in an eastbound Queen streetcar waiting at a red light at University Avenue. The night's mist had cleared and beams of sun rushed through gaps in fast-moving clouds. At Campbell House, a bulky west wind churned the tops of blossoming crab apple trees.

When the light turned green, the streetcar edged into morning traffic. At Bay Street, Paul elbowed his way to the back doors and got off. He walked south, the wind lifting his wavy hair. At the Bay-Wellington Tower he let two elevators pass before squeezing inside a third. The doors closed within an inch of his nose and he held his arms close to his sides so the shoulders of his bargain-basement suit wouldn't be crushed.

He got off at the thirtieth floor and walked down the northeast hallway. He found his officemate loading pads of paper into a new briefcase. "Don't take off your jacket," he said to Paul, "and get your stuff. We got a full day on Platz's deal." Paul didn't mention he already knew that. "Everyone's been exempted from the last day of orientation," the officemate added.

Twenty minutes later, all eight summer students were gathered in the thirtieth floor lobby. Furtive glances accompanied muttering about working on "due diligence". Paul puzzled over what the phrase meant, exactly. He knew

Collins, Shaw represented the underwriters of an initial public offering by a software company, and that they were heading to the company's head office a few streets over to read stacks of documents. And he remembered the humourless, ever-preening Roberta Carnegie, head of legal research, who, in their orientation, had lectured about understanding an organization's legal obligations. But now he had to help find them. With a deep breath, Paul hoped no one was relying on him.

At lunch in his office after a morning with a mountain of corporate minutes, Paul picked up the message. "*Hi, it's Kate. We're on for tonight. My place, nine. I've arranged for him to arrive an hour or so later. You must come, Paul.*"

This obligation was easy to find but he hated it.

Close to five, the summer students were corralled into a meeting room with the junior associate in charge of diligence. It was apparent that an enormous amount of work needed completion in a short time. The weekend was shot.

Paul returned to his office and laboured over a memo summarizing what he'd found in the minutes. All day, he hadn't been as sharp as usual. The memory of his altercation with Art had stolen his concentration and twice he'd taken long walks outside to deal with it. At eight, with a headache coming on, he called it a day. The sun was a half hour from setting when he emerged onto Wellington Street.

The morning wind had fallen. The skies were clear and the temperature was dropping fast. Though he knew it would make him late for Kate's gathering, Paul wanted to go home first. He worked his way northwest to Queen and Bathurst. At his apartment, he ditched his suit and leather shoes for jeans, a plaid shirt and runners and made a few preparations for a busy time ahead.

It was 9:40 before he stood in his windbreaker in front of the door to Kate's condo. She lived in the west building of The Summit at King and Bathurst Streets. Her parents had helped her buy unit 1201 so she could walk to her new city planning job at Nathan Phillips Square. From inside the unit, Louis's voice boomed into the hallway.

Before Paul knocked, the second elevator opened. Lee, diminutive but muscular in casual pants and a jacket, surged ahead of Mark, whose torso filled out a sharply cut grey suit. Each carried a gym bag. Lee broke into an unrestrained smile, while Mark looked reserved.

Nodding toward Mark, Lee said, "This guy wanted to do squats all night on his gimp knee rather than come here."

Mark smirked. "Glad to see we're not the only ones late."

"We did *a lot* of squats," Lee added with a laugh.

"I'd rather be anywhere else, too," Paul said, lifting a fist to rap on the door.

"I heard you beat the shit out of Art last night," Lee said.

Paul knocked. "He came after me. Let's keep the record straight."

Kate flung open the door wearing tight jeans and a blouse. Paul didn't think of her often, but when he did, it was that she was maternal and pretty. Her striking green eyes, long brown hair and high cheekbones reminded him that she was beautiful, a near equal to Art. As he took off his windbreaker, an ache to lie alongside her again flitted through him.

Somewhere between agitated and excited, she gave everyone fond hugs. "Okay, okay, you're all here," she said.

"*Finally.*" She led them down a short hall into a kitchen where a breakfast nook looked onto a spacious living room. Louis perched at the end of a couch, knees bouncing, still in a suit with the top button of his shirt undone and his tie loosened. He broke into a large smile and rubbed his moustache. More casual and slouched in a neighbouring chair, Cyril flicked a bottle of beer. Beside him was a pair of crutches, and one of his ankles was wrapped in an elastic bandage and rested on a coffee table.

Kate pushed Paul, Mark and Lee toward seats and went to the kitchen for beers.

"What happened to you?" Mark asked Cyril.

"Louis elbowed me off the bottom step in front of our building," Cyril said, wincing. "Twisted my ankle."

"You were supposed to be on the street to greet the investors when they arrived," Louis said.

"I was *there*," Cyril replied.

"Sorry, but you weren't even close." Louis opened his hands to the room. "Everything needed to be goddamn perfect."

"It *was* perfect," Cyril said, his voice jumping a pitch. "Until *you* suddenly decided *you* needed to be the first to greet them and fucking elbowed me to the side. I'm sure leaving for the doctor partway through didn't impress the investors."

"How'd the meeting go?" Paul asked, dropping into the middle seat of the couch next to Louis. Mark pulled a nook chair up to the group and Lee took the remaining seat on the couch. Kate put three open beers on the coffee table then sat cross-legged on the floor.

"Great. Excellent," Louis said, rekindling his smile. "Too bad about Cyril leaving early, though. I wanted to show them our depth."

"Yeah, yeah," Cyril said, shaking his head.

"I think the money will come in. I really do. *Rot-A-Tot-Tot*—here we go."

Kate clapped her hands together. "Boys, we're here for *Art*," she said.

"I don't have much time," Louis said. "I need to get back to the budget. Cyril, do you think—"

"Louis, *please*," Kate said. "He'll be here shortly. He was a wreck this morning. I've had enough of him. This is it. We have to plan."

"Plan what?" Lee asked.

"What we're going to say, of course," Mark said. "He'll run like a quarterback being blitzed if we don't do this right."

"Exactly," Kate said. "Paul, what did your parents do with David?"

"That was a bit different," Paul said. "He binged on alcohol and dope. Ended up in detox at Toronto General. A friend of our family doctor put my father in touch with a treatment centre. David was so ashamed, he agreed to go—until he checked out again."

Kate bit her lower lip. "We have to convince a person for whom everything has come easily, who's had the world at his feet, to listen to us."

"To drop his arrogance and listen," Mark said.

"Good luck," Cyril said. "I like the odd bit of cocaine myself but it owns him."

"Don't get like him," Louis said, glancing to his side. Cyril snorted. "I'm just saying," Louis added. "Especially not now."

They spoke for several minutes, Kate lobbing out idea after idea on how to pull Art onside.

"You're throwing Hail Marys, Kate," Mark finally said.

"Like I explained on the phone last night, Kate," Paul said, "he'll only listen to you."

"I'm so angry with him. I need your backup. I *need* you to repeat to Art what I say." Everyone went silent and looked behind her. "What?" she asked, turning on her crossed legs.

Still in his barista uniform, Art had walked into the condo like he owned the place. He stood tall at the living room's threshold, his eyes dark and compressed with suspicion.

8

"Repeat what?" Art asked. His squint deepening, he looked at everyone in turn, ending with Kate. She jumped to her feet and pulled the other chair from the nook toward the group. "Repeat what, Kate?" he growled.

"Sit," she said, pointing.

"Why is everyone here?" Art added. He pointed at Paul. "Especially *him*."

"Settle down, pretty boy," Paul said.

"Fuck off."

"*Please*," Kate exclaimed. "Art, sit and listen to me."

To everyone's surprise, Art did as asked. On the chair, he smoothed his auburn hair with both hands, and like a lion in a cage, eyed his audience.

"Art," Kate continued, slowing her words for impact, "we all love you." Paul nearly gagged on his beer. "You know *I've* loved you for a long time. However much of an asshole you've been to me." A sardonic smile stole onto Art's face. She sighed and bit her lower lip again. "Just listen to me. You *can't* continue like this."

"Like what?"

Kate threw her hands at Art. "Like *this*. Using coke all the time. Wasting your life. Of all of us, *you're* the one with the gifts, with the charisma, with the—everything. You've got it all and you're damn well throwing it away." Art shrugged. "No, don't just *shrug*. This is it, Art. I don't have it in me anymore to watch you watch you fall into—into this abyss. It makes me so angry."

"Abyss? Are you serious?"

"I am. And I don't want to watch it anymore. You have to get help. *Professional* help."

Art looked over at Paul, but it was Lee who shocked everyone.

"She's right," he blurted with an embarrassed half-smile, grabbing each bicep with a hand. "Do you know what I'd give to have what you have?" His grin broadened. "To have a girl want my attention?"

"It's not like that, Lee," Mark said.

"It is," Cyril said.

"What do you mean?" Lee said, glancing at Mark. "Of course it is." He looked at Art again. "I shouldn't have given you money in L.A. Big mistake. Not just for me—because I really need the money—but for you, too."

"Everyone's right, Art," Louis boomed. "You've exhausted all of us. Rehab. That's what you goddamn need. Now."

"I'm with them," Mark said.

Art looked around, his expression blank. He got up from his chair and sauntered to the kitchen. Self-aware like on a film shoot, he opened the fridge, took out a beer and twisted off its cap. Then, standing tall, he took a long slug and wiped the corners of his mouth with the back of his free hand. For a moment, Paul thought Art would relent.

Then Art's sardonic smile reappeared. "Man, you've all got way bigger problems than me," he said. "You scratching me like a girl last night, you with your stupid movies, you with whatever happened to your ankle, and you with your pathetic body. And Kate, I don't even want to start about how you flaunt yourself." Art's eyes landed on Mark. "And, fuck, you got the biggest problems of all."

"You're a complete asshole," Kate hissed.

Art shrugged once more. "If you want to know the truth, I don't give a shit. I have to make a phone call."

"You're calling your dealer, aren't you?" Kate asked.

"You bet."

"Not with my phone."

"Yes, with your phone. In your bedroom." Art went into the neighbouring room and closed the door behind him.

"Asshole doesn't even begin to—" Mark said. "I should fucking annihilate that guy."

They fell into a pained trivial conversation broken only by the murmur of Art's call. Kate paced the living room.

"We're wasting our time," Louis finally said.

"My ankle's killing me. I need to go soon," Cyril said.

"Yeah, it's a quarter past ten already," Louis continued, eying his watch. "I want to get to that budget."

"Don't go yet," Kate said.

"What are you going to do?" Paul asked Kate. "He's made up his mind."

"I'm going to give him a piece of mine," she said and stormed into the bedroom.

Paul wondered why Kate bothered slamming the door shut; her rant with Art might as well have been right in front of them.

"*Get off the damn phone, Art.*"

"*I'm in the middle of the call, Katie. Leave me alone. This guy is a pain in the ass—he never gives me enough.*"

"*You drive me insane.*"

The shots continued back and forth. Lee flexed his biceps and Mark walked to the solarium at the end of the living room to peer down King. As Cyril rubbed his ankle, Paul ground fingertips into his temples.

Kate swung open the door and marched back into the living room.

"*Katie,*" Art yelled from the bedroom. "*Eleven fifteen. That's when I'm meeting Tony. That okay with you, Katie?*"

She resumed pacing. Louis looked at Cyril, tugging at his moustache. "I don't want to be here," he said. "Let's go." He lifted his stocky body from the couch and walked to the front hall.

"I was going to say the same thing," Cyril said. Fumbling into an overlarge jacket, he pulled himself out of the chair and inserted a crutch into each armpit.

"I'm going, too," Mark said. He returned from the solarium and picked up the gym bag he'd left beside his chair.

"Kate, do you have any Aspirin?" Paul asked, getting up from the couch.

She stopped in the middle of the room, her hands clenched. "In the first cupboard." As Cyril joined Louis and Mark in the front hall, Kate threw her arms up in the air. "What are we going to do?" she asked.

"Nothing," Paul said, walking around the nook into the kitchen. "Things will have to take care of themselves," he added, shaking out the pills.

"Actually, life is what you make it, Paul," Art said, returning from the bedroom. He picked up Kate's car keys from the nook. "I'm not sticking around either. Your car got gas, Katie dear? Tony doesn't like it when I stand in front of his house, and I want to keep warm."

"I'm gone, Kate," Mark said, his gym bag strung over his shoulder. "You coming, Paul?"

"No, I'm going to stay with Kate for an hour or two, I think."

"You're *not* taking my car," Kate yelled at Art.

"As a matter of fact, I am," Art said, smiling at Kate. "Coming down?" he asked, joining the others in the hall.

"We'll catch the one after," Mark said.

The front door thumped shut behind Art. Paul sprawled across the couch; his watch showed it was ten thirty. Lee jumped up. "Mark and I can catch a cab," he said, grabbing his gym bag. "We're both near the university." The door slammed again as the others left.

Kate shoved Paul's feet up the couch and sat next to him. "Thank you for staying," she said, her face flush and fierce. "*You* at least have been good to me."

"I'll stay as long as I can," he said. Rubbing his temples again, through the residual ugliness in the air, Paul felt another ache of lust for Kate. His yearning for her was the first for another woman in six weeks. "Let him go, Kate," he added. "For Christ's sake, he's hurt you enough."

"That's it, Paul. I'm done. I'm not having anything more to do with him."

Paul rubbed harder. "I already decided that yesterday," he said. "I think I have to go and get some sleep." He got up and found his windbreaker.

Kate took on a look of furious determination. "And I'm going to tell him that to his face."

But she never did.

9

Tony Rivera had a sense of community. Along Richmond, where he rented his Victorian, he picked up litter from the neighbouring school's students. He kept his postage-stamp-sized front yard tended and told the landlord to repair the peeling paint on the front of the house. And when he saw someone picking on a loner, he would jump in to fix the imbalance of power.

His sense of community was why he didn't like his clients visiting too late. In an ideal world, the evening cut-off would be ten. The neighbours shouldn't have to deal with loud voices or honking cars in front of his house after that. *He* shouldn't have to deal with that, he thought, watching the Blue Jays in New York City, his obese body leaning back in a lounge chair in the back room with his feet propped up.

Jennie had gone to bed, leaving him to munch on as many cheese puffs as he liked. The cellophane bag was almost empty, and his white undershirt and three-day-old beard were covered with specks of mutant orange. The game was deep into extra innings; the Jays' shortstop popped up. Rivera muttered in dismay and crunched the bag between his meaty hands.

He pulled himself out of the chair and walked down a hall to the base of the stairs near the front door. "Two men on and they popped up for the third out," he yelled to the bedroom upstairs.

"I'm trying to sleep, Tony," he heard. "And why do you have that game on so fucking loud?"

"I'd like to sleep, too," he said under his breath. But he had his deadbeat movie star client at eleven fifteen, then another client a half hour later. Then he would fall into bed next to Jennie. She was way overweight, swore too much and was pressuring him to make something of himself, but he knew the place would feel empty without her.

It was a few minutes after eleven. He walked into the living room and snuck a finger under a blind in front of one of three tall, narrow windows looking onto Richmond. A small car, maybe green, was parked on the other side under a young ash. The headlights were on and white puffs coughed out the exhaust. "Fuck, this is what I mean," he muttered. "People are going to get woken up."

Rivera returned down the hall to the top of the basement stairs. Leaning to one side, he looked at the TV. It was the bottom half of the inning and the Yankees already had a man on first. Rivera shook his head, sighed and headed downstairs.

At the front of the basement was a tool room. Rivera entered its darkness, feeling for the light's metal chain in the centre of the ceiling. After a few swipes, he found it and tugged hard; the chain emitted a raspy, grinding sound. In the sixty-watt light, he went straight to the wooden workbench, gouged and blotched with paint. He turned on a lamp, then, from one of the shelves along the top of the bench, he pulled down a large tin. Across the front was the fading name "Bristol Flour" and an image of a smiling woman stirring a large spoon in a bowl.

Rivera had a bad feeling about the movie star. From November to March, he'd built up a debt of more than ten thousand then dramatically slowed his purchases to the point where Rivera got worried he wouldn't get paid. In the last two weeks, he'd started buying again, but the evening before, he'd only paid a lousy thousand against what he owed. That's why Rivera had asked his brother to make an impromptu visit that evening when Rivera passed over the bag. His brother could be intimidating. And the movie star was—well, he was in the film business. He *must* have the money to pay … if given a little motivation.

Twisting off the tin's top, Rivera withdrew a large bag of white powder. Then he opened a drawer in the bench and removed one of many small plastic bags strewn inside and a measuring spoon. Three minutes later, everything was wiped down and put away, and Rivera had a small bag of blow in his pants pocket.

On the TV upstairs, the Yankees' designated hitter was in the arms of teammates, being congratulated for his game-winning RBI. "Aw, jeez," Rivera said. He went back to the living room window. Across the street, the car was still running. He shook his head in irritation. Before his brother showed, he would give the movie star a piece of his mind.

Rivera grabbed a jacket off a hook on the wall next to the front door then stepped outside. In the yard beside the freshly painted wrought iron fence, tulips had closed to fend against the night's bracing air. He heard the engine and a rattling exhaust. *What the hell is he doing?* Rivera crossed the street and slipped past the back of the car. Stepping onto the sidewalk, he saw the driver's side window was down.

From alongside a neighbouring commercial building, the dark form of Rivera's brother approached. Rivera held up a hand for him to wait, then turned. He wanted to put both elbows on the sill of the car door and get as close to the movie star as he could. Then he'd motion his brother to emerge with his weapon and make the movie star shit his pants.

"Holy fuck," Rivera uttered. Still strapped in a seatbelt, the movie star was slumped over the centre console. Above his left ear in matted auburn hair was a gaping hole that revealed flecks of bone and greyish-white matter. Blood bubbled out and down the side of his face onto the front of his barista uniform, pooling in his crotch.

Rivera stood, his lips hardening, and forced down nausea. He waved both hands at his brother and hissed, "*Get the fuck out of here.*" Looking up and down Richmond, he saw no one. He had enough time to flush his cocaine down the toilet and clean up. Then he would make an anonymous 911 call, because that's what responsible citizens did.

TORONTO

May 6, 2013

10

Louis's text read: "*Dying soon. Cleaning slate. Visit me. Princess Margaret Hospital.*"

In his condominium, Paul put his smartphone down on a small table next to the reading chair where he sat. Though mid-morning, floor-length drapes on the other side of the living room were pulled shut in front of sliding glass balcony doors. Lights in the front hallway to his left, and in the kitchen and dining rooms to his right, were off. John Coltrane's aching sax played from the stereo. Though Louis loved drama, Paul believed his words. But at that moment, all he cared about was finding serenity.

An hour later, Paul had only gotten up once, to replay Coltrane. His smartphone vibrated and Rachel's name showed. He hesitated, sensing her news would bring renewed agitation. Louis *was* dying, though. Paul dragged the phone to his ear.

"How are you, Paul?" Rachel asked.

An answer escaped him. "How are *you*?" he responded.

He lifted himself out of the chair and walked to the balcony doors. Reeling aside one of the drapes, he squinted as early May sun flooded the living and dining rooms.

Rachel paused. "Did you get the text?"

"Yes." Paul cleared his throat. "Just now."

"He really wants to see you."

At the end of February, Louis had insisted Paul visit for coffee. They'd never gotten out of his office. Tugging at his moustache from behind his overlarge desk, Louis had blurted, "It's a fucking tumour in the liver. Size of a goddamn baseball." Tanned, wearing an Armani jacket, his face was drawn and his eyes were restless, jumping from one film award on his desk to another. Paul had known right away that Louis wasn't quoting his current project's script.

Paul looked to the ground five floors below his condo. A crab apple tree was bursting into white bloom at the perimeter of Victoria Memorial Square Park. He changed focus to his reflection in the balcony door. His wavy brown hair was askew, his six-foot frame sagged and his angular face was unshaven and waxen. A large sigh escaped.

"I know you're taking time for yourself," Rachel continued, "but couldn't you—"

"Sure," Paul found himself interrupting. "I'll come by tomorrow."

Rachel's voice became stern. "Tuesday's too late. This afternoon. It has to be this afternoon."

A shower, shave and cab ride later, Paul was barely through the door of the private hospital room when he heard, "You could have goddamn visited earlier."

The words were Louis's, but the voice, gravelly and weak, was alien. Paul shot a nervous glance toward the bed. Propped up, ensconced in a morass of tubes and monitors, Louis was a collapsed mass except for distention around his abdomen.

"What have they done to you?"

"*They* haven't done anything to me. It's my fucking liver. Piece of shit. And all the fucking chemo and radiation." Louis grabbed for a deep breath. "They're good people here. Very good people."

Paul looked out the window, feigning interest in Toronto's western skyline. He was all nerves.

"That bad that you can't look at me?" Louis asked. "Sit next to me. My voice doesn't travel like it used to."

Paul pulled a chair to the bed. Louis looked ahead and let his eyelids drop. A young nurse came in as Paul sat.

"Hello, sir," she said to Louis with a brimming smile. "Another visitor? That's nice. If you want to sleep, he can wait here or in the waiting room. There's a TV there."

Louis opened his eyes and a scowl crossed his face. The whites of his eyes and skin were yellow. His thick hair and moustache were gone and sorry red blotches covered his scalp. "I don't need to sleep," he croaked.

"Of course you don't, sir," the nurse said, reorganizing the crumpled edges of the bed sheets. "But if you do, now your friend knows about the TV."

As the nurse left, Rachel moved into the doorway. Her face was haggard and her long red hair was stringy and dry. She smiled at Paul then waved at him to stay put and disappeared, closing the door behind her.

With a feeble push of his hands, Louis sat up a few inches and let a cough rip through him. Exhausted, he fell back into the bed. Except for the hum of the IV pump and Louis's laboured breathing, there was silence.

Paul fought off rising revulsion. He began driving a hand through his hair but stopped, thinking it was a provocation. Tugging at an ear, he struggled for words. Finally, he offered, "I'm sorry, Louis. I had no idea things were like this."

"Neither did I," Louis said. "What's going on with you? Rachel said you took time off work."

Paul nodded. "Just after we met in your office. But this visit's about you. There's nothing they can do?"

"Lots of pain medication. I'm tripping." He paused to grab air. "No, nothing."

His eyelids fluttered and Paul thought it better to let him rest. A half-minute later, Louis rolled his head toward Paul. His eyes stuck on Paul's chest.

"You're the last one I wanted to see," he said.

"The last one?"

"Saw Kate and Mark yesterday. At first I didn't want my old friends to see me like this. But I'm not proud."

"I understand," Paul said.

Louis's eyes lifted to meet Paul's and flared. "Do you?" He paused. "Well maybe *you* do."

"You saw Lee, too?"

"Even him. Day before. Talked some but mostly he just stood there and smiled at me. Of course, Cyril I see every goddamn day. Actually, we had some good chats in the last month."

Paul nodded again, then after a few seconds, said, "I can't remember the last time I saw Rachel."

"Yeah, and all of a sudden I've seen a lot of my family, too. *Now* they want to make things right. But by their goddamn definition, of course. You can't wait till the last moment to untangle complicated lives, you know?"

"Are you talking about Rachel?"

Louis rolled his head back and stared at the ceiling. "Ah, well, not her. She's been a good sister. Helped a lot at Dagger Films. I made that into my real family, especially after my tramp ex left." A rasp escaped his throat, then he went on. "I've been lying here, trying to come to terms with what's happening to me. And I can't. Sorry, but I can't. Maybe I'm not spiritual enough or something. But I'm fucking forty and I'm going to die. Complete bullshit."

"It's—it's …"

"Exactly, there are no words." Louis turned back toward Paul. Again his eyes flared for several seconds, reprising his famed clenched determination. "I've got a lot of movies left in me. Nothing I can goddamn do about that now—except protect my vision for Dagger."

"How?"

"I gave all my ideas to the three directors on my board, which includes Rachel. And to Cyril. He can be so good, and I know better now than ever how he thinks. But he likes those substances too much. I hope the two of them don't let me down."

"Maybe you can—"

"Direct from the grave? I thought of that. If it's possible, I will," Louis said with a hoarse chuckle. "That'd be a great movie, actually."

"Involve your father, I mean."

Louis contorted his face. "My time with that fucking philanderer is up."

Paul's eyebrows popped. He wanted an easier topic. "What's your favourite movie you made?"

Louis relaxed again. "I've been thinking about that. I don't know. They all become your children, you know, and

I don't want to say I liked one better. I'll tell you what movie I regret *not* making."

"Which one?"

"*Robert Street Rage.* That could have been great, but then that whole thing with Art happened, and it seemed wrong to make it."

"However it turned out, you would have told me it needed more blood."

Louis chuckled. "Ah, the motto. 'When in doubt, add blood.'" The start of a cough stole the chuckle but Louis supressed it. "I should be in the entertainment section, not the obituaries," he said after a few seconds. "Anyway, up to Rachel and Cyril now."

The nurse stuck her head in the door, her smile on full. "Don't need your help," Louis wheezed.

"Just use the buzzer if you do," she said and disappeared.

"I can't get rid of her," Louis said, glancing at Paul, shaking his head. He struggled for air. "Anyway, I asked Rachel to tell everyone to come and see me. I wanted to let all of you know that you've been my source of comfort."

"What do you mean?"

"In these last months. Not my youth. Certainly not my parents. Not working on films, though I had some winners. Not even the early days of my marriage, before that all went to rat shit. The times in undergrad when we all got together. That's where my mind keeps going. At Kate's place, Friday and Saturday nights. You know why?"

Paul shook his head.

"Sounds corny, but the future was exciting and fresh. Every one of us had something going on. All my good ideas came to me then."

"Child baby-killers?"

"One of my best."

"You drove us crazy, talking about your shots, making us act them out."

"I know, but I didn't care. I loved every second of it. And of course out popped *A Cannibal's Eyes*."

A gurgle mocking a laugh emerged from Louis's lungs. As Louis worked to subdue mucous, the nurse reappeared.

"Maybe I should go," Paul said, beginning to feel agitated. "I'll come back tomorrow."

"The TV, sir. The TV," the nurse said.

Louis leaned in the other direction, struggling with the distention around his gut, and landed sputum in a shiny aluminum dish. "Two more goddamn minutes," he said, waving the nurse away. She dropped her smile, shook her head and left.

Louis reached out a trembling, veiny hand and touched Paul's forearm. "Listen up," he whispered, grabbing for energy like a flickering light bulb. "I meant what the text said. I have to clean slate."

"I don't understand," Paul said.

"I did it with the others, too. I'm walking into the next world, whatever it is, without any secrets. They fuck everything up. I've seen it. Everybody should get rid of them."

Paul would have preferred to walk out. "What's so important?"

"I didn't treat you right."

Paul compressed his eyebrows and tugged his right ear. "I still don't understand."

"Don't you? I wasn't your goddamn friend. I stayed away."

"When?"

"Oh, fuck, you know."

Paul stretched for words. "Lots of people did."

"I wasn't goddamn sure. When you were charged with Art's murder, I just wasn't sure. I'm sorry. The whole fucking thing got to me."

Drawing his arm away from Louis's touch, Paul tried to laugh things off. "Apology accepted. Honestly, I didn't notice."

"Really? I tried to make it up after."

"You did. It's been a good friendship, Louis."

Paul stumbled over his acknowledgement of Louis's end, but he doubted Louis had caught it. More mucous had forced its way up Louis's throat, leading to a raucous cough. The nurse strode in and said, "You need to take your medication and sleep, sir." She pulled Louis forward as best she could. As he wrestled with heaves, she gave him a forceful back rub.

Paul saw a chance to leave. "Louis, I'll come back tomorrow."

Louis's eyes were red-rimmed and teary with exertion. As he caught his breath, he held out a hand for Paul to wait. "One other thing," he whispered. Paul made his way to the door then looked back. Louis's lips moved but only air emerged.

"*Enough*, sir," the nurse said, "you have to rest."

Feebly, Louis waved his fingers. "The Foxy Lady," he said. Gripping the door handle hard, Paul pushed his free hand through his hair. "She always liked you best. I was a prick. I told her to stay away." Louis shook his head a few times. "That was wrong."

That could explain a few things, Paul thought. He wanted to ask Louis more but he knew he'd run out of time. "See you tomorrow, Louis," he said. As he bolted out the hospital room, painful tears blurred his vision.

11

Paul trudged down Princess Margaret Hospital's front steps, his heart racing with the poison of Louis's decline. The air was fresh and warm but wisps of cirrus clouds dulled the sun. Glancing at his watch, he calculated he could make his appointment by taxi. He fell into the hollowed-out back seat of the first one at the hospital post.

Fifteen minutes later, Paul entered his psychiatrist's office. She was on time, and once he was seated across from her, she offered her customary first question. "So how are the meds?"

"They're helping," Paul reported. "I'm sleeping better."

"That's good," she said, taking notes on an electronic pad. "Any other side effects?"

"Vibrant dreams. Long, involved, sometimes unpleasant."

"I see. Do you feel better, do you think?"

"I suppose. Still a lot of wasted hours. Still out of sorts, mind wandering, not focussed like I'm used to."

"We've talked about this. 'Wasted' may not be the best word."

Paul tried not to smirk. "Up at six this morning. Didn't calm down till eleven and then only until something got me going again. Honestly, seems wasted to me."

The psychiatrist nodded. "What are the dreams about?"

Always unsure of how to fill their sessions, for more than half an hour Paul described his dreams in graphic detail: pressure at the law firm and falling behind on files; accusations by his ex that his drop in alimony was a ploy; an inexplicable long, silent visit from David. When he finished, an expectant hush filled the room.

The psychiatrist stepped in. "The meds seem to be helping but I think we should increase the dosage. From fifty milligrams to seventy-five. That should reduce your anxiety further. The main point of anxiety is still the fear of falling back into depression?"

"Yes," Paul said, nodding. "I feel it creeping up on me again. God forbid I end up where I was in 2002. The firm won't tolerate another full year off work."

"I think you've taken the right steps. Some time off work to reverse the trend. Coming to see me. Anti-depressants. And like we talked about, do the things that give you pleasure. Stay engaged. It can be the antidote, so to speak. Falling into depression is *not* inevitable. And the first step starts by engaging with me more."

"I just told you about my dreams."

"Your dreams are expressing your sense of alienation, of being apart from everyone else. That's why I'm pressing you to engage."

"I'm not keen on talking. Ask my friends."

"I don't need to. That's obvious to me. But if you want to start practicing law again, I think you need to interact. *Do you want to keep practicing?*"

"At this point, yes, although when I get like this, I question what the point of everything is." Paul sucked in air. "I just came from the hospital. A friend of mine is dying of liver cancer." The psychiatrist stopped taking notes and lifted her head, eyeballing Paul. "I doubt he'll live more than a few days."

"You haven't talked about him before."

"I have, actually. Louis was one of my housemates at the University of Toronto. On Robert Street. Art, Mark, Lee—and Louis. I haven't talked about his illness, though."

"Why not?"

"I visited him in February, right after his diagnosis. After that, I ignored him. I could hardly get to the hospital today. Terrible, right?"

Back at the electronic pad, the psychiatrist shrugged. "Why did you ignore him?"

"Didn't feel I had the capacity. And seeing him made me wonder why him and not me."

"But you went today."

"His sister texted and called me. He said he was cleaning slate."

"Cleaning slate?"

"He's been doing that in the last few days with all his friends. He said he wants to walk into the next world without any secrets."

"And what secret was he keeping from you?"

"That he stayed away as a friend."

"Recently?"

"No, he put himself back in touch in the last years."

"Oh. When you were charged? And after?"

"Yes." Paul paused. "I told him I didn't notice, which wasn't really true."

"People treated you differently?"

"Oh, yeah. A lot. They still do, I think."

"How can you tell?"

"There's a reticence. A doubt. You know, whether I did it."

"You feel that?"

"I do."

"What I'm getting at, is it real, do you think, or is it your perception?"

Paul smirked. "I don't know how to distinguish the two. Feels real. For example, Kate. I think she has doubt. Or did anyway."

"Kate? She was—?"

"Art's girlfriend in university. I had a short fling with her that started just before Art came back from Los Angeles, before he was murdered."

"Yes, you told me."

"She said she never had doubt. Didn't believe her then and still don't."

"You could take people at face value. Especially friends."

Paul eyed his doctor. "I suppose."

"We have to wrap up soon. Did your friend, Louis, have anything else to say?"

"He talked about the Foxy Lady," Paul said with a laugh.

"The—?"

"Foxy Lady. She was a girl in university we both lusted after. Terribly."

"I see. And what did he say about her?"

"Turns out he discredited me with her so she would lose interest."

"Oh."

"She was interested, though. For one afternoon. Kind of. Then never again." Paul felt puerile and tugged at an ear. "It's not important. It was a long time ago. I don't have more to say today." After booking his next visit, Paul left the office faster than Louis's hospital room.

Throughout the evening he wandered his condominium, looking for distractions. But Louis hovered over him. As he prepared for bed listening to music on his smartphone, he thought back to university.

"I can't do this," Paul yelled on the fifteenth take of the first scene of *A Cannibal's Eyes*. "I'm not a fucking actor. Art is an actor. Get him."

"I don't want him," Louis shot back. "I want you. If you want to be a goddamn lawyer, you're going to have to be an actor."

"That's bullshit."

"Is that what you're going to do with your life? Become a goddamn lawyer?"

"*Yes*. What's wrong with that? Anyway, it doesn't matter. I don't have the marks to get into law school."

"We need more blood, that's what we need."

"More blood? I'm *dripping* in this paint."

"I say more goddamn blood. *Bring more blood.*"

Paul pulled back the sheets from his bed and sat at the edge. In his earbuds, Coltrane played again and he tried concentrating on the melody line. But his mind veered off. He wondered if *he'd* have the courage to clean his own slate before the reaper opened its arms.

A group text came through. "*Louis is in a coma,*" Rachel wrote. "*He won't make it to the morning.*"

Paul's thumbs hung over the keyboard. He gave up on a reply and rolled into bed, looking for the mercy of sleep.

12

Four days later, Friday, Paul lingered by himself, thinking that Louis's funeral service had similarities to Art's.

The differences were obvious: the fifteen years between them; the midtown condominium rather than the downtown United Church; the jazz instead of church hymns. But the month and spring air matched. The same core of friends—minus Louis—was there. And sorrow hung again like pregnant clouds.

In the centre of the condo's large, austere living room, a laptop and projector on a box faced a wall stripped of art. Rachel separated herself from the crowd and stood beside the box. Her red hair was formless and heavy makeup couldn't hide dark rings under her eyes. She clapped her hands to settle the din, sending a ripple through her fleshy arms. "Everyone," she said, "can we begin?"

Glancing toward the other side of the room, Paul's eyes met Kate's. Her husband stood next to her. Her ten-year-old son, unable to stay still, was in front. Kate flicked her head for Paul to come over.

In a dark suit, the first he'd worn since taking his leave, Paul wandered behind the crowd then pushed in between Kate and Mark. She landed him a generous hug; her husband shook his hand. Mark slapped him on the back. Pointing to the person beside him, he whispered, "You remember my husband, Charles?" On the other side of Mark, Cyril waved and Lee nodded and smiled.

"Many of you knew my younger brother, Louis, well," Rachel continued, a quaver in her voice. "It should come as no surprise that he's left us with a little production. Cyril, can you turn down the lights?"

Hunched in an ill-fitting jacket, Cyril dodged guests to the condo entrance and tapped a global dimming switch. As the lights fell, the front door handle turned. A silhouette slipped in and melted into the other side of the crowd. Another similarity, Paul thought.

"Let's not make this too goddamn sad."

Paul looked up amidst a wave of gasps. On the wall, Louis sat straight at the desk where he'd told Paul of his cancer. His coarse hair was full but his face was yellow. His hands were joined together, tense with his trademark pugnacity.

"You weren't supposed to see *this* movie of mine. But if you are, well, things haven't gone as planned. I'm sharing the highlights of my life. What I want you to think about when you hear my name after I'm six feet under."

A picture shot up of a young Louis standing next to Rachel in front of their parents. Laughter rippled through the crowd at the children's awkwardness. Paul noticed Louis's parents standing three feet from the laptop, absorbed in the image. His father, thin with a narrow face and slumping shoulders, held on to a cramped, crooked smile. With a tissue, his mother whisked away tears from a pudgy, defiant face.

"My parents, Jack and Dana Grey, have both been dear to me. My father, the very successful investment banker, my mother the local politician. You all know them. He's a WASP, she's Jewish, and both are agnostic. We never knew what to do with that, so we all ignored it. That's why the service is at my condo." The laughter was louder, less apprehensive.

For fifteen minutes, the erstwhile Louis lobbed out images of his life, working the crowd's mood and memories. When a picture of the front lawn of a Victorian semi appeared, even Paul felt a stir. He stood with Louis, Mark, Cyril and Lee, all crowding around Art and Kate, and thrusting open beers bottles and magnified smiles at the camera. Broad-shouldered, long-legged and with an assured half-smile, Art tilted his head toward Kate and pulled her close with an arm around her shoulder. Her eyes held love and wariness.

"Undergrad. University of Toronto. September 1991 to April 1995," Louis bellowed. "With my buddies at Robert Street. Kate Baxter, Art Featherstone, Paul Tews, Cyril Coeur, Mark Koslovsky and Lee Chiu. These were my formative years. Every good idea I ever had is from then."

"Who's that, Mommy?" Kate's son asked, looking up.

"Just a friend, Kyle," she said with a smile. She turned to Paul, and cupping a hand around one side of her mouth, whispered, "Oops, didn't see that coming. God, to look like that again."

"But you do," Paul said. Kate batted her eyelids in mock appreciation.

"And a clip of the first contribution to my oeuvre at Dagger Films," Louis continued. "*A Cannibal's Eyes,* winner of the University of Toronto Film Society Award in October 1994. Made at Robert Street."

In the thick of a stormy night, Art stood soaking wet in a cape. His hands were outstretched and in one he held a knife, blood dripping from the edges of its blade. He wiped rain from his eyes, then screamed, "I have my revenge. *I have my revenge. Now—dinner.*"

"We lost Art in 1998," Louis continued, more quietly. "A potential star. Truly sad. I'm just saying."

"He's dead, *too*, Mommy?" Kyle said, his squeaky voice carrying.

"Shhh, sweetie. Yes, he is," Kate said, biting her lower lip.

When the last image faded from the wall, Cyril raised the lights. Some pushed back tears, others let them flow. Next to the laptop, Rachel stood like a forlorn child. "I can't top that," she said. "He made the best schlock movies, he was larger than life and he was a great brother. He's been taken much too early. Let's just spend some time together to celebrate him. The burial will be family only."

The crowd's murmur resurfaced. Paul started to look across the room but Kate enveloped him in a second hug. A light tremor ran through her body.

"How *are* you?" she asked, pulling away.

"Everyone keeps asking me that," Paul said, attempting a casual smile.

Her eyes penetrated too hard and he looked the other way. Mark had removed his glasses and blew debris off the lenses. Lee was speechless and pale. Looking straight ahead, Cyril's eyes were glassy and expressionless.

Kate tugged at Paul's shoulder to re-engage him. "I'm worried about you," she said.

"It'll pass."

Kate was interrupted by her son. "Who was he again, Mommy?"

"You heard of the movie *Crawlers*?" Paul jumped in. "From last year?"

"Think so."

"Louis made that movie."

"Oh." The boy looked away, sizing up whether he'd heard something important.

"I'm going to talk to Rachel," Paul said.

"We'll see you tonight, right?" Kate asked, putting a hand on Paul's shoulder.

Paul nodded and pushed out of the crowd. He found Rachel as she was closing the laptop. Spotting him from the corner of an eye, she clutched him. Too many hugs in a short space of time were making him feel antsy.

"Thanks for coming Monday," she said.

"Thanks for calling me," Paul said. "Where are your parents? I wanted to give them my condolences."

"They're on the balcony getting some fresh air. Looks like Mark and Lee are going to talk to them." Rachel looked bewildered. "I wish Cyril would come over and help with this equipment. Anyhow, Louis felt such urgency. I'm glad you got to see him."

"Did he get rid of all his secrets?"

"Hah," Rachel said, "I have no idea."

"And how are you holding up?" Paul asked, saying the right thing.

"Oh, you know."

"We could have coffee tomorrow."

Rachel looked Paul in the eyes. "I can't tell you what a burden this has been. And no help from anyone. It would be good to talk."

Paul was crestfallen Rachel accepted his offer. "There's that little bistro around the corner, on the south side of St. Clair close to Yonge," he said. "Say eleven?"

"I know the place. Yes, thanks."

On the other side of the room at a table with food and refreshments, a tall, lissome figure stood alone and poured herself a glass of wine.

"She still wears black," Paul said.

"Pardon?"

Paul nodded at the table. "One of the secrets Louis and I shared."

Rachel followed Paul's eyes. "Oh, her. It wasn't much of a secret. For Louis."

"You know her?" Paul asked, surprised.

"Just remember her from university. And Louis stayed in touch, I think. Cyril knows."

"Really?"

"Grace, isn't it?"

"Yes. Grace Campbell. But Louis and I knew her as the Foxy Lady."

Rachel snorted out a laugh. "*So* juvenile."

Paul tilted his head and smiled. "I'd have to agree. Louis claimed it was the Hendrix song playing when she came to the first Robert Street party."

He had enough of Rachel and let other guests intercede. He retrained his sight on the refreshment table, but now its perimeter overflowed with people he didn't recognize. He decided it was best to leave.

She appeared out of a shadow, halfway to the door. "Hello, Paul."

He turned to meet his name. Straight, long black hair parted in the centre covered the shoulders of her slim body and cinder eyes smoked against the pale, smooth skin of her symmetrical face. A flush rose in Paul's face and a catch formed in his throat.

"Gra—Grace," he blundered.

"Having trouble with my name?" she asked with a cautious smile, tossing back some hair. One arm crossed her abdomen, while in the hand of the other she held her glass.

"No. Just—I had no idea I would see you here."

"I wouldn't be surprised if you didn't remember. How long has it been?"

Paul pretended to think. "Fifteen years. Nearly to the day, actually."

"That long? My god. Are you leaving?"

"I am, actually."

"Will you walk me to my car?" Grace asked, setting down her glass.

Once she'd found her jacket stuffed in a closet, Paul held open the front door. He glimpsed Kate eyeing them from the side of the room, her hands tight on Kyle's shoulders.

Paul felt a ping of excitement underneath his sediment of self-doubt. As the elevator arrived, he fumbled for a question. "Where do you live these days?"

"You might remember I moved to Rome in 1998. My Italian mother lives there."

"I do."

"I danced at a company for a while. My prime passed years ago. Now I'm an administrator there." The elevator stopped for the condominium lobby and they exited.

"You came to Toronto for Louis?"

"Not for the funeral, for a project. Even though he was so sick, Louis wanted to continue discussing some crazy idea to use Rome as a location for a new production. I did a little work on it last year." She shrugged. "I guessed he wouldn't be well enough to see me. Cyril and I met and it's all been delayed. But I did have time to visit with my brother. And of course come here. What have you been doing?"

They walked out of the lobby and the sun hit their eyes. Paul deliberated what to disclose. He felt comfortable telling her he was a lawyer taking a sabbatical.

She nodded. "I think I knew about your law career." She stopped in front of a rental car, reaching into her purse for sunglasses. "I leave early Sunday evening," she added, looking at him.

Paul took a chance. "Perhaps we could have dinner? Tomorrow night?"

To his surprise she didn't pause. "That would be lovely," she said. He clutched an earlobe and gave a small chuckle. "Why are you laughing?" she asked.

"I don't suppose you remember the last thing you said to me fifteen years ago?"

Reaching into her purse again, this time for her smartphone, Grace said, "Remind me at dinner. Give me your number so I can text you." After she sent her text, she smiled. "I'll wait for your thoughts on a time and place. Ciao."

Paul watched Grace drive away. He shook his head. For three months he'd done everything to avoid social engagements. Now he had three. Only one interested him.

13

Paul rang the doorbell. He stood on the steps of a faux-Tudor, two-storey house. Pink luminescence saturated the sky. In High Park down the street, past the jagged outline of roofs, treetops were fuzzy with buds.

Cool air nipped Paul's hands and he rubbed them together. Subdued laughter and hints of music came from inside. A few seconds later, footsteps scampered to the door. Kate's son pulled it open and stared.

"Hello," Paul offered.

Kate appeared from a room right of the centre stairs and hurried to the door. "Talk to Paul, Kyle," she said. "You met him yesterday, remember? One of my university friends?"

Kyle made room for his mother and shot upstairs. "He didn't inherit your social graces," Paul said.

"Obviously not," Kate said with a laugh. "It's so nice to see you." Her eyes were sad yet inviting. She embraced him then led him to the room. "Paul made it, everyone," she announced. "It's important. Our little group has gotten so small."

Mark hulked next to Charles on a couch across the room. Kate's husband was crouched in front of audio equipment and tossed a behind-the-back wave. From the side, Lee pushed himself off a loveseat. Wearing one of his ludicrous grins, he introduced a small, pretty woman next to him.

"I invited Rachel, too, but she was tired," Kate said. "Paul, I'll get you a beer."

"Sure," Paul said.

He sat in an uncomfortable dining room chair dragged from down the hall. Kate's husband stood from his crouch. "There," he pronounced, looking around for reaction as "I Will Always Love You" began playing. Lanky and bald, he looked older than his ten-year age difference with Kate.

"What's that shit?" Cyril asked. Close to a speaker in a corner, he was slumped in a lounge chair, his arms folded across his bony frame, eyes mere slits.

"A number one song in the fall of 1992. When you guys started hanging out at Robert Street, right?"

Kate returned with Paul's beer and sat next to him in another dining room chair.

"We didn't listen to *that*," Cyril said.

"Try grunge," Lee said with a squeal of a laugh.

"I tried to tell you, honey," Kate said. Looking at Paul, she tilted her head toward her husband and added, "He does what he wants. Set in his ways."

"I might have grunge, actually," her husband said.

Cyril pulled himself up from his slouch and walked to the middle of the room. "Anyone want to smoke some ganja with me?" he asked. There were no takers.

"Smoke out back on the deck, please," Kate said. "Sit where the neighbours can't see you." "Smells Like Teen Spirit" blasted over the speakers. "Honey, turn that down," she added. "It's not the night."

Conversation paused and Paul sucked at his beer. "People are asking about you at the firm," Mark said. "We miss you. It's like playing a man short on some transactions."

Paul shifted on his chair, glaring at Mark. "Can't imagine."

"Sometimes you have to get away," Kate said.

"What are you talking about?" Lee asked. He looked at his date for insight but she shrugged.

Mark snapped his head in Lee's direction, early jowls shaking under his chin, and adjusted his glasses. "Lee, I told you. A time-out."

"You did?"

"I took a sabbatical in early March," Paul said.

"Sorry," Mark mouthed toward Paul. He cleared his throat and said, "Others at the firm have done it."

"What's going on, Paul?" Lee asked.

For a second, Paul distracted himself with the perfect placement of each strand of Lee's jet-black hair. "I suppose I'm recharging batteries."

"You mean you're depressed again," Lee said. "Can't take time off for that at my company. Lose the customers."

"Not depressed," Paul said. "Recharging."

"You lawyers," Lee said, laughing. "Your clients think they need you. Data management customers aren't like that. Got to stay real close to them. No time to recharge."

Mark's face stiffened. "You're doing better than the rest of us, Lee."

"Let's talk about something else," Kate said.

"That would be appreciated," Paul said.

"And you city guys are the worst," Lee continued, turning to jab a finger at Kate. "You know what I read the other day? The public service is *twice* as likely to call in sick as the private sector."

"I don't know where you got that from," Kate said. "We work hard."

"Making sure every condo building looks the same?" Lee laughed, looking at his date again for understanding. "Because they do." He stared at Paul. "So are you going back?"

"Yes, soon. Please, let's talk about something else."

"How about Louis's confessions?" Kate asked.

"Sure," Mark said. "He would have wanted us to."

"I was only at the hospital for ten minutes," Lee said. "Just talked about our families, which was weird. I had no idea Louis held such a grudge."

"What about you, Mark?" Kate asked.

Mark shrugged. "He said he suspected I was gay all along."

"So did *I*," Kate said.

"What the hell, Kate, I hardly knew myself."

"Mister football and hockey. And you threw in the odd date with a girl. You were as close to the vest as they come. But I knew."

"I had to be careful till I understood myself," Mark said. "Anyway, Louis said he knew by third-year university. That was even before I told Paul."

"I knew at age seven," Charles said.

"You were different, I guess," Mark replied.

"How does it matter if Louis knew in third year?" Paul asked.

"He thought he could have been more—supportive and encouraging."

"Louis?" Kate said with a laugh. "You know, if he'd really known earlier, he'd only have jabbed and teased you more."

"That would have been okay compared to Art," Mark said. "He tried to make me feel mentally deficient for being athletic. Remember? 'Jock man' is what the prick called me."

Cyril reappeared, a waft of sweet air following him, and slumped back into the chair near the speaker. He turned up the music but Kate got up and dialled it back down. "We're talking about Louis's confessions," she said.

"Great," he said.

"What about you?" Kate asked Paul.

"You first," Paul said.

A sad smile crossed her face. "He told me that he was jealous of Art. Being with me."

Lee laughed. "You okay with this?" he asked Kate's husband.

"We've talked about him," Kate's husband said with a fabricated sigh. "The great Art."

"You should have been there," Mark said. "Everyone wanted a piece of him. At least at first. Like honey to bees. And your wife got him."

"My wife is a beautiful woman."

"She is," Mark said. "But don't take this the wrong way, Kate. Art could've had anyone he wanted."

"Louis was a horny bastard," Cyril said from behind closed eyes. "Don't take *this* the wrong way, Kate, but he had an eye for beautiful women. And he was routinely jealous."

"Thanks, Cyril," Kate said. "And I thought I was the one with jealousy issues."

"Yup," Paul said, "when Louis set his eyes on a woman, he wanted to be the centre of her world. He told me he undercut me."

"How?" Mark asked.

"He convinced the Foxy Lady to avoid me."

"The who?" Lee asked.

"Where were you?" Mark asked. "The skinny dancer girl from Annesley Hall. The one who started coming to our parties in fourth year."

"Louis thought she was beautiful," Cyril said. "Lots of other girls, too, but *especially* her."

"Well, that puts me in my place," Kate said, smirking.

Cyril laughed. "She stayed in touch after university but only because she wanted a movie part. Drove him crazy."

"I didn't much like her," Kate said. "She was at the funeral service. I saw you talking with her, Paul."

"I'm having dinner with her tomorrow night," he said.

"Whoa, that'll help you out of your rut," Mark said.

Kate stared at Paul and put a finger to her chin. "I—I don't know what to say to that," she said. "Just be careful."

Paul shrugged and gave a half-smile. "And what was Louis's confession to you, Cyril?"

Cyril snorted and took a gulp of beer. For the first time his red eyes opened wide. "That despite his promise, I won't be president of Dagger Films. Not any time soon anyway." A gasp went around the room. "Yeah, yeah. Too many drugs, he said. I'm destined to be an assistant producer, I guess."

"Oh, how disappointing for you, Cyril," Kate said.

"That's one way of looking at it. Speaking of cocaine—"

"Not here, Cyril. I got a kid upstairs, right?" Kate's husband said.

"*I* have a confession," Lee blurted, glancing around the room. "I went to see Detective Beecham two years ago. On the anniversary of Art's murder. May 8."

"Why?" Kate asked.

Lee gripped his biceps so hard, his fingertips turned white. "I had a theory about what happened to Art. Who shot him."

14

Lee had everyone's attention. He glanced at his date, who, for the first time, looked genuinely absorbed in him.

"Thirteen years after?" Mark asked.

"Yeah," Lee said. "Just came to me that day. I guess because I was thinking about Art."

"And why didn't you tell us?" Mark demanded.

"I didn't want to open up old wounds," Lee said, flashing a look at Paul. "With the murder and Paul's arrest and everything."

"Well, what *was* your theory?" Kate said.

"I—I'm not supposed to say," Lee said.

"Seriously?" Mark asked.

"Yeah," Lee said, squeezing the life out of his biceps again. "Detective Beecham listened but he said he doubted it went anywhere. When I called him back a few months later, because I hadn't heard from him, he said the case was closed as far as he was concerned. And he told me to keep it to myself, out of respect for Art's family. But I really want to know what you think. Maybe I'll tell you one day."

"What Beecham meant was he thought he had me dead to rights," Paul said.

"Good on you, Lee," Kate said. "That you tried, I mean. You know what? I'm going to call Detective Beecham myself, just to keep up the pressure to solve Art's murder. In fact, I'm going to do it every year. May 8 is as good a day as any."

"This guy really lives with all of you still, doesn't he?" Charles asked, looking from one face to another.

"He made an impression, there's no doubt about that," Mark said.

"Great for parties," Lee jumped in, back to one of his insidious smiles. "The girls that came over when he threw a party at Robert Street. Remember, Kate?"

"Ha-ha," Kate said.

"But he knew who was helping him out with rent, right, Kate?" Lee said, his smile broadening.

"More or less," she said.

"Aw, I'm just playing with you," Lee added.

"You gave him *rent*?" Kate's husband asked.

"Occasionally."

"But I thought his father—"

"Never mind, honey."

"If you want to know where the money went," Lee said, "it was partying, especially at our place. The cocaine, too, of course. Here's the thing, though. Art got straight As. They were artsy courses but he was smart. He knew what he could do well, and when he did it, he was the best at it. I've never seen a guy who could *focus* like that. It was almost beautiful."

"He *was* beautiful," Mark said. "A total prick sometimes, but beautiful."

"It's true. He had the looks," Kate said. "Sorry, honey," she added, tilting her head toward her husband.

"Do you want me to leave?" he offered with half a chuckle.

"You know, this is ancient history. Besides, you said you wanted to know about my past."

"There are limits, right?"

"I've never seen anything like it since," Mark continued. "His proportions were perfect. Like a statue of Adonis." Charles turned to eye Mark. "He was only a friend. But I admit I admired him from afar. And he was a flirt, with everybody."

"I was completely insecure," Kate said. "'What's it like to be with him?' other girls asked me all the time. You know, 'damn nerve-wracking' is what I said."

"Louis used to say he had the talk and the walk—and everything else," Cyril said. He sat up in his chair, his face drawn. "So I quoted the Delphic Oracle back to him. The most beautiful is the most just."

"Louis was interested in one thing—that his movies were successful," Paul said in a subdued tone. "Art helped him incredibly with *A Cannibal's Eyes*. He carried a shot like I couldn't even pretend. That's why they fell out so hard when Art went to L.A."

"I repeat, the most beautiful is the most just."

"What does that *mean*?" Lee asked.

"For the ancient Greeks," Charles said, "inner qualities were highly important. Know thyself. Avoid excess. Both mottos on the walls at the temple of Delphi. And what Cyril is saying is that the Oracle associated beauty with being just. Not appearance."

Mark wiped his glasses again. "Charles is a professor of history, in case any of you didn't know."

"Art was a lot of things," Paul said, "but just was not one of them."

"Exactly," Cyril said. "He routinely ridiculed me. Called me 'little man', among other things, all the time."

"'Jock man' was worse," Mark said.

"I don't think so," Cyril countered.

"It wasn't *that* bad," Kate said.

"Bad enough," Mark said. "Like being punched in the face every five seconds."

"For Christ's sake," Paul said, "ridicule, aggression, harassment—they were part of Art's competitive strategy." Kate eyed him. "Well, it's true," he added.

After smirking, she said, "Somehow this all misses the point."

"Okay, that's enough for me," her husband interrupted. "The barbecue needs cleaning."

As he left, Kate waved a hand after him like she was swatting a fly. Lee burst into laughter. A few seconds later, putting a finger to her chin, she said, "Of course Art was physically striking but, you know, his real beauty was what he *did* to you. Burn his eyes through you, until you were helpless, or romance you by giving you a hundred and ten percent of his attention. The passion he sent your way could be completely consuming. He made you *part* of him. I miss him to this day."

"With the greatest of respect, Kate, he wanted to fuck you," Cyril said.

"Is that what you reduce everything to? And what's wrong with that, you know?" she asked.

Sniggers spilled through the room but Paul felt the hum of his agitation grow louder. He got up and said, "I think I'll go watch your husband clean the barbecue."

He walked halfway down the centre hall then noticed Kate following. She pulled close to one of his ears. "I want to talk to you about something, soon. Not here, though," she whispered. "Something of mutual interest. It might make you feel better."

Paul tugged at the lobe of the other ear, puzzled. "Anything would be welcome. I'm supposed to be looking for an antidote."

"More later," Kate said, smiling. She dashed back to the room.

Paul shrugged and continued to the kitchen, where he stepped out onto the deck. Kate's husband stood in front of a picnic table cleaning a barbecue grate overtop newspaper.

"Reminiscences don't bother you, I hope," Paul said. He looked up at a silvery half-moon and the stars able to penetrate city lights. The smell of hyacinths rose around him.

"Truthfully, not a bit. I came to terms with what I offer Kate a long time ago. And it's not what Art offered. I'm an accountant, right? I help with a good lifestyle." He returned to the grate, scouring it with a metal brush, sending bits of carbon flying. "I wonder if Kate will call the police."

"Knowing Kate, it's not 'if' but 'when.'"

"It's true, right? She takes her responsibilities very seriously."

Paul paused, then said, "Art certainly deserved as much."

Kate's husband nodded. "I gather Art was quite the druggie. Cocaine, right?"

"Druggie?" Paul repeated, thinking that was a word only an accountant would use. "He had a yen for coke in undergrad, but his crowd in L.A. really laid it on."

"Your friend Cyril has the same yen."

"The one thing they enjoyed together. As far as I can tell, Art's habit got much worse."

"Did she pay for that, too?" Kate's husband asked, raising his head from the grate.

Kate was walking into the kitchen. Paul saw no point in saying Art took money from anyone he could. "No."

She opened the sliding door and stuck her head out. "Ooh, it's cold. You know, that thing must be clean by now, honey."

"Nearly done."

"I hope Beecham is more helpful to you than he was with Lee," Paul said.

Kate shrugged. "He must be retiring soon."

"Glad to hear it."

"I know. But it won't help the case."

"He's an incompetent, obnoxious asshole," Paul said. "Someone else needs to take a crack at it."

Kate's husband looked away. Kate started for the kitchen then turned. She raised the thumb and pinky of a hand to her mouth and mimed "call me" to Paul.

15

"I have a funny feeling," Detective Beecham said.

Paul apprehended a bedpost, a perimeter of light around the blind of a window, a crack in a door to a hallway, but he didn't recognize them. He wanted to rouse himself and examine his surroundings. But every ounce of energy was sucked out of him.

Beecham hovered to Paul's left, heavy and indolent. A film of sweat was smeared across the elevated brow of his thick face. "I can tell when things don't add up. I have a funny feeling about how things are going."

Art, crouched behind Beecham, peered around. Beecham didn't see him. Lee pointed and grinned at Mark. With a fearsome glare, Mark slapped down Lee's hand. Kate, Louis and Cyril gaped at each other. Paul wanted to raise himself and greet Art but he was in complete torpor. He wondered why he was the only one lying on his back.

"You don't get this type of sixth sense without experience," Beecham went on. Art mouthed the identical words then suppressed a laugh. Kate put a hand over Lee's mouth to stop him cackling.

"If it's a sixth sense, you don't need experience," Mark said. Rage was colouring his face but Beecham took no note.

"Let the man get this done," Louis said.

"That's right," Cyril added.

"Like I said, I got a funny feeling."

"I got a funny feeling," Art mouthed.

"What about, exactly?" Kate asked.

"Your friend liked drugs. A lot of drugs."

"A *lot* of drugs," Art repeated, nodding in approval.

"Forty-eight hours into the investigation? *That's* what you got?" Cyril asked.

"Like I said, I got a funny feeling."

Art shook his head and shrugged.

"Make him stop, Paul," Louis said.

Paul wanted to explain that, as much as he wanted to, he couldn't. But his voice failed him.

"For goodness' sake, Detective Beecham, what are you trying to say?" Kate asked.

"I'm not *trying* to say anything. I *am* saying your friend liked a lot of drugs but—"

"But?"

"That may not be relevant here."

"What do you mean?"

"I think one of you—"

"One of *you*," Art repeated.

"—knows something you're not telling us."

Art extended a forefinger, and pointing at everyone in succession, said, "Knows—something—you're—not—" He reached Paul. "Telling."

Paul's legs thrashed. Exhaling hard, he rolled onto one side and fell back asleep.

16

Wisps of Coltrane's sax floated in the back of Paul's mind. He glanced at his smartphone's screen. It was eleven fifteen Saturday morning and he wondered if Rachel would show. He sat at a table beside the front window of the self-serve bistro on St. Clair West where they'd agreed to have coffee. Two other patrons sat alone swiping tablets. It didn't much matter to Paul if Rachel forgot their appointment.

He looked for a reply text from Grace. He'd resisted suggesting a time and place for dinner until early that morning. Putting the phone down, he puzzled why she hadn't responded. He wondered if offering to pick her up had been too bold. But it wasn't like they were meeting for the first time.

Amidst swirling wind, rain spat onto the sidewalk, leaving black imprints that merged. Drivers turned on wipers and pedestrians hurried their steps. As Paul tasted his lukewarm coffee, a cab lurched to a stop in front of the bistro. Rachel eased her heavyset figure out of the back door and dashed for the entrance. She spotted Paul and gave him a hug, whispering, "Sorry I'm late."

"You took a cab?" Paul asked, smiling and sitting again. "From a block away?"

Rachel laughed, removing a thin coat. "Well, he was right there, just waiting for me." She put the coat on the back of the chair across from Paul then looked at the empty plate in front of him. "What did you order?"

"A bagel with cream cheese."

"I think I'll just have a coffee," she said. A minute later, she returned with a cappuccino and took her seat, shifting several times to get comfortable. "It was creepy staying at Louis's last night."

"I can imagine."

"I only have a little time. There's much more to do than I ever realized."

"That's too bad," Paul lied.

Rachel's face became serious. Deep wrinkles scattered from the corners of her eyes, making her look older than forty-five. "How did you enjoy Louis's grand post-mortem production yesterday?"

Paul reflected. "I don't know. The thing is, it was very like Louis. Taking charge of the project himself. Got to admire his bravado."

"I don't," Rachel said, controlling a rogue strand of red hair. "I'm tired of it."

"I suppose it was the last time."

Rachel looked at Paul doubtfully. "Don't get me wrong. I feel such grief that he's gone. We weren't that close and were very different, but still," Rachel said. "But the whole thing yesterday—it was a sham, a reinvention of the past. It left me terribly cold."

"I don't understand."

Rachel took her coffee cup and put it near the centre of the table. Then she dragged Paul's cup level but six inches away. "It's like this cup is the family that Louis presented," she said, pointing to her cup, "but this cup is the *real* family," she added, pointing at Paul's.

Paul laughed. "That's everyone's family."

Rachel pushed the cups until they were at opposite edges of the table. "Now?"

Paul shrugged and opened his hands for help.

Glancing around the bistro, Rachel continued. "He wanted the rest of the world to think that our family was happy and loving and *tight*."

Paul gave a rueful smile. "Yeah, at the hospital, he didn't have kind things to say about your father."

"Father was a very successful banker and hardly ever home. My parents grew apart. Once Mother figured out she was basically single, after raising us she did her school trustee thing. But there was a coldness and a distance in our house. Like a hospital almost, sterile. Louis saw our parents—and maybe even me—as unsupportive and self-interested. Loyalty was a big deal to him."

"Except maybe when it came to other men's female interests," Paul said.

Rachel sized him up for a few seconds. "Exactly. That's why his marriage fell apart eventually. His ex and he were mortal enemies to the end. Did you notice she wasn't at the funeral?"

"Keep going."

"Anyway, that's what his montage yesterday was designed to do. Make our family look tight, for lack of a better word. And *I* participated in the whole charade." Rachel sighed. "Plus he made me executor of his will at the last minute."

"Now I really did expect your father would do that," Paul said.

"They had a terrible falling-out in the end. Louis wanted to air all these little family secrets and my father wanted no part of it. Did your family have these secrets, too?"

"My father died when I was eighteen. A year after my brother. There was no time for secrets. We were reeling."

"Oh yes, I'm sorry. I forgot."

"Except for my brother's addiction issues. *They* were a big secret."

Paul's phone vibrated on the table and his heart bounced.

"Do you have to take that?" Rachel asked.

Paul thrust a hand through his hair. "No, it can wait."

Rain pelted the bistro's west window and a neighbouring tree bent to the will of the wind. Rachel continued on about her week ahead. After several minutes, she paused.

"So Cyril isn't becoming president of Dagger?" Paul asked.

A slanted grin crossed Rachel's face. "Oh, there's all that, too. You heard about it already?"

"Cyril told us last evening."

"He was *very* upset. I'm on the board of Dagger and Louis entrusted us to find the right person for his vision."

"Louis mentioned," Paul said. "He always said how good Cyril was. But can he be president? Imagine the pressure of living up to Louis's dream."

Rachel tilted her head. "Louis thought he could. Not only is he really good but he was loyal to Louis, as Louis was to him. Cyril has to come across as *stronger*. He needs to get out from underneath Louis's shadow and take charge. It's hard for him, I guess. Louis was his male role model. And he had a difficult childhood—raised by a single mother."

"He's got another problem."

"I know, of course," Rachel said. "Cyril's not well. But Louis did say that if he can get those substances under control, the president's job is his." She checked her watch. "I'm sorry, Paul, I really do have to go. But tell me about you first. When I tried to reach you at work, they told me you've been away for a while. It's not the same problem again, is it?"

"I just needed to take some time." *She wants more*, Paul thought. "I like the phrase 'recharging my batteries.'"

Rachel eyed Paul. "Is this related to your divorce?"

"Oh, no. That was three years ago and very amicable. Two introverts who'd gotten bored with each other. Easy. No kids."

"Can't imagine that being easy," Rachel said. Paul shrugged. "But then I'm pretty much a spinster. You don't like being a lawyer, do you?"

Paul smiled. "How many lawyers *like* what they do? The money, for those who get it, yes. The stress, the hours, not so much. It just was time to hit reset for a little bit. The firm has been great."

"You know, if I'd been put on trial for murdering a friend when I was twenty-five, I doubt I would've had the strength to continue like you did." Paul squinted to dissuade Rachel from more. "Returning to law school and all."

He shrugged. "I didn't see a choice." He glanced at his smartphone.

"That thing is burning a hole in the table," Rachel said. "Not from the Foxy Lady, by any chance?"

Paul smiled. "How very astute of you."

"How very predictable of *you*."

Four young women entered the bistro, asserting their adulthood with loud gab. Paul wished their noise would drown out his conversation and induce Rachel to leave.

"Go ahead," Rachel said. "Look at it."

Paul hesitated but took up the offer. *"Restaurant and time are fine. I'm at the Hotel Beaux Arts. Ready any time after 8:00. Looking forward. Grace. :)"*

For the first time in a long time, Paul found himself analyzing a woman's words for intrigue.

"Well?" Rachel asked.

She really should go, Paul thought. "What did Louis say about her?" he asked.

"I don't remember the specifics. It was the fact she came up in conversation so regularly that struck me."

Paul nodded. "We thought she was an iconic beauty. I'm having dinner with her this evening." A shrill laugh among the young women obscured Rachel's reply. "I'm sorry?" Paul asked.

"Danger, I said. She has danger written all over her."

Paul stared at Rachel. *Danger? Why would she say that? And compared to the last three months, how could it matter?*

17

The short distance from Paul's King West condo to Hotel Beaux Arts didn't justify the use of his silver Lexus sports sedan. But the bulbous clouds and his desire to make an impression did. All day the rain had come and gone; for the moment it held off. But a constricting humidity had arisen, and to the west skies growled. Everywhere, evening drivers and pedestrians looked up toward a giant, imminent release.

Paul parked illegally in front of the hotel as the first splotches of rain slapped against his car. A valet approached with an open umbrella. "I'm okay, thanks," Paul said. He jumped out of the car, grabbed his own umbrella and scurried under the hotel's front overhang. Under warm pot lights, he turned back and watched the rain rally into a mass of drops bursting as they struck pavement. Thunder rolled above, ending with an echoing thump.

Automatic doors in the hotel's glass façade sensed Paul and opened. He darted into a high-ceilinged lobby. Guests looked uncomfortable in square furniture, some pausing conversation to stare at the downpour. Paul wiped a few drops from his blazer shoulders.

He approached the black marble registration desk, gave his name and asked for Grace. A short phone call later, he was told she would be five minutes. Not far from the bank of elevators, he found a place to stand and feign calm.

Six or seven elevators later, she arrived at ground level. Her long dark hair flared over bare shoulders and a string of pearls, and an off-white floor-length dress hugged every curve of her dancer's body. Seeing Paul, an even smile spilled over her pale face and she tossed her hair back. She strolled toward him in stilettos, a clutch peeking from under a jacket hung over her left forearm. Extending a hand, she pulled him in for a light kiss on both cheeks.

The rain pounded. Holding the umbrella above her, he led her to his car and opened the passenger door. He drove back to King West, where he'd made a reservation at Vignoble. Traffic inched along but the rain lightened. Across from the restaurant, a car swung out of street parking. "Divine intervention," Paul said, quickly backing in. Minutes later, they were at their table examining tall menus and the wine list.

When the glasses of Burgundy arrived, they toasted to undergrad. Out loud, Paul recalled Grace when they met in fourth year: quiet, off in a corner, fences up. To himself, he remembered the evenings he lost three years later thinking of her smell, the softness of her skin—and his embarrassment with her.

"It's true," she said with a giggle. "I'm very shy in a group." Her bare shoulders rose and fell. "Actually, I'm simply shy. You know that. At Annesley Hall, I just hung out with a few friends in their rooms." *Like me*, Paul thought.

After their appetizers arrived, Paul said, "So you stayed in touch with Louis over the years?"

"Well," she began, fighting an escargot, "it's a bit embarrassing, really."

"What do you mean?"

Grace scrutinized Paul, who'd started in on potato leek soup. "What I love is dancing."

"I remember."

"No, but *love* it," she said, flicking her hair. "Not ballet. Jazz, modern. I've done it since I was a young girl and all during university on the side. It gets me out of myself and my world."

"You were in a dance company in Toronto when we last spoke, weren't you?"

"I was too embarrassed to tell you, but it had just ended. As I mentioned yesterday, I went to a dance company in Rome and danced there for a while. Never got more than minor roles." She paused to stab another escargot and sighed. "I always thought I was really good, but you get old, right? On my twenty-eighth birthday, I just knew it was over. At least I got a good administrative job there."

"So what's embarrassing?"

"I kept in touch with Louis because I imagined being an actress as an alternative to dancing."

"I'm sure he was very receptive."

"How did you know?"

Paul ran a hand through his hair. "He liked to work with people he knew. People he felt he could control, I suppose. He tried me for a short while. Then he realized I couldn't act if my life depended on it. That's how Art got his start. They irritated each other, but he knew Art and that he'd be a great choice." Paul smiled. "In your case, it was adoration. You know that, right?"

Grace's face reddened. "I had an idea," she said. "But I certainly wasn't going to let him control me."

After a pause, Paul asked, "What's it like for a woman when she has so many men interested in her?"

"So *many*? There weren't many, Paul."

"My father used to say—I think he stole it—that for a beautiful woman, finding a man is like waiting for a bus. There's always another one around the corner."

Grace frowned. "It's not like that. It's not meaningful unless someone's important to me. And that doesn't happen overnight. And almost never now." She paused. "And bless his heart, Louis was only meaningful to me for career opportunities. I did some location work for him a few years ago. But acting—nothing worked out. Being in Rome. And having a son."

"A son?"

"Yes," Grace said, smiling, taking a sip of wine. "I have a fifteen-year-old son."

It was Paul's turn to redden in the face. The concept of the Foxy Lady with a child had never occurred to him. "Before I become too entranced again, are you—married?"

"Again?" Grace stroked her ring finger. "No, I'm not attached. Italian men and me, it doesn't work out. Not with the father of my son. Not with anybody. And you?"

"No," he said, shaking his head. "Divorced. Three years ago. Friendly, no kids." They pushed appetizers to the side and reclaimed glasses of wine. Paul took a long sip for courage. "So, *do* you remember the last time we spoke, Grace?"

"I remember the gist of it," she said, nodding slowly.

"Honestly?"

"Why wouldn't I?" she said. "It was right after Art's funeral, on the steps of the church."

"I asked if you had any interest in me."

"And I said, no, it wasn't the right time."

"It was what you said after. I asked why not. And you said, 'I just don't feel the passion.'"

Grace's face crinkled. "Ouch. Nasty brush-off. I'm sorry."

Paul laughed, pulling an ear. "Well, at least I didn't kill myself."

Grace twirled the wine in her glass. "No woman is worth that," she said. "But, my god, I went for the jugular there, didn't I?"

With a flourish, the waiter arrived with the mains, Arctic char for Grace and beef tenderloin for Paul. "Is there anything else I can get you? Some pepper? Perhaps more wine?" he asked. They ordered two more glasses of Burgundy.

"I thought maybe it was because of something Louis said," Paul continued.

"I didn't take what he said too seriously. I did like you, actually."

Paul waited a few moments, digesting. "I never knew why you left for Rome."

"Ah, now you're imagining some Roman lover? The ultimate, painful insult."

"Two or three. Honestly, not even I'm that masochistic."

Grace giggled then took a forkful of fish. "My mother had found the opportunity for me at the dance company. I didn't really want to take something my mother had found for me, but I realized it was something special. You'd recognize her if she walked through the door. I look just like her. Her family was well known once, in Lazio, almost aristocratic and quite well off. The money's long gone but she still has connections. I became pregnant soon after I got there. My mother was furious. Didn't help my career either. One of the other dancers, of course."

"I wonder, Grace—" The waiter interrupted with the glasses of wine. Paul waited for him to leave. "When we spoke the last time in 1998, at Art's funeral—the thirteenth of May, if I remember—you probably know that the police had spoken with me."

Grace pondered. "Yes. I knew from friends that you'd been interviewed. Everyone was talking about it. Art was so well known."

"Did that make a difference? Was that the reason for the brush-off?"

Grace took another bite of char and shook her head. "The police had nothing to do with it. I *had* to take the job in Rome, especially after things in Toronto fell apart. I told you, dance is what I love. Maybe if we'd had coffee in March instead of late April. But I had no ties to keep me in Toronto. My father and I fight easily. And my brother wanted nothing to do with me at the time." Grace paused. "I'm sorry I said, 'I just don't feel the passion.' That wasn't really true. But I was embarrassed what was happening with my dancing career, and sometimes men need to be hit over the head to understand it's not the right time."

Paul realized he hadn't touched his food. He picked up his knife and fork and held them above the tenderloin.

"Of course," Grace continued, "never in my craziest dreams did I think you'd lose two years of your life right after." She paused. "I guess the bright side was you were acquitted."

18

Paul stabbed one side of the tenderloin with his fork, then pressed the knife on top of the other. Blood rushed to the meat's surface. After hesitating, he thrust the knife back and forth until a slice curled to his plate. It was cooler and less flavourful than he'd expected.

He wanted to kick himself. He'd drawn her to the worst topic possible. *What the fuck was I thinking?* Now conversation would stupefy to the point where one would say, "Wow, that was *some* thunderstorm, wasn't it?" Anxiety crept under his skin.

But Grace surprised him. "Even though I left, there was part of me, after your arrest, that thought I should have been there for you."

Startled, Paul put down his cutlery and sat back. "Why? We hardly knew each other."

She threw her hair back with a snap of her neck. "We did a bit, didn't we? And I already told you. Whatever I said, I *did* like you."

Paul's mouth went dry and he took a sip of wine. "That's a long way from wanting to be there for me."

Grace smiled. "It was fifteen years ago. I'm just telling you what my reaction was." She put down her cutlery as well then dabbed the corners of her mouth. "I might be quiet and shy. But what you don't know about me is that's not always true. Not if faced with certain things."

"Like?"

"Don't threaten me. Don't threaten my son. If you do, get ready. And injustices upset me. I want to respond. I want to right the wrong."

"And that was one? How could you know?"

Grace shrugged again. "I knew everyone involved. Maybe not as close friends but I did know them. I just *felt* it couldn't be you. In every fibre of my body. I thought it had to be related to Art's drug problem."

Paul sat forward again and cut another slice of meat, "You couldn't know that."

Her eyes bore into him. "I could, actually," she said and resumed eating the char.

"The police—that prick, Detective Beecham—called it tunnel vision."

"Tunnel vision?"

"Someone becomes so convinced of what happened, they don't allow for anything else."

"My god, Paul, it happened right in front of his dealer's house."

"And Art owed his dealer."

"Exactly," Grace said, nodding.

"Ten thousand."

"A lot of money. Even today."

"And he was so screwed up," Paul said, "everyone had cut him off. So Art ends up with his head blown off. Except, in the end, that story didn't hold up."

"I never understood why not. I followed as best I could in Rome at an Internet café."

"Really?"

"Really. But the coverage on Toronto newspaper sites was sporadic. There were some stories about the trial, though." Done with her food, Grace laid her knife and fork across the plate. "It's shocking what Art brought out in people."

"Adoration."

"I meant murder." Grace scanned the buzz of the restaurant. "He had an extraordinary arrogance. I'll never forget what I witnessed once. It was after university, early 1996 or so. My father, atoning for past sins, was still feeding me money and I was working at that little retail place, The Papery, trying to make ends meet on my own while I was at the dance company in Toronto. It was the tenth time Louis had contacted me about acting, and I decided to listen. So I went to his office, if you could call it that. He was casting for a new movie, and I knew exactly what he wanted, but I thought there was a chance at a career. Then Art walked in."

"That must have been before he went to L.A. That was *Rot-A-Tot-Tot.*"

"I guess. I had just started talking to Louis, but when Art walked in, Louis went right after him, in front of me, asking him how he could do this to him."

"What?"

"Art's father had found him an agent and he had an opportunity to audition," Grace said. "But Louis kept saying that he had a contract with him for his next movie."

"Christ, I remember that dispute well," Paul said.

"Do you? Art just pushed Louis aside and told him that he was going to do what he wanted. And Louis, crazy mad, asked Art for his father's phone number, and got on the speaker phone and had it out with him. It was the most embarrassing thing. But the arrogance—Art just sat there, chatting with me, a hundred percent confident things would go his way. And they did."

Paul smiled. "For a while. Cocaine got in the way and then the auditions dried up. Everyone lost interest. He ended up doing porn."

"I remember now."

"Until the cocaine interfered with even that."

For the rest of the meal, Paul swung the conversation to the safety of reminiscences of undergrad at Victoria College, of his serious efforts at Commerce and hers at English with a History minor. When they emerged from the restaurant, the rain had stopped. As the air stirred, droplets bulging from telephone wires and leaves plummeted to the sidewalk.

Close to Paul's car, Grace hooked one of Paul's elbows and said, "Let's keep walking. I've got a few more minutes in me before I simply expire of fatigue."

She drew in close and he felt the easy sway of her hips. They stopped to peer into a store. The stirs of air gathered into a gentle, fresh breeze that toyed with strands of her hair and pressed her dress against her legs. When she asked, "What is your time off about, Paul?" he was imagining running his hands along the sides of her waist.

He thought for a moment and shrugged. "Four months or so of not drafting documents."

"No, what's it *about*?"

He released his fantasy and they walked on. "Some of it's about being free from wondering why I'm helping already rich people lower their tax rate. Some of it's about believing I'm worthy and avoiding dark places I can go to.

Some of it's about not feeling guilty, like those who've been persecuted can."

She was quiet for several seconds then said, "Can you resolve all that in four months?"

Paul tugged at a lobe. "I'm running out of time."

A few steps on, Grace asked, "Do you remember that time after we had coffee in Hart House? Three or four weeks before all that stuff happened with Art? When we snuck into that vacant room?"

Paul cleared his throat. "I was hoping you'd forgotten. I've carried that embarrassment with me for a long time."

Stopping him, she put a hand up to his cheek. "Oh, come on. You were an excitable young man. Just a little *too* excitable. But very cute." King West was busy with club-goers, men in glossy suits and women in thigh-high dresses, but Paul noticed none of them. "I have an idea that might help with your time off," Grace said. "Why don't you visit me in Rome? Have you been?"

"No."

"I have this coming week off, too, and an extra room in my place. It's a little cramped but I'm sure you can make do."

Lost for words, Paul stepped back in surprise and ran a hand through his hair. "That's—that's so generous." *An invitation to Rome from the Foxy Lady and that's the best I have?*

"Yes, it is," she said with a laugh. "I hope you come. Now drive me back to my hotel. I'm still on Rome time and in desperate need of sleep."

19

Two months earlier, Lee had the idea that Paul and Mark should join him on his Sunday morning jog at Queen's Park Circle. Every Sunday after, at 8:00 a.m., he woke Paul with a call telling him that Mark was game. And each time Paul said, "No," and hung up. When Lee called this time, Paul already lay awake, infused with a carnal hum from his dinner with Grace. "I'm there," he said.

He rummaged through his bedroom closet and found track shoes, clean shorts, socks and a shirt. With them on, he stared at himself in the mirror. Though he hadn't exercised in months, his shoulders looked well-formed and his legs strong. Lactic acid might plunder his muscles, but he didn't care. He left his bedroom and went searching for his favourite David Bowie CD.

He'd poured a glass of orange juice and smeared a piece of toast with jam when a text arrived. Licking his fingers, he stared at the smartphone screen. "*Thanks for a delightful dinner. What day are you arriving in Rome?*"

He grinned and felt a surge up his spine. *Why not? After the last months, why the hell not?* "Will check for flights later this morning," he typed. "*Pleasant dreams?*"

A few seconds later, "*Yes! Text me your arrival time so I can pick you up at Fiumicino.*"

With a whip of energy, Paul locked his condo, took the elevator to P1 and drove east on King. He rolled down the driver's side window and crisp, dry air fluttered through the cabin. A cloudless, cobalt sky drenched the world in sunlight.

After parking, Paul traversed Queen's Park west to east. Not far off, wearing stretchy everything, Lee thumped out leg pumps. Mark stood several feet away in a voluminous tracksuit, returning his glasses to his face after a cleaning. When he saw Paul, he opened both hands, appealing for mercy. With a huge smile, Lee belted out, "Okay, Paul's here. Let's go. We're going to get you as fit as you were in university, Mark."

They followed a groomed path that encircled goliath oaks and maples. The recent sun and warmth were enticing buds into leaves, and a multitude of squirrels, alert for dogs, foraged through young grass. Lee went into a trot.

"Easy pace, Mark," he said from the front. "Kick those legs nice and high."

"Eat shit, Lee," Mark said. Paul chuckled, sending his stride off-kilter.

They made the first round of Queen's Park. Lee barely broke a sweat. He began jogging backwards, lifting his glaring track shoes high. Mark was hunkered down, pushing through heavy steps and grabbing for air. When Lee barked at him to keep up the good work, Mark looked up with a scowl and showed him a middle finger. Lee cackled in delight.

Paul's heart throbbed and his quads smouldered. Lee yelled that there were two more rounds. Tired of Lee's control, Paul increased his pace and elbowed past, causing Lee to stumble. "Is that all you got?" Paul asked.

"Oh, smartass," Lee said, catching up. "We Asian guys are not only smarter, we're faster, too." He ran onto the grass to the left of the path and bolted by. Mark was left to his solitary hell.

Paul took the bait and accelerated. Several yards behind Lee, his lungs heaving, he notched Lee's rhythmic stride. As they passed other runners, sweat bubbled across his brow and a drop fell into each eye. He flailed away the sting without losing pace.

At the end of the second round, Paul remained close to Lee. But the burn in his quads intensified and his calves were losing their push. Inch by inch, Lee gained distance on him.

"Is that all *you* got?" Lee yelled.

Paul's chest hurt and his arms thrashed, but the competitiveness he'd learned at Robert Street kicked in. *Just keep up with him for the first half of the last round, then kick past him.* Paul gulped for air and willed himself faster.

They entered the last half-round and closed in on Mark, his legs churning like he was caught in quicksand. Lee's breathing was more laboured and every few seconds he checked Paul's position behind him. Paul eased back, lulling Lee into thinking he was done. Straightening for the final three hundred yards, with Mark only two hundred ahead, Paul sucked in every bit of oxygen he could and found his last reservoir of energy.

He surprised Lee on the inside of the path. "You prick," Lee gasped, pulling alongside him. Mark was fifty yards from the end of the round. Paul and Lee approached, both swinging left of Mark onto grass. Lee's thrashing left elbow pushed against Paul's right arm to make room to pass. Paul didn't relent. Twenty-five yards from Mark, Lee punched his shoulder against Paul's, sending Paul into a stumble, giving Lee the room he needed.

Paul licked saltiness off his lips and forced his legs back into stride. With his last dollop of energy, he caught up to Lee, passing Mark. Lurching right, he pummelled Lee's shoulder. Lee fell toward Mark, catching his roiling left leg. He tumbled, and Mark, with wheezing expletives, pitched hard right to avoid him. Alone at the finish line, Paul doubled over for breath then strutted, arms to the gods of victory.

In no time, Lee was at Paul, pushing his chest with both hands.

"Like, what the fuck was that? Huh?"

"Just protecting my space, that's all."

"It was sweet," Mark said, collapsed on all fours in the middle of the path, oblivious to the inconvenience he caused other runners. "I beat you. Victory snatched from the jaws of defeat."

"You ran one round less than us, asshole," Lee said, making small circles, his chest heaving.

"When it counted, I beat you."

Paul sidled up and put a hand on Lee's shoulder. "Relax. Just relax. We're having fun. Besides, you pushed first."

"That's bullshit," Lee said, pushing away Paul's hand.

"*Come on*," Paul said.

"Not fair, man, just not fair."

Mark shifted to a cross-legged position at the side of the path. "Take a chill pill, Lee. So, did you get some loving from the Foxy Lady last night, Paul?"

Lee cast a look of half-interest at Paul.

Paul smirked. "What is this? High school? No."

"Neither did I," Lee said. "Friday night. Neither did I."

"With all that stuff about Louis and Art?" Mark said. "What did you expect?"

"It was our *fourth* date," Lee said.

"Why'd you even bring her to that?" Mark asked.

"She says she wants to get to know me first."

Mark shook his head.

"But I *am* visiting Grace in Rome," Paul said. "She offered me the spare room."

"She lives in Rome?" Lee blurted.

"What the fuck, man?" Mark said. "There are signs of life in you after all."

"The thing is, it'll be good to get away."

"With the Foxy Lady?" Lee said with a large smile. "She'll eat you up."

"I hope so. Or maybe I don't. I don't know. I'm just going."

"It's a great idea," Mark said. "It's what you need. Rome is a great city to forget life."

"Make a meal out of you."

"Gotcha, Lee."

"I have a client who lives in Rome, with a sister here," Mark said. "Emilio Di Strata."

"He's the guy you're always jetting off to see?" Paul asked.

"Yes. Old aristocrat—great guy. You should meet him. Very connected."

"Mafioso?" Lee asked with a burst of laughter.

"You remember how I used to tell you what a pain in the ass you are?" Mark asked.

"Every day. Like clockwork."

"Nothing's changed, Lee."

Mark struggled to get up while Lee looked ready to run another three. Though parked east of Queen's Park Circle, they decided to walk Paul to his car.

At the statue of Edward VII, Mark stopped. He pulled a leg back to stretch his quads, looking like an obese flamingo. Paul and Lee continued on. Lee leaned in, and snapping his head back toward Mark, said in a low tone, "Something's wrong with him."

"What are you talking about?" Paul asked, looking straight ahead.

"Chippy. Very chippy. Even my date noticed it."

"Lee, I hate to tell you this. He's been like that with you since university."

"It's different now." Lee caught Paul's eyes. "And he asked me for money."

"He asked you for *money*?"

Lee nodded. "Not *that* much. He says it's to tide him over for six months. I got enough."

"But he earns—" Paul trailed a hand through soggy hair. "I mean, he's been a partner for more than five years."

"He bought real estate. In the U.S. In 2007. *A lot.*"

"Oh, shit, I didn't know."

"Don't tell him I told you."

"What about Charles?"

"What about him? He's just a prof. He's got nothing—except a giant pension. Paid for by our taxes." Lee leaned in even closer to Paul. "Hey, do you want to hear what I said to Detective Beecham two years ago? Between you and me?"

Paul shrugged. "If you want." Uneasiness traced his spine.

"Well, I thought Art planned his murder."

"*Planned* his murder?"

"Listen to me," Lee said. Words tore out. "Two years ago I was in L.A. trying to find a dealer for our software. I had some spare time, and on the anniversary of Art's death, I decided to drive by the motel where he and I hung out when I visited him in 1996. Just to kind of remember those times. And when I saw the pool, I remembered a conversation I had with him there. He said if he ever decided to take his life, he would do it *dramatically*. He said he'd choose to die in a hail of bullets like Bonnie and Clyde. And my read of Art is that, when we finally intervened, he was done. He'd given up. And planned things."

"What are you saying? He *hired* someone to shoot him? As some kind of weird, dramatic statement?"

Lee slapped Paul's shoulder with a hand. "Yup. In L.A., he even said *I* could do the shooting, like, to impress some girls. He was half-joking but I could see the connection."

"Geez, Lee, what are you *talking* about? Art wasn't done. He was too busy being the victim. Blaming others. Lashing out. I hate to say it, but for once, Beecham was right. That doesn't go anywhere."

Lee wanted to say more, but Mark caught up, glancing at them both when they went quiet. They crossed Queen's Park Circle to Hoskin Avenue. "I've got some documents for Di Strata," Mark said. "Maybe you can take them with you, Paul?"

"Can't you courier them?"

"They're family documents. He'll see it as a big favour if you do this. You'll get a nice dinner for it."

At Paul's car, they exchanged stiff hugs. "When are you leaving?" Mark asked.

"I'm thinking of Tuesday evening."

"I'll get the documents to you before then."

"Give me a call," Lee said, trying to look casual. "To talk more."

Paul fell behind the steering wheel of his car and retrieved his smartphone from the glove compartment. He called Collins, Shaw's favourite travel agency. Ten minutes later, he had a flight to Rome.

She picked up almost immediately. "I'm arriving Wednesday morning at 10:20 a.m.," he said. "And leaving the following Wednesday. Is that okay?"

"That's fine," Grace said. "I'll leave you to your own devices the last few days. I want you to know, you're doing me a favour, too. It'll be nice to have some company. My mother wants some extra time with her grandson, and I tend to be very reclusive."

Paul waited several seconds. Then he said, "Maybe I could see you before you leave today?"

She paused. "I don't want to cancel my final *arrivederci* with my brother." Dropping a tone, she added, "And I like the anticipation of Wednesday. See you at Fiumicino."

20

Sunday afternoon, Paul decided to escape Toronto's concrete and noise. His car's navigation system guided him an hour west to Highway 6. From there, he was led up the Niagara Escarpment to Rock Chapel Road. Spring in rural Southern Ontario enveloped him: young leaves cloaking trees; cacophonous birds swooping; thick coverings of blue scilla, white trillium and purple violets. At the top of the escarpment, farmland undulated and he was directed onto Harvest Road.

The day gleamed. Flush with fantasy about visiting Grace in Rome, Paul managed to enjoy the drive for its own sake. Only in the deep recesses of his mind did he acknowledge that the drive held another purpose.

His call so soon after their coffee had surprised Rachel, and her offer of hospitality had been hesitant. On the north side of Harvest Road at a metal sign marked '505', the navigation system announced that Paul had reached his destination. He turned right onto a gravel lane that ran straight and steep to an old red-brick house. The lane ended in a bulge under a sprawling maple where Paul parked his car next to two others. As he got out, a golden retriever ran from behind the house, vigorously wagging its tail amid muffled barks, and landed its snout in Paul's crotch.

Rachel came out the front door in a cardigan and baggy jeans and stood with her arms crossed at the top of a three-step landing. Her face was more haggard than at the bistro, and Paul began to feel unwelcome.

"You don't mind?" he asked, reaching her.

"No," she said with a faint smile, offering a cautious hug. "But I have a guest."

Rachel led Paul into the house, the retriever squeezing in first between her and the door. In the front hallway, she pointed left. "Have a seat in the living room," she said, continuing past stairs down a hallway. "Coffee?"

"Sure," Paul said, edging into the room. "I didn't realize how far into the country—"

He chopped his words and stood still. On the other side of the room, lying on a worn corduroy couch with an arm across his forehead, was Cyril.

He pulled out earbuds and glanced at Paul. "Surprise," he said. His eyes were red-rimmed and dilated. The retriever ran up to the room's threshold and barked at him, then scampered down the hall. "Rachel is following orders from Louis to watch over me," he added.

Paul found the couch's matching chair. The room smelled musty. Thumbed magazines were scattered over the faded finish of a veneer coffee table, and in the corner an old tube-type TV with dust streaked across its screen sat in an entertainment centre. To his left, a framed portrait of Louis stood on top of a cabinet, his grin so extravagant, Paul was forced to turn away.

Rachel returned carrying a tray with coffee mugs, spoons and cream and sugar containers. She used some magazines as coasters. The retriever reappeared, first barking at Cyril again, then landing its snout in Paul's crotch a second time.

"You sure I'm not intruding?" Paul asked, protecting himself with his hands.

"I told you I don't mind," Rachel said. "And Dante, *you're* going in here," she added, tugging the dog by its collar into the dining room across the hall.

"She does a bit," Cyril said, removing his arm. "She was just trying to beat me into going to rehab. Tuesday. Apparently I'm an addict, Paul." With a sigh, Cyril sat up, reached for the closest mug and took a sip of black coffee. A faded T-shirt swamped his upper body and several days of stubble dotted his gaunt face.

Returning from the dining room, Rachel stood across from Cyril and glared at him. "I'm not your mother," she said. "Do whatever you want." She looked at Paul, disconsolate. "Another request from Louis."

"I heard," Paul said. He looked at Cyril. "Why didn't you deal with this when Louis was alive?"

Cyril shrugged. "Always too busy at Dagger. Not that there isn't a lot to do now. Someone needs to run that place. Crazy time to leave." He looked Paul in the eyes. "Do *you* think I'm an addict?"

"A hundred and ten percent."

"Thank you," Rachel said. "We'll get by without you for a month, Cyril."

"And what makes you an expert?" Cyril asked Paul. "Watching Art?"

"Watching my brother. I should have been as direct with Art as I'm being with you."

Cyril looked through the front window of the living room and took another sip of coffee. "I'm not convinced."

"Neither was my brother—or Art. Denial."

"And your brother went to rehab?"

"Yes. He got it for a while."

"And then?"

"Died drunk—car accident. Twenty-five years old. I was seventeen. My father never recovered from the heartache. Thought he could have done more."

Cyril snapped his head back toward Paul. "What's the point then?"

"The point is some people recover. Shit, Cyril, the thing is, Louis held you in high regard for your work at Dagger. And I think you were his closest friend. But you're one step away from becoming like David—or Art, for that matter."

Cyril snorted. "Most days I was just the little man on the team. And I'm nowhere near becoming Art. I can handle the stuff and he couldn't." He looked back at his coffee. "And I don't know anything about your brother."

"What happened to him took a huge toll," Paul said. "Branded me for life. Are you lit up now? The last hurrah before rehab?"

Cyril shrugged again and lifted the mug to his lips.

"Of course he is," Rachel said, exhaling hard and throwing her hands in the air.

"Why? Because Louis died—and didn't make you president?"

Cyril squinted at Paul, then Rachel. "I just like the stuff."

"Louis wanted you to have that job, and Dagger needs you," Rachel said. "It's yours if you act responsibly and get better. Time to stand tall. Go to rehab. Take that spot Tuesday."

"I still don't understand why you use so much," Paul said.

"I've been using coke since first-year university. We have a long, happy history together. Art learned from *me*, if you want to know."

"I already knew that," Paul said. "No male role model in your life? Daddy issues? Or in your case, not having a daddy issues?"

Cyril sent eye daggers at Paul. "You're way out of your depth."

"Geez, Cyril, what man *doesn't* have daddy issues?"

Cyril looked back at his coffee. "I'll tell you this. The coke gives me power. It helped me meet Louis's demands."

"*I* should use some," Rachel said.

"I'll give you credit," Paul said. "At least we're talking about what's going on with you. With my brother—never."

"I've had enough," Rachel said, looking between the two men. "This is the kind of thing rehab is for." She shook her head then picked up her mug. "How much is one person supposed to take? I'm going to the kitchen," she added, and left.

Tension began infiltrating Paul. He wished he'd stayed home. "Louis told me he wanted you to complete his vision," he said.

Cyril put down his mug and lay on the couch, placing an arm across his forehead again. "Yeah, yeah. Scary stuff, especially without my crutches."

"I think you can do it. Go to rehab. Figure your shit out."

"No choice, I guess."

"Apparently," Paul said.

Cyril dropped his arm and looked at the ceiling. "But once I run Dagger, that'll show people," he said.

Paul shrugged. "I'm going to find Rachel."

He walked out the living room and down the centre hall, finding the kitchen at the back on the right. The walls were a garish green and the appliances at least forty years old. The morning's dishes were stacked in the sink under a leaking faucet. At one end of a bare table in the middle of the room, Rachel sat in front of her coffee looking out a back window.

"I need to go," Paul said. "Bad timing. Sorry."

"There's nothing wrong with your timing, Paul," Rachel said with a blank face. "Give me ten minutes. Sit down."

As Paul sat, Rachel got up, closed the kitchen door and returned to her seat. "I'm just overwhelmed right now." She kept her eyes steady on the cup in front of her.

"Something I can do?" Paul asked, surprising himself with his offer.

"Thanks. But I've just got to get through this. I have *so much* to do. Now I've got Cyril here, arguing back and forth with me. And I haven't even had time to grieve."

"Why is he even here?"

"A month or so ago, when Louis knew he wasn't going to make it, we had a heart-to-heart. He'd told Cyril he could run Dagger *only* if he went to rehab. He should have gone right then, but Louis didn't let go till the last second and then everything was in disarray. Louis made me promise I'd do my best to convince Cyril. So I lured him here. I wanted to speak to him right away, so he doesn't think I'm going to relent."

"It would be easier if Louis's father was involved."

"You're right, but that's not going to happen."

"I think he'll go. He's just scared."

"I hope you're right." Rachel scrutinized Paul. "Anyway, you didn't come here for this."

Paul pushed a hand through his hair. "I'm visiting Grace Campbell in Rome."

A crooked smile emerged on Rachel's face and wrinkles flared. She cleared an errant strand of red hair from her face and put a hand on one of Paul's forearms. "My, my. The Foxy Lady. I hope you have the time of your life."

Paul examined Rachel's face for veracity. "Then why'd you say that she has danger written all over her?"

Rachel stared back. "Let me show you something."

Cyril didn't move when they walked back into the living room. From the dining room, the retriever whimpered for attention. At the cabinet where Louis's picture sat, Rachel bent over to open the lower drawer. On top of an old laptop was a cardboard box overflowing with photos.

"Louis wanted a few of these for his post-mortem production," Rachel said, spreading images over the top of the cabinet. "And there's one I want to show you. Ah, here it is."

Without looking at Paul, she handed him a fading four-by-six. He laughed out loud. The picture was from a party at Robert Street. "I remember this," Paul muttered. "Kate took it."

Art leaned forward on a ratty couch, throwing a smile at the camera. Behind him, Cyril's sallow profile stared into the distance. On the other side, Paul slumped in a chair holding a beer, and behind, Lee piggybacked on Mark pretending to strangle him.

"Do you see who's in the back?" Rachel asked.

Two people stood in a corner near the front door. "Oh, yes," Paul said. With a voracious grin, Louis held a beer toward the camera. Next to him, elegant, looking away, was Grace.

"Look at that face, Paul. That's a dangerous face."

"What are you talking about?" Paul asked. "She looks beautiful."

"There's no emotion there. It's like looking into a pool of impenetrably dark water. You have no idea what's going on underneath."

Paul laughed. "'Still waters run deep', as your brother said."

"How well do you know her?"

"She's not impenetrable."

Cyril surprised them and said, "Let me see." Paul handed him the picture and Cyril sat up again, stared for a few seconds, then scowled.

"You know her quite well, don't you?" Paul asked. "She told me she did some production work for you guys in Rome. And that she talked with you about doing more."

"Yeah, yeah," Cyril said. "The project's been delayed. I think Louis paid for her to fly over so he could see her one more time. Then he chickened out when he became too sick. Anyway, she's a bit of mystery." He slapped the photo with the back of his free hand. "Drove me crazy. How pathetic I looked next to Art."

"Stop being so hard on yourself," Rachel said.

Paul took the picture back. "We all did next to Art," he said.

"You wanted to be his equal, too, didn't you, Paul?" Cyril asked.

Paul compressed his lips and thought for a second. "Equal or better."

"And he put you through a lot of shit for that. But now, it's like you admire him."

Paul shrugged. "Like all of us he was flawed, but there was a lot to admire."

Cyril snorted. "Fuck, it was because of him you lost two years of your life waiting for a trial that lasted a couple of months."

Paul paused. "Cyril, Art was the victim. *He* didn't choose to prosecute me. That was Beecham and the Crown."

21

To his left the bedpost floated, surging higher then slowly dropping, again and again. Behind him, a dim orangey-brown light snuck past the edges of a blind drawn over an unknown window. A door, not three feet away that led who knew where, was open a crack. He pushed himself up and hung his feet over the edge of the bed. The aim was to get to the door and escape the menace massing around him. *But my legs—my entire body—are too heavy.*

"What can I do for you?" Liebowitz asked with only a glance. He sat behind an enormous desk in a leather chair that engulfed three quarters of his thin, stooped frame. He was mostly bald, with yellow-white hair springing from above the ears. His watery grey eyes looked down at a fountain pen that lay in a small open space on his desk between piles of documents. With emaciated fingers, he picked it up, then pulled off the cap and snapped it back on three or four times.

"What am I doing in here?" Paul asked.

"You've been arrested and charged with first degree murder," Liebowitz said. "A serious offence, indeed."

"I'm aware of *that*. What am I doing *here*?" Paul asked, feeling his mouth curl in dismay. Now he sat on a hard bench in an enclosure with floor-to-ceiling clear plastic on all sides. In front of him, attached to a prong of metal that disappeared into the floor, was a small microphone that quivered with each word he spoke.

"Not so loud. That device is very sensitive."

Paul's dismay intensified. He spread his hands toward the walls either side of him. "*This*."

"Oh, that," Liebowitz said. "That's just to get you used to things. In case matters don't go as planned."

"But I'm here of my own free will."

"Who posted bail for you?"

"No one posted bail."

"Then you should be in custody. That part I don't understand. I have a good mind to ask you to leave. Anyway, I'm safe while you're in there."

"You're my lawyer, aren't you?"

"That's what I'm told. Do you have any assets or income?"

"No. I'm in law school. I worked for a year after undergrad but my savings have gone to tuition and rent."

"Your parents?"

"It's just my mother. She's not much use to me at the moment."

"Another Legal Aid file, then."

Liebowitz continued working the pen cap. Since they'd begun talking, he'd shrunk a size and the stacks of paper on his desk had grown higher. *Why won't my legs move?*

"What am I supposed to get used to?" Paul asked. "You're going to get me off, aren't you?"

"I will do my best."

A phone rang from somewhere on Liebowitz's desk. He set down the pen with its cap on, and pushed a stack of documents aside until they teetered at the desk's edge. A black rotary landline emerged.

"Yes?" Liebowitz said. Paul wanted to shift on the bench to ease a growing pain in his buttocks. But he couldn't—he'd lost control over the lower half of his body. "Tell them I'll be there in a second," Liebowitz added.

He put down the receiver and retrieved the pen. It had become so large in his hands that he had trouble pulling off the cap. Piles of legal-size papers had filled the back wall's dim corners either side of Liebowitz's dusty, framed academic degrees.

"Aren't we reviewing my case?"

"Not today. I have to be in court," Liebowitz said, his voice fainter.

"The thing is I need to understand what's going on. I'm starting to lose my mind."

Liebowitz gave up on the fountain pen. For the first time, he concentrated his gaze on Paul. "Mr. Tews, I am not a therapist." Paul squinted to see Liebowitz's eyes. Either Liebowitz had become half-size or his chair double-size, Paul was not sure which.

"I wasn't asking you to be one," he said. "I need some guidance."

"You'll get it when you really need it. Right now, other clients' matters are more pressing. I am sure you understand my predicament."

"Aren't you supposed to represent me to the best of your abilities? Is this it?"

"No need to get snarky, Mr. Tews. I must go."

Documents were stacking up in front of Paul and Liebowitz had been reduced to the size of a gremlin. *I need to get up. I need to leave.*

"Something, anything, Mr. Liebowitz."

Paul heard Liebowitz exhale, more like a squirt of air from a balloon than a human sigh.

"Reasonable doubt."

"Reasonable doubt?"

"That's all we have to show. That's the burden of proof for the Crown in a criminal case. A very high standard to meet. Much higher than in a civil case." Liebowitz was gone from sight, his voice no more than a squeak. "Of course, you said some very unhelpful things to Art Featherstone. Especially at the end of the fight. And that story you wrote is an oddity. We shall see if we can deal with all that."

Paul sat glumly. "The story *explains* what I said to Art at the end of the fight. It gives context."

"I remember your point full well. As for representing you to the best of my abilities, needless to say, I will. That, I'm afraid, will have to do." Liebowitz paused a moment. "One other thing, Mr. Tews. Did you do it?"

Paul compressed his eyebrows and ripped at his right earlobe. "I don't think so."

There was a pause. "You don't think so? That's not helpful, Mr. Tews. Like I said, don't get snarky."

Paul heard a rushing sound. Liebowitz had evaporated.

"Hello?" Paul said. "Are you there, Mr. Liebowitz?" He heard nothing. His body seemed cast in iron. *Is someone going to get me out of here?*

22

Paul awoke Monday morning, groggy from a fitful sleep. Lying in bed, he visualized the world beginning its week by taking kids to school, going to work and tackling errands. Like other recent Monday mornings, he wanted to pull the sheets back over his head and find calm.

He tried to imagine Grace collecting him at Fiumicino Airport. He couldn't conjure the scene as easily as he had Sunday. What value would he be to her if he felt so little worth himself? "You're blocking. You're creating obstacles," he muttered under his breath and swung his legs out of bed.

After showering and shaving, with a pot of coffee on, Paul assembled his best clothes for his trip, setting aside those that needed express cleaning. He then prepaid some bills and left his psychiatrist a voicemail postponing their next appointment. At one point he thought of texting Grace to test her continuing interest in his visit but couldn't think of what to say.

Around eleven, Mark called to say that he was couriering Signor Di Strata's documents. Paul assured him he would deliver them personally. To his surprise, Mark set aside the Monday morning demands of his practice for small talk. Despite soreness from the waist down and blisters on his feet, Mark said he'd repeat the run just to see Lee humbled.

"Paul, going to Rome for Grace is the right thing. You got to get out there and circulate," Mark went on. "Even Lee said so, and what the hell does he know?" Paul remembered he needed to call Lee—and Kate for that matter. "This stuff with Louis has gotten to everyone, but you can't let it take you down."

"My issues were there before Louis got sick. It's not the first time. You know that."

"You're seeing a professional, aren't you?"

"Of course."

"Keep circulating. You'll get back to the firm sooner."

"Maybe I'm not cut out to be a lawyer."

"Don't give me that shit. We're a team here. We're missing one of our best players."

Paul chuckled. "Lots of talent on the farm team."

After moving his conversation with Mark to a quick conclusion, Paul called Lee.

"I didn't think I'd hear from you," Lee said.

"Why not?"

"People don't always call me back. For business they do. Not for other stuff."

"Here I am."

"Plus you and Rome and the Foxy Lady."

"I'm calling her Grace now."

"'Calling her Grace now.' That's funny." Wirelessly, Paul saw Lee's smile.

"So you lent Mark money," Paul said. "He's not telling me anything about this."

"I was going to. Now he says he doesn't need it. Big bonus at the law firm, I guess."

"I wouldn't know."

"We had a long talk after we left your car yesterday."

"Really?"

"Sure, we talk all the time," Lee said. "Mostly about sports. That's when he told me he didn't want the money."

"I don't understand what's going on with him. He's highly regarded at Collins, Shaw."

"What do you mean? He wants to be the big man. Practicing law for him is just a step to bigger and better things. All about the injury, Paul."

"The knee?"

"You didn't know?"

"Yes—I guess—" Paul stumbled.

"Like he was *so close* to a football scholarship and maybe the big time, and it all fell apart for him. That's what he thinks. That's why he's out of shape, too. The pain in his knee reminds him."

"Maybe you shouldn't be asking him to jog, in that case."

"I told him to stop being a baby," Lee said. "You know what else he told me? He would've never come out if he'd gotten the scholarship. Never."

"You're a good guy, Lee. Especially for the grief he gives you."

"Just banter. Also, Charles knows shit about sports." Paul wanted the call to end but Lee continued. "Darlene hasn't called me back."

"Sorry to hear that," Paul said. "Mark was right. You brought her to the wrong event."

"She said she wanted to go. I don't understand women."

"You're not alone there, Lee."

"Just for me, have the best time with the Foxy—I mean, Grace. For me. No, for Louis, too. Actually, for all mankind."

"Depending on what happens," Paul said, "Louis will roll in his grave."

"I don't think Darlene will call back." Lee sighed. "You know, the pressure from my parents is *intense*. I got to get married. They thought not getting into med school was a disaster. This is worse for them. And my business is successful."

"They should be proud of you."

"What they want, Paul, is grandkids. Remember, I'm an only child. Hell, I want kids."

"Call Darlene again."

"I already left four messages."

"So a fifth won't hurt," Paul said then paused. "Well, I suppose it could."

"Don't you want kids?"

Paul chuckled. "Not the top thing on my list."

"I don't get that. You're forty. Doesn't your mother want grandkids?"

"I don't speak to her that often. Not her decision anyway."

"Maybe Grace?"

"For Christ's sake, Lee," Paul said. "Anyway, she has a son."

"Really? You're just depressed. It's from the thing with Art, right?"

"Where'd you get all this insight from, Lee?"

Lee paused. "I read books. About emotional health and stuff. To connect with girls."

"Now I see why Darlene didn't call back."

"Really?"

"Honestly, if you talked to her like you're talking to me now, you probably scared her the fuck away."

"Shit. I asked her a lot about her relationship with her parents. That's what the book said to do. *Hotwire to Women.* Good book. Want my copy?"

"Ah, no. I have to go, Lee. Mark told me to circulate and that's what I'm going to do."

"Like I said, it's that whole thing with Art that gets you down. Remember, the jury saw it your way. It worked out in the end."

"I don't always see it that way."

"Did you think more about my idea about Art? About the Bonnie and Clyde thing?"

"Not for another second. Sorry, I don't buy it. Art was more of a survivor than me."

"I think you're a survivor. You just have crazy thoughts sometimes. Why don't you just accept somebody else did it?"

"Lee, I already see a psychiatrist. But thanks."

As he pulled the phone from his ear, Paul heard, "Really?" He pressed "End Call".

23

Kate returned Paul's early afternoon message within the hour. She was out of one meeting, going to another, but she sounded excited to grab a few minutes with Paul at the expense of responsibilities. After he told her of his travel plans, she grew quieter then suggested a drink that evening when her husband took Kyle to piano lessons.

Near seven, Paul was back at the High Park house he'd visited Friday night. Kate's son and husband were on their way out the front door. Kyle walked past Paul without acknowledging him, stamping his feet in rage. "We haven't practiced," her husband said with a raised eyebrow. "This'll be fun, right? I told Kate you're here. She's in the shower. Go on in."

Closing the front door, Paul stood near the centre stairs. Water drummed from the second floor. He went into the formal living room with yellow walls and creamy, hefty furniture, across from the room where they'd remembered Louis. Paul was about to take a seat when the shower stopped.

"Paul?" Kate yelled down. "Are you there?"

He walked out the living room and most of the way up the stairs. The bathroom door was half open. "Hi, Kate, I'm here."

"I'm missing a bath towel. Can you get me one? They're in the closet beside the bathroom door."

It was an oversight that surprised Paul but he finished his climb and located the closet. After choosing a towel, he knocked on the door.

"Come in," Kate said, "but look away."

The bathroom was a quarter the size of Paul's condo. Plumes of steam made him squint. To the right was a voluminous shower stall with slate walls and a glass door. A silhouette of Kate's left side stood behind millions of water beads on the door. Her head was tilted back as she wrung water from her long hair. After several seconds, he looked away as asked.

Kate turned toward him and said, "Toss me the towel overtop the door." Paul walked over, and she lifted her hands to receive the towel, revealing an opaque outline of her breasts. "There's wine in a cooler and some glasses in the kitchen," she added.

Downstairs again, Paul pulled off the cover of a Sauvignon Blanc and withdrew the cork. As he poured two glasses of wine, he ran over the snapshots of Kate's body. Fifteen years ago, her breasts had been a bit firmer and her hips a bit leaner. But her attractiveness was just as real and a stir of lust grabbed him.

Ten minutes later, Kate joined him in the living room. Wearing a light dress, her hair damp and tangled at the fringes, she gave Paul a lingering hug and a kiss on both cheeks. Two couches sat at a right angle, and she dropped into the one closest to the room entrance while he took the other. He had put the cooler and glasses of wine on a coffee table. After a large sip from her glass, she crossed her legs in his direction.

"It's so nice to relax," she said, plucking at her dress while eying him. "You look better today."

"You worry more than my mother."

"What can I say? You're very dear to me." She bit her lower lip then continued. "The past is the *past*. You know, ancient history. Paul, it's *really* time to be done with it."

He stared at her and shrugged. "I don't choose to feel this way. It chooses me and I have to fight it." He needed something else to land on. "I wanted to tell you, Kate, you look lovely."

"Oh, please, after a child," she said, patting her stomach. "But I'm glad you noticed. So Rome, huh?"

"Yes. I visited Rachel yesterday. Cyril is looking at rehab, by the way."

"About time."

"She doesn't like my plans. Mark and Lee, on the other hand, love the idea. Anyway, I only booked for a week."

"Uh-huh. I hope you have fun."

"That's the idea. Except Rachel thinks she's dangerous somehow. She says her face is like looking into a pool of impenetrably dark water."

"You know, that's a bit dramatic—but you're a big boy." Kate reached for the cooler and topped off their glasses of wine. "As long as you know Grace can't be trusted."

"What do you mean?"

Kate paused. "I've said enough." She ran three fingers hand through her drying hair. "I enjoyed our romance together. Did I ever tell you that?"

"Changing the topic?"

"Damn right. It was uncomplicated. I can't remember why we let it die off."

"Art was back at the wrong time," Paul said. "And I needed to make sure my law school marks held up."

"Art was a mess. Mr. Boy Toy and his lost career."

"Boy Toy? Really? He had your heart and I'm sure he still does. It might have been uncomplicated for you but it felt kind of passionate to me."

Kate moved couches and sat close to Paul. He smelled her freshness and took in her green eyes. Putting a hand on his knee, she said, "I'm interested in something with a bit of passion now. But also uncomplicated."

She leaned over and he glimpsed her breasts. She kissed him on the lips and he held it for five seconds before pulling back.

"*This* is your antidote?" he asked.

She smiled. "For both of us."

"But you're married. You have Kyle."

Kate furrowed her eyebrows and rushed out words. "Oh, don't misunderstand. I have no intention of leaving any of that. But I need some fulfillment and satisfaction. This whole thing with Louis—it's had me thinking of the past, and yearning."

Paul smiled. "For Art, you mean."

"Yes, but not just that. My husband's a good man and my life is orderly. But there's—there's no damn excitement. I get more thrill choosing wallpaper than being intimate with him. Which he has little interest in." She paused and smiled again. "I don't come to this easily, Paul. But you and I, we had fun. Some time, you know, together, would actually keep me in the marriage. And I'm guessing you could use your release, too."

Kate was right. Being with a woman would calm him like a warm blanket dissolved shivers.

"Maybe this visit to Rome complicates things," she continued.

"Let's not jump to conclusions," Paul said.

"She likes you. I saw it at Louis's service." Kate pulled back a few inches. She sighed and leaned over for her glass of wine. "Despite what you think, when we first got involved, I was over Art. It took two years after he screwed off to L.A. but I was feeling free of him. And I felt safe with you, as I would now. Anyway, you think about my idea."

"When he came back, it felt like you were going to rub me into his face."

"More likely you rubbing me in *his* face. And it was *you* who told him, not me, I'm sure you'll recall." Kate put down her glass and crossed her arms. "But you're right, I *did* want to. Jealousy, I guess. Even when he returned. Just seeing his face again. Which is where the Foxy Lady, as you boys call her, came into it."

"What do you mean?"

"She hooked up with him when he came back from L.A."

Paul reached for a lobe. "Really? Are you sure?"

"I'm pretty sure," Kate said, nodding. "I bumped into Art and her twice. It felt awkward, like she was involved with him. *He* was rubbing *her* in my face. There was something going on there."

"I don't think you're right about that."

"I think I am. Have I taken the charm off your visit to Rome?"

Paul finished his wine in several gulps, set the glass on the coffee table and ran a hand through his hair. "It would have come up before," he said finally.

"I had no reason to tell you. Or do you mean at the trial?"

"Yes. But I guess—why would it?"

"It was very discreet, Paul. If it happened." Kate looked across the room at a clock on a cabinet. "They'll be back soon. It's only a half-hour lesson." Paul put his palms on the couch, preparing to stand. "I'm having doubts about calling the police. About Art," Kate continued. "If Beecham told Lee the case is closed, what's the point? Art's murder hasn't been solved in fifteen years and it won't be now. I've stopped thinking about it."

"Beecham gave up because he thought he had his man. Like I said Friday, when he retires, maybe someone else will bring a fresh set of eyes. What I want is for Beecham to rot in hell."

"You know, if *I* don't care what happened to Art, then who does?"

"His father maybe." Paul paused. "Did you think it was me, Kate?"

"Didn't you ask me this years ago? I never did."

"Kate, to be honest, I've never been sure."

She bit her lower lip again and her voice dropped a tone. "It was very complicated for me, Paul. I desperately wanted Art's murderer found. And I *desperately* didn't want it to be you. I was sure it wasn't. When you were acquitted, I was both happy and sad. Can you understand that? It was a *torturous* time."

"I suppose."

Kate sighed and looked at Paul warily. "It *also* was complicated because when you told me that Thursday evening you wanted to punch Art until he stopped breathing, I *understood*." She held up a hand, showing a small space between the thumb and forefinger. "And that Friday night, I was *this close* to following Art to his dealer's and just strangling the shit out of him. *That's* how much I understood."

Car doors slammed in the driveway. Kate looked up then bolted from the couch to the front door. Seconds later, Kyle flew by upstairs.

Kate's husband followed in and she turned a cheek for a smooch. "Mmm, you smell good," he said. Paul stood, yearning to leave.

"How'd it go?" Kate asked.

"Not well," her husband said, taking off a thin jacket. "I read him the riot act. Practice or else no camp, right? I'm going to talk to him some more. Nice to see you again, Paul."

Once Kate's husband had climbed the stairs, Paul joined Kate. She hugged him again. "Remember, the past is the past," she said, patting his chest. "And think about my suggestion. In the meantime, go have your fun in Rome. I don't need to know the details. And I won't tell you to be careful a second time."

24

The post belonged to his bed. Dawn created the orangey-brown perimeter of light around his bedroom window. And the door in front of him, ajar a crack, led to the hallway and living room. Paul's surroundings didn't confuse him this time. Still, he sat paralyzed at his bedside, beholden to the dream.

The courtroom felt like an auditorium; from the front, the back rows of seats were blurry. The walls were panelled in wood only slightly less dirty and worn than the creaky oak floor. Dust-speckled light angled down from grimy windows at the fringe of the ceiling.

At one end of the front row, Kate and Art's father sat together, each stern and apprehensive. At the other end were Louis and Mark, huddled together in a private chat, then Cyril and Lee, yakking it up. A court guard in a pressed blue shirt leaned in and told them to be quiet.

Paul sat in the witness box. The Crown prosecutor had made a strong case, harping again and again on Paul's words to Art at the end of their fight: "*Get out of here. Honestly, I used to care. Now I just want you dead.*" Liebowitz had said they were so damning, he had no choice but to call Paul as a witness. *But they're done cross-examining me and the trial is almost over. Why am I still in the witness box? I should be next to Liebowitz.*

Paul stood to walk to the defence table but two other court guards rushed in front of him, pulling guns from their holsters. Amid gasps from the crowd, standing strong and steady, they pointed their weapons at Paul's heart. He fell back into his hard wooden seat. Liebowitz held up his emaciated hands, palms facing Paul, urging calm.

From the bench, the judge cleared his throat and the chatter in the courtroom subsided. He looked at the Crown prosecutor, then at the members of the jury. In a voice familiar to Paul, he said, "We are ready for the closing arguments of the Crown. Ms. Daly?"

The judge looked down at Paul, as if ensuring he was paying attention. Paul's eyes bulged. It was the drawn face, sunken eyes and shiny scalp of Art's father. *Wasn't he in the front row of the courtroom?* But he was there, too, still next to Kate, still stern and apprehensive.

Paul snapped his head toward the jury stand. Of the twelve jurors, six were Art's father as well, in varying poses. And beside each, completing the jury, was the same woman, bouncing on her seat, eyes darting between Paul and the Crown prosecutor. Paul recognized six versions of Art's mother, of her auburn hair and her narrow, symmetrical face. *How has Liebowitz missed that the deck has been stacked against me?*

The Crown prosecutor, Ms. Daly, a perky young woman in a black robe and with a mountainous perm, stood and approached the jury. She locked herself into one spot and spread her arms in a welcoming gesture.

"Ladies and gentlemen of the jury, it is my job to convince you beyond a reasonable doubt that Paul Tews is guilty of the charge for which he has been indicted: first degree murder. There is no more serious charge under Canadian criminal law. Under the *Criminal Code* as it applies to this case, a person commits homicide when, directly or indirectly, by any means, he causes the death of a human being. *Culpable* homicide, that is, blameworthy homicide, includes murder where the person who causes the death of a human being means to cause his death. And murder is *first degree* murder when it is planned and deliberate.

"Before I continue, let me say that it is *not* my job to make social commentary on what Parliament has deemed a fit penalty for first degree murder. If it were up to me, Paul Tews would die, just like Art Featherstone did. Sadly, in Canada, we don't have capital punishment, though many would agree with me when I say it would be an appropriate punishment for this heinous crime."

Several of Art's fathers in the jury nodded.

Daly sighed and took a deep breath. "Now, the defence would have you believe that there is reasonable doubt that it was Paul who murdered Art. And if that's true, you must find Paul Tews not guilty." Daly's voice dipped with gravity. "But ladies and gentlemen of the jury, *all* the essential ingredients of first degree murder have been met. Everything is quite simple. Let me show you."

Daly smiled at the jury. "For me to succeed in showing that Paul is guilty of first degree murder, I must prove beyond a reasonable doubt these five things. One: it was Paul who was the offender. Two: the time and place of the murder. Three: that Paul committed an unlawful act. Four: that the unlawful act caused Art's death. And five: that Paul *meant* to murder Art. In addition, to show it was *first de-*

gree murder, I must prove that the murder was planned and deliberate."

Nodding her head with understanding, Daly said, "A little complicated, I know. But let me point out to you that the second, third and fourth ingredients are simple to prove. From police testimony, we know that Art was murdered on May 8, 1998 on Richmond Street West in Toronto. We also know that, if Paul was the offender, shooting Art was an unlawful act. And from the autopsy report and testimony, we know that the shooting caused Art's death. So what this comes down to is showing that it was Paul who committed the offence, that he intended to commit it and that it was planned and deliberate.

"So, was it Paul?" Daly asked, spreading her hands again. "*Of course it was.*" She paused. "Now, I'm aware that the murder weapon has not been found and that that may bother you. But here is the key point. To find Paul was the offender, you don't need to have direct evidence that Paul shot the bullet that killed Art. It is enough to have circumstantial evidence. We need to know that Paul had the *opportunity* to commit the crime. And he did.

"Immediately before the murder, Paul was with Art and their friends at Kate's place. Those friends tried to convince Art to seek professional help for his unfortunate cocaine habit. Irritated by them, Art decided he actually needed more. He told everyone, including Paul, that he was going to wait in Kate's car to buy cocaine at 11:15 p.m.—from the same dealer, at the same house, that Paul learned of *the evening before.*

"Now, every guest left Kate's place before Paul. Paul said he was going to stay with Kate to help her with her resentments toward Art. But then, all of a sudden, he needs to leave after all. Because of a headache. Hmm. He'd already taken an Aspirin at Kate's for that. But he chose not to wait around for it to take effect.

"So Paul leaves. What was Paul wearing when he left? The same large windbreaker he'd arrived in. A windbreaker certainly large enough to easily conceal any type of handgun that shot the calibre of cartridge that killed Art.

"Then what happens? Paul waits at a coffee shop at King and Bathurst Streets, supposedly for a coffee to help his headache. Now, the time Paul left is most interesting for two reasons. First, when Detective Beecham interviewed Paul—which was videotaped under oath—Paul said he was at the coffee shop *for half an hour*. In fact, he went on to say, he probably was at the coffee shop at the time Art was murdered. But Detective Beecham was too good. He ordered surveillance video from the shop and we see Paul stopping in at 10:45 p.m., then leaving at 10:58. 'Oh, oh, I forgot that I left that early,' he claims. Ladies and gentlemen of the jury, Paul was lying. *Lies*.

"But the time Paul left the coffee shop is interesting for another reason. It *proves* Paul had the opportunity to murder Art. Remember, a neighbour heard a shot at 11:05. And it's only a six-minute walk from the coffee shop to Richmond Street where Art died. Paul waited at the coffee shop, left at 10:58 and walked north on Spadina. At Richmond, he spotted Kate's car, and around 11:05, he shot Art in cold blood as he sat in the driver's seat, a young man whom we all agree had a brilliant future.

"Let me make one final point about opportunity. We know Art died from a bullet to the head. Now, shooting a handgun isn't the easiest thing in the world." Daly mimicked the shape of a handgun with her right hand and pointed in the air. "You don't just go bang, bang. A bit of practice beforehand can help a murderer be sure his awful deed will get done. And Paul had that practice. With a handgun that his Granddad owned and taught him to use as a teenager. We don't know what happened to the murder weapon, but we know Paul had experience with a type of gun that shot the calibre of bullet that killed Art."

Still locked in one position, Daly gave a violent nod toward the jury to assert her last point. She let drama accumulate before continuing.

"Now, ladies and gentlemen of the jury, let's consider Paul Tews's motive. In summary, Paul killed Art because he felt unstoppable malice toward him.

"Let me start with what we know about Paul at Robert Street, where he first met Art in September 1993. All his housemates say that Paul was friendly but also very competitive. *Especially* in relation to Art. Paul always had an eye for what Art was doing, and often tried to better him. Sometimes, Lee Chiu said, they were like two lions circling each other, taking swats and jumping into fights.

"Indeed, in September 1994, Paul writes a story that was published in the *Acta Victoriana* in February 1995. And what is the story about? It's about feelings of malice one young man has toward another, about jealousy, about envy, and about his extraction of revenge through an awful, premeditated murder. By *gunshot,* for goodness' sake. The defence wants you to believe that it is just a story. But I submit to you that John is Paul and Greg is Art. The story is evidence of the growing malice Paul felt toward Art. The similarities are simply too eerie.

"And isn't it interesting that, of all the women available to him while Art was in Los Angeles developing his film career, Paul chose Art's former long-time girlfriend, Kate? He *admitted* in testimony that that gave him some satisfaction. In a sick way, Paul was looking to get back at Art with Kate.

"Indeed, Kate was the reason for that terrible fight between Paul and Art on the evening of Thursday, May 7, 1998. The defence wants you to think of it as a 'disagreement', members of the jury, but it was a *brawl*. And how do we know that? Because of the testimony of Mr. Chen, who watched his basement apartment become damaged. Because in Art's autopsy, scratch marks were found on his wrist—claw marks really—and in samples from underneath the fingernails of Paul's right hand, Art's DNA was found.

"And how did the fight end? Paul kicked Art out of his apartment with these words: '*Get out of here. Honestly, I used to care. Now I just want you dead.*' Have more chilling words ever been spoken? *And* a few hours later, on a call with Kate, Paul said, 'I was this close to punching his pretty face till he stopped breathing.' Yes, below Paul's calm, friendly surface, his malice toward Art, the malice that had grown inside him for years, was exploding, and on Friday, May 8, 1998, he pulled the trigger of the gun that killed Art."

Daly's voice rose. "Ladies and gentlemen of the jury, I have shown you the opportunity and motive Paul Tews had to murder Art Featherstone. That means that the first ingredient of murder, identity of the offender, is established. It was Paul Tews."

Her voice settled down again. "The last ingredient for murder is to show that Paul meant to kill Art. That's not a problem. You're entitled as a matter of common sense to infer that Paul, sane and sober at the time of the shooting, intended the natural and probable consequence of shooting the handgun. That is, that Art would die."

Once again, Daly's voice gained strength. "I am left with one other thing to prove. And that is that Art's murder was planned and deliberate, and that therefore Paul Tews is guilty of *first degree* murder. I said earlier that everything about this case is simple and it is on this point, too.

"We've already established that Paul hated Art. We know about the Thursday night fight and Paul's awful words to Art. And Paul testified that the fight made him angry the next day, to the point where the anger interfered with his ability to concentrate on a transaction he was working on at Collins, Shaw. He even took two walks 'to deal with it', as he said in testimony. And, in the evening, he was late for Art's intervention. Why all this strange behaviour? Well, he was putting the final touches on his plan for Art, likely acquiring a gun if he hadn't gotten one before. When he finally arrived at Kate's place, he had his eyes and ears open for the right opportunity. And what better one could come along? Art waiting for his dealer on Richmond, a man whom Paul knew Art owed ten thousand dollars. He immediately realized everyone would assume Tony Rivera was settling a score. Paul's plan came together very nicely."

Paul twitched in the witness box. *Damn, she's good. It's dark in here.*

"Ladies and gentlemen of the jury, all the ingredients of first degree murder are met. I urge you to find Paul Tews guilty of that crime and throw the proverbial book at him." Once more, Daly nodded sharply then twirled around and returned to the Crown table.

"Marvelous job," Art's father, the judge, said. "Mr. Liebowitz, does the defence have any useful closing arguments?"

Liebowitz pushed himself out of his chair. Stooped, his gait arduous, he made his way to the jury box, nearly tripping over his black robe. He stopped, took a deep breath and started pacing back and forth. "First of all, ladies and gentlemen of the jury," he began, "just look at my client. Does he *look* like a killer? Those blue eyes, the wavy hair, the solid, lean six feet. That's not what you'd expect a murderer to look like. So I say set him free."

"I hope that's not the best you have," the judge said.

Paul leaned forward in the witness box and hissed at Liebowitz. "Art had fights with others, too. Remember?"

"That's *right*," Liebowitz said, throwing a finger in the air, continuing to pace.

"Excuse me," the judge said. "That is highly irregular. No talking with counsel during closing arguments."

Liebowitz continued. "In the days before his death, Art was a very difficult young man. He picked fights with Kate, Louis and others, and insulted nearly everyone he encountered. So why are the police and the Crown focussing just on Paul? Why, I ask you? Art provoked malice toward himself from *many* people, and they also had motive."

"And the murder weapon," Paul hissed again.

"That's the last time I'm permitting that," Art's father barked from the bench.

"*Another* good point," Liebowitz said, still pacing. "*Where* is the murder weapon? I'll tell you. *Nowhere.* It's never been found. So there's no evidence directly linking my client to the murder. This so-called evidence about Paul stopping off at the coffee shop and having the opportunity to murder Art, it's weak, it's insufficient to convict. Right there, you've got reasonable doubt.

"*But* there is one other point I'll make and I don't even require my client to remind me of it. My client has *explained* those awful words the Crown keeps reminding you of. '*Honestly, I used to care,*' blah, blah, blah. Paul wrote those words in his story, and they were adopted by Art and Paul, in rather dramatic fashion, as their own code to say, 'Leave me alone. Give me my space.' We have testimony that they *often* said it to each other, loosely, cavalierly, as competitive, brash young men who mix it up once in a while might. Before May 7, 1998, if Paul used those words, it didn't mean a body would show up the next day. And it didn't mean that on May 7 either.

"Ladies and gentlemen of the jury, you have reasonable doubt who murdered Art Featherstone. Use it to set my client free from the clutches of this charade." Liebowitz stopped pacing and appeared ready to collapse. Slowly he returned to the defence table.

Those are the weakest closing arguments for the defence ever rendered. I'm done for.

"Right then," the judge said. "It is time for me to give my instructions to the jury."

"Excuse me," a jury member, one of Art's fathers, said, standing.

"Yes?" the judge, his mirror image, asked.

"I am the foreperson of the jury and we know our decision."

"Oh, you do? Well, technically, I need to give instructions, but it's obvious, isn't it?"

Paul's mouth went dry as sand and his heart rattled like a baby's toy. *I can hardly see him, it's so dark.*

"Yes, the decision is obvious. Paul Tews is guilty of not caring sufficiently for my son."

All Art's mothers nodded in agreement.

Maybe it's dark enough to escape.

25

Twelve hours to departure, Paul awoke from his dream with an overhang of unease. Instead of going to Rome, shouldn't he be doubling psychiatrist's appointments and gearing up for professional obligations? And what about the mistrust Kate felt for Grace and the danger Rachel saw in her? He got out of bed and went looking for music to crowd out his thoughts.

Of course Kate would say that, Paul told himself next to a rack of old CDs. She wanted him as a safe sidebar dalliance and Grace complicated that. As for Rachel, knowing what to do with her words had always been a mystery.

But if Louis knew of his plans, besides being envious as hell, he'd howl at Paul, "*Go, goddamn it, go.*" And Mark and Lee had both given a strong thumbs up. Paul felt the grip of quandary.

Art would have known what to do. The Art from before L.A. The one who actually followed through after saying, "Life is what you make it." In Paul's circumstances, that Art would have gone to Rome, jumped into the pool of impenetrably dark water and enjoyed life.

Paul thought about playing Coltrane but opted for Soundgarden and started downloading his electronic boarding pass on his smartphone.

ROME, ITALY

May 15, 2013

26

"Well, good morning, everyone," the pilot began. "We'll be landing at Fiumicino Airport in about twenty minutes, where the local time is ten fifteen. It's already twenty-two degrees Celsius in Rome, heading for a high of twenty-seven. Thanks for flying with Air Canada. We know you have a choice."

The plane flew above wisps of clouds that seemed to follow it like dolphins accompanying a ship. Paul roused himself and lifted the window blind to let in the morning sun. Below were green and yellow fields bounded by tall bushes and dotted with farm vehicles. In the distance, the sky's trenchant blue touched the grey-blue of the sea. The plane's landing gear released with a thump.

Paul rubbed his face, concerned with the stubble and fatigue that Grace would see. He imagined her greeting him, standing still and alone in a milling crowd of greeters, wearing all black, her face opaque. That would be okay, he thought. He could work with that.

Forty-five minutes later, he'd deplaned at Fiumicino's Terminal 3, taken the inter-terminal train to customs and retrieved a suitcase. With his carry-on slung over a shoulder of his jacket and pulling his suitcase behind him, he walked at a deliberately casual pace toward frosted glass sliding doors. They parted and he went through, feeling more defenceless than going into the psychiatrist's office.

He preferred not to stand like a fool in front of hundreds of well-wishers interested in someone else and turned left. Seconds later he heard, "Paul—Paul, this way. Over here."

Grace emerged from the crowd in a casual, mid-thigh-length white dress and sandals, and skipped a few steps toward him. She clutched sunglasses and keys in one hand and a small purse in the other. "Welcome to Rome," she said with a large smile, throwing her hair back, then kissing him on both cheeks. She took his free elbow and hustled him away from the crowd. "Come," she said, "I'm parked this way."

Soon after, they were on the second level of a parking deck. They strode between rows of cars until Grace stopped at a small white Fiat. She opened the trunk and Paul pitched in his suitcase then closed the door. He squeezed past a neighbouring car into the passenger seat and put the carry-on on his lap.

In the blaring sun, they joined dense traffic to Rome. Conversation was light and noncommittal. As they grew closer, they hit wild convergences of vehicles and Grace worked the manual shift hard. She managed through expertly and he sensed she was at home.

"So, how should I think of you? As Italian or Canadian?"

She smiled. "I still feel like a foreigner here. And certainly not Roman. No, your family has to be from Rome to be considered Roman. They make that *very* clear. But with Justin born here, more and more, there's distance from Toronto."

Soon traffic slowed to a crawl and Grace pointed. "Over there. You can see the top of St. Peter's. There are hundreds of churches in Rome, of course. I'm going to drive along Viale Aventino. You'll catch a glimpse of the Palatine Hill—where the she-wolf kept Romulus and Remus alive—and the Colosseum. Do those things interest you?"

"Yes," Paul said. "But you're the one who took history in undergrad. I'm just a lawyer."

"My real interest was the history of dance, not this. I'll show you some of the main attractions in the next few days. But I warn you. After a while, I simply can't take all the people and you'll be on your own."

Tourists were thick on Viale Aventino and buses belched out more. Hawkers commanded large sections of the street, many trying to sell the same cheap souvenirs.

"Okay, we turn here, onto Via del Circo Massimo. I live in Trastevere, on the other side of the Tiber. Do you know it?"

"No."

"It was working class once. Very buzzy and charming now. It's my father's place, actually. He was going to give it to me—I couldn't possibly afford it on my own—but I insist on paying proper rent."

Several minutes later, they crossed the Tiber at Ponte Palatino, south of Isola Tiberina. The river was swollen with fast-flowing, green-brown water.

"Levels are still high," Grace said. "There was flooding earlier in the year."

On the other side, she pushed into Trastevere, putting her car through a dizzying set of turns, avoiding pedestrians and scooters. She headed up a narrow street on a grade that dodged left, then right, creating a small square. "It's really just a jog in the road but I call this my little piazza," Grace said. She made a U-turn and drove back a short distance along the wall of a house to a tiny opening between motorcycles parked at a slant and another small car. She inched her car in, pushing up against the other car's bumper to make room. "Welcome to parking in Rome," she said, laughing.

Paul squeezed out his side of the car. Inserted above him in the wall was a stone plaque with "Via dell'Arco de' Tolomei" in capital letters. They retrieved Paul's suitcase and walked into the piazza, the wheels of the suitcase thumping over the road's dark grey irregular rectangular stones. Two- and three-storey buildings in hues of brown, orange, yellow and pink, some freshly painted and others blistering, surrounded them. Grace swung left and walked toward a two-storey coral house with open green shutters, young vines on trellises around the doorway and a wrought iron lamp anchored above the entrance.

She unlocked and opened the front door. The air of the hallway inside was cool. Either side was a door with a number above a doorbell. Grace walked to stairs at the other end of the hallway and took Paul's carry-on from his shoulder. Climbing five steps in one direction, then five in the other, they reached the second-floor landing. A short distance to their right, Grace stopped in front of an apartment marked "3". She ratcheted a key into the lock and turned her wrist; the lock banged open, echoing through the hallway. Pushing the door with her shoulder, she led Paul in.

After setting down Paul's carry-on, Grace opened two large windows that looked onto the piazza. Paul closed the door behind them then released the grip on his suitcase and surveyed the apartment. He stood in a spacious living room with a plush beige sofa in the middle and two chrome-and-black leather chairs on either side. In front of the sofa was a glass-topped table on a large Persian carpet. Left of the front door was an overflowing wooden bookcase; right, beyond a wide doorway, was a modern white kitchen. At the far end, next to the entrance of a hallway, a large grandfather clock ticked sonorously. Etchings of clocks and colour blotch studies hung on the walls.

"You have your choice of rooms," Grace said. "I have a sofa bed in my cubbyhole of a study. Or you can use my son's room."

"He hasn't left because of me, has he?"

"Like I said, my mother's stolen him from me. I bet you're up for a nap and shower."

"Maybe quick ones."

Two hours later, Paul woke in Justin's room, his suitcase and carry-on dropped in the middle of the floor. He lifted himself from the narrow bed and opened the window and its shutters. Noise from the piazza and eddies of warmth roiled the room's quiet and cool air. Rested, he rekindled his fantasy after their King West dinner of sliding his hands along the sides of Grace's waist. But it burst at the sight of pictures of bands and girls on the walls, a guitar in the corner and a work desk with Italian school texts.

After hanging some clothes in a closet, Paul showered off the grime from his flight and shaved his morning stubble. In a fresh shirt and jeans, he went looking for Grace but found he was alone. On a side table under a large, ornate mirror hung on the living-room wall next to the kitchen, a note read, "*Buying groceries. Back shortly. If you want espresso, press the top button on the coffee maker. G.*"

It was close to one. Espresso in hand, Paul wandered about Grace's apartment. A fan of fashion magazines lay on the living-room table. He glanced at one, puzzling over Italian descriptions. At the middle row of the bookcase, he ran his hand across the spines of English, French and Italian books about ballet, examining a few covers of dancers striking impossible poses.

A small wooden desk with a closed laptop on an inlaid green leather surface sat below the living room's right window. Tiny drawers were built into the back and a collection of antique hairpieces lay along the top. Paul picked up the centre one. It was long and made of rigid metal with a sharp tip. At the other end was an oval cameo of a woman's face, blonde hair piled high.

Grace strolled into the piazza holding a plastic grocery bag in each hand and looked up at her apartment. Paul waved out the window and she smiled, picking up her pace. A minute later, the front door lock banged open again. He returned the hairpiece to its spot and walked toward the door.

Grace struggled through with the bags. Paul took them from her and set them on the floor as she closed the door. He slipped his hands around her waist and drew her toward him. She didn't resist and he strengthened his embrace until her body was tight against his. He snuck his lips toward the crevice of her neck, and parting her long, fresh-smelling hair, remembered the smoothness of her skin from fifteen years before.

Pulling away, he found her lips, open and protruding. The kiss began slowly, interspersed with short, hard breaths. Every few seconds she pulled away and made him find her again, each time allowing him to separate her lips further. He ran one hand between her shoulder blades and the other to her lower back.

A sharp knock startled Paul. "I know who that is," Grace whispered.

He released her and stepped back. She opened the door partway and began an animated discussion. After walking the groceries to the kitchen, Paul crossed the living room back to the small desk under the window. An older woman stood in the doorway, her hair pulled back in a bun and strands of jewellery hanging from her neck over a black wool dress. Catching sight of Paul, she paused her rapid-fire monologue and gesticulations. Grace stepped in front of her line of vision.

A few minutes later, Grace freed herself. She walked over to Paul, who watched the comings and goings of tourists in the piazza, cameras around their necks and guidebooks in their hands.

"I'm sorry," she said, putting a hand on Paul's shoulder and pulling close. "That was my meddling neighbour, Signora Di Grotto. She was talking about some city work planned for the piazza this fall. Really she just wanted to know who you are."

"How does she know I'm here?"

Grace chuckled. "She watches everything from her window. She saw us this morning."

Paul stared. "That's—disturbing."

Grace shrugged. "That's life here. No privacy, unless you never go out. 'Signora Campbell, you have to be so careful these days.' As if I would just let any man into my apartment."

"Where is Justin's father?"

Grace pulled away and began a slow walk toward the kitchen. "He lives near Turin," she said with a wave of a hand. "Hardly a factor in our lives. I feel sorry for Justin."

Paul sensed he'd stumbled onto soft ground and abandoned the topic. He looked across the piazza toward the second floor of a three-storey house with peeling ochre paint. At one window, from behind parted shutters, half a shadowy face emerged and paused. Paul squinted to discern facial features but seconds later the shutters flew shut.

27

After a quick lunch, Paul gave Grace free hand to choose sights. They spent the afternoon parsing the narrow streets of Rome's medieval city, standing in the still vastness of the Pantheon, lingering at an outdoor café at Piazza Navona and fighting crowds at the Fontana di Trevi. The sun was relentless, inducing films of sweat and stops for gelato and cold espresso. By mid-afternoon, fatigue from his spotty sleep on the plane crept over Paul.

Near six, they took a taxi to Grace's apartment to rest before dinner. They strolled to the entrance of Grace's building under the bore of Signora Di Grotto's eyes.

In her apartment, exhaling a rush of air, Grace kicked off her sandals and lay on the sofa. She held open her arms for Paul to lie beside her. He lay on his back, and as she filled the crevices next to him, he put both arms around her. Fatigue and longing combined into delicious anticipation. Both fell into a heavy slumber.

It was after eight when Paul stirred. He felt for Grace but didn't find her. She sat reading next to him in one of the metal-and-chrome chairs, her feet tucked under her. Looking up and smiling, she flicked her hair back over the black dress she'd changed into.

"Up for dinner?" she asked. "Let me take you to my favourite spot in Trastevere. It's close by."

Rousing himself, Paul went to the bathroom and splashed water on his face. In Justin's room, on a small table next to the bed, he found a spare set of apartment keys that Grace had left for him. After choosing a light jacket and slacks for dinner, he pocketed the keys.

Twilight had fallen and the air outside was temperate. They ambled deeper into Trastevere along Via della Lungaretta, finding locals teeming in the narrow streets. At Piazza del Drago, Grace guided Paul toward a small restaurant with patio seating under umbrellas behind a fence of large potted plants. The proprietor came to the door, greeting Grace with a smile and a dip of the head. Without asking, he led them to an outdoor corner table for two.

The patio was more than half full. Wafts of tomato, basil and garlic rolled past them. Grace ordered two glasses of a Frascati recommended by the waiter. When they arrived, Paul swirled the wine and drew in its bouquet before holding out his glass for a toast. "To passion," he said.

Half a glass later, they ordered appetizers, pasta and mains. His fresh greens and vinaigrette before him, Paul looked at the woman across the table and felt a smile creep onto his face. "This is unbelievable," he said. "I could never have imagined finding you alone."

"I'm not alone," Grace said. "I have Justin." She sipped a spoonful of minestrone soup. "I have a little surprise for you. Tomorrow I'm taking you to my favourite place in Rome. The Galleria Borghese. You have to pre-book tickets and I ordered a pair for tomorrow afternoon—two o'clock. Some of the most beautiful art in the world and my favourite sculpture."

"Lovely," he said.

"It's nice to see you relax," she continued after a few seconds.

Paul cocked his head to one side then ran a hand through his hair. "Have I been tense?"

Grace circled her spoon in the soup to dissipate the heat. "I'd say so, yes." Paul raised his eyebrows. "It's like you're waiting for something bad to happen. I had something similar as a dancer, before a performance."

Paul pulled a lobe. "You know, I've had this problem since March. When I told you in Toronto that I took a sabbatical—it was because I needed to. Just so you know. I've been trying to shake this apprehensiveness."

"Tell me more."

Paul waved in the air above him. "It's like a bird is circling above me, ready to attack and take a piece out of my side. And I'm stuck to a rock or something, unable to avoid it. I hope that doesn't bother you."

"That's why I suggested coming here. To relax. It's the vestiges of what you went through, isn't it? That would leave me wary forever."

"Or maybe unfinished business. That's out of my control."

"After I came to Rome, when I searched for information about you on the Internet, I kept saying to myself how awful it must have been to come under suspicion like that," Grace said. "Having the whole world turn against you all of a sudden."

"I had Liebowitz," he said with a chuckle.

"Liebowitz?"

"My lawyer. The oddest, tiny fellow. I never knew if he and I were on the same page. Actually, in the end, he wasn't so bad. I should be more grateful." Paul looked around Piazza del Drago. Most buildings were painted deep yellow but the one directly across was dirty and covered with graffiti. "Anyway, the whole thing was surreal and utterly alienating. It still is."

Grace took her last spoonful of soup then threw some hair over her shoulders. "I felt empathy. Useless empathy. Like I said, I wanted to help. It should never have happened."

Paul finished his salad and put down his fork. "I suppose the police and Crown had grounds," he said, draining his wine.

"Grounds for what?"

"To be suspicious."

Grace thought for a moment. "I mean, I assumed they had *some* reason to arrest you. As I told you in Toronto, I thought it was that drug dealer."

"Tony Rivera?"

"Yes."

"That's what we thought at first, too. Early Saturday morning after Art was shot, after my first police interview, Kate insisted we all meet at her place. To comfort each other. And that's what everyone said. It had to be Rivera. The previous Thursday night, before a bunch of us met at a pub, Art made a detour with me to Rivera's place. That's when I heard Art owed him ten grand."

Grace nodded.

"But soon it stopped making sense to me. And to Liebowitz. Why would Rivera murder Art right in front of his house? And unless he had a death wish, a guy like that wouldn't do it himself. He'd hire somebody. And why kill

Art at all? Rivera wasn't going to get his money back that way."

"Because he didn't think he was going to get paid anyway? To prove to other—customers—that they couldn't take advantage of him?"

"Maybe. Except when I saw Rivera as a witness, he came across as very *thoughtful*. Not just methodical and cold-hearted." Paul paused. "Obviously, at trial, Liebowitz tried hard to discredit him, to suggest to the jury that it was him. Maybe it worked. What an odd place to talk about all of this."

"We're speaking English. I don't think people will listen in." Grace circled a finger around the top of her glass then finished the wine. "There was an argument, wasn't there, Paul? With Art?"

Paul nodded. "Yes. And worse, he attacked me."

"I remember."

"But Art liked to pick fights. Especially around the time he was shot. That was another reason Liebowitz doubted it was Rivera. Others had bones to pick with Art." Paul sighed and cleared his glass of wine. "Liebowitz said Beecham was right not to have tunnel vision. That we needed to think who else could have murdered Art. The thing was, most of them were my friends. I couldn't wrap my head around that."

The evening's warm air drifted past Paul's face. The waiter stepped in to take empty appetizer dishes, then brought spaghetti alla carbonara for Paul and bucatini all gricia for Grace.

"I've picked some Amarone for us," Grace said.

Paul nodded. "How well did you know Art?"

"Well enough to want to go to his funeral," Grace said, looking into the distance. "Mostly from English lit classes and a few parties. But I did bump into him shortly before he died. He was struggling but didn't say why."

"I told Kate, Art's old girlfriend, that I was coming here. She mentioned she'd seen you with Art before he died, actually."

Grace shrugged. "We had coffee once or twice. He had a lot of anger and self-pity. Very unattractive. Let's enjoy the pasta." A few forkfuls later, after the server had brought the red wine, she went on. "Tell me, what did Art and you argue about?"

Paul laughed bitterly. "It was about Kate."

"Really?"

"You know they were together a long time before Art went to L.A. and dumped her, right?"

"I knew something about that."

"Kate and I had a fling. It started just before Art returned from L.A. It ended after three months. Before—"

"Before we made out in Hart House?"

"Yes," Paul said, releasing a cautious smile. "It was nice but nothing special. Her heart was still with Art, even after he'd been away for two years. Codependents in the worst way."

"And *that* was what the fight was about?"

"Yes. That was Art, right? Incredibly possessive and self-centred. Even after two years, he thought Kate was *his*. He could really drive you crazy."

"You thought you could change that? In this fight?"

"Not at all. But I thought I didn't need to put up with his shit anymore. Before he went to L.A., we accepted Art's arrogance as the price to pay for being his friend. The parties alone. Well, you remember."

"Lots of pretty girls for you."

"They wanted Art's attention. We tried to compete. I know I did, and so did Louis. Generally, they treated us like aliens."

"You should have shown more confidence."

"The point was we let Art treat us how he liked because he brought the pretty people in. He just knew how to be the centre of attention. Lee said something similar after Louis's funeral. You never saw Art throw a baseball or football. He never sat down with the guys to watch a Leafs game. But he finished at the top of most of the English lit classes he took at Vic."

"I remember he got better marks than me," Grace said with a smirk.

"And he knew details of Scorsese films that even Louis didn't. And he got the lead at the Victoria College Drama Society."

Paul paused to sip his wine. "But not only that, he was the master of negative spin. Back in the day, Mark was in good shape, not like today. And he was a good athlete. If he hadn't blown out his knee in high school, he could have gotten a scholarship to a U.S. college. Anyway, he did what he could in university, played a lot of sports and stayed fit. But the thing was, to Art, he was just 'the jock man'. And he said it in a way where there was no comeback. Anything Mark countered with just made him look more pathetic. Or when he saw Cyril, Art would say to him, 'How many phone numbers did you get today, Cyril?', knowing it was zero. Or after *A Cannibal's Eyes* actually got a bit of local distribution, he'd ask me, 'How's *your* film career going?' And many times, at parties, in front of others. We were all at the end of Art's barbs. And we just let it happen. Because they were from Art."

Paul took another sip and shrugged. "Honestly, who isn't self-centred when they're twenty-one or twenty-two? But Art? He wanted to captivate—no, capture and rule. And he could and he did."

"Until he came back from L.A.?"

"Exactly. He came back like one of your Roman statues. Parts of him missing, his surface pitted, a shadow of himself. And he felt he'd been *victimized*. The world was out to get him and he hadn't gotten his due. No catharsis. No humbling. Just an angry fuck, ripping people apart, relentlessly, especially the ones close to him. Honestly, we tried to help him. In their own way, everyone gave it a go. And as thanks, he would provoke us. Come to think of it, I'm not sure why we cared. As crazy as it sounds, I guess we were looking for the old Art."

"But the fight?" Grace asked.

Paul ran a hand through his hair and leaned in toward her. "The thing was, in university, because of who he was and his successes, Art had the *right* to be arrogant. But in L.A. he *failed*, as abjectly as anyone could. With that, he lost his right to treat people like he did. So yes, we tried to help. But, like I said, we also didn't take his shit anymore."

Paul sat back and drew in a long breath. "I've thought about that a lot. Fighting Art with words and fists. Maybe it was the wrong thing to do. Maybe I should've helped more. If I had, I probably wouldn't have gotten into such an ungodly amount of trouble."

28

They finished their pasta in silence. Paul drank the last of his wine as the waiter arrived with saltimbocca for Grace and pollo con peperoni for him. His head felt thick.

"I should have ordered a bottle," Grace said. "Do you want another glass?"

Paul shrugged. "Sure," he said.

After testing her dish, Grace asked, "What actually happened to Art in L.A.? All he told me was that his agent got him a few roles. They were small but, my god, they sounded like *good* projects. Recognizable names in the major roles."

"Art really didn't tell us much. We hardly heard from him in L.A. Mostly what he did was taunt Louis when things looked promising. But Lee was our spy. And Louis visited a few times."

"Lee?"

"Yes. Art went to L.A.—let's see," Paul said, looking skyward, "it was late March '96 or so. Lee followed him maybe two months later."

Grace paused eating and wiped her mouth with a napkin. "I didn't know Lee at all."

"I suppose Lee comes across as superficial, even childish," Paul said, picking away at his chicken dish. "But he's very smart and he's got a heart of gold. He was going through a crisis at the time. His parents immigrated to Canada from Hong Kong when he was five and they put enormous pressure on him to succeed. Honestly, *enormous*. Forced him to learn violin. Always the best grades in school. And going to med school, that was just a given.

"It was very hard for Lee to assert himself. I remember his parents visiting us at Robert Street just after I moved in. His mother wanted him to move out because she was concerned that his marks would suffer from living with four other guys. University is for the future, not for fun, she kept saying. It took every ounce of willpower Lee had to say he was staying with us. Actually, it was Art who gave him the courage to do it. After that, well, Art was a god to Lee. He even went with Art to music clubs for a while, circulating amongst the musicians and übercools with his giant, goofy grin.

"Anyway, Lee did really well at computer engineering, but when he graduated, in '95, he missed the GPA for med school by a hair. His parents were crushed, and they crushed Lee in the process. I remember him coming to us, asking us what he should do. And it was Art again who said, 'Do what I do. Do what you do best.' Which for Lee was programming. So he did that for about nine months, at a big tech company, partly in Ontario, partly in Silicon Valley. Then, the following year, he *was* accepted into medical school."

"And what happened?"

"Well, Lee talked to Art in L.A., and to me, and it was clear he didn't want to do it. He liked programming and he had dreams about starting something on his own. So after just about having cardiac arrest, he told his parents he'd turned down med school. Then he ran for L.A. After two weeks, he quit the tech company and stayed with Art for three months. Lee had the time of his life. He'd call us once in a while about the parties he'd been to and the women he'd said 'Hi' to. He was the one who told me that Art landed his first role. I think it filmed in September '96.

"Lee eventually got bored, surrounded by wannabe actors, and visited some friends from engineering school in San Jose. That's where he came up with the idea for his company. He came right back to Toronto and started it. Honestly, he's much more successful than he ever would've been as a doctor."

"And Art?"

"Well, as you know, Art had an agent in L.A. It was someone his father knew, though having *A Cannibal's Eyes* on his résumé must've helped. Lee said Art went to a lot of auditions, mostly for horror movies, before getting his first part. It was a bit part but still a part. I don't remember the name of the movie now. So things looked like they were going Art's way, as always. I remember that Louis ate humble pie and went to see him in L.A. late in '96. Cyril was still trying to be a stockbroker but he was helping Louis on the side, and they both flew down for a weekend. Louis was trying to make connections through Art, but I think Art took him to one party, then told them both to leave him alone.

"To hear Louis and Cyril tell the story, the whole time they were there, Art was a smug bastard. He had a second role lined up by then. But Louis was right. It was a step down for Art from the first. A real bit part with maybe two lines. And they both noticed that Art was using cocaine quite heavily. Now for *Cyril* to say that—because he liked his drugs and they'd shared at more than one party—was something. But Lee said the same thing. In fact, Lee paid for some coke when he was in L.A. because Art's monthly allowance didn't cover everything.

"And then, in '97, Art went AWOL. No one heard from him for months. It was Louis who tracked him down. He flew down to L.A. looking for distribution for his first film and financing for his second. He looked up Art and was shocked. He called me that very evening. The work had stopped coming for Art. Christ, that wasn't a big surprise. He was competing with thousands of people as attractive and charismatic as him. And for the first time he was failing. Even Lee saw that, and Lee doesn't see anything until it's right in front of his face. The thing is, Art didn't know how to deal with it. He didn't adjust his strategy. He just thought snorting more coke would give him the power.

"Partway through '97, Art's father wondered why Art's monthly expenses kept going up. Mr. Featherstone is a smart man. He spoke to the agent and figured out his son was in trouble. But like my father with David, he didn't know what to do about it. I'm sure it tore him apart, but all he did was rant and rave and keep sending cheques. Art continued to fall behind on his expenses. Remember, Lee wasn't there anymore to help him."

"And so the porn?"

"Exactly. A niche. Bi films. When the producers found him, they thought they'd died and gone to heaven. I mean, he was a god on screen. They supplied some coke and enough cash for Art to get by. Eventually, Louis went down to L.A. once more and came back shaking his head. Art's agent had long given up and the coke was starting to interfere with Art's porn shoots. November '97, he returned to Toronto.

"We had a party to welcome him back, at my old place on Wolsley because Kate's place was being renovated. It was a complete disaster. It was a dreary day, and Art was trying to stay off coke and was the dreariest guest. Mr. Chen didn't even have to tell us to be quiet."

"Eat your chicken before it gets cold," Grace said. "My god, what I wonder is, where was Art's mother? Didn't she care?"

Grace had finished her saltimbocca. Paul toyed with his food.

"Honestly, Art's mother was enigmatic, to say the least. American. An actress, always trying to find a job. I only talked to her a few times when she visited at Robert Street and at Art's funeral. She and Art's father split up when Art was a teenager and she moved back to New York City. Art stayed in Toronto. I remember thinking how beautiful she was. Art got his auburn hair from her and she had a delicate, narrow face. Mr. Featherstone, on the other hand, looked like an accountant. They were a complete mismatch. He was one of Canada's highest-profile businessmen, steady and tough, and she was hyper and flighty, focussed on being an artist. I always had the sense that Art was just an inconvenience for her. I heard she died about five years ago."

Paul laid his knife and fork across his dish. "When Art returned to Toronto in late '97, his father had had enough and cut him off. Even threatened to take him out of his will. Art became a leech on everybody and could barely hold down a job as a barista. Well, you saw him. My great competitor—the guy I could never measure up to—had fallen to earth. Hard."

The waiter came over to remove plates and offer a dessert menu.

"Some tiramisu?" Grace asked. "It's very good here. Maybe a liqueur, an Averna?"

"Yes to both."

"I'll join you," Grace said and ordered.

Silence fell between them once more. Paul reflected that all evening they'd been immersed in the topic he hated most. But in Rome, with the Foxy Lady, the world floating with the power of wine, he didn't much care. He was feeling comfortable in his own skin. The waiter returned with the dessert and liqueurs.

Paul took a gulp of Averna, sensing Grace's penetrating eyes.

"There was a threat, wasn't there, Paul? When you and Art fought? Wasn't that the real problem?"

Paul released a derisive snort. "And I quote, 'Get out of here. Honestly, I used to care. Now I just want you dead.' Was that a threat? Beecham certainly thought so. And so did Liz Daly, the eminent piece-of-shit prosecutor. Except it really wasn't."

"But what else could it mean?"

"I wrote a story that was published in the *Acta Victoriana*. The last two sentences were from that. Art, trying to make fun of me, started using them whenever he wanted to tell me to get out of his face. And then I started using them back when he pissed me off. We must have said them fifty times. More. I was put on the stand at trial to explain that."

Grace's smartphone on the table lit up. She glanced at the caller ID then picked up the phone, holding her free forefinger in the air for Paul to indulge her. She spoke in

Italian for more than a minute. Paul felt some escape from the past and the desire to dip his toe into warm water with the woman across from him. But as she put the phone down, worry invaded her face.

"Something wrong?" he asked.

"That was my mother," Grace said. "My god, Justin hasn't come home."

29

Grace's thumb darted over the smartphone's keyboard. Her call rang through to voicemail and she left Justin a rushed message. Then she said, "I need to go to my mother's."

"Is her house close by?" Paul asked.

"She's in an apartment not too far from here."

"I can get to your place by myself. If I go along Via—"

"Via della Lungaretta."

"Yes, and continue on, I'll get to Via dell'Arco de' Tolomei and the piazza."

"Then I'll take a taxi. We have to find Justin. You brought the extra keys?"

Paul checked his pocket. "Yes."

He insisted on paying. When he was done, they hurried out of the restaurant then stopped on the street in front of the patio. Grace frantically waved at a taxi.

"If Justin is worried about being without you, bring him back home," Paul said. "I'll move to the other room."

"He and I had an agreement. I've given him everything. Now he can help me out. At the most I'll stay at my mother's one night. Just leave the apartment door open in case I come back. That way I won't wake you with that old lock." Grace flung open the rear taxi door and jumped in the back seat. After lowering the window, she said, "Are you sure you know how to get there?"

"I can always look at the map on my phone. Off you go."

The taxi made a harrowing U-turn and tore away, its tires slapping against the road's stones. In a flash, pedestrians reclaimed the taxi's path. Paul shook his head and laughed out loud, startling a couple walking arm-in-arm, who gave him a wide berth. He was supposed to be exploring the Foxy Lady. The streets of Trastevere were no substitute.

His watch swam into view. It was close to midnight and he yearned for bed. He began an unsteady stroll in the direction of Grace's apartment, taking longer to find Via dell'Arco de' Tolomei than he expected. In the slow ascent to the piazza, the cacophony of the crowds behind him receded.

A distant rumble rolled through the sky and heavy raindrops began spotting the stones at Paul's feet. Most shutters in the buildings around him were closed, many with interior light piercing through slats. But in one of the buildings at the end of the piazza, a pair remained open on the top floor. A pot-bellied old man in an undershirt stood at the window, watching Paul. For several seconds Paul stared back, and when the old man realized he'd been spied, he growled then slammed the shutters closed.

Above the front door of Grace's building, the wrought iron lamp emitted dim light intersected by more drops. The front door lock turned easily and the bolt slammed open. Paul put a shoulder into the door.

In the first-floor hall, a motion sensor caught the door opening and a faint ceiling light came on. The air smelled dank and the door thudded shut behind Paul, sending an echo through the building. Muffled television voices escaped from the apartment to the right. After swiping drops from his shoulders, Paul walked to the stairs at the other end.

He ascended in one direction, then the other, his left hand gripping a cold metal railing and his feet feeling for steps. As he reached the second-floor landing, another ceiling light came on but he struggled to see the opening of the lock in Grace's door. Leaning in, he dragged the key along the lock's surface. The tip of the key caught and ground in. After several exploratory twists, the lock's bolt yielded with a loud metallic bang.

The door slammed into its frame behind Paul, causing a second echo. He cringed. He turned the lock shut, then, remembering Grace's instructions, flipped it back open.

The ticking of the grandfather clock filled the apartment. His eyes adjusted to the darkness of the living room. To his right, in the kitchen, LED displays on the microwave and espresso machine pulsed 12:13. He walked toward them, correcting his path after stumbling into the side table beside the kitchen entrance.

He patted down the inside kitchen wall and found a switch. Cold fluorescent light flooded the white, windowless space and he covered his eyes with a forearm. Then he found a glass in a cabinet and a bottle of water in the fridge. He filled the glass and gulped.

Leaning against the kitchen counter across from the fridge, Paul glanced around groggily. A corkboard covered with a child's paintings hung on the wall. In the bottom right of each piece, "Justin" was written, the letters large and sloppy on the faded and curled pieces at the top, but smaller and sharper on the newer pieces below.

A second rumble roiled the sky, this time much closer. A moment later, lightning cavorted through the slats of the living room's closed shutters. The air inside was weighty and the shirt underneath Paul's jacket stuck between his shoulder blades. Somewhere above the apartment, rain started gurgling through eavestroughs, and the clap of a lock opening resounded. Paul couldn't tell if it was from the building's front door or another apartment. The thought jumped into his head that Grace had made it home. He waited, listening for steps. When he heard nothing, he let the disappointment sit for a few seconds, then put the glass in the sink, turned off the light and walked to the bathroom down the hall.

The bathroom light was even starker than the kitchen's. Paul used the toilet then washed his hands and face. He stared into the small mirror above the sink. Another thump of thunder startled him, tingling his nerve endings. For an instant he saw primal fear: eyes protruding, jaw tight, muscles taut.

Shutting off the light, Paul's skull felt thick and throbbed. Lightning took rapid snapshots of Justin's room. He hung up his jacket and wondered if he should take Aspirin but decided he was too tired to care. He dropped onto Justin's narrow bed and pulled off his shoes and socks.

A remote click and thud reached his ears. Paul tried to understand the unfamiliar sounds. Grace was back after all, he guessed, a smile curling his lips. Justin had been found and was fine. She was relieved. She was still a little drunk. She was happy to see him. Arousal grabbed him, and forming fists, he pushed himself up from the bed. It was time for a dip in warm waters.

Paul padded out of Justin's room and looked down the hallway. Again thunder smacked, so close the building shook. He walked to the end of the hall. Short, sharp slaps of rain punished the living room shutters and lightning flared. As the room fell back into darkness, Paul glimpsed a heel disappearing into the kitchen. He imagined Grace's supple figure, wet and slippery from the storm.

Smiling again, Paul snuck to the brink of the kitchen and peered in. The only light was dim pulses from clocks on the microwave and espresso machine. After several seconds squinting, Paul distinguished the edges of the countertop and cabinetry across from him. Then there was another glance of lightning, enough for his eyes to dart around. In the far left corner, a silhouette of curled fingers reached toward the corkboard with Justin's artwork.

The kitchen fell dark once more. There'd been a supplication in the curled fingers that gave Paul pause, but his lust drove back. He approached, imagining spinning Grace toward him, finding her lips and exploring her body.

He swung behind, close enough to hear breathing, and formed Grace's name in his mouth. Then he heard a whisper, "*Justin—Mario*," and a small sob. Instead of embracing the sides of her waist, compassion invaded his arousal and he touched both shoulders with his hands.

She screamed as the thunder walloped. With fingernails like vulture's claws, she turned for his eyes, lunging high, scratching open the skin on his forehead. He shrieked, putting up both elbows in defence, and she began to punch at him, mostly striking his elbows but also his jaw and chest. He stumbled back against the countertop but she continued the flurry of blows.

Lightning blazed through the kitchen doorway. Signora Di Grotto's rabid face bore down on Paul. Darkness resumed, but her image was burned into his neurons: tears rolling down from watery, blue eyes; twisted thin lips, receding gums and yellow teeth; grey hair, flailing free from its bun. Amidst a volley of sour breath and sputum, she punched and punched again.

Paul pushed back with his forearms, forcing her against the counter underneath the corkboard. Then he rushed out the kitchen into the living room, and gasping, ran to the other side of the sofa. The rain continued to splatter against the shutters.

His eyes adjusted to the poor light. She appeared in the kitchen doorway in a knee-length nightgown and bare feet, holding an iron frying pan in both hands. Spying Paul, her eyes steady and breath caught, she stooped like an old cat ready to pounce. Paul watched her every move and held up his hands. For some reason, he broke into remnants of high school French. "*Arretez. Arretez. Je suis le guest.*" Then he lost sight in one eye and swiped at it with a hand. Blood from his forehead had trickled in.

She hissed at him, "*Dove è Justin? Huh? Dove è Justin?*" then moved into the living room.

Other than making out Justin's name, Paul had no idea what the woman was talking about. She charged after him, running toward the end of the sofa closest to the front door. He kept his distance, lurching to the other end. She stopped, waving the pan back and forth, and arched her back, readying her next attack.

He wondered what he could do to end the insanity. He tried English. "I'm Paul. Grace's friend. We met yesterday. Don't you remember? *Paulo. Paulo.*"

She reversed course and came at him again. As Paul chased back, one foot slipped on the Persian carpet and he stumbled to his knees. The cat was on him, swinging the pan. Paul scrambled but she clipped the back of his head, sending him staggering toward the front door. He turned to deflect another swipe of the pan with a foreman, feeling it sting with pain.

For an old woman, she brought an endless supply of energy. He needed to be more aggressive. He lunged at her, and dodging the flailing pan, grabbed her wrists, thin and breakable as matchsticks. He shook them until the pan fell and bounced over the wooden flooring.

"*Dove è Justin?*" she spat at him again.

Her lips looked stiff and serrated like the edge of a saw. He pulled her to the front door. She fought every step, tugging to tear herself free, breathing fire. Letting go of a wrist, he swiped at the door handle. Her free hand instantly started pounding his face but he had the door open.

With a swing of his foot, he kicked the door open further. Then he thrust the old feline through the opening, and releasing her other wrist, pushed a shoulder and propelled her into the hallway. For a second, he worried she would fall, but stumbling toward her apartment door, she caught herself. He shut and locked Grace's door, then fell with his back against it and fought for air.

"*Dove è Justin? Dove è Mario?*" she screamed at the edge of Grace's door. Paul caught his breath and waited. A few seconds later, Signora Di Grotto's door slammed shut, echoing through the entire building. He checked and checked again that the door was locked. Then he wiped blood from his forehead and eye, slipped to the floor and focussed on the ticking of the grandfather clock.

30

Paul was startled from the foetal position in Justin's bed by a hand stroking his shoulder. Wary of another attack, he threw up a forearm.

"It's okay, it's me," Grace said. She sat at the edge of the bed. "That's an awful bump." Paul dropped his arm and turned to look at her, his eyes adjusting to the morning light. "Oh, and your forehead. My god. What *happened*?"

Grace smelled fresh and the ends of her hair were moist. She wore a simple red dress and was in bare feet.

"Is Justin okay?" he asked.

"Yes, he's fine. Just pouting like a baby because no one's paying attention to him. Now, are you going to tell me what happened? You said in your text that a neighbour *attacked* you. I didn't take it seriously. Signora Di Grotto? You mean *her*?"

"Yes, her," he said. He explained.

After he finished, Grace said, "I'm going over there right now. This is outrageous."

"Why was she asking about Justin? And who is Mario?"

"I—I don't know. I'll be back."

When Grace left, Paul got out of bed and saw on his watch that it was ten fifteen. He shuffled across the hall and looked at himself in the bathroom mirror. Before he'd gone to bed, he'd wiped the blood off his face, but three angry red diagonal scratches were carved across his forehead. He felt the back of his head and winced when he found the protrusion from Signora Di Grotto's swing of the pan.

Grace hadn't returned even after Paul showered and shaved. He helped himself to coffee and ate a bun with jam, then went to the small desk beneath the living room window. The sky was an implacable blue, and after the night's thunderstorm, the air was breezy and vibrant.

Grace returned and locked the front door behind her. She looked at Paul, then out a window. "She doesn't remember anything."

"*What*?" Paul said. Grace walked to the sofa and sat. "But how can that be?" He took one of the neighbouring chairs.

"Nothing. Nothing at all. And I believe her."

"You do?"

"I do," Grace said, nodding slowly. "She sleepwalks, very actively. I've found her in the hallway at night a few times, walking around, in a different world. You said she was in her nightgown, right?"

"Yes. But that wasn't sleepwalking. That was an attack."

"I understand. I'm just explaining what I think happened. She must have found her way into my apartment because I told you to leave the door unlocked. But to make matters worse, her wrists are blue with bruises. She didn't know why. Now she does. But she says she won't call the police."

"Won't call the police? *I* should be calling *them*."

"An elderly woman? A stranger from another country? It doesn't look right. Anyway, she's not going to call. But I apologized on your behalf."

Paul was stupefied. He ran a hand through his hair, wincing again at the bump on his head.

"That must be awfully sore," Grace said. Paul said nothing. "There is one other thing you need to understand," she continued. "Signora Di Grotto's only son, Mario, was killed years ago when he was a boy. An awful car accident in which her husband died as well. She idolizes Justin because he's the same age now as when her son died. You said she was in the kitchen when you found her."

"Yes. She was looking at Justin's artwork. She reached up to it with her hand. Maybe I startled her."

"I think you must have. Not that it justifies what happened. But I have her over for coffee every once in a while, even though she's a total busybody. She's so lonely. And every time she's here, she goes into the kitchen and stares at Justin's paintings. Often she starts crying and talks again about Mario. You can understand. It's ripped her heart out."

Paul sucked in air. "I suppose."

Grace got up from the sofa and sat on an armrest of Paul's chair. She ran two slender fingers up the back of his neck and over the bump. Then she brushed them across the scratches on his forehead. "I have to tell you, I think this makes you even more attractive than usual. I'm just going to imagine it was a street fight, not a fight in an apartment with a sixty-five-year-old woman."

Paul's stupefaction eased and he managed a smile. "I have better luck with the old women." He paused, then added, "Are you sure Justin shouldn't be here?"

"Yes. He just misses me and can be very possessive and jealous. I want to have some time away from him, for romance. Understand?"

Paul felt he'd been accommodating enough. "I do."

"And the Galleria Borghese today, at two. Remember?"

"Yes."

Grace stood and went to the desk. She opened a drawer and pulled something out. "But I want you to meet me there. I need to go pay the property taxes for this place for my father. I have this map of Rome." She returned to the sofa and opened the map on the coffee table. "Here's the Tiber, which we crossed yesterday," she said, running a finger along the river's meanderings. "Trastevere is down here, in the southwest corner. Galleria Borghese is in the Villa Borghese, the large park in north Rome, here. Take a taxi. It shouldn't cost that much. If it does, you're being ripped off."

From inside Justin's room, Paul heard his smartphone. "Take that," Grace said. "I'm going to finish my makeup, get my purse and go."

Paul hurried into the bedroom. The caller ID showed Mark Koslovsky.

"I'm glad I caught you," Mark said. "Guess you're having fun there?"

"Yes and no. I'll explain later."

Mark laughed. "Okay, I won't pry. The documents I couriered you—have you dropped them off yet?"

"I got here yesterday. And it's only a few minutes after eleven in the morning."

"Well, it's five in the morning here, but I just got an email. A family member is ill and the client wants to review the documents right away. Can you drop them off today? Somehow? I'd really appreciate it."

"Okay, let me try to figure this out with Grace. Can I give her the name?"

"Sure. Just don't tell her what it's about. Call me back?"

"In five."

In his carry-on luggage, Paul found the thick envelope with the documents. He stepped out of Justin's bedroom in time to see Grace unlocking the front door. She wore sunglasses and black shoes with long, thin heels that showed off her legs below the red dress.

"Grace," he said, walking toward her. "I promised Mark I'd drop off some legal documents with a client here in Rome. I need to do it today." He showed her the envelope. "To this address."

"That's close to Via Veneto." She paused and took off her sunglasses. "That's a very nice address. Is that *the* Emilio Di Strata?"

Paul shrugged. "I don't know."

"We can drop off the envelope late this afternoon, on the way back from the gallery." Grace gave Paul a peck on each cheek. "See you shortly."

Paul called Mark back and told him the plan. "That's great," Mark said. "I'll tell Signor Di Strata."

"Grace wondered. Is he *the* Emilio Di Strata?"

"Yes, probably. He comes from an old aristocratic Roman family. He's well known in the art world as a collector. Only the best stuff for him. His sister's in Toronto. Loves her dearly, but she was banished from Rome for some misdeed no one ever talks about."

"Ah, yes. Misdeeds."

"Paul, be good to him. He's one of my best clients."

"Of course."

"I mean, *really* good. If he invites you for dinner, or anything social, you *must* accept, regardless. Take one for the team."

"I'll be on my best behaviour."

"Okay." Mark's voice sounded doubtful. "It's the best I've heard you in a while."

"You should see the scratches on my face."

"I don't need to know about that."

"Not what you think. From a sixty-five-year-old woman sleepwalking."

"The idea I had was better," Mark said and hung up.

31

In jeans and a light jacket, Paul stepped out of a cream-coloured Fiat pulled to the side of Via Pinciana with Grace's map of Rome and the envelope from Mark. As best he could, he'd followed the taxi's route on the map from Trastevere to the entrance to Villa Borghese. When he asked about Galleria Borghese, the driver pointed to a white building across the street a few hundred yards beyond wrought iron gates. Paul attempted a *"Ciao"* but the driver was already accelerating hard into traffic.

He waited for a clearing then crossed the street and hurried along a concrete walk, past a garden with a tree in purple bloom behind, and lemon trees and blue irises in front. Opposite, the park sprawled and undulated, umbrella pines hovering over coarse grass and crisscrossing pathways. A boulevard led to the gallery where stairs rose from both sides to a terrace and the first-floor entrance.

He stopped in front and reread Grace's text. *"I'm inside. They sell tickets in the basement and yours is under my name. Find me on the first floor."* At the dispensary, an unsmiling woman handed Paul his ticket, looking away from the scratches on his forehead.

A minute later, he walked up the stairs to the terrace and gave his ticket to the attendant. The entrance salon featured fourth-century A.D. floor mosaics of fighting gladiators and the second-century *Satiro Combattente*. High up on the far wall, Marcus Curtius threw himself on his horse into the chasm. Paul told himself to savour the art, that he would find Grace when he found her. But after a few minutes, jostled by a multitude of tourists with craning necks and cameras they couldn't use, he escaped to the next room.

In the middle, there was a large sculpture of a woman reposing on a pillowed chaise. At the far end, Grace circled, smiling and blissful in intense concentration. Paul walked to the sculpture's signboard. By Antonio Canova. Paolina Bonaparte Borghese, Napoleon's wayward sister, as *Venere Vincitrice*. Even to a lawyer, the sculpture shone with sensuality. Paolina lay on the chaise, nude from the waist up, propping her head with her right hand. Her left arm lay along her side, delicately holding an apple. She stared ahead with a slippery, daring look.

Still circling, Grace caught Paul's eyes. Her smile expanded and her lips pressed forward. He remained in front of the signboard, allowing her to find him. When she did, she brushed her shoulder against his arm then flicked her hair back.

"Isn't she just lovely?" she said.

"Yes, though I don't know a thing about art."

"You don't have to in order to appreciate this. The perfection of the lines. The expressiveness in the face. It just consumes you. You want to reach out and touch."

"Who do you think she's staring at?"

"I don't know. An admirer? A lover? Someone in the pain of desire whom she's chosen to toy with? Just for the fun of it?"

"I'll take the admirer."

"I'll take the lover," Grace said and walked away.

They worked their way through the rest of the gallery. In Paul's mind, oils, marbles, names and scenes swam together. Grace stayed close to his side, nudging up against him, whispering into an ear, running fingertips along a shoulder. Lust was forcing out the last months' tensions. Paul wondered if sweat on his fingertips would penetrate Mark's envelope.

An hour later they emerged from Galleria Borghese, stepping onto the terrace and looking across the park. "Time for gelato," Grace said, putting on her sunglasses. "Then we can drop off those documents you're carrying around." They walked arm-in-arm down the gallery's steps and the front boulevard to several red trailers with treat-filled windows. Grace bought Paul coconut and pineapple gelato and chose strawberry for herself. A class of young children approached, and they stepped aside from the screaming bedlam that engulfed the trailers.

Grace wiped her hands with a napkin and said, "Let me see the envelope." She stared at the label. "Via Sicilia. It's not far. We can walk there."

She led Paul out the park and across the busy Corso D'Italia. Ten minutes later, they stood in front of a three-storey villa, stuccoed with white, block-stone trim, and surrounded by a wall of yellow brick. Grace's mouth hung open. "Do you have any idea what this is *worth*?"

At the left of the building they found a wrought iron gate. In a neighbouring brick post, Grace pressed a button beside a sign "Di Strata". A female voice squawked "Sì?" over a speaker next to the sign. Grace spoke Italian.

"*Un momento per favore,*" the voice, harsh and grating, responded.

Half a minute later, the gate buzzed. After a brief hesitation, Paul pushed it open. Grace and he walked along a path of small square stones, reaching stairs that led to the front door. A tall, thin woman in a wool suit peered with a tilted head from the landing at the top.

"Good afternoon," Paul said, walking up a few steps and reaching the envelope toward her. "These are some documents from my colleague, Mark Koslovsky, in Canada. Mark asked that I deliver them to Signor Di Strata."

Grace began repeating the words in Italian but the woman interrupted. "Of course I speak English," she said. "I am Signor Di Strata's secretary. I will take the envelope to him."

An older man in a dark suit appeared from the entrance, shorter than the woman, with a full head of hair streaked grey, glasses and a narrow moustache. "*Buongiorno,*" he said with an engaging smile, coming forward and holding his hand out for Paul. "Di Strata," he said. "You are Mr. Koslovsky's partner, are you?" His English had only a trace accent.

Paul stepped to the top of the stairs. Feeling underdressed in jeans, he shook Di Strata's hand. "Paul Tews," he said. "I'm a senior associate at Collins, Shaw. It's very nice to meet you."

Di Strata nodded. "And who is this lovely lady?"

Grace skipped to the top of the stairs. She took off her sunglasses, introduced herself and reached out a hand.

"Signorina Campbell, it is a pleasure," Di Strata said, taking the hand and kissing it. "Won't you please come in?

For a coffee perhaps?" His secretary looked at him with surprise.

Paul wanted nothing more than to be back in Trastevere with Grace, but he remembered Mark's warning to venerate his client. He turned to Grace and said, "Do you mind?"

"Of course not," she said, her eyes alive with curiosity.

With a noticeable limp, Di Strata led the way through a small foyer into an enormous room with a white marble floor and matching staircase at the end. The walls around them were covered with paintings. Grace couldn't help but gasp.

"These are some of my ancestors," Di Strata said, stopping and waving a hand. "Nothing special here. Signora Tramente, can you ask Carlotta to bring coffee into the salon?"

"Of course," Di Strata's secretary said, a smile yet to crack her meagre lips.

They followed Di Strata into a large room at the back of the villa. "Do you like art, Mr. Tews?"

"Please call me Paul." He looked at Grace. "To be honest, I'm just learning."

The room was painted a deep pastel yellow and sunlight flooded the end. Roman busts stood between the windows. Grace gasped again.

"I am an old man, Mr. Tews. I stand by formalities."

"May I ask," Grace said, "are those—?"

"Originals, yes," Di Strata said. "First century A.D. Of course, you see these everywhere in Rome. Not my ancestors," he added with a laugh. "The middle one is of Nero.

He was a controversial fellow but the sculpture is quite well done."

"And this, here, on the wall?" Grace asked, pointing.

"Ah, Signorina Campbell, I see you have good taste," Di Strata said.

Grace walked closer to a luminescent mid-size oil of fruit and vegetables scattered on a wooden table then looked at the signature. "My god, a Caravaggio?"

"It is," Di Strata said with an appreciative smile. "It is a beautiful piece. And also one of the reasons I had that ridiculous security system installed. You are being carefully monitored," he said, laughing again.

As Grace stood dumbfounded, Paul cleared his throat. "We were at the Galleria Borghese earlier today. Grace's favourite piece is by Canova."

"Well, of course it has to be the sculpture of Paolina Borghese," Di Strata said, looking at Grace, his eyebrows raised.

She turned with a large smile. "Oh, it is."

"Truly lovely," Di Strata said.

Grace went doey-eyed and Paul felt a nag of irritation. "I gave the documents Mark—Mr. Koslovsky—sent with me to your secretary," he said.

"Yes, I appreciate that." A younger woman brought in coffee on a silver tray. "Thank you, Carlotta. Signorina Campbell, Mr. Tews, please have a seat." Di Strata pointed at two sofas at right angles. Grace and Paul took one and Di Strata the other. Carlotta put the tray down on a centre table, poured coffee, then left. Di Strata sighed. "I don't know what Mr. Koslovsky told you about me," he said, looking at Paul.

"That you're a very important client of his," Paul said, "and a renowned art collector."

Di Strata chuckled as he struggled to raise his cup to his lips. "As I said, I am just an old man but one who's been blessed with a good life." He took a sip then returned the cup to the table. "Allow me to say, however, that getting old is not pleasant." He threw a hand toward the Roman statues. "Unlike my friends here, I don't get more valuable with age. Just my belongings. And that of course creates complicated family matters."

"You have a sister in Toronto?" Paul asked.

"Yes, my younger sister. In a barbaric place known as Woodbridge. I hate going there, but I love my sister and try to visit her once a year. She will get part of my estate. Which is why I have dealings with Mr. Koslovsky. Tax authorities. It seems the Canadian ones are just as bothersome as the Italian ones. Always making simple matters complicated. But enough about that. Are you here on vacation, Mr. Tews?"

"Yes. Just for a week."

"Visiting this lovely lady?" he asked, dipping his head toward Grace. She smiled.

"I am," Paul said.

Squinting at Paul, Di Strata paused, his moustache quivering. "Mr. Tews, please forgive me for asking such a bold question of someone I have just met. But you are only here for a week, and I am interested, most interested. Mr. Koslovsky once told me the story of a friend—from university I believe—with the same first name as you. It was a most startling story. It reminded me in a small way, a very small way, of something that happened to me. Would you be that friend?"

Grace looked straight at the cup of coffee in her hand; Paul set his down on the table. *What the hell was Mark thinking, gossiping about him?* Paul gave an almost imperceptible, stoic nod. "Quite probably," he said.

Di Strata continued to stare at Paul. "I must review these documents now. But I would like to extend an invitation to both of you to join me for dinner tomorrow night."

"We would be delighted," Grace said. Paul's heart sank.

"Tomorrow evening at seven then," Di Strata said. "I am very much looking forward. I only hope I can make it sufficiently interesting for you."

32

"That was *stunning*," Grace said from the back seat of a taxi, her smile wide open like she was ten years old. "That was a rarified look at an old Italian aristocrat. My god, in all my years here, I've never seen anything like it."

Paul looked out the window on his side. "Don't be fooled by him."

"What do you mean?"

"Maybe it's different here. But I bet it's not. The upper crust, the elite. The thing is, they may be charming and engaging, but they're not guileless. My experience is that they know exactly what they want from you."

"I meant his villa and the treasures."

"I suppose they were impressive," Paul said. "I need to text Mark that I accomplished his mission and that I'm taking a bullet for him tomorrow evening."

"Aren't you looking forward to it? I am. I have to think about what I'm going to wear."

It was close to five and the taxi inched through traffic. Several times Grace encouraged the driver to take an alternate route and raucous discussion followed. It was like her hands had different lives, one in Toronto, always close to her body, and one in Rome, fingers pursed and wrists flapping.

In Trastevere, in the piazza in front of Grace's apartment, the taxi driver made a sharp U-turn and came to a severe stop, scrambling a group of Asian tourists. Stepping out, Paul looked around, feeling like a fish in a bowl. The old man in the undershirt stood in front of his window, his eyes peering through curling cigarette smoke and piercing Paul's skin. Paul stayed close to Grace as she made her way into her building.

As they reached the second floor, Signora Di Grotto's lock smacked open. They hurried for Grace's apartment, but Signora Di Grotto darted into the hallway before they could get through. "*Buongiorno*," she said.

"*Buongiorno*," Grace replied, nodding and raising a key to her lock. Signora Di Grotto approached them in a light coat and holding an umbrella. Paul looked away, a film of sweat forming on his forehead and burning his scratches. He edged closer to Grace, running a hand through his hair, grimacing when his fingers touched the bump on the back of his head.

Signora Di Grotto pressed Grace into conversation and Grace curtly responded as she unlocked the door. Eventually it came. "*Dove è Justin?*" Paul braced himself and broke for the door, opening it himself. But the tenor of her words was soft and caring, and the threat Paul felt eased.

He slipped into the apartment, and a few seconds later, Grace followed. "Jumpy, aren't you? She still says she remembers nothing," she said. Paul tried to wrap his head around the idea and failed. "Very worrisome. I don't even know if she has any relatives alive."

Grace went to the kitchen and returned with two glasses of sparkling water, handing one to Paul. "I'm going to have a quick shower and then show you what I might wear tomorrow night." She kissed Paul on the cheek and scurried to the bathroom as he sat on the sofa, sipping.

With the thrum of the shower in the background, Paul checked his smartphone. *"Thanks,"* Mark wrote. *"The client is delighted (in part with Grace I have to tell you). BTW, I may have a surprise for you shortly. Stay tuned."*

Ten minutes later, Grace strode into the living room in a knee-length black dress, a crashing bustline through the tight top and swaying folds on the bottom. In towering heels, she walked to both living room windows and drew the shutters partway closed. Then, from the top of the desk in front of the right window, she took an antique hairclip, and arching her back, accentuating her breasts, clipped her hair into a long strand.

She walked toward Paul then made two expert pirouettes, sending a gust of citrus perfume toward him and the dress into a mid-thigh twirl. Lust hit him like a sledgehammer. He got up from the sofa and with both hands drew her face close and kissed her. Her lips swelled into his and separated. A single time, she pulled back and let him find her. Then she crushed his mouth and pushed him toward the sofa.

He bounced into the sofa's plushness. Lifting her dress, she spread her legs and straddled him. He found a zipper at the back and slowly pulled it down. Leaning forward and kissing him, she let the dress fall from her shoulders, revealing a black lace bra.

She drew back, and while grinding into his crotch, unbuttoned and pulled open his shirt. Then she dropped her face and ran her lips along his shoulders. She found the tip of his belt, and as her mouth returned to his open and yearning lips, she undid his pants and felt for his hardness.

Breathing in short, sharp bursts, he lifted her off him and whispered in her ear, "I've got to have you now. Right fucking now." As he swung behind her, she straightened and let her dress fall to the ground. Then she undid her bra and dropped it onto the dress.

He pushed her forward and she kneeled on the couch, laying a side of her face along the top edge, her mouth parted and eyes closed. Her breasts, nipples stiff, swayed. Arching her back, she inched her legs apart. He tugged at her panties until they were taut at her knees.

He kissed her lower back, licking microscopic swirls of hair. Then he snuck his lips up her spine, and curling his hands over her breasts, he stroked her nipples. As his lips reached the base of her neck, he grabbed her hair bound by the hairclip and tugged. At the same time, he stroked the inside of her upper thighs then drew his fingers up. She arched her back further and gasped as his fingers found the edges of wetness between her legs.

Kicking off his pants and underwear, he moved the tip of his hardness up and down her lips, again and again. Then, holding her hips, he penetrated slowly but firmly, his own gasps obscuring hers. He began to thrust, praying to himself that he could check his excitement.

She reached behind and removed the hairclip, letting her hair spill across her shoulders. Then she pressed back to stop him thrusting. Squirming left and right, gulping, she used him as her toy. A short while later, catching her breath, she whispered, "There's something I must do."

Pulling away, she turned him and shoved him against the back of the sofa. Straddling him once more, tonguing her front top teeth, she guided him into her and bucked against his body. He held on to her hips, accentuating her movements. Then she dragged two fingers along the scratches on his forehead where early crusts had formed. Her bucking intensified and he clutched the sofa pillows. It was too late, and he came. In the midst of his pleasure, something scraped across his forehead, but at that moment, he didn't care to know what. Seconds later, Grace arched in climax then collapsed toward Paul.

They held each other, eyes closed, collecting their breaths. Then Paul felt it again: warm wetness around one eye. He tried to swipe away the irritant. When he blinked open his eyes, he saw a red smear on his fingertip.

Grace pulled back and stared. She pursed her lips and blushed. "Oh dear," she said, "I got a bit carried away." She opened the palm of her right hand and revealed the hairclip, bits of Paul's early scab clinging to its prongs. Tossing the clip on the sofa, she used a fingertip to remove the rest of the blood from the corner of his eye.

He knew he looked shocked. She kissed him twice on the lips, and pulling herself off him, cuddled against his side. Darting her tongue across her fingertip, she stared at him, unflinching, and said, "I hope you don't mind too much. It's one of my weaknesses."

33

Paul dabbed at his forehead. Wariness from Grace's use of the hairclip, which half aroused and half riled him, tempered his physical bliss. He tried to recall the last time he'd had sex. Off the top of his head, he couldn't, an admission he would keep to himself.

"I'm glad you didn't come in your pants before you got my clothes off," Grace said, giggling.

Paul added embarrassment to his recipe of feelings. "Let's never talk about Hart House again. I've been trying my best to forget it. For fifteen years."

"Okay, I won't go there again," Grace said with a soft smile, "but if you want to know the truth, I was a bit flattered." She leaned across the sofa, collected the hairclip and pressed the rumpled black dress against her chest.

"Are you really wearing that to Di Strata's for dinner?" Paul asked.

"My god, no. That would be entirely inappropriate." Naked at the back, Grace skipped to the hallway and into her bedroom.

They changed into casual clothes and found one another in the living room. Grace replaced the hairclip on the top of the desk. Then she opened the window above, letting in a rush of fresh evening air. After staring across the piazza for a few seconds, she returned to the sofa, folding her legs and nestling close to Paul's shoulder.

"Paul, there's something I've been wondering. About Art."

Paul tugged his right lobe and looked straight ahead. "I feel that bird of prey circling above me again."

"Your apprehension?"

"Yes. Is this about the arrest?"

"I'm sorry. I didn't mean to—"

"It never goes away. Some people just need to ask about it. Others don't ask, but I know they want to."

"We talked about it last night."

Paul shrugged and his forehead began to throb. "I'm just trying to make you understand. I usually don't talk about it. Our conversation last evening—I felt comfortable with you. And the wine helped, too."

"You know what I think?"

"No."

"Your feeling of apprehension, your concerns about what other people think, will only go away if you *do* talk about what happened, what that whole mess left you with. Then that bird will stop taking a piece out of your side every day."

"What's there to talk about? I was arrested and charged with first degree murder. I was put on trial. I was acquitted."

Grace raised a hand and stroked Paul's cheek. "And how long did that take?"

Paul pressed his lips together harder. "More than two years."

"Two shit years. Filled with anxiety, I'm sure."

"I was *tortured* by fear."

"I can understand that."

"Can you?" Paul asked. "Do you know how *close* the jury came to convicting me?"

"How could anyone know?"

"From their eyes. After they announced the verdict, Liebowitz and I hugged. But I saw over his head and snuck a look at the jury. They were still watching me. Still wondering."

"But it's over. And it's been over for a long time."

"People still watch—and doubt."

"That you murdered Art?"

"I can see it in their eyes, too. I can *feel* it." Paul turned and stared into Grace's dark brown eyes. "Don't you wonder, just a bit?"

Grace swallowed then shook her head. "No."

He looked away again. "You see. It's that hesitation."

"Paul, I had to swallow."

"I could have done it, you know."

"What are you saying?"

"That the jury got it wrong. And the police got it right."

"You're making this up now."

"I'm just saying out loud what crosses everyone's mind when they meet me. And some of those around me, too, I'm sure."

"No, you're wrong," Grace said. "It's the horror of the event. They put themselves in your shoes and they—they *empathize*."

"I don't think so. Di Strata?"

"That's exactly what I mean. He wants to know. He wants to understand."

"If I did it," Paul said, sighing. "The bird of prey circles."

"No, what it was *like*."

"I feel tainted, Grace. That's what I feel like." Paul snorted. "I just made more progress with you than I have in two months of psychiatric appointments."

"Psychiatric appointments?"

"Something to take the shine off any new relationship." Paul released a stiff laugh. "Okay, sorry. You get a freebie for that. Ask anything."

"I don't want to know now."

"Ask away. Please."

Grace guided some hair back. "The police never found the murder weapon, did they?"

"No."

"Then how could they arrest you without a murder weapon? That just seems so basic."

Paul regretted his offer. His forehead throbbed more. "Beecham and the Crown thought they could rely on motive and circumstantial evidence of opportunity for a conviction. They would have loved to find a weapon. And I would have, too. Because it would have pointed to someone else. But they didn't."

"The motive was revenge against Art for the fight?"

"It started with that. But their theory became that I had an uncontrollable malice and hatred toward him, which grew over the years I knew him. To the point where I planned first degree murder. All bullshit."

"And then you were in the vicinity. That was the opportunity, right?"

"Yes, I left Kate's place that night because I had a terrible headache. I stopped in at a coffee shop around the corner from Kate's to rest because I felt so unwell and had a coffee. Sometimes I find that helps. A short walk from where Art was killed."

"It doesn't seem enough to put you through what they did. Without a weapon."

Paul's throat began to feel raw like his forehead. "Actually, there were other things that led them to charge me. Things I couldn't change." Paul paused. "I'm going to get some water."

"Let me get it for you," Grace said.

"No, I'll do it." Paul went to the kitchen. Taking the first sip, he looked again at Justin's artwork in the corner. It spoke of a boy unbridled and guilt-free. Gulping down the water, he tried to remember how that felt.

Paul returned to the sofa. Grace took a tissue and dabbed his forehead. He ran fingers through his hair, then folded his hands and looked down. "We were a nice family from Willowdale, but except for me, it was emptied of men in three years."

"What do you mean?"

"Three deaths in three years. David, my older brother in '89. My father in '90. And my grandfather, the one who meant a lot to David and me, in '91."

The bubble of anxiety that always arose when Paul mentioned David filled his gut.

"David was nine years older than me. He was brilliant in math. Won prizes in high school and got several scholarships to universities, including Yale. Did really well there. Then he was accepted into business school. My father was very proud and had huge hopes.

"But David was very quiet, very *into* himself. He was good about letting me hang around him, though. And a few times, pretending it was no big deal, he talked about voices—he used to call them his 'ghosts'—that jabbered at him insanely. I had no idea what he was talking about and I was scared to ask. I just didn't know what to do with it. He started drinking and drugging, I think, to obliterate them. And then the whole damn thing spun out of control and we lost him. He drove drunk into the back of a truck when he was twenty-five, four months after rehab. I was only sixteen. To the best of my knowledge, he never told anyone but me about his ghosts.

"My father struggled terribly with David's death." The anxiety bubble in Paul's gut burst. "He just didn't recover. My mother fell into her own grief, expecting him to comfort her, but he didn't have enough strength for himself. Eventually, he fell into himself like a damn house of cards. Dropped weight, never laughed and walked around in a daze, putting one foot in front of the other."

"Who could blame him?"

"I suppose. I wanted him to snap out of it, to be a man, to be *strong*. I was naïve. He was crossing the street about a year after David died and was hit by a car with the right of way and busted his skull open on the pavement. The driver said he stepped right in front without looking. My father survived for four weeks, in and out of a coma. When I visited him in the hospital, he looked like he *wanted* to die. Honestly, I think he let the car hit him."

Grace kept her eyes intent on Paul.

"My grandfather, my mother's father, was a big guy, burly, usually with a stubble on his face. Kind, with a soft voice. Quiet, like David." Paul paused, letting a feeling of warmth douse the anxiety. "Grew up in Northern Ontario, near Kirkland Lake, and raised his family there. My mother moved to Toronto when she married my father, but my brother and I always loved going up north to visit Granddad in the summers. He was an outdoorsman. Showed us hiking, fishing, canoeing. And how to use guns."

"Really?"

"Yes. Granddad had a few rifles, a shotgun and a couple of handguns he'd collected. And he taught us how to shoot them, somewhere out in the woods with thousands of mosquitoes.

"He was a very perceptive guy. He saw that David was becoming more and more closed off. He insisted David and I visit, even in the summers when David was in university. When we were on the lakes or tromping through the woods, it was the only time David came out of his shell. Granddad's presence allowed him to breathe and relax. To be free of his ghosts, maybe. The thing was, when David died, I think Granddad took it as hard as me and my father. He called me once a week after it happened. While my father was checking out.

"Not long after my father died, Granddad was diagnosed with colon cancer. My mother insisted he come live with us, to get the best care at Princess Margaret. He was a fish out of water in the big city and went downhill very fast in the summer before first-year university. My mother took us to Kirkland Lake for the last time, in August, to clean out his place. One evening, when my mother was out donating things, he gave me a few of his belongings. He kept saying, 'You oughta have these. To remember me by.' A framed picture of my grandmother and him in front of the first shack they built together outside Kirkland Lake. A hunting knife, which I still have. And one of the handguns David and I had used, with some cartridges, in a nice black case with green velvet inside. It was a .38 calibre Smith and Wesson revolver, the very same the cops used to use."

"A handgun?"

"Granddad said he would have given me his hunting rifle, too, but he'd given it to his best buddy in Kirkland Lake before he came down to Toronto. Anyway, he wanted me to have it, as a remembrance of him, of what he was. You know, an outdoorsman, a hunter, a bit of a collector. And in memory of David."

"So you had this—when Art was—"

"No, I didn't. A few days later, I made the mistake of telling my mother that Granddad had given me the gun. She went berserk and made him take it back, and then somehow he must have gotten rid of it before he died. I protested like a spoiled child for days. But I sort of understood. She'd lost David and my dad and was about to lose her father. The last thing she wanted was for me to hurt myself with that gun.

"So after Art died, at my first interview at 14 Division—to see if I was a witness—they asked me if I'd ever owned or shot a gun. And I was very open with them, of course. I wanted to help. I told them how Granddad had taught David and me to shoot guns and even that he'd wanted to give me the Smith and Wesson. And they asked me quite a few questions about that. 'How often have you shot a handgun?' they asked. 'Tell us what the circumstances were.' They even asked if they could speak to my mother to corroborate my statement."

"Yet they still arrested you."

"Like I said, other things came up. For one, Art's autopsy. He was shot Friday night and they did the autopsy Saturday morning. And they found the bullet in Art's skull and knew it was from a .38 cartridge, which is the type my Granddad's Smith and Wesson used. At trial, the Crown went on and on about that. 'Yes, the murder weapon hadn't been recovered,' they said, 'but he knows guns, and specifically, a type of revolver that *could* have been the murder weapon.' But the thing was, there were hundreds of guns that could have shot that cartridge. And the police had searched my place high and low once they'd gotten a warrant. There was no gun and there was no trace of me firing one. That's one of the reasons the jury acquitted me, I think. They wanted something more than the circumstantial evidence the Crown was relying on.

"But Beecham sure thought he had enough to arrest and charge me. You see, the other thing that came up was that Beecham thought I was lying to him."

"Why would he think that?" Grace asked.

Paul let his shoulders slump and looked at Grace. "Things didn't go well at the second interview, where I met the great Detective Beecham from Homicide for the first time. I'm sure he thought I wasn't being straight with them. That's what they look for. Vagueness, inconsistencies, lies. Stepping into your own shit. That really gets them thinking they're on to somebody."

"What were your inconsistencies?"

Paul stayed quiet for a bit. Anxiety pinged around his gut like electrons around an atom. "I'll finish. But let's make this the last time we talk about Art or anything related to him. At least for a few days."

"Okay."

"When the police interview someone after a murder, even when they're just interviewing for witnesses, before anyone's a suspect, they like to take what's called a K.G.B. statement. It's a videotape interview under oath at a police station. The name isn't the Russian secret police. They're the initials of an accused in a case that went all the way to the Supreme Court of Canada. The case decided that a statement made at an interview that is inconsistent with testimony at trial is admissible for its truth. Not just as an inconsistency to attack the credibility of a witness.

"That case doesn't matter. What mattered is that the police interviewed me three times—three K.G.B. statements under oath—before they arrested and charged me a few hours after Art's funeral.

"The third interview is irrelevant. I had Liebowitz with me by that time and said nothing. The first interview was the one with the detectives at four in the morning Saturday, the 'get-to-know-you' session where I talked about Granddad's gun. They'd already interviewed Kate, because Art had been shot in her car. And of course she'd told them about the evening before, when we'd gotten together at her place and implored Art to get help for his cocaine habit, and how he just blew us off. And she also told them about the previous Thursday evening when he'd come over to my place, and Art and I fought. So they were pretty interested in talking to me. Of course she told them about Art leaving the party for his dealer, too. So different detectives interviewed Rivera and me at the same time.

"When I got home from the first interview, just as I was going to bed, Kate called and said everyone was coming over to her place for a group hug. So we got together around seven in the morning, shocked and numb with what had happened. Eventually, Louis, Mark, Cyril, Lee—they hadn't been interviewed yet but they knew they would be—asked Kate and me what the detectives wanted to know. I told them exactly what I'd been asked but then I left. I got really tired and I needed sleep. I was expected at Collins, Shaw by noon to work on the diligence for a large transaction.

"So I worked on the transaction most of the day Saturday and Sunday. Then, around 5:00 p.m. on Sunday—I think I was writing a memo summarizing various leases I'd read—I got a call from 14 Division. Did I mind coming back for a few clarifications? The thing was, what was I going to do? I still wanted to help. So I went back for the second interview. Back to the same small room with a few lights on, and bare white walls with chips in them, being videotaped, under oath. And for the first time, I met Detective Beecham. Somehow, I knew that was a bad omen.

"And as I said, things didn't go well. You see, in the first interview, I'd told them about having the headache when I left Kate's place after Art's intervention, and that I'd stopped off at the coffee shop at King and Bathurst to get a coffee. And I told them I was there for a half hour or so. That put me in the shop at the time Art was shot. Well, by the second interview, they'd pulled the surveillance tapes from the coffee shop and they showed me arriving at 10:45 p.m. and leaving at 10:58. In time, in other words, to swing by Richmond on the way home and pop Art in the head. They didn't have to say it to my face; they were concluding that I'd had the opportunity to murder Art when I'd said in the first interview I didn't. I could see their temperatures starting to rise, just about that. 'Were you lying to us, Paul?' they finally asked. 'I had a bad headache and I *really* don't remember the exact time I left the coffee shop,' I kept saying.

"And then they started asking more questions about the fight I had with Art. At the first interview I described it as two friends from university sparring. But I didn't mention the last words I said to Art after the fight. 'Get out of here. Honestly, I used to care. Now I just want you dead.' Those words."

"But why not?" Grace asked.

Paul shrugged. "They really didn't ask me anything in the first interview for me to tell them. And I tried to explain that they were words from the story I'd written. That Art and I used as our own code to say, 'Fuck off and leave me alone.' Beecham couldn't seem to wrap his head around my explanation, and his temperature went up more.

"And then they told me that scratches had been found on Art's wrist at his autopsy and asked whether I'd give a sample from under my fingernails, for DNA. I gave it to them, still thinking the police were my friends, and told them that the scratches were probably from me. I knew they were going to find Art's DNA, so I thought I might as well tell them. That seemed to agitate Beecham even more. I think he thought I'd played down my fight with Art in the first interview.

"I didn't do a good job, I suppose. The thing was, I thought I had things under control. Instead I started to realize that Beecham was having, well, real trouble with me. He was a stocky guy, quite short. At first he was very friendly. 'Just help me out here,' he would say. Or 'Just one more question.' But he also perspired easily, and halfway through my second interview I saw some sweat on his forehead.

"By the end of it, I sensed I was in trouble," Paul said, his heart skipping beats just as it had fifteen years earlier. "I asked him, 'Am I a *suspect*?' And when Beecham looked straight at me, sweat all across his brow, and said, 'Well, what I would say is that you're a person of interest,' the earth just fell out from under me, and I knew it was time to get the hell out of there and hire defence counsel."

34

A day later, early Friday evening, Grace was darting between her bedroom and bathroom, adding final personal touches before the dinner with Emilio Di Strata. Paul, elegant in a summer suit they'd bought that morning off Via del Corso, sat at the small desk in the living room, reading his emails on Grace's laptop.

Grace emerged and pranced in front of Paul. "What do you think?" After a morning meandering through Rome and an afternoon sharing their bodies, he would have found her alluring in scuba gear and flippers. Instead she wore a green dress and matching jacket that teased out the shape of her body, with a slim gold chain around her neck.

"Beautiful," he said. "Beautiful as you were all day."

She studied herself in the mirror above the side table near the kitchen, her lips pursed. After several moments, she said, "That's the best I have today. Just give me five more minutes."

Paul turned off the laptop, and folding it down, he stared out the window. The light of another brilliant day was receding, and high in the atmosphere, some cirrus clouds gathered like feathers on the wing of a swan. It was quiet and beckoning in the piazza, the interval between visits from tourists and strolls by locals. It also was Paul's favourite time of the day. Feeling calm and open, he thought to enjoy it.

His eyes fell on the ochre, three-storey house directly across from them. Some of the six pairs of shutters had been closed for the night, but others were still open or ajar. Twice a shadow immersed in its own life flitted past a window.

Wanting to check Grace's progress, Paul began turning his legs but stopped. In the right second-floor window across, a closed shutter eased open. Behind it a dim silhouette appeared, becoming still as a mannequin. Paul thought for a moment he'd conjured the shape. But then there was a small perceptible shift, a straightening of posture, and he knew he hadn't.

The outlandish thought arose that eyes were on his. He shook his head, but the more he stared, the more certain he became. He shifted left to make himself harder to see and waited. Sure enough, seconds later, the silhouette realigned itself. A shiver ran the length of Paul's spine.

"Grace," Paul called out without moving.

"Yes?" she said from the bathroom.

"Is there a voyeur in the house across the piazza?"

"A what?" she replied. "Just a minute, I'll be right out."

Paul tilted his body farther from the window. Grace walked into the living room then stopped, observing him. "What are you doing?" she asked.

A moment later, the shutter across the piazza opened more. Some hair and a sliver of face were visible. "Look," he said. "There's somebody watching me. In that orangey-brown building. He just moved because I did."

"I don't understand," Grace said, standing behind Paul. Instantly, the silhouette disappeared. Then a hand emerged, grabbed the shutter and drew it closed.

"Ah, he saw you," Paul said. "Someone was watching me from that window on the second floor. It's a bit weird, actually," he said, squirming.

For a second Grace stared. Then she tossed a hand through the air and said, "Oh, these neighbours. If you stop paying attention to them, they'll leave you alone."

"Really?" Paul said, thinking of Signora Di Grotto and the pot-bellied old man.

"No one can see inside here anyway."

"I bet you can."

"We should go," she said, glancing at the grandfather clock. "I don't want to be late."

A half hour later, right at seven, Grace pressed the button next to the wrought iron gates of Di Strata's villa. Signora Tramente emerged, haughty and hawk-like, on the front door landing. With a cool dip of her head, she led Grace and Paul into the centre hall and held a hand toward the open doors of a room facing Via Sicilia.

It was spacious, with light blue pastel walls. Grace's eyes went to several abstract paintings while Paul, pushing a hand through his hair, combed for Di Strata. He sat facing them at the other end of the room in a sumptuous white chair, one of four centred by a small table. Interrupting a conversation with someone across from him, Di Strata smiled at his new guests. In another dark suit, he pushed himself out of his chair and limped toward them.

"Welcome, welcome," he said with outstretched hands. His eyes were glued on Grace. "Oh my, even more beautiful than yesterday," he added. They met him partway, Grace receiving a peck on both cheeks and Paul a firm handshake. The echoes of a familiar voice resonated in Paul's head. Rising across from Di Strata's seat, turning with a large smile, was Mark.

"My god, that's a *Gauguin*, isn't it?" Grace asked, putting a hand to her mouth.

"Ah, you certainly have an eye for the best," Di Strata said with a smile and slow nod. "Yes, a little something I picked up years ago. When I could still afford such things. Extraordinary, isn't it?"

Paul walked toward Mark, taking in his well-cut suit. "For Christ's sake, what are you doing here?"

"Be careful with your language," Mark said, cringing. "Told you there might be a surprise."

As Paul and Mark huddled off to one side, Di Strata took Grace by the arm and showed her around the room. "What's going on?" Paul asked.

"His older sister is on her deathbed and there's been a huge falling-out between him and her husband about some of his belongings that she has. So he called his lawyers together—mostly from here but also me—to redo his estate. He wants nothing to go to the older sister's family now. Everything to the younger sister in Woodbridge. It's a fortune. And when he dies, there'll be a lot of taxes to pay. He's planning how to raise the cash."

"And he flew you over?"

"Just decided after he read the documents. I hardly made the flight."

"I didn't think clients did that anymore."

"This one does. And he invited me to stay for dinner, too. You're stuck with me this evening, I'm afraid."

Grace came over with Di Strata. "You remember Mark?" Paul asked. "Did you meet at Louis's service?"

"No," Grace said. "Nice to see you again, Mark. It's been so long."

Mark rubbed his large stomach. "Yes, and many pounds. But you haven't changed at all."

"Oh, please," Grace said.

Carlotta entered carrying a silver tray with a bottle and four flute glasses. She set the tray on the table centring the chairs.

"Ah," Di Strata said, moving toward the table, "this is a little prosecco grown in some vineyards in which I have interest. I hope you like it. It's usually quite good." He double-checked the label of the open bottle. "We must enjoy the good things in life," he went on, pouring into the flutes, "while we still can. Come, let's sit."

They each took a glass, bubbles surging to the top, and sat in a chair. Next to them there was a view through a tall window onto a small grass terrace and Via Sicilia.

"I do not say things like that lightly," Di Strata said. "Mr. Koslovsky just told me the very sad story about your friend, Mr. Tews, the film producer. That is the type of thing—well, I am seventy-five. I have been very fortunate that nothing like that has happened to me. My older sister is very sick but she is nearly eighty-one. Of course, there comes a time when enough is enough. When the curtains close, so to speak. But until that time, I say *enjoy* life." Di Strata lifted his glass, and the others joined him then sipped.

"I wish it were all prosecco and beautiful villas like yours," Grace said with a light laugh.

"Of course it can't be," Di Strata said, "but it is a question of balance. Naturally, we all have our troubles. In fact, I must tell you," he said, pinching together the forefinger and thumb of a hand, "that this whole business with my sister has been most upsetting. But in general, with the right balance ... yes, it's about the balance."

"But how?" Paul asked. "Many of us can't *choose* a balance."

Di Strata eyed Paul. "Naturally, I understand what you mean. Many things are out of our hands. I fully appreciate that. But I think *you* are doing exactly the right thing."

Paul yanked a lobe then gave a compressed smile. "I'm sorry. Can you elaborate?"

Di Strata took another sip then smiled and gestured toward Grace. "You are putting yourself in the company of beauty. That is what I have done over the years. I have surrounded myself with beauty, whether the company of a lovely woman, wonderful art, Puccini or whatever it might be." He paused and Carlotta magically appeared with more wine. "Thank you, Carlotta. Most importantly, beautiful women. Not just pretty, but *striking* and *bold* and *consuming*. You understand what I mean, of course," Di Strata said, looking back and forth between Paul and Mark.

Both cleared their throats and said, "Yes."

Di Strata nodded and a more hesitant smile crossed his face. "Ah, to be *consumed* by a woman one more time. Do you know what the hardest thing is for a man to accept as he grows old?" he asked, again looking back and forth between Paul and Mark. "It is how quickly his attractiveness fades. When he is young, he receives attention for his looks, his strength and his courage. Fifty years later, it is for something called 'experience', whatever that is worth." Di Strata downed his glass of prosecco. "I can tell you, not a lot, of course."

Carlotta approached the group and stood next to Di Strata. "Ah, dinner is ready," he said. "Come, let's go into the dining room. Carlotta will bring our glasses." Di Strata limped toward a wide doorway that led to the next room. Paul fell behind Grace and whispered to Mark, "I take it he doesn't know about Charles?"

"None of his business."

"Then how is it he knows about my past?"

Mark adjusted his glasses. "He has his own story, Paul. It came up in that context. By the way, your face looks like you were in a bar fight."

Paul wiped two fingers along his forehead and felt the scabs forming. "You have to watch out around here, Mark," he said and walked into the next room.

35

The dining room was narrow, with deep green walls and cascading palms in the far corners. Di Strata approached the head of a walnut table laden with four settings of translucent white porcelain plates and lustrous silverware. The scent of spring flowers on a buffet filled the air. Carlotta put the flutes next to wine glasses then darted through a small door.

"Signorina Campbell, you are here, next to me," Di Strata said, "and Mr. Tews, you are beside her. Mr. Koslovsky, you are on the other side."

Carlotta returned with a bottle of white wine and poured half an ounce for Di Strata. He swirled, smelled and tasted. "That's fine," he said. "Another little something from a vineyard I own. I'm sure you'll enjoy it."

A few minutes later, small plates of fresh greens drizzled in lemon and olive oil arrived. As they ate, Di Strata went around the table asking everyone about their professional lives. Grace, bubbly and opinionated, talked at length about the travails of a dance company with reduced government funding. Paul started to shrink inside, and when Di Strata came to him, he spoke in vague generalities, deciding that his sabbatical was none of Di Strata's business either.

They were served whole sea bass, the skin a slick black, mouths open in protest and eyes cloudy, with a side of small buttered potatoes sprinkled with chives. Carlotta circled the table and fileted each fish. The woman who had kept to corners at university parties bloomed like the flowers on the buffet. Back and forth, Grace and Di Strata discussed the merits of this and that artist. Paul sensed that she was in over her head with a master looking to be consumed. Wishing he'd paid more attention to art, Paul fell into a pout as he swallowed his last bit of bass.

Di Strata wiped his mouth with a cloth napkin then sat back with a wizened look on his face. "Mr. Tews," he said, "I understand that you have been through your battles."

Paul looked at Di Strata. *Here we go. Here we fucking go.* He wondered how to divert the conversation and threw a hostile glance at Mark, who stared back, hard and stern.

Di Strata raised a hand and Carlotta began to take away plates. "We will have some dessert, and cognac and coffee. Then I am afraid I have to take care of a few things, and soon it will be time for an old man to go to bed." Di Strata sighed. "It was not always like this, of course."

There was a pause in the conversation as Carlotta returned with small bowls of strawberries and heavy cream.

"Perhaps I am raising a topic, Mr. Tews," Di Strata began again, "that you are very tired of. If it were me, I would wish every day that, like any scourge, it would leave me forever. So forgive me that I even speak of it. But I want you to know that you have my admiration."

A strawberry covered with cream fell off Paul's spoon onto the table. "Why is that, Signor Di Strata?" he asked in a low voice.

Di Strata pinched a finger and thumb again and flicked the hand at Paul. "Because you were persecuted, and you *fought and won.*" Paul telegraphed more anger at Mark, who dropped his eyes to his dessert. "Please, Mr. Tews, I was the one who asked Mr. Koslovsky all the questions. I forced him to reveal some of your confidences. If you are irritated, it should be with me."

Paul collected the strawberry and put it to the side of his bowl. "You're right. It's a topic I'm tired of." Underneath the table, Grace placed a hand on his thigh. He sighed. "There's nothing admirable about what I did. I endured. Anybody would have done the same. Actually, they probably would have handled it better. Much better."

"Why do you say that? You are alive, you are with a wonderful woman and you have an excellent profession. You fought and you won. Me, my anger nearly split me in two. If I had been a young man, I would have become a criminal lawyer, a defence lawyer, just to fight the state." Paul raised his eyebrows. "I see you are surprised, Mr. Tews."

Paul set down his spoon. "I had a similar idea," he said. "When the Crown finally decided not to appeal, and I returned to third-year law school, I was going to change all my courses and article with a defence law firm. But in the end it was too close for comfort. I didn't think it was the way to redemption."

Di Strata looked Paul up and down. "In this country, Mr. Tews, we have our own scourge. They are called the Comando Carabinieri Tutela Patrimonio Culturale." Di Strata looked at Grace.

"Something like—the Italian Cultural Heritage Protection Unit," she said.

"The TPC," Di Strata said. He shook his head then held open his palms and raised his shoulders. "They're like crazy people. They came after me with such vengeance and hatred, it was shocking. I have collected for years. My father did, too, and so did my grandfather. I do not need to be associated with any disreputable activities. And yet, what they accused me of, it was absurd. A farce, the entire thing, from start to finish."

"You should tell them what happened," Mark said.

"Do you know this unit of the Carabinieri?" Di Strata asked, leaning forward in his chair, his voice quivering. "They try to protect Italy's national cultural heritage. Of course, for centuries there has been a terrible problem with people stealing cultural artifacts. I am the first to admit that. What has left this country over the years—with the English, the Germans and of course the Americans—it is an outrage, an obscenity. That is one reason why I am such a careful collector. One of the *main* reasons." Di Strata waved both hands in giant semi-circles. "So this beauty, this magnificence, this splendour stays in our country, where it belongs."

"As it should," Grace said.

"Yes, exactly, as it should. You see, for years, I have only dealt with the best-known dealers. *I* do not need to deal with anyone else. The dealers know me not just as a man of means but one of discerning taste. Many of them have visited here, sitting where you are today. Why would I ever deal in stolen goods? Why? There is no reason."

"Stolen goods?" Grace asked.

Di Strata's eyes narrowed and his voice became rigid. "Say some farmer digs in his field, for whatever reason a farmer digs, and he stumbles onto something. Some coins. A piece of jewellery. Maybe even a statue. This is Rome.

This is Italy. Do you have any idea how much history there is here? It happens all the time. Now, who owns that? Of course the farmer thinks *he* does. That would be natural, actually, wouldn't it? And he keeps it and maybe he sells it. The TPC thinks he should turn it over to them. That is what *they* think. I don't know. I wonder about that circumstance.

"But there are chains of people—*cordata* we call them—who bring goods to market from illegal excavations. The chain starts with tomb raiders, and that is what they really are, tomb raiders. They go to a site, in Lazio, Campania, Sicily, and just dig with heavy equipment. What is lost and the damage that is done, it is terrible. Then there is someone local who sets up a 'collection centre' and they in turn report to a 'collector' in the area, who understands what has been found and what its value is. Then, magically, a provenance is created, and dealers—not my dealers—take what is found into their inventory and sell it to collectors.

"Some people who buy these things, well, they know the item has been illegally excavated or perhaps stolen and do not care about provenance. Others look at the provenance without asking the right questions. For the TPC, they are just part of a giant illicit trade. As for the purchaser, again, I don't know. What would happen to these items if someone did *not* buy them? I'll tell you. They would be lost, discarded when they cannot be sold. Or end up in the hands of a Chinese or Russian private collector. Is *that* honouring our country?

"In any event, I was never one of those. I only bought from dealers I trusted. And over time, especially as I saw the TPC gain power, I bought only from dealers who were *friends*. I do not make friends easily. You have to gain my trust over a long time. Isn't that so, Mr. Koslovsky?"

"Yes is the short answer."

"Exactly. And even then, for me to trust someone one hundred percent, well, that is rare. My sister in Toronto, maybe. You understand, of course.

"In any event, in 1999, a beautiful September day, there was a knock on my door as I was having breakfast, right in this chair. Signora Tramente answered and two men from the Carabinieri were there. Very pushy, of course. Insisted on speaking with me. So I let them into my home. We sat in the room where we had prosecco earlier.

"At first I thought there might be a problem with an export licence or something like that. Anything of cultural heritage cannot be exported without a licence, and it can be nearly impossible to get one. I have had long fights when I wanted to auction something outside the country. But instead they asked me question after question about a Sicilian vase I had bought years before from a very well-known dealer here in Rome. It was a beautiful vase." Di Strata's voice started to soar. "Ancient. First century A.D. Splendid—the condition, the work, the artistry—magnificent." His voice fell again. "The dealer knew right away I was prepared to pay.

"But I did not buy it without asking questions. I made all the inquiries a seasoned collector would." Di Strata looked out the dining room window into the falling dusk. "But he lied to me. About the provenance of that vase. That might have been the most disappointing thing of all. A person who I thought was my friend, taking advantage of me like that. Sensing my appreciation for this object. Vulnerable to his greed. Vices like greed … it is awful what they do to a man."

Di Strata looked at his three guests in turn, then leaned forward, his voice even lower. "I tried to explain to the Carabinieri. That I had asked the right questions, that I thought I was dealing with a friend. But they charged me under Article 712 of the Penal Code: purchasing or acquiring objects of uncertain provenance. *Five* years of my life, Mr. Tews, age sixty-one to sixty-sixty, lost, until I won based on the—what is it called?" He spoke in Italian to Grace.

"The statute of limitations, I think. Is that right?" she asked, looking at Paul and Mark.

"Probably," Mark said.

"*The statute of limitations*," Di Strata roared, landing a fist on the table. "I waited a long time for that persecution to end. A very long time. That was *vindication*." He looked around the table, his eyes ablaze, licking his lips. "You must know that feeling, Mr. Tews. That type of victory. It is sweetness, honey, the nectar of the gods."

There was a long pause. Paul cleared his throat. "As I said, I only felt that I had endured. Not relief. Not happiness. Not the sweetness you're talking about. Just that I had endured … and the knowledge that I had a lot more to endure after."

Di Strata looked at his guest in astonishment. He pressed the fingertips of his hands together. "Forgive me, Mr. Tews," Di Strata said, his voice metallic, "but those sound like the words of a guilty man."

36

Near eleven the gates to Di Strata's villa clanged shut. The air on Via Sicilia was bracing, the fragrance of spring blooms mixing with the rank smell of combusted diesel. Gathering in one of Paul's elbows, Grace shivered and drew close. Mark, a thick leather lawyer's briefcase in his right hand, looked back and forth between Paul and the sidewalk, slathering Paul with annoyance.

Paul glanced at Mark. "Something wrong?"

"Jesus, man, it's with *you*," Mark said, shaking his head, his early jowls trembling.

"You're supposed to watch your language around here, Mark."

"Oh, fuck off."

"I don't understand. What's going on?" Grace asked, looking at each of them then tossing her hair back. "It was an amazing evening."

Mark ignored Grace and kept his eyes on Paul.

"I agree," Paul said, hoping he didn't sound too facetious.

Mark's massive chest deflated with a giant sigh and he set down his briefcase. He snagged the glasses off his face, and with the bottom of his jacket, he began cleaning them. "I know everything you went through was a burden. Trust me, no one knows better. But what the hell, can't you just be a little social? When you have to be?"

Paul felt anger flare. "He called me a murderer."

"He didn't."

"As close as you can get."

"Oh, for fuck's sake."

Grace patted Paul on the chest. "I'm sure he didn't mean it that way. And you *were* a little morose."

Paul looked at her. "He was charmed by you. The same wasn't true for me."

"This could be my biggest file this quarter," Mark said, "and he's going to think my colleagues at the firm are all head cases."

Paul rolled his eyes. "Not all of them. Just one. Anyway, Mark, he won't see me again."

Mark had cleaned his glasses to within an inch of their lives and put them back on. "That's where you're wrong," he said.

Paul stared. "What do you mean?"

"You're flight's Wednesday, right?"

"Yes, for now."

"Di Strata wants to visit his sister in Woodbridge, to explain things in person. He feels unsafe. He wants to come on the same flight as you, just in case."

With a sneer, Paul nodded toward Di Strata's villa. "What about the bird woman in there?"

"She has to be here. I told him it was okay. I *assume* you can generate the social graces to handle that situation."

"If I have to," Paul said. "But no more talk about my past. Tell him."

Mark released more volumes of air. "I'll try. Which way is Via Veneto? I'm at the Hotel Aria."

"Di Strata is taking good care of you," Grace said, pointing west. "That way. We can walk with you and catch a cab from there."

Grace and Paul strolled ahead of Mark, dodging cars half parked on the sidewalk. A few blocks later, Grace aimed them north. Round street lamps glowed warmly, sending shimmers of light into the black sky between leaves of tall trees. The designer stores had long closed but noisy throngs still filled restaurant patios dotted with heat lamps.

At the front of the Aria, Paul and Mark shook hands, looking at each other awkwardly. "You've got to understand, Paul," Mark said, "it's like a car wreck. People don't want to know about it, but at the same time they *do*. It's a kind of sick fascination. You know what you need?"

"What?" Paul asked.

"A simple summary of that episode in your life. That'll fix people's curiosity and then you can move on to another topic. Don't leave it hanging in the air." Mark turned to Grace. "Great to see you again, Grace. I'm going to get some sleep. I'm whacked from jet lag."

Hotel attendants and patrons sidestepped Mark's mass as he receded into the hotel. "Let's walk a bit," Grace said. Like the Roman couples around them enjoying the onset of the weekend, they strolled arm-in-arm along Via Veneto, soaking in the city's pulse.

"Mark seems like a good friend," Grace said after a while, glancing at Paul. "I have a feeling he really cares about you. Whatever he just said."

Paul shrugged. "I suppose. I hardly see him at Collins, Shaw. You get so immersed in files. But he did check in with me a lot when I took the leave. As did Lee. I should have returned their messages more often." He paused. "But what you saw tonight, his concern that I embarrassed him in front of Di Strata, that's a different Mark. He's very edgy."

They stopped at a store window. "Oh, look at that purse," Grace said, pointing. "That's snakeskin. Actually, that's barbaric. But it's beautiful." Paul tugged her along and she returned to their conversation. "How is it different?"

"I don't know. Something's going on with him. He was always very ambitious. Granted all the partners at Collins, Shaw are. Just comes with the territory. But it's intensified with him."

Paul tilted his head. "The time he *really* was caring was when I was arrested. Nobody knew what to do with me. Actually, Kate was good to me, too. She came by often when I was out on bail. She was crushed about Art. Crushed. Imagine—the guy charged with murder telling the woman who's loved the victim with all her heart that everything is going to be all right.

"Mark was different. He was all business. Forced me over the facts time and again to make sure I didn't miss anything with Liebowitz. Talked over strategy. Even tried to reconstruct things to figure out who did do it. 'There's somebody from Art's past whom we don't know about,' he'd say. 'Maybe someone in L.A.' He wanted to go down there and ask questions, because the police hadn't. We were always good friends … but we were really close at that time. Then, at the end of the trial, we had a falling-out."

"A falling-out?"

"Yes. The entire goal at trial was to create a reasonable doubt in the jury's mind that I had committed the crime. If there was reasonable doubt, they'd be forced to acquit me. So Liebowitz worked up several strategies.

"One, which I already mentioned, was to put me on the stand to explain my so-called threat toward Art. Another was to argue that I had no connection to the murder weapon, because no weapon had been found.

"So Liebowitz's other strategy was to emphasize how many people Art had pissed off in the week before he was murdered. To show that there were *other* people who had motive. And I don't just mean Tony Rivera. Mark was right at the top of that list."

"He was? Mark?"

"The night before Art was killed, Mark had come out. You know Mark's gay, right?"

Grace furrowed her eyebrows. "I think so. I think I saw him with another man at Louis's funeral service."

"That was his partner, Charles. A complete knob. FYI, Mark's status is not for Di Strata's ears."

"*I* won't be seeing Di Strata again."

"On the Thursday night before Art was killed, all the guys in our group were at The Salty Dog, a pub we often went to, and Mark announced he was gay. It was a big deal for him. When Art and I were walking home, Art suggested to me that Mark came on to him right after, in the bathroom. Art flirted with *everybody*, so it was possible. The next evening, before Art was shot, we told Art he needed help. He rejected all of us viciously. Louis, Cyril, Lee, even Kate. But he mocked Mark the most, about his sexuality. Very two-faced of Art. Mark was extremely pissed off."

"My god."

"Well, Liebowitz ran as hard as he could with that at trial. He made sure that the jury heard how *everyone* was angry at Art. Kate, for example. Because she'd had a huge blowout with Art the day before I did. And Mark. He ended up testifying about being gay and coming out, and what exactly had happened with Art, which was nothing more than a short exchange of words. I guess Mark thought I should have put Liebowitz on a leash. But I was up for first degree murder, and there was no question what Liebowitz had to do. Reasonable doubt. But it took some time before Mark came around. Quite some time. He did, though. A good friend."

Grace kissed Paul on the cheek. "Let's continue this at my place," she said. At the next corner they found a taxi. She held Paul's hand as they tore through Piazza Barberini to Via delle Quattro Fontane. Via Nazionale swarmed with taxis and pedestrians but in the inky night it felt menacing to Paul. He was lost until they crossed the Tiber and stopped in front of Grace's building a few minutes later.

It was almost midnight and most shutters around the piazza were closed. Paul caught errant sounds as he stepped out. Behind him, as neon light penetrated shutter slats, a television audience released an affected roar. Elsewhere, a couple shouted a crescendo of insults at each other while their neighbour above tried to drown them out with "The Ocean Song".

From the top floor of the building at the end, the old man in the undershirt looked down from an open window, a cigarette dangling in his mouth. He removed the cigarette and released a whistle that started quiet and ended shrill, then grabbed his crotch. "Ignore him," Grace said. "He's rude and has problems."

As Grace fumbled in her purse for her front door key, shutters above opened, releasing pulses of an aching aria. Oblivious to Grace and Paul, Signora Di Grotto leaned with both forearms on her ledge and stared ahead. The lamp above the door threw a dim light on her ashen face, tears trickling down sagging cheeks.

When they entered Grace's apartment, Paul said, "Keep the lights off." He walked over to the window above the desk and gazed across the piazza. Grace came up behind, and when she touched him on the shoulder, he flinched.

"Jumpy," she said. "What are you looking at? Friday night in the piazza?"

At first, Paul saw nothing. "Just wait," he said, squinting.

"Oh, are you on that again?" Grace moaned. She kissed his cheek. "There's nothing there," she whispered. "It's your paranoia."

"Just wait," he repeated, keeping his eyes steady. "I can feel it on my skin."

With arms crossed, she followed his gaze. "I'm serious. There's nothing there. It's like a little village here. Sometimes people don't respect your privacy." She looked back at him and tugged at his arm. "Come on. Let's not do the exact thing you're worrying about."

"Look, there," he said. "Honestly, at the same window I showed you before we left. A small light is on and there's someone standing there, watching us. Who lives there?"

"Paul, I don't have the slightest idea," Grace said. Her tone had become irritable. "Now please, let's step away."

The shutters across the piazza closed, and a moment later, the light went out. An eerie stillness settled in, interrupted only by the ticking of the grandfather clock.

"For Christ's sake, isn't that freaky?"

"Don't be silly," Grace said. "You're tormenting yourself. Now let's close all the shutters and go to bed. I'm going to have a glass of water. Do you want one?"

"Yes."

By "go to bed", she meant her bed, queen-sized with a goose down duvet and white pillows and sheets. It had cradled and cloaked him the night before for his deepest sleep in months. Holding her there mesmerized him like the sticky sweetness of sponge toffee he'd had as a boy with David. With a last glance at the ochre building, he pulled tight the shutters above the desk and closed the windows.

When he got to bed, Grace lay on her side facing a lamp on a table next to her, reading a small Italian book. On the table on his side, there was a glass of water with bubbles cavorting to the top. He took a long sip then put down the glass and stole into bed. Curling an arm around her, he form-fitted his front to her back and found her in a bra and panties. A few seconds later, she let the book fall shut.

"Paul," she said, "can I say something to you? Something you may not want to hear?"

Paul shrugged. "Will you kick me out if I say 'no'?"

"Very likely."

"Then talk away."

"It's simply this. The *only* way you're going to escape the shroud you live under is to talk about it. With someone you trust. And you *need* to escape the shroud. It's choking the life out of you."

"That's why I see—"

"Yes, I know, the psychiatrist. I don't mean talking about things for an hour once or twice a week. I mean intensive discussion, probably with a friend." Paul stayed quiet. "And that friend could be *me*. At least while you're still here."

Paul's stomach seized. "Actually, sleeping like I did last night is very healing. And making love." She turned and lay on her back, her body stiff like an ironing board. He hadn't said the right thing. "Okay," he said, "I'll think about it. I'll think about disclosing everything to you. If I can."

"You can," she said, "and you can trust me."

"Can we sleep now?" he said, faking a yawn. "I'm dead tired."

37

To Paul's dismay, sleep evaded him. It was like an alluring woman interested in his attention but unsure of his offers. To avoid waking Grace, he resisted tossing and turning. At his wit's end, he snuck out the bedroom into the kitchen to refill his glass of water. The LED on the microwave flashed 1:13.

He returned to bed, drank half the water, then put the glass on the side table and lay on his back. He heard Grace's steady breathing and imitated it. Relaxation followed, and cloudy remembrances of Di Strata slamming his fist on his dining table swam with images of decapitated Roman statues and Grace's pale skin. Sleep was ready to possess.

But he was startled awake again. His eyes shot open and he stared at the ceiling, trying to place himself. *Rome. I'm in Rome.* The sound that had awakened him echoed in his ears: it was the bolt of the apartment front door. *Jesus Christ, Signora Di Grotto is back.* He sat upright, his body stiff with vigilance, shivers pulsing through his limbs.

His mouth dry, he licked his lips. With shallow and choppy breaths, his eyes started adjusting to the bedroom's darkness. There was no Signora Di Grotto and his shivers began to scatter. He looked left. There was no Grace either. Her side of the duvet was pulled back and the sheet where she'd lain was creased. He touched the sheet and it was still warm. The shivers pulsed once more.

Probably having a drink of water herself. Or in the bathroom. But there were no matching sounds. Instead an echo came from the building hallway, feeble like someone had suppressed its source. Paul recognized the building's front door closing shut.

He threw his half of the duvet onto the middle of the bed as well. Edging out of the bedroom, he slid down the hallway to the threshold of the living room. When he saw nothing, he hurried to the small desk. Opening one window above, he leaned forward and peered through a tiny crack between the shutters. As a wisp of cool air curled past his face, he saw her. In stretchy black athletic pants and a matching jacket, Grace stood at the front door of the ochre building across the piazza, inserting a key into its lock. A second later, without glancing around, she slipped inside.

He stood in the same spot for ten minutes, his eyes trained on the building. No lights came on; no shutters opened; no one slipped back out the front door. It seemed like millipedes were scurrying across his skin. *What the hell is Grace doing in the voyeur's building? And why so long?*

He paced the living room, the grandfather clock's ticking infiltrating its silence. Every thirty seconds or so he bolted back to the crack in the shutters and looked for answers. A maggot of a thought bore into his brain. *She has a lover there. Of course she has a lover in Rome. How could a beautiful woman like that not?* He burned with the hot shame of naiveté. What a fool he'd been. *What a fucking fool.*

He returned to Grace's bedroom and sat at the bedside. Apprehension continued to parch his throat and he finished his glass of water. It was all he could do not to switch to Justin's bed. But that would give her a read he didn't want to reveal. He lay down and pulled the duvet over him, grinding his teeth, knowing sleep had lost interest in him completely.

He closed his eyes, but now all he saw was Grace fucking the hell out of a swarthy, well-built man with a crooked nose. What had he been thinking coming to Rome? What kind of geographical cure had he duped himself with? He would check flights in the morning. He was sure he could return to Toronto the next day on standby.

A few minutes later, the front door of the building echoed shut again. Ten seconds after that, the bolt of the apartment door found its internal metallic receptacle. He lay stiff on the bed, attempting normal breathing. Soon she would return to bed smelling of another man's sweat and semen.

He didn't need his eyes open to know she'd arrived. The bed shifted, then the duvet was pulled taut. He wanted to stay still, feigning REM sleep so she would drop into blissful slumber. Her breathing slowed and once again he matched each inhalation and exhalation. He told himself to be patient. Soon he would be alone with his thoughts and able to collect himself for the morning. But his throat was dry again. So dry that when he tried to swallow, he gagged up a cough.

"Are you *awake*?" Grace whispered.

He knew he couldn't fool her. "Yes," he said, his body rigid.

"For how long?"

He cleared his throat. "Since you left."

She caught her breath. After several seconds, she said, "So you're wondering what I was doing." He said nothing. "Justin's father lives there," she said. "If you're feeling jealous or angry or anything like that, you don't need to. He lives there as a matter of convenience—for Justin."

Again Paul said nothing, processing the news and her tone. The proximity of Justin's father made sense; the timing of Grace's visit didn't. "Why did you go over there in the middle of the night?" he asked finally.

"I'm extremely angry with him." Grace turned on the lamp on her side table. Paul shielded his eyes from its invasive light. "That's who's been watching us. I guess curiosity is getting the better of him. He can be so damn dominating, so *patronizing*. It's none of his fucking business who I'm spending time with. I don't watch as women troll through his place, do I?"

"But you went over there at *one thirty* in the morning."

"I got up to go to the bathroom. You were asleep. At least I thought so. And I went to the window and looked again. Within thirty seconds, he was back, opening those damn shutters a little way. He's watching. He's checking up on me. So I just put on some clothes and went over there and confronted him."

"You have a key?"

"Of course I do. For Justin, if he wants to visit." Grace's eyes bore into Paul's. "Justin's father had nothing to do with him for years, Paul. I mean for years. He continued his dance career then eventually failed, like so many of us do, and returned to Turin. I had no wish to see him ever again. I wanted to be left alone and raise Justin on my own, by myself, without interference.

"And then one day he appears at my front door. Old, out of shape, like a broken man. He'd had a revelation that he needed time with his son. And then he pleaded. And made threats that he would pursue his rights. Three times he appeared," Grace said fiercely, "and three times I sent him away. It was quite a show for Signora Di Grotto.

"But my mother always said, 'A son needs a father.' And Justin is an awkward fifteen-year-old—handsome, but dreadfully shy like me—and sometimes I can't connect with him. Eventually my mother's words convinced me to let Justin's father see him. And then a year later, he moved in across the way. What could I do? I thought about filing charges for harassment, but is that the right thing for Justin? Sometimes it's a good thing he's there.

"So I'm sorry. When I saw him again just now, I had to go over there and give him a piece of my mind. He denied everything, of course, but at least I don't think he'll bother us anymore." Grace pulled up beside Paul and hugged him. "Believe me. He means *nothing* to me. *Niente*." Feeling Grace's body, hearing the urgency in her voice, Paul grew calmer. "I should have told you. I simply thought you'd have a hard time relaxing with him there. Or worse, that you wouldn't believe me."

They lay together in silence. After a few minutes, Grace said, "It's time for sleep." She reached over and turned off the light. It was her turn to lie awake much longer than she wanted to.

38

Grace's nocturnal wandering left Paul skittish much of Saturday. Vatican City and the Sistine Chapel were spellbinding but the clog of tourists aggravated his edginess. Waiters overrun by lunchtime crowds seemed abrupt and slippery. And his plays at affection after lunch felt forced. Grace sensed his detachment. Like the heavy cumulus clouds that appeared, she moved in close, suppressing him. By late afternoon, he longed for the rest of the day to himself.

In the evening, Grace picked out another restaurant in Trastevere for dinner. The warm air smelled of rain and they agreed on a patio table under a canopy. During appetizers, she tried to lead him down the alleyway of his past but he didn't let her get far. He turned the conversation to Justin, a topic she grabbed and where his mind could drift.

"Are you okay?" she finally asked, at the end of their main course.

"I'm 'okay', whatever that means," he said. "There's a lot to take in here. I feel overwhelmed."

"Do you want any dessert?"

"Just a coffee, I think. Decaf." A few spits of rain fell on the ground beyond the canopy. "Actually, let's make that a cognac."

"I'm asking if you're okay because I don't take rejection well."

"Rejection?"

The waiter arrived and took their drink order. "Yes, rejection," she said in a low tone, her eyes glued on Paul.

"Are you suggesting I'm rejecting you?"

She pursed her lips. "I'm not sure."

He let a few seconds pass, confused. "I'm not."

"I never feel I'm quite good enough. That's a problem I have."

"Join the club."

"No. I really feel that. And when there's proof I'm not good enough, I—I don't do well."

The rain fell harder, forming rivulets between stones. "Me, I just withdraw," Paul said. The cognacs arrived. Paul took a large sip, swirled it around his mouth and enjoyed the burn down his throat. "But you *are* good enough. Probably too good for me, if truth be told." Grace sent him a cautious smile.

They decided to wait out the rain and ordered two more cognacs. The drinks warmed Paul to the world and to Grace's charms. "What did you and David talk about?" she asked.

"What did we talk about?" Paul repeated, running a hand through his hair and watching a sheet of drops fall straight and hard. He shrugged. "Like I said, not much. School, I guess. Girls. The thing was, he had quite a few girlfriends and I was envious. Sometimes he picked on me ruthlessly, and I wanted to kick him to a pulp, but he was too big for me. But despite that and all his problems, I thought he was the coolest guy. Smart, good-looking, intense, misunderstood."

"That's you as well," Grace said.

"Nice try," Paul said with a trace of a smile. "When I started writing, it was about his world. As I saw it. Not mine."

"You never told *anyone* about his voices, his ghosts?"

"No. I was a kid. I didn't understand and it scared me. And he made me swear not to tell. And not to tell anyone how much dope he was smoking. I took that very seriously, because I thought we had this sacrosanct brotherly bond. Trust me, I haven't stopped berating myself for keeping quiet."

"But why?"

"You never know what might have changed."

"My god, that's a hard way of looking at things."

Paul shrugged again. "I feel the same about Art. Another exceptional person gone in a flash."

"But what could you have done about *him*? Somebody murdered him."

"I could have been a better friend when he came back from L.A. Ignored his arrogance and provocations and helped him face his demons. There was a lot to save. For him, for everyone who'd looked up to him. Honestly, he'd become vulnerable and I didn't take it seriously enough."

"And you could stop a drug dealer from acting insanely?"

"I told you, it wasn't Rivera. And that misses the point. How did things get so out of control with Art? How did he end up owing ten grand to a dealer in the first place? If I'd acted, even before he left for L.A., maybe the whole chain of events would have unfolded differently."

"You really think so?"

"I'm not usually a fatalist, but on that point, I am. We sized each other up when we met in third-year undergrad. We were instant competitors, but then we became friends, too, with a mutual respect. At least, that's what I thought. Really, for me, it was admiration. I shouldn't have been so damned impatient when he came back from L.A."

Grace furrowed her brow. "You said your lawyer—Liebowitz—wanted the jury to think others had motives to murder him. You must have thought it could have been another friend of Art's. Maybe even someone you know?"

"Well, I suppose that's what Liebowitz was implying. I don't know. I don't want to think about that. I just know it feels like I bear responsibility."

Grace paused. Paul could tell she had more questions. He needed to shut her down. The rain had reduced to a drizzle so he said, "Let's walk home."

"Our shoes will get wet," Grace said.

"I'll buy you a new pair tomorrow."

"Hmm. You do care after all."

After paying, they headed to the edge of the patio canopy. Grace popped open the umbrella she'd brought along and handed it to Paul. As they stepped onto the street, she snuggled in and looped an elbow through his.

Ten minutes later, they entered the piazza drenched from the knees down. "Oh, screw this," Grace said. She slung off her light jacket and took off her shoes. Clamping them at her side with her elbow, she pulled her keys from her purse and handed the purse to Paul. With a squeal, she dashed in bare feet to her building. He ran after with the umbrella outstretched, laughing, trying to protect her from the drizzle. By the time they were beyond the front door, strands of hair clung to her cheeks, and the darkened shoulders of her white cotton blouse stuck to her skin.

The dim ceiling light came on. He closed the umbrella and let it drop with her purse to the ground. Turning her toward him, he kissed her hard, feeling her lips grow into his. Then he pulled her close and pushed his hands down the wet back of her blouse to the curves of her tight jeans.

Somebody inserted a key in the door. Grace pulled away, picking hair off her cheeks. She handed the umbrella and purse to Paul, grabbed his elbow and raced him up the stairs to her apartment.

The grandfather clock's ticking filled the darkness. Dropping her jacket and shoes, Grace grabbed Paul's face and crushed his mouth with her lips. Her tongue, slippery and probing, funnelled around his, and he let her umbrella and purse fall. Then he began to undo the buttons of her blouse. They stuck to the wet fabric, and after several seconds of fumbling, Paul ripped the blouse open by its collar.

"My bl—" she started, but his lips obliterated her words. She pulled away. "Wait," she said, catching her breath. "I want to share something with you." Leaving him bulging his pants, she turned on a living room lamp then scurried to the bedroom.

A minute later she returned wearing only a crimson strapless bra and panties. Each hand clenched, she pulled close, suppressing a smile. As their legs touched, she opened her hands, revealing two coiled blood-red silk ropes.

Looking down, a flush intercepting the paleness of her face, she asked, "Do you know what to do with these?" She walked to the chrome-and-black leather chair closest to the lamp and faced him. "Tie me up," she whispered.

He spun her a hundred and eighty degrees then with two fingers prodded her lower back toward the chair. She knelt on its seat. He prodded again and she bent over, raising her ass and lying on the back cushion, her shoulders and head hanging over the edge. Her black hair released to the ground, obscuring the sides of her face.

Walking around, Paul took the ropes from her hands and said, "This can't be that hard. Don't move." He took one rope and knotted an end around her slender left wrist. Then he took the other end and tied it around a horizontal bar at the bottom of the chair. She tugged but the rope was taut. With the other rope he tied her right hand the same way.

"Please be—" she started.

"I'll be careful," he interrupted. He gathered her hair into a strand and gently pulled. The ropes quickly confined her. "This will do just fine," he said, and released the hair.

Feeling more calm and in control than he had in months, he returned behind her. The crimson panties were stretched tight over each buttock. He ran fingers along both her calves, into the bends of her knees and along the insides of her thighs. Then he slipped his hands under her panties and drew the panties up into the crevice between her legs. Her hips began to writhe.

He snapped his hands free and inched them up her spine to the roll of her shoulders over the chair. Leaning over her, he kissed her back then tugged at her bra strap with his teeth. His hands slipped around her, pulling her bra down and cupping her breasts.

"Jesus," she said, "how much longer do I have to wait?"

"As long as I please," he said. "Be quiet." He undid her bra and it fell to the chair. He pulled her up at the waist, forcing her to arch her back. "Stay like that."

"It's hard," she said.

"I said stay like that." He pushed her legs apart and between them mounted the chair on his knees. Leaning over, pushing the erection in his pants between her legs, he returned a hand under each breast and coarsely kneaded her nipples. The arch in her back collapsed and she started to squirm.

"Come on," she hissed, "use me."

He unzipped himself from his pants. Pulling her panties to one side, he entered her as deeply as he could. He stayed still, gritting his teeth, letting her push from side to side and absorb him.

"Stay close to me," she said, beginning to thrust back and forth. "Don't go anywhere." Her thrusting increased and he joined. "No," she said breathlessly, "don't move." As he held onto her hips, she accelerated the violent stabs toward him, constrained only by the ropes chafing her wrists. In a final plunge, her body seized and shivered, and he felt multiple spasms. Three bucks later he released, proud he'd conquered the Hart House curse again, and fell into a heap overtop her.

After a few seconds of collecting their breath, she said, "Move, you're too heavy. And get me out of these." He eased himself off her, zipped up his pants, then walked around the chair and untied her. When she returned from the bathroom a few minutes later, he lay on the sofa. She joined with her back to him, pulling a blanket over them. He put an arm around her and she collected his hand between hers. The first blissful strains of sleep crept around his eyes.

"Did you really give the gun back?" she asked.

Paul flinched as sleep fled. "What are talking about?"

"The gun your Granddad gave you. Did you really give it back to him?"

He felt irritated. "Yes, of course. I testified as much—under oath."

"It just seems the men in your family were all taken from you. Your Granddad gave you the gun not long after David and your father died. In a way, it was a remembrance of all of them. You must have wanted to keep it."

Paul sighed. "I did," he said in a quiet tone. "But like I said, when I told my mother about it, she went berserk." He paused then added in a whisper, "Did anyone ever tell you ask too many questions?" He closed his eyes but listened carefully.

"No," she said. "They complain that I'm too quiet. I just like connecting with you, I guess."

"You want to know something?" he asked.

"Yes."

"When Granddad taught me how to shoot that handgun, I never felt so powerful in my life."

39

Sunday, the skies hung out their dirty laundry. A thin, steady rain fell without interruption. Water curled between stones and gurgled into a sewer at the lower end of the piazza. For the first time Grace suggested they stay indoors. Paul contented himself checking world events and emails online, then dipping into *Brave New World*.

At first, having Grace look over his shoulder at the laptop and cuddle beside him reading her own novel felt cosy. By early afternoon, however, Paul noticed that she followed him everywhere. When he made himself a sandwich in the kitchen, she was beside him, helping out. When he moved to one of the chairs, she stretched her legs from the sofa onto his knees. And when he napped in her bedroom, she snuck in and lay beside him.

Isn't that what lovers do? he asked himself. *Maybe it's just me. Drawn to isolation like the rain to the sewer.* But it was something different, he decided. Her eyes had a beat on him like he was a husband who'd just had an affair. Her circumspection made him feel guarded, and he turned aside several attempts at in-depth conversation. After the last, she sighed and watched him for several seconds, as if trying to understand. He kept his eyes on the alphas, betas and epsilons of his book.

Late afternoon, he walked over to the small desk and looked out the window at the unrelenting rain. Her eyes were trained on him again and he decided he needed to get out. "Do you have any beer?" he asked, knowing she didn't.

"No."

"Can I buy some around here?"

"I don't really feel like going out yet."

"Just tell me where," he said. "I'll get it. I'm going to take a walk, too." Her lips pressed together and her eyelids batted with unsaid inquiry. "I won't be long," he added. "Maybe half an hour."

She gave him her umbrella and directions to a store open Sundays. After an enduring kiss on the lips, he stepped out of the apartment with his spare keys and galloped down the stairs and out the building. He waved to her standing at a window as he left the piazza.

Paul found the store without difficulty and fumbled his way through buying three bottles of Peroni Red. With gesticulations and bastardized words, the clerk told him how to find the Tiber. The umbrella open in one hand and the three beers in a plastic bag in the other, Paul found Lungotevere degli Anguillara and walked along until he was across from the Ponte Palatino. He waited for the pedestrian signal to turn green. The rain pelted the umbrella and he caught spray from whining motorcycles and jockeying cars. Dampness crept into his bones. He decided the Tiber could await a sunny day. With a decisive turn, he began retracing his steps to Grace's apartment.

Not long after, he turned up Via dell'Arco de' Tolomei in a scurry. He cursed, realizing his second and last pair of shoes was getting wet. Through a barrage of rain, he looked toward the piazza's entrance fifty yards away. At the ochre building, two men, one inside and the other stranded outside, struggled to get a refrigerator on a dolly over the front door's threshold. The second man, his shirt dark across his shoulders from the rain, made grand sweeping motions to show they needed to approach the door the other way around. They shouted back and forth until the man in the rain yelled "*Basta*" and began pulling the dolly away from the door.

Paul's smile at the struggle plunged from his face and he lurched to a stop. Grace had scampered into view, holding a shawl over her head. With a few words and gestures, she indicated she needed to get into the building. The two men, quickly charmed, pulled the dolly out far enough for her to slip by.

Paul saw no reason why Grace needed to talk to Justin's father. She'd disclaimed all interest in him, and though Paul had kept an eye out, he hadn't noticed any silhouettes behind shutters that day. He needed to understand better, he told himself, and walked toward the building.

The two men were turning the dolly with the refrigerator around. The man inside had stepped out and held open the door with a hip, shielding his face from the rain. Immersed in their struggle, they didn't notice Paul step by with his open umbrella. The first-floor light was feeble, and Paul stopped to let his eyes adjust, holding his breath, worried he would stumble upon Grace. There was nothing except an apartment door on each side and dried-out palms in the front corners.

On the second floor, Grace uttered rapid-fire Italian, then a door closed. Paul's first thought was to collect himself, abandon his scepticism and return to Grace's apartment. He turned toward the front door, but it was blocked again by the two men, the other end of the dolly against the threshold. The man in front, noticing Paul for the first time, looked mistrustful. Paul held up the three beers and smiled. He spun around while closing the umbrella and headed for the stairs.

He ascended six steps then doubled back another six. The stairs continued to the third floor, but Paul stopped, guessing Justin's father rented the apartment to the left. Two more palms sat in the far corners of the second-floor landing and between them was a window with a view of Grace's building.

He stole forward, making sure the three Peroni Reds didn't clink together. At the apartment's door, he stopped and listened. He expected to hear a heated exchange inside and even imagined bursting in to protect Grace. But all he made out were temperate, unhurried murmurs.

He put his right ear a few inches from the door. A voice approached from the other side; it belonged to Grace. No man's voice came from the apartment, and Grace's tone was calm. Confused, Paul felt his mouth go dry and he licked his lips.

The door handle twitched. Suspending his breathing, Paul darted to the stairs. He started down but stopped because the two men had blocked the bottom steps manoeuvring the dolly into an apartment. The door creaked open and Grace's elegant rear lines showed. Paul bounced back up the stairs to the second floor and continued halfway to the third, stopping on the landing where the stairs doubled back. His back against the wall, his heart hammering, he breathed in silent spasms.

Conversation between Grace and another woman spilled out. Occasionally, a third voice, cracking and dim, added some words. "*Ciaos*" and the smacks of kisses then shot back and forth. The temptation was overwhelming. Paul squatted and peered down to the second floor.

Though he strained, everyone was too far left for him to see. Then he noticed a reflection in the window at the far end. It revealed Grace sending air kisses then scampering down the stairs. Once she was gone, Paul saw the reflection of the back of an older woman. He leaned around a bit more, enough to sort out her appearance from the front as she spoke a few words to someone else. She reminded him of Grace, but with twenty-five more years. And pounds. Disappearing into the apartment, she left the other person, standing alone.

That person made a half turn toward the stairs, and Paul jerked back. For a moment he heard only falling rain. Sweat surfaced on his brow and he feared he'd been sussed out. Then the other person shuffled toward the second-floor window and his back came into Paul's view. A young man looked out the window and waved cautiously. Paul squinted at his reflection.

His gut seized like he'd been tasered with a million volts. It was Art's auburn hair. It was Art's handsome face. It was Art's proportions. But all in the body of a teenager.

40

What in goddamn hell. What in goddamn *hell.*

The teenager had disappeared into the apartment. On the landing, Paul dragged his legs out from under his squat and sat on his ass. Then he put down the umbrella and beers and slumped against the wall. That was Art incarnate. That was Art redux. *Fuck, that was Art embodied.* Paul ran both hands through his hair twice. *Art is alive.*

In a way.

Paul's gut ached and his chest felt like it supported a hundred-pound weight. *Take a breath, get another, grab a third.* He let his head fall back against the wall, wincing when he grazed the bump from Signora Di Grotto. Then, several times, he rotated his head and rolled his shoulders. Composure seeped in and his brain began processing again.

Do the math. Justin was fifteen. Add nine months of gestation and it was possible. And there were supporting details. Grace had admitted that she and Art had met in the months before Art died. Plus Kate's instinct was that there'd been more between them than they'd let on. And of course, Grace had been at Art's funeral. It wasn't just possible. It was undeniable.

A cavalcade of implications marched into Paul's brain. He threw himself back to Art's funeral, where the idea that he was a "person of interest" in the murder had consumed him. Even so, at the end of the service, he'd been driven to find Grace by the residual heat of their Hart House encounter. Pawing the front steps of the United Church with the tip of a shoe, he'd asked if she had any interest in him. Now he understood why she'd told him she didn't feel the passion. She'd slept with his rival and had an enormous problem to deal with. Wrestling so long with her fearsome rejection in the squalor of male insecurity had been a stunning waste of time.

And could he say that Art was alive? Of course not. An extension of him was. One that was just entering his formative years, who would exert his own being. The way Grace spoke of him and with his first glance, Paul guessed that Justin would be less effectual than Art. Justin probably was an intimation, a tease, an underachieving distortion of his father.

But pushing all other thoughts aside was the realization that Grace had lied to him. Kate had been right: she couldn't be trusted. Grace hadn't just thrown a lazy lasso around facts; she'd developed an entire scheme of deception about Justin's father. Paul's confidence in her exploded like a crystal glass crashing onto a marble floor. *Why hide that she's the mother of Art's child?*

Paul stood with the beers and umbrella and walked down the stairs. Rachel had been right as well: Grace *was* a pool of impenetrably dark water. If he couldn't trust Grace, there was no point in confronting her. Instead, he had to get the hell out of there. He longed to be back at his condo, alone in his reading chair, in the dark. And in the meantime he'd have to outdo Art as an actor.

On the first floor, the two men had the dolly and fridge in the apartment but the door was propped open. Paul looked in, more to release nervous energy than out of curiosity. The man who'd spotted him earlier looked up, and mistrust clouded his face again. Paul hurried into the rain and bolted to Grace's building.

Holding the spare key at her apartment door, Paul finished his fabrication for flying back to Toronto early. His mother was seriously ill and he had to take the next flight; lovely time and all, hope to see you soon, but he had no choice. As he opened the door, Grace came over from the sofa to greet him.

She looked wary. Paul handed her the beers and placed the umbrella into a metal can next to the door. She'd brushed out her hair and changed her clothes to remove evidence of being outside in the rain. To assure her of his affections, he conjured the best smile, kiss and hug he had. Like a good scene in one of Louis's movies, she seemed to buy his act.

"You were gone quite a while," she said.

"I walked to the Tiber and across the Ponte Palatino," he said. "It was beautiful."

"In the rain?"

"Very stagey. Very dramatic. The blue water against the grey sky."

She tilted her head. "The water looked green-brown yesterday, I thought," she said.

"You're right. Kind of grey-blue-green-brown."

He cleared his throat and walked over to the desk. He picked up the dagger-shaped antique hairpiece with the oval cameo that lay on top of the back drawers. Turning its sharp tip into the palm of his other hand, he said, "I just need to check my emails. My mother sent me one yesterday. She was unwell."

"Of course," Grace said. She eyed Paul like she wanted to join him but instead she took the beers to the kitchen. "Do you want one now?"

He sat down in front of her laptop and entered the URL for his email. "Sure, yes," he said, pretending to be immersed. Moments later, he added, "Oh dear, my mother's been in hospital."

"What?" Grace said from the kitchen.

"My mother's been in hospital," Paul said louder, minimizing the email program.

Grace hurried back holding a glass of beer. "My god, what's wrong?"

Easing back in the chair, he rubbed his chin as if in deep thought. "Grace, if she doesn't get better soon, I may have to leave early." Her eyes narrowed as if reacting to sudden bright light, and her lips hardened. "She's had a bad heart for years."

"You should call her," Grace said, setting the glass on the desk. "Go into Justin's bedroom if you want privacy."

"Good idea," Paul said. He stood, gave Grace another light kiss on the lips and headed down the hallway.

He circled around Justin's room, wondering what he would say to his mother. They spoke at most once a month and he hadn't told her he was going to Rome. For the first time, he noticed there were no photos of Justin in the bedroom. The only picture was a headshot of Grace on the night table next to the bed. Indeed, as he thought it over, in the entire apartment, except for the artwork on the corkboard in the kitchen, all evidence of Justin had been removed. *Part of her scheme of deception.*

Then Paul remembered he'd only minimized his email program and not closed it. Gulping, he charged out the bedroom and down the hallway. Grace spun around, sucking in air, her right hand flying off the laptop's touchpad. Blood rose to her cheeks, overwhelming her usual paleness.

She picked up the glass on the desk and met him halfway in the living room. "Did you make the call already?" she asked, handing him the beer. "How's your mother?" Then, with a sudden air of insouciance, she turned and churned her hips away from him.

He yanked a lobe. When she was almost in the kitchen, he said, "You know I haven't spoken to her, don't you? You checked my emails."

She turned and gave him a quizzical look. "Excuse me? What did you say?"

He wanted to say, "*Grace, why are you lying to me about everything? What the fuck is going on here?*" But he couldn't get there. Someone he thought was a friend was gaming him, and an ugly remembrance took shape. The back of his mouth tasted bitter and metallic. He took a sip of beer.

He saw again the square white interview room at 14 Division. It was the second interview and Beecham was across from him, sweat on his brow. Each time Paul answered a question, Beecham nodded and said, "I see. Now I understand better." Then Paul shuddered, recalling the worst moment. It was after Beecham said for maybe the twentieth time, "Now, just one more question." The moment when Paul realized he'd been played for a fool and said too much.

"Nothing. I, ah—I left her a message to call me," he said.

Grace kept her quizzical look for several more seconds. Finally she smirked and said, "Really, Paul, sometimes it's hard to figure out what's going on in that head of yours." She walked into the kitchen.

What was going on was that, unseen and untouched, he wanted to get the hell out of there. It was the same wish he'd had when the third interview with Beecham ended. The interview where Liebowitz had instructed him to say nothing and after which Beecham arrested and charged him with first degree murder.

41

The trick for Paul was to play his role as Grace's lover yet find a private moment to move his departure from Wednesday to Monday. If he couldn't make the change online or by phone, he would just show up the next day, bright and early, at Air Canada's ticket counter at Fiumicino. Yes, early, before she had any opportunity to continue playing her games. And then he'd be on the plane to Lester B. Pearson International Airport before the new world dawned on her.

"You're very quiet this evening," Grace said at the tail end of their dinner. The rain had continued unabated and the outside air was cold and clawing. They were inside the restaurant, in a corner, away from the small Sunday crowd. "You hardly touched your wine."

I'm not going to explain to you that I need my wits about me. "Bit of a headache tonight. It's the weather," Paul said. "You look especially beautiful tonight," he added, planting a smile on his face.

Grace returned the smile. "Why thank you. I didn't think you'd noticed."

I fucking notice everything you're doing. "Of course I did."

"I thought about driving to Pompeii tomorrow. It's supposed to be sunny and warmer. After we buy those shoes, of course."

Not on your life. "That sounds nice. But I have a better idea. Why don't we do that Tuesday? I might go see the Colosseum tomorrow. I can't imagine visiting Rome for the first time without seeing it. I know you said you're tired of it. I'll go alone."

"You don't mind? I took three more days' vacation to be with you until you leave Wednesday. I could drop by work tomorrow morning to make sure there aren't any emergencies. The director would appreciate that, I think."

Stay there all day if you like. I won't be here when you get back. "I don't mind at all."

Paul wished the minutes along. They traded meaningless words and fell into a long pause, scanning the restaurant for something of interest. He wondered what kind of sex he'd have for her later if she sought it. Then, staring hard at him, she said, "You said you'd think about disclosing everything to me."

"Disclosing what?"

Her brown eyes bore into him. "Remember? You said that Thursday night. When I offered to be your friend? Your listener?"

Not in a goddamn million years. "I suppose I could tolerate a cognac," he said.

"I'll join you."

After their first sips, she looked at him expectantly. "You know what I think is going on with you?" she asked.

"No idea."

"I think you had more malice toward Art than you like to admit. I think that maybe, at some point, you did want him dead." Paul started. "Don't get me wrong," Grace added. "I'm not saying you harmed him. I'm just saying that he aggravated you so much from time to time that it at least occurred to you. That's a hard cross to bear."

Now you're the prosecution, too. "That's quite a thing to say."

Grace laughed, mockingly, Paul thought. "*Thinking* about it isn't unnatural, Paul. I mean, there have been one or two situations where the idea of wanting somebody dead dropped into my head for a second." She wet a forefinger with cognac and rimmed the top of her glass until it sang a chilling tone. "And also, with you men, there's all that testosterone. It does peculiar things. I know, I know. You admired him and all, but mostly he was your keenest competitor. Sometimes your arch-enemy."

Her eyes sliced into him, like a cat spying a lonesome bird. "None of that makes me a murderer, of course," he said.

"I know the malice *I* can feel toward my father. He's just been abusive. Paid everything for me, but otherwise, made me feel horrible as a woman because my mother left him. I wish I hadn't been so cowardly all the time."

"I'm sorry. How did we get onto malice?"

"Paul, I read your story. I read it the day it appeared in the *Acta Victoriana*. It was really well done, and I was jealous. I had sent in a story, too. Yours was published, mine wasn't, and I was the damn English major. I remember it. It was *rife* with malice."

"Grace, it was a rant. Yes, Art was a seed for it. But not as a victim. For the type of relationships he imposed on people. There's nothing new to that. I said as much at the trial."

Grace smiled. "I hardly knew each of you then, of course. And I'm sure your lawyer played everything down. That's what he was hired to do, wasn't it? To make sure no one knew you harboured thoughts of murdering Art."

"I didn't harbour those thoughts, Grace."

"Never once? You should reread your own story, Paul." Anger welled up inside him. He licked his lips and took a sip of cognac. "Well, if it's not that," she continued, "then it's about the gun."

What the fuck is it with you and the gun? "What's this theory?" he asked, shifting in his seat and pulling at a lobe.

She smiled. "I see your body language. You get defensive when this topic comes up. Pulling at your ear like that."

Caught out, Paul put his hands around his cognac glass. His lips constricted and the metallic bitterness returned to the back of his throat. "I don't think you can convict somebody for body language."

Grace laughed with the same mocking tone. "Oh stop, Paul. I was just pointing it out so you talk to me more freely. It's clear your Granddad meant a lot to you. And I have a funny feeling that you wanted to be an outdoorsman and a collector like him."

Paul shook his head and crossed his arms. "I'm urban through and through. I can't tell the difference between a deer and a moose. Never hunted anything except myself."

"It's true. You are urban. You never owned your own gun?"

"No." His anger at the endless questions mounted. "And what about you? Have you ever owned one?"

"Me? I wouldn't know which end it fires from. Of course not."

"Don't tell me you couldn't aim and fire one if you had to. Say, to protect Justin."

"My god, what an awful thought."

"When pressed, people do the oddest things. If not Justin, then say in self-defence. You could do that, right?"

"In self-defence, sure. For Justin, certainly. But as I said, I wouldn't know which end to point. I've only seen one once."

"You've seen a gun? A real one, up close?"

"Yes, but I don't want to talk about it."

Why the hell not? That's what you make me do all the time. "Speaking of funny feelings, I think you knew Art better than you told me, Grace."

She shrugged, too overtly, he thought. "I told you. We shared a few English classes at Vic. I mean, who didn't know him?"

"Well, there's a difference between knowing who he was and knowing him as a friend."

Grace paused. "Would say he was a friend? An acquaintance, someone who I would stop and talk to if I ran into him when I was walking across campus."

"Were you drawn to him?"

Grace took another pause. "He had his charisma. I was too shy. And I didn't want to be part of a fan club, if you know what I mean."

"I don't."

"There were lots of girls who tracked his every move. I didn't want to be just another one. I wanted to meet someone unique, different, out of the ordinary."

Liar. "Don't we all?"

"Well, people weren't as selective with Art. He did have the power to lure you into his world, if you let him. He just knew the things to say to make you feel special, even though, rationally, you knew he'd simply used the same damn lines with a hundred others. I don't know how Kate put up with it."

"She didn't especially well. He often tore her up. The thing is, I'm saying you knew him better than I realized."

"Not really."

Liar, damn liar. "And you spent time with him when he came back from L.A.?"

"Just a few coffees. Don't you think it's time we paid and went back to my apartment?"

"Soon. I have to tell you, Kate is certain the two of you had a fling."

Grace's face seized with surprise and she looked down at her cognac. "Well, we didn't," she said, then gulped down the rest of her drink. "And I'm not sure what business it is of hers anyway."

Liar, goddamn fucking liar. "But you saw him for more than a few coffees."

Grace exhaled a long breath and rolled the fingers of her right hand over the table. "All right, Paul, I don't know what the point of this is, but we did become better acquainted when he came back from L.A. We had dinner a few times, hung out a bit, but nothing serious at all."

"Not lovers?"

Grace's face became rigid. "It's not even your business, Paul, but no. I realized quite quickly that he was hunting around for friends and probably money. He told me that his father had cut him off. Once I heard that, I grew very wary and stopped seeing him."

"So when I recounted his time in L.A.—for Christ's sake, you knew all about that."

"Just bits and pieces. I don't even think he was telling me the truth. He was after money. He knew my father was supporting me and he was after a piece, through his guile and manipulation. And I didn't fall for it. I was gone as soon as I figured that out."

"When was that?"

"March of that year. I don't even remember exactly." Grace waved at the waiter for the bill. "I really don't want to talk about this anymore." Her eyes darted around the restaurant for a distraction.

"Let me get this one," Paul said.

"I've got it," she said, agitated. "I want to talk to him about the quality of the food."

Grace became engrossed in a conversation with the waiter. Several times he looked at Paul as if Paul were responsible for lies about the dishes they'd chosen. Paul ignored him and processed. Say Art and Grace had had sex early or mid-March 1998. Then Grace must have known she was pregnant with Art's child before he was murdered. And what if she'd told Art? What would his reaction have been? Throbbing with cocaine, self-centred, believing his fate was greatness … Paul guessed it would not have been understanding.

Words from Liebowitz's summary to the jury jumped into his mind. He'd stressed that Art had been hateful toward many friends in the week before his murder. "*Probably toward many others we don't even know about. And of all those people, who felt the kind of malice to think of murdering Art? Knowing the reaction Art brought out in people, probably quite a few. Surely that's enough for reasonable doubt."*

Kate had been one who'd felt Art's barbs, worse than most. Wednesday evening, May 6, 1998. Art and Kate had had a huge blowout. Yes, that evening, Art had taunted Kate about other women. Without naming her, they must have included Grace.

Yes, Art, down and decrepit in his final months, had still held the beauty to attract, like a carnivorous plant in a filthy bog. And the Foxy Lady had fallen in, with one giant, unexpected consequence—and without the time of day from Art afterwards.

Yes, Liebowitz had been spot-on. Who *had* felt the kind of malice to conceive of murdering Art? *Maybe the woman sitting across from me?*

42

When they got to Grace's apartment, Grace served cake and herbal tea in the living room. She was pale and guarded, a throwback to her undergrad days. Eventually she went to her bedroom to change for the night.

"I'm going to call my mother again," Paul said from the sofa. He waited for a response but none came. After finishing his cake and tea, he got up and walked to Justin's room.

Closing the door, he turned on a small lamp on the night table. First he texted Mark about his plans for early departure. Then he looked for Kate's contact and entered her number with country code. Back and forth he paced, eyeing a few stuffed animals, waiting for the call to connect. "Come on, come on," he muttered under his breath. He was surprised how tired he felt.

He wouldn't tell Kate about Justin or who Justin's father was; that would be far too upsetting for her. He just needed a bit more information to satisfy his curiosity and inform his fears.

"Hello," Kate answered.

"Kate, it's Paul."

"Paul, where are you?"

"In Rome still."

"What time is it there?"

"After midnight."

"I was just thinking of you."

"You were?"

"Lee just called me. Rachel's been on the phone to him because Cyril pulled himself out of rehab after five days. Now she doesn't know who can run Louis's company and thought Lee could give her some ideas. Of course, Lee being such a sweetheart, he tried to help but just made things worse. I thought, you know, with what happened to David, you might have ideas for Rachel—"

"Kate, I don't have time to talk about that. I need to ask you something."

"Okay," she said, her voice apprehensive. "What is it?"

"The thing is, I know this is weird, but I need to talk to you about the days before Art's murder."

There was a break. "Why?"

"I just need to, Kate. Do this for me?"

"Something's wrong."

"Nothing's wrong. Just answer a few questions."

Kate sighed. "Okay."

"The fight you had with Art the Wednesday night before he died—"

"Oh, not this again."

"It was because Art taunted you again, right?"

"Yes, he was being an asshole."

"Details, Kate. Give me some details."

"I'm going to move to another room." Some seconds later, Kate's voice reappeared. "There. You know, this better be important, Paul. I don't enjoy talking about this."

"I wouldn't ask except—"

"Anyway, I'm sure you remember, after he came back from L.A., Art's landlord kicked him out because he couldn't pay rent. Quite often he showed up at my place to sleep on the couch for the night, you know, without calling. At first it didn't bother me, but he wasn't *tidy*. I had to pick up after him and even washed his clothes once or twice. Of course, it was completely *natural* that I do this for him. And then all those feelings of being taking advantage of started coming up for me again. More intense than ever, because he'd left for L.A. without telling me, and then shows up two years later and just treats me like a friend. All that *stuff* you know, Paul."

"But that Wednesday night, didn't he provoke you? About other women? That thing he did to goad you."

Kate's voice grew icy. Paul imagined her biting her lower lip. "You'd think I'd forget after fifteen years, but, yes, that was it exactly. I was *so* tired of cleaning up for him that I really let him have it. And then he did what he always did when he wanted to be the biggest asshole to me. He told me *other* women treated him better. He could be such a *prick*."

Paul felt bad for ruining Kate's evening. Also, fatigue was overwhelming him. He focussed on an oval throw rug in the centre of Justin's room, white in the middle with orange diamonds around the edge. Like clouds on a blustery day, the diamonds moved closer and absorbed one another. He needed to get Kate to the point.

"So he made you jealous."

"Extremely."

"Did he name names?"

"Of women?"

Kate paused. Paul decided he needed to sit and plopped himself on the edge of Justin's bed. "I think I know what you're getting at," she said. "You mean did he talk about the Foxy Lady?"

"Yes."

"Not specifically. But you know, as I told you, I'd seen them together before. I assumed she was one of them."

"So they *were* lovers, like you said."

"Lovers? I'm sure he fucked her. I don't know why you believe me all of a sudden, but I hope it doesn't break your heart. It was a long time ago, Paul."

His eyes ached to close, his mind demanded sleep. He lay on Justin's bed, his head on a small, stiff pillow, and he watched the ceiling rotate. "So Art never mentioned a problem with another woman?"

"With the Foxy Lady, you mean?" Kate asked. Paul shut his eyes, feeling consciousness ebb away. "Now that you mention it, you're reminding me of something."

"Wassat?"

"Pardon me?"

"What's that?"

Out of the corner of his eye, on the other side of the room, Paul thought he saw movement. He tried to sit up but his head fell back to the pillow.

"During the fight that Wednesday night, Art did say—it was something like, yes, it was, 'You women are all the same. Demands, demands, demands. I wish you'd all go to hell and let me be who I want to be.' God, it just makes me *so* angry even now. You know, like I didn't let him be who he wanted to be."

Paul turned his head, trying to blink away the fog settling over him. The door to Justin's room was half open. Above the knob, fingers gripped the edge so hard, their talon-like nails were white.

"Paul?" Kate said. "Are you there?" The phone slipped out of his hand and plunged to the throw rug. "*Paul?* Oh, for goodness' sake."

Before slipping into nothingness, he glimpsed Signora Di Grotto at the doorway staring at him with a fierce smile, and Grace, ashen and expressionless, looking over her shoulder.

43

Consciousness approached, fuzzy like an oncoming car's headlights in mist. He looked for the bedpost, the perimeter of light around the window blind, the crack in the door to the hallway, but none was there.

He had no idea where he was. As if blowing air into a deflated balloon, he forced consciousness to expand. Slowly he made out the forms of stuffed animals, a sliver of light under a door, dim hints of dawn through overhead shutter slats. He had it. Rome—he was in bed in Justin's room. It was okay. He was leaving shortly.

Then discomfort rose. His legs were strangled at the ankles, and his feet ached and felt bulbous. Both hands were tight against the bed, swollen, fingertips pricked by a thousand needles. His mouth and throat were raw like he'd eaten sand. He realized he lay naked without a blanket.

He pushed his tongue between his teeth to lick his lips but his mouth was taped shut. As alarm leapt through him and he tried to raise his head, he gagged on a rope across his neck. He tried to thrash his legs and pull his hands, but something like coarse rope stripped skin from his ankles and wrists.

He visualized his bare, trapped body on the bed. His breathing became rapid and sharp, and alarm turned to panic because he couldn't get enough air through his nose. An involuntary scream rose in his throat, but with his lips held shut, only a long, guttural grunt emerged. His face ballooned with exertion and sweat crept onto his brow.

The door opened and Grace, wearing a loose floor-length dress, stepped into the threshold. Her hair was pulled back, held in a bun by the antique dagger hairpiece with the oval cameo. "There, there," she said. "Just stay calm. That's the secret."

Paul lifted his head as far as the rope across his neck allowed. He tried to say, "*What the fuck is going on?*" but again, only a long grunt surfaced. He dropped his head, and flaring his nostrils, he tried to control his breathing.

"That's better," Grace said. "Relax." She approached the bed and opened the room's windows and shutters. As Paul squinted against the flood of light, she sat on the edge of the bed. She leaned across him and dabbed the sweat from his brow with a moistened washcloth. Her eyes were crystal-clear and alert, and their lids fluttered. "Despite what you think, I've always found you very attractive. Especially now, naked and tied to the bed. If other things weren't so urgent, I'd have my way with you. Oh, look at you, all excited and the veins on your neck bulging out. Calm, I said. That's the only way."

With a forefinger, Grace touched the scabs forming across Paul's forehead. More sweat had bubbled up between them and she dabbed his brow a second time. "I didn't want to do this, you know. I thought we had a chance for real *amour*—I know I felt that way—and that I'd also get the information I need without any fuss. Wednesday, Thursday, Friday, everything was fine between us. And I told you to confide in me and it seemed you would. At least you started to. Then something happened. I don't know what it was. Something caused by your damaged brain, no doubt. Suddenly I realized, my god, he's going to leave early, before I have what I need. I just *felt* it. I told you I know your body language. Of course, the text you sent Mark last night about not being able to take Di Strata with you made it clear, too." She straightened up. "I'm truly sorry I had to do all this. But it'll be over soon, and maybe you can forgive me.

"Now, I need to explain a few things," Grace continued, her eyelids fluttering again. "The first thing is don't struggle. The more you struggle, the more you'll hurt that beautiful body of yours and I *really* don't want that to happen. Let me assure you, Paul, everything has been properly tied. And if I have to wait for you to tell me what I need to know, I will, within reason. I'll be patient and take good care of you. I'll feed you. I'll wash you down. I'll help you go to the bathroom if I have to. But only within reason. Don't test my patience too long.

"The second thing is, when this is done and I'm prepared to let you go, don't even think about the police. Signora Di Grotto was here last night. Maybe you saw her? I told her that you were unstable before you arrived. So *anxious* and under so much *stress* for the last few months. That's why you took the sedative last evening—the one I crushed into your tea. She understood and was quite keen to help me undress you and get you onto the bed. I mentioned your state to Signor Di Strata, too. And then, last night, I told the waiter how angry you were with me and how you were *harassing* me." Grace held her wrists up in the air; the chafing marks from the blood-red silk ropes were still there. "And these. Well, I took pictures right after and yesterday. If I need to, I'll tell the police how someone I invited into my home, whom I was just trying to help with an offer of love and attention in Rome, *abused* me. Poor Canadian. You won't stand a chance here.

"The last thing, Paul," Grace said, her eyes wide open. "Just *tell* me what I need to know when I ask you. Keep things simple. Now think about that for a few minutes, and I'll be back with a pee bottle and some breakfast. And then we'll talk."

Grace walked out the room without looking back and closed the door behind her. Panic swept through Paul again. He pulled his arms and legs as hard as he could and was rewarded with new tears in his flesh.

It was a half hour before she returned. Her face was humourless and sombre. She carried a large tray with a glass of orange juice, a sliced and buttered croissant and a rectangular plastic container. She set the tray on the night table.

"I'm sure you have to pee," Grace said. "Let's get that out of the way." Attached to the plastic container was a long tube with a small funnel at its open end. She stretched the tube between his legs, set the container on the floor and guided the tip of his penis into the funnel. "There," she said, "get little willy working." He gritted his teeth and crunched his eyebrows in humiliation. "Come on," she said, "we don't have all day." He sent warm liquid down the tube. "Very good," she said. "I'll be back after I wash my hands."

A minute later, she sat next to him on the bed again. "Now, breakfast. You might think you can scream for help." She held up a cloth napkin from the tray. "If you do, I won't hesitate to stuff this down your throat. Got it?" Paul stared straight at the ceiling. "I said, got it?" After a few moments, he nodded. "Good," she said.

She inserted a finger under one corner of the tape over his mouth and pulled hard. "*Ouch*," he yelled. Blood oozed along his lips.

"Quiet," she said. She reached half a croissant to his mouth.

"I don't want any goddamn breakfast," he hissed. "What the *fuck* is going on here? What do you think—?"

An instant later, the napkin was in his face. He tried to dodge it by thrashing his head back and forth, but Grace forced his head to one side and clamped his nose shut. When he finally gasped for breath, she stuffed the napkin into his mouth. He grabbed for air through his nose.

"Don't be foolish, Paul. We're going to do this my way. Now, do you want breakfast or not?" He threw his head back and forth. "Fine. I really don't care. But I don't think you've grasped this situation yet. I'm going to leave you by yourself a while longer. When I'm back, I'm sure you'll be ready to help me."

Alone once again, try as he might, Paul could not get the napkin out of his mouth. It didn't matter, he told himself. Even if he yelled, no one would arrive to help and Grace would be right back to reinsert the napkin. For the first time, he realized he could hear the sound of the grandfather clock in Justin's room. He followed its ticking to steady his breathing. He had no choice, he decided. He had to appear obliging and find out what Grace wanted.

Hours passed without any sign of her. The room became bright and warm and he started to feel thirsty and hungry. He breathed evenly so he wouldn't choke on the napkin. At one point a new worry—that she wouldn't return—crept into him. He tugged once more at the ropes and immediately his ankles and wrists stung as cuts and burns deepened. He calmed himself, telling himself she had to return. It was the only way she could get what she was after.

Paul guessed it was close to noon when she walked into the room again. He felt a surge of relief, and with his eyes he tried to signal a willingness to cooperate. She stood next to the bed, severe like a nun in front of religion class. "Are you ready?" she asked. He nodded. "Okay. Not a word out of you unless I ask."

She withdrew the napkin and crumpled it onto the tray on the table. "Now. Do you want food or something to drink?" Again he nodded. "All right." He gulped from the glass of orange juice she held to his lips, letting her wipe his face when some juice spilled out. Then he chewed down the partly stale croissant. "Now, shall we talk a bit?" she asked.

"Yes," he said, his voice hoarse. "What do you want to know?"

She became very still. "This is what I want to know, Paul," she said, her eyes burning into him like lasers. "Where is the gun?"

44

Paul's mouth fell open. Then he licked the blood off his lips. "What are you talking about, Grace? I don't. Have. A gun."

She crossed her arms and leaned over the bed. "Actually, I think you *do*. And I think you've had it since before Art was murdered."

Paul licked his lips again, trying to see a way out. "Grace, you're making this up."

"*I'm not,*" she hissed. "*Where is it?*"

"Honestly, Grace," Paul pleaded, "*I don't have a gun.* I haven't had one since I gave Granddad's Smith and Wesson back. That's the truth."

Panting and glaring, she dropped her hands to her side and clenched them into fists. "Look, do you want me to phone up this Detective Beecham and tell him that I *know* you have a gun? That you've always had one? You know what he'll think? That he was right all along. That you murdered Art. And that you should have been convicted."

"He already thinks that, but I didn't kill Art," Paul said as evenly as possible.

"My god, it's easy to think you did, given your fucked-up relationship with him." Leaning forward, Grace grabbed the cloth napkin off the night table and forced it back in Paul's mouth. "I'm giving you one more chance, Paul. That's it. Either tell me where the gun is or I talk to Beecham. Or worse." She stomped out of Justin's bedroom.

Hours came and went. Unable to move, his neck and limbs stiffened and the throbbing of his wrists and ankles worsened. For a while he shut his eyes, resorting again to the grandfather clock's ticking for calm. Now, however, as it counted down the time to Grace's return, the clock sounded ominous. He wouldn't know what to say.

The daylight in Justin's room eventually faded, and Paul's bladder forced his hand, filling until it was too painful to bear. His vengeful side wanted to piss all over Justin's bed, but he guessed that was the last way to solve things with Grace. He tore his throat out trying to scream loudly enough for her to hear him. Finally, she burst through the door holding a small, thin book.

"What? Are you ready to talk?" He groaned, looking at his crotch. "Oh, that. I guess I said I would take care of you." She put down the book, left the room and returned with the plastic container. When he was done relieving himself, Grace pulled the napkin out of his mouth and laid it beside his head. "Well, what do you say? Where is the gun?"

"Grace, please listen to me," Paul said, his voice a mere rasp. "There is no gun. I didn't commit murder. What you hear in me is guilt. As bad sometimes as if I did do it."

Grace picked up the book and stuffed the front cover in his face. He recognized the *Acta Victoriana* from early 1995. "Remember this?"

"Fuck, Grace, it was just a story."

Standing overtop him, she said, "It's *not* just a story." Grace opened the book at a crease in the spine. "Listen. *Listen* to the final paragraphs.

"'*I wanted to. I needed to. I* had *to.*

'He had humiliated me too many times. He'd made me the object of his endless jests, the target of his ceaseless disgraces, and the recourse against his countless insecurities. He had stolen the woman I loved, dashed my hopes, and neutered my confidence. They said he was the most beautiful, the most capable, and the most likely to succeed. Beautiful, I say, like a venomous snake about to strike; capable, like the female praying mantis about to eat its mate; and successful, like the grizzly standing on its hind paws, preparing to gore. He was cruelty in beauty's cloak.

'The use of the object in my hand? It was out of my hands. It had potency greater than anything I had ever experienced. I became a fatalist, prepared to let life take its course. I said, 'Honestly, I used to care. Now I just want you dead.' And I pulled the trigger.'"

Grace looked at Paul with triumph. "'*Cruelty in beauty's cloak.*' Your words, Paul. Words of *malice*. The rest of it is crap, by the way."

"Grace," Paul moaned. "I heard all this in the stand. *I didn't do it*. Sometimes I *sound* or *act* like I did it. Because of the guilt—"

"My god, the guilt of a murderer?"

He shook his head. "*No.* Sometimes I *dream* I did, and when I wake up, I have to *convince* myself I didn't do it. It's like part of me wants to suffer a murderer's punishment because I let him down. One of the two people I admired most."

"Oh, I want to believe you. But it doesn't matter. All I need to know is where the gun is. *Just tell me.*"

Paul sighed. "There's no gun. It's that simple."

"That simple, is it?" Throwing the book to the ground and sitting on the bed, with her right hand Grace pulled the hairpiece out of her bun of hair. She flicked her head twice, fluffing hair over her shoulders and chest. For a moment, her black hair against the smooth, pale skin of her face caught Paul's eye as it always had. Then she lurched forward and stuffed the napkin in his mouth yet again. He flared his nose for air.

Staring at Paul, Grace turned the hairpiece's sharp end into the palm of her left hand. After four or five twists, she spread her palm inches from his face. Blood oozed from a puncture. "Paul, I damn well mean it," she said. "Last chance."

She leaned forward. Holding the hairpiece by the cameo, she dangled it inches above his heart. Without warning, it dropped. Paul squealed and recoiled. The hairpiece bounced off his skin without piercing it, then fell flat on his chest. "That was gentle," she said. "We didn't even draw any blood."

Grace picked up the hairpiece. She lowered the dagger tip to his chest and dragged it several times from one pectoral to the other. Then she circled each nipple; against every ounce of Paul's will, they became erect. "My god, I think you're enjoying this," she said. She poked the top of each nipple two or three times. "Still no blood," she said. "What *do* I have to do?"

Poking him under the Adam's apple, she dragged the hairpiece tip toward the middle of his chest. A red scratch pouted open and specks of blood appeared. His back arched and he thrashed back and forth. "Oh look, what have we here? Don't move. You'll only hurt yourself more."

Grace pulled up on the hairpiece so it didn't cut anymore, but to Paul's horror she kept dragging its tip, slowly, all the way to his lower abdomen. He lifted his head but the rope didn't allow him to see. "Men are *so* sensitive about their private parts. I guess it's the thousands of nerve endings that make the dick the centre of male existence." She lifted the hairpiece and swung it back and forth by the cameo. "Let's play," she said.

He began to grunt. She carefully held his penis then dragged the dagger tip of the hairpiece from the top to the beginning of his scrotum, increasing the pressure as she went. He thrashed and screamed through the napkin. "Stop," she ordered. "I'm not moving this. You'll gouge yourself." On she went, over the ridge of his scrotum. "Oh, who knew this could bleed?"

She stopped with the tip of the hairpiece pressing into the skin between his scrotum and anus. As far as the ropes let him, he pressed toward the upper end of the bed. But she pushed the hairpiece harder, eliminating whatever space he'd gained and making the skin under its tip taut. Leaning over him again, holding the hairpiece steady, she brought her face within a few inches of his. "Paul, I told you I'm not always quiet and shy," she said, her hair falling into his eyes. "Are you ready? To tell me the truth?"

He shrieked and nodded. She grabbed the edge of the napkin with her teeth and tore it out of his mouth. He gasped as the hairpiece pierced his skin. "Goddamn it, you're right," he said. "I *did* keep Granddad's gun. I still have it."

"Where?" she asked. "Answer me. I can press a lot harder."

"In my condo. The ceiling above my laundry machine."

Grace smiled and released some pressure from the hairpiece. "*That's* a good boy," she said. "Hmm. Your lawyer—what was his name?—Liebowitz? He put you on the stand. And you lied. And to Beecham, too. What do they call that again?"

Paul squeezed his eyelids, holding back tears. A few escaped from the corners of his eyes and rolled down the sides of his face. "For Christ's sake," he hissed, "it's called perjury."

45

A failure, a fraud, a fiasco. That's what he was. Practiced the wrong profession. Misled a court and officers of the law. Harmed his brothers. He'd waited so long to get it all out to one person. Too bad it was the wrong one.

He kept his eyes closed, letting darkness swirl inside him like spewing volcanic ash.

"Perjured yourself?" Grace asked. "I don't know much about that, except that in the movies it's bad. I guess you simply did what was necessary to save your world, right?"

She withdrew the hairpiece and set it down on the night table, its bloody tip perched over the edge, pointing at Paul. She left the room and came back with the washcloth freshened. When she dabbed his forehead, his eyes flew open and flared at her.

"There, there," she said. "Don't be too angry with me. I had to do what was necessary to save my world, too." She moved the washcloth across his lips, then along the scratch on his chest. "It wasn't such a big deal, was it? You should have just told me. Days ago." Dabbing him between his legs, she added, "You were supposed to *confide* in me." An irrepressible rage seized him, aimed as much at himself as her. "You're *shaking*. Calm yourself. Most of it's over."

"I need some water," he whispered.

She crumpled the washcloth in one hand and offered a smile, compressed and contrite. "It's the least I could do."

She returned a minute later with a large glass of sparkling water. She helped him lift his head as far as the rope across his neck allowed, and he managed to gulp down half the contents.

He lay back and tried to restore normal breathing. He located the grandfather clock's ticking again; he needed to be calm and quiet. "What are you going to do with me, Grace?"

Standing beside the bed, she smiled again. "I'm going to teach you about forgiveness."

"Now you want me to forgive you?"

"Yes."

Paul swallowed. "Why do you care about the gun?" he asked in a low, even voice. "What difference does it make to you?"

"I just do, Paul. I'm not crazy. It's just that there are some things that are very important to me, that I need to protect. And I was put in a position of having to do that. Sometimes you forgive, even if you don't understand. A child throws a precious vase to the ground in a tantrum. Eventually you forgive because it's your child. I'm asking for something similar from you. Out of affection or caring. Or something like that."

He saw a path. "Or love?"

She glanced at the hairpiece. "That would be a bit too remarkable," she said. "Though of course I always knew you felt *something* for me. As I did for you."

He avoided looking at the hairpiece. "If you really had to save your world, whatever that means, I guess I could accept what you've done to me. I'm not the easiest person to deal with right now." He paused. "Can't you let me go?"

"I have a few other things I need to do first. By the way, I didn't really mean that stuff about you being the murderer. I was trying to provoke you to talk. And I understand better now that I know about the perjury. I can see how that would weigh you down, being a lawyer and all."

She turned to leave. "Grace," he said hurriedly. "The rope across my throat. Does it have to be there? I need to move my neck. It's incredibly sore."

Turning back, she said, "I guess not." The rope ran around the bed mattress. She returned to the side of the bed and fumbled with the knot for a few seconds. With a gasp of relief, Paul lifted his head then turned it from side to side and rotated his shoulders. "Is that it?" she asked.

"The rope around my right wrist—"

"I can't take that off now," she interrupted. "I'm not sure when."

"Just loosen it a bit. It's cutting me."

She looked and grimaced. "There's blood," she said. "All right, a bit." She played with the knot, and he felt the rope loosen and the pricks in his fingers ease.

"Last thing," he whispered.

"It's time for you to rest."

"Please," he said, motioning with his head for her to sit next to him. "I need—"

She sat and asked, "What? I can hardly hear you." She leaned in, turning an ear toward his mouth.

Paul hurled his head up and struck his forehead into Grace's temple. She recoiled, her mouth falling open and her eyes rolling back. Swaying from side to side, she collapsed overtop his body.

"Oh fuck, that *hurt*," Paul spat, his forehead throbbing. He fell back, letting the pain settle for ten seconds. But he knew Grace could recover any time.

Sucking in a long breath, he pulled at his right hand. She'd loosened the rope enough that there was slack. Gritting his teeth, the cuts encircling his wrist searing with pain, he fished the rope toward the base of his hand. There, the rope strangled on his widening finger bones and the base of his thumb.

Pushing himself up against Grace's weight, he examined the rope, ignoring the blood dripping to the ground. He twisted his wrist further, and his second and third fingers, severely curled, were able to claw at the knot. He dug like he was ripping at earth after being buried alive. The nails of both fingers tore but he didn't let up. Eventually his second finger bore into a crevice in the knot. A minute later, the knot loosened enough that he could pull out his hand.

He snapped his hand and crunched the fingers, stifling groans as full circulation returned. Grace moaned and he knew his time was running short. The knot around his left wrist yielded quickly. To get at the ropes around his ankles, he moved her, gently for fear of rousing her. His feet, blue and purple, were swollen twice their normal size. When he released the knots at his ankles, blood released from his feet and an excruciating tingling ran throughout.

Grace moaned again and stirred. His time was up. He swung his legs over the bed and tried to stand. His feet crumpled under him, and he fell across the room, nearly striking his head on the closet door. She moaned a third time. Crawling to her on all fours, the cuts around his wrists splitting further, he stretched her slender body in its long dress across the bed. Quickly, he tied her down as he had been and pasted her lips with adhesive tape from a roll he found under the night table.

Slumping against the side of the bed, Paul examined the cuts on his wrists and ankles, then rubbed his feet. After a minute, he was able to stand, and he walked out of Justin's room into the bathroom. In its harsh white light, he examined his face in the mirror. Above his day-old stubble, deep black lines hung like hammocks under his eyes. Amid the scabs across his forehead, a large blue and red bump was emerging where he'd struck Grace. He stepped into the shower and washed his damaged body, collecting himself.

Dried off, he re-entered Justin's room. Grace looked at him wide-eyed and fearful. "Well, look who's up," Paul muttered. "Fun, isn't it?" In his suitcase, he found his last clean clothes. "Here's what we're going to do. I'm taking the next flight out tomorrow. When I'm back in Toronto, I'll make a call to someone—I don't know who yet—and they'll free you. I've got to get out of this godforsaken city while I can."

He sat down on the bed beside her. Her eyes expanded further and she began to thrash. "Don't. You'll hurt yourself. I speak from experience," he said, holding his wrists in the air. "Don't worry. I'm not going to hurt you. You might think I'm a murderer but I don't have any desire to harm you.

"What I *am* going to do is ask *you* a few questions. The tape is coming off, which will hurt, and the napkin will go in your mouth if you scream. You know the drill. Ready?" He ripped the tape off her pouty lips. Instantly she began to cry. "Stop. I told you. I won't hurt you."

Her crying worsened to sobs. "Sorry, Paul, I'm *so* sorry. Don't hurt me. Just let me go. I didn't want to hurt you. I had no choice."

"Oh, you had *lots* of choice. In fact, you fucking enjoyed that."

"I *didn't*."

"*Why* do you give a shit about the gun?"

Her sobs multiplied. "I shouldn't tell you."

Paul smirked. "I'm not sure what choice you have."

"To protect Justin," she blurted.

"*Justin?*"

"You don't understand."

"I do more than you realize. He's Art's son." She stopped sobbing and every red blood cell vanished from her face. "Yes, I know about that," he said.

"*How?*"

"I checked a few things out and saw him. Figured out he was the voyeur. He's a dead ringer. That's your mother who lives across the way, isn't it?"

"Yes," she whispered.

"And let me ask you this." Paul's voice became more forceful. "Did Art know you were pregnant with his child?" Her eyes darted around the room. "You just answered that for me. So Art knew. And let me guess, he wasn't interested in having it." Her sobbing returned, harder, hacking at her throat like a saw ripping through wood. "Come on, Grace, out with it." He made sure she saw him look at the hairpiece.

"No. He—he insisted I have an abortion. *Insisted.* I wouldn't do it. I said he had to help me with the child or leave me alone. I never saw him again after that."

"So you were the other woman making demands on Art."

"Pardon?"

"When was this?"

"Early in the week before he died."

"You're the one. And then you fled to Rome?"

"Yes. I only went to his funeral because—"

"Because it would've looked odd if you didn't?"

"Yes."

"Had he threatened you?"

"I don't want to talk about this anymore."

"He didn't? Art would have done that if he needed to." Paul picked up the hairpiece. "I wonder how you would feel if I did to you what you did to me."

She looked at him, her eyes wide. "You would do that?"

"In a heartbeat." He pressed the dagger end of the hairpiece into the palm of his left hand just as she had.

"He said he would find me at all costs. To make sure I didn't have the baby."

"Motive, I'd say, Grace. Motive."

"You don't know what you're talking about."

"Beecham would find it interesting."

"He'd find your gun more interesting."

Paul paused. "How *does* this relate to the gun?"

Grace's chest heaved with a sigh. "Someone else learned about Justin. Being Art's son."

"Who?"

"Paul, please, it doesn't matter. They just wanted to know where the gun is. I don't know why. They never told me. They threatened me, about Justin, and forced me to find out from you. I had no choice."

Paul moved the hairpiece toward Grace's face. He waved the tip back and forth over her lips. "Tell me who, Grace. Tell me who."

She bit down hard on her lower lip then licked blood from where the tape had torn her skin. Looking toward the ceiling, tears welling up in her eyes, she whispered, "It was Louis."

46

"*Louis?*" Paul hissed. Grace nodded. "For Christ's sake."

"I'll explain. But you have to promise to let me go," Grace said, grabbing breaths.

"You're not in a great bargaining position. But I will."

"I lied to you," she said.

"You have a habit of doing that."

"I told you I didn't see Louis before he died." Grace tongued more blood from her lower lip. "I did. On May 4. I landed on Friday and saw him Saturday. Paul, you mustn't tell. There's a lot at stake here."

Paul gave a laugh. "Just tell me the story and I'll decide what to do. You mean there was no production work in Rome? All lies as well?"

"There *was*. I did work for him last year, scouting locations for some churches. And then the project got more serious early this year and he called me again. A script about a murderer in the Vatican who channels a fourteenth-century serial killer." Grace grimaced. "Paul, these ropes. They're making my hands and feet hurt."

Incredulity passed over his face. "Live with it. Keep going."

"In March we made plans for me to come to Toronto in early May for more scouting work. The idea was to make some decisions, and then I would contact the authorities and see what we could use." She looked at Paul expectantly but he said nothing. "He called me a week before I was supposed to arrive to tell me that he was sick."

"He waited that long?"

"Yes," Grace said. "He insisted I come over anyway, saying I could meet Cyril alone if I had to."

"Cyril said Louis chickened out. That he was embarrassed by how he looked and he didn't want you to see him."

Grace nodded. "That's what Cyril told me Saturday morning when I met him at their office. The meeting with Cyril wasn't very productive. Everything was put on hold. But then Louis called me at the hotel in the afternoon. I didn't even recognize his voice. He implored me to visit him at the hospital without telling anyone. And I did, late in the evening."

"What room was he in?"

"He was in 1501. He looked awful. My god, his eyes were so sunken and yellow. He could hardly speak three sentences. I knew it was very serious."

She was right on all counts. "Keep going," Paul said.

"After a few minutes of useless catching up, he said he had a favour to ask."

"A favour?"

"My problem was that Louis had met Justin a year and a half ago."

"What?"

"Louis visited me, here, in Rome," Grace said. "November 2011."

"I didn't know about this."

"I don't think he told anyone. He simply showed up one day. Basically his intention was to ask me to be in a relationship with him. Justin answered the door. It was the most embarrassing thing. I always wondered if people would see the resemblance to his father."

"I'm sure he did."

"Instantly. The whole thing was a disaster. I had to find a way to explain I had no interest. And then explain why no one had heard of Justin. It was the pregnant question in the room."

"And what's the answer?" Paul asked.

"I don't want anyone interfering with how I raise Justin. Except maybe my mother. My son is mine. No one else's."

"What do you mean? His grandfathers? Don't they deserve to know their grandson?"

"Powerful men like both of Justin's grandfathers do the wrong things to their sons and grandsons. They think they know how they should be and what they should become, and what those men are really worrying about is their legacy. It's best to keep quiet about Justin."

"I still don't understand," Paul said.

"Art told me how his father treated him. How possessive and dominating he was." Grace's eyelids compressed. "I don't want any part of that man. I worry he'll be just like my father and do to Justin what my father did to my brother. My father *neutered* my brother when he didn't follow in his footsteps. Reduced him to nothing but an excuse for a man who craves solitude. Or, when faced with people, craves their approval. Justin needs to be his own man. And strong."

"So, let me get this straight," Paul said. "Justin doesn't know who his father was? And hasn't met *either* grandfather? This is crazy. Art was just being a bitter prick, complaining about his dad."

"You remember I told you I've seen a gun?"

"Yes."

"My father had one," Grace said, her eyes now wide and blazing. "He brought it out one evening and taunted my brother with it. Told my brother to shoot it to prove he was a man. And when my brother didn't, my father tossed it back and forth between his hands, like he was going to shoot it himself. It felt like it would be at my brother. That's how sick things were."

"We're talking about Art's father now. Justin's *grandfather*. I know he was a powerful businessman and could be a hard-ass, but I don't think he'd do to Justin what your father did your brother."

"Have you seen him since the trial, Paul?"

"No." Paul said. He sighed. "I'm sure—I'm sure he didn't know what to do with me. But I still think Justin deserves to get to know him."

"*No, he doesn't.* I have nothing but distrust for men like him. What Art said is enough for me not to want to take a chance. Justin is not getting close to Art's father. And not to my father either."

Paul shook his head but thought it best to move off the topic. "Anyway, what favour did Louis ask?"

"Louis said he thought you had a gun. That you'd had it for years, even at the time Art was murdered. I was shocked. It made me wonder—"

Again Grace looked at Paul expectantly, but he said nothing. "Anyway, I simply didn't see what that had to do with me."

"The favour, Grace."

"He asked me to have an affair with you in order to find out where the gun is. He told me that you were so, ah, smitten by me, that you would divulge the information. You went a long way there ... but not far enough."

Paul tasted metallic bitterness in his throat again and pulled at each lobe. "Louis? What a fucking kick in the teeth." He paused then added, "How would he know about the gun?"

"I asked him that. He said it was none of my business."

Paul looked at Grace, tied to the bed. The most attractive liar he knew. "And why did you agree to do it?"

"To have you as my lover?"

"Yes."

"Carrot and stick."

"Stop with the games."

"If I got the information," Grace said, "Louis promised me not to tell Art's father about Justin. He also promised two hundred and fifty thousand dollars."

47

Paul's head bulged like a bike tube pumped with too much air. Louis was a bastard, Grace had humiliated him and his secrets were coming out all wrong. *Get the fuck out of here. Now.*

"Ah. Money," Paul said. "*That* explains things."

Grace scrutinized him. "You said you would release me," she said after a few seconds. He turned to leave the room. "*Paul*, you *promised*."

He spun around. "I did," he said. He grabbed the napkin from the night table and added, "I just didn't say when." Her mouth fell open in dismay and he jammed the napkin in as far as he could.

Paul took his suitcase, dropped it on the throw rug and stuffed it with his dirty clothing and shoes. Then he grabbed his carry-on and checked for his passport and ticket. Grace grunted several times. Without looking at her, he walked with his belongings out of Justin's room into the living room.

For the first time Paul noted how dark it was outside. The grandfather clock ticked louder than ever; it was close to nine thirty. The air in the apartment was stale and he didn't dare open any windows and shutters for fear Justin was watching. Instead he sat at the small desk and opened Grace's laptop.

As it loaded, Paul checked his smartphone. Among other communications, Mark had called six times and texted three. The first text twenty-four hours before said it all: *"Paul, if you're leaving early, Di Strata must join you. MUST. Please call me ASAP."*

Paul set down the phone and searched for his airline's website. After paying a stiff fee, he was able to move his flight to twelve noon the next day, Tuesday.

Another text landed from Mark. Paul called him, and Mark's assistant put Paul through right away.

"Did you get back already?" Mark barked.

"Nope."

"Then where the *hell* have you been?"

"Seeing the sights," Paul said.

"Let me close the door." After ten seconds, Mark's voice reappeared. "Do you know how many times I called you? Texted, emailed. Nothing. You can't just drop off the face of the earth like that."

"I've been indisposed in ways you can't imagine."

"Fucking your brains out, no doubt. I need your help, Paul. I'm *counting* on you."

"It's not what you imagine."

"Look, all I care about is that Di Strata comes back with you."

"Someone else needs to fly with him."

"I *told* him you'd do it. He's an old man. He trusts you and he doesn't like change. If you don't come through, this will look bad on me."

"He *trusts* me? He called me a murd—"

"We've been over that."

Suspicions of him in Rome were high, Paul thought. "I hope you set him straight."

"What he knows is he's flying with you."

"Well, I just rebooked for tomorrow at noon Rome time."

"Paul, what the *fuck*? How am I going to get him ready now? I've got to try and reach Signora Tramente. She'll bust my balls."

"What the hell is wrong with you these days? I know clients are important but this is out of proportion. Let Di Strata find someone else. Things haven't worked out here and I need to get back home."

"You don't understand," Mark said, raising his voice. "You *don't*. He's one of my best clients, and I need to make sure I keep every client and get a bunch more."

Paul paused. He'd sooner have a cavity filled without freezing than open another can of worms, but he saw no choice. "Lee told me you wanted him to lend you money. What's going on?"

Mark caught his breath. "That little bastard. I'll kill him."

"He's a good guy, Mark. He's worried about you. He told me you bought real estate in the U.S."

"Little prick."

"Tell me, for Christ's sake."

"I started flipping houses in the U.S. in 2005. I made a lot of money at first. At the peak in 2007, I bought five houses in Palm Springs. Then the market crashed. There's a personal guarantee, so they have recourse. I'm underwater and I can barely keep up the mortgage payments. I'm on the brink of elimination."

"Does Charles know about this?"

"No, and he's got no money anyway. He's just a history prof. What do they make?"

"Lee would say it's all in the ridiculous pension."

"I don't give a shit what Lee says. Fuck, if I have to file for bankruptcy, what's Ted Collins going to say?"

Paul sighed. "You know, this is a *really* bad time but all right. I'll get Di Strata if you set it up with the bird woman."

"I'll tell her you'll be at Via Sicilia at nine in the morning. Don't be late, Paul, and treat him like he's your father."

"Turns out fathers aren't revered that much anymore."

Mark paused. "Mine was. I don't know what you're talking about." He hung up.

During the night, Paul grabbed a few hours' sleep on the sofa. Otherwise, he ignored Grace's occasional muffled cries and paced her apartment like a prisoner waiting for his gates to freedom to open. The same questions rooted around in his mind. *How did Louis know about the gun? Why did Louis enlist Grace against me? How can I avoid another arrest and trial, this time for perjury or some obstruction charge?*

And the same images played in front of him. Granddad handing him the rectangular box painted in black lacquer, saying, "Specially made for her, that box is." Paul opening it as Granddad, stroking the grey stubble on his worn face, watched. The box lined with green velvet, and the .38 Smith and Wesson lying black and handsome in a cavity with six brassy cartridges pinned in slots to the lower left. "You know, your mom had a hissy fit when she saw me give her to you in Kirkland Lake, and made me take her back. But I'm givin' her to you anyways. I want you to have her. Even though your mom's been through a lot, what she doesn't know won't hurt her. Our little secret, eh?" Paul nodding, Granddad still stroking his stubble. "Never been registered or nothin'. Damn government always interferin'. Just keep her to yourself, eh? And treat her with God's care. She'll blow your head off if you're not payin' attention."

Our little secret. Paul remembered how shooting Granddad's Smith and Wesson had been one of his favourite stories in university. But he'd kept his grandfather's wish and never told anyone he still had the gun. In criminal law in first-year law school, he'd reviewed Part III of the *Criminal Code—Firearms and Other Weapons*—and it gave him a giant lump in the throat when he read that the penalty for possessing the Smith and Wesson without proper registration was up to five years in prison. So, May 9, 1998, the day after Art's murder, when the 14 Division detectives asked in his first interview if he owned a gun, Paul had said no. He hadn't seen the need to stress his mother or risk firearms charges when only he knew about the gun. And right after the interview, as a precaution, he'd made sure no one could find it.

But the following day, going to 14 Division for his second interview, Paul's lie had made him queasy. *For Christ's sake, I was under oath*, he'd told himself. Right from the start, though, the interview went off the rails, and Beecham ended it by telling him he was a "person of interest". Rigid with alarm, Paul had decided then and there that revealing "our little secret" would only make him a full-fledged suspect. So he'd kept it to himself, to die with, he thought.

After fifteen years, how did Louis know? Nothing made sense except that truth was in short supply while ulteri-

or motives weren't. What he did know after a quick check online was that perjury was punishable by up to fourteen years in prison, and that he'd become vulnerable to Grace. He needed to get home, lay low and take care of Granddad's gun. And maybe, as a parallel measure, cut a deal with the beautiful liar.

When dawn emerged, Paul opened the windows and shutters in the living room for fresh air. Mile-high storm clouds filled the sky and reluctant grey light snuck into the apartment. He went into the kitchen and assembled Grace's usual breakfast of tea and buttered toast.

He startled her when he pushed open the door to Justin's room holding a tray. Her wrists and ankles were chafed deep red but she'd been asleep. Her eyes roused with anger that dissipated slightly when she saw breakfast.

"I suppose I've thought things over," he said as he put the tray on the night table. "We need to talk." He pulled the napkin from her mouth. "No screaming," he said, wagging a finger.

She gasped and rotated her lower jaw. "I thought you'd never come back," she finally said. "You have to let me go. I'm in pain. I have to pee."

"Grace, you've lied to me endlessly. I need to know. What was Louis's interest in the gun?"

"*I told you. He said it was none of my business.*" Grace rotated her jaw again. "Of course, I've constantly wondered about that myself. First I thought that if you *did* have a gun, you—you might have used it for Art. But I just couldn't believe that. Then when you told me the story about your Granddad, I thought it just was a secret you were keeping from your mother. But why would Louis care about that?

None of it makes sense to me. The most important thing for me is to protect Justin."

"And to make some money, I'd say."

"It would overjoy me to be financially independent of my father. I could even buy my own place in a suburb and be out of his life entirely."

Paul reflected. His sense was that she was being truthful. "And what are you supposed to do with the information you get from me?"

She paused and pursed her lips. "I'm supposed to send it to an anonymous email address Louis gave me. And then I'm supposed to receive a bank draft."

"I suppose we could make a deal, Grace."

"A deal? Look at me. What choice do I have?"

"I'm not going to leave you here to die. You do have a choice. But now that I know who Justin's father is, the thing is, I also could reveal Justin to one or both grandfathers. And Art's father knows me and probably will believe me."

"My god, you wouldn't."

"I won't if you send an email to that anonymous address saying you tried everything to get the information about that gun, but you can't. Say because I'm a total head case right now. *And* if you promise me not to tell anyone else about the gun. If you *do* tell them where the gun is—and I'll know, because trouble will come my way—I'll tell everything. What do you think? And how about some food? I'll loosen the rope around your neck. I hear that's a good thing."

When he was done, Paul gave Grace the tea and toast. She munched, deep in thought.

"I don't know," she said. "It throws me to think that Art's father isn't like Art said he was. Maybe I've underestimated him."

Paul wanted Grace onside, if only temporarily. "Like I said, I haven't seen him since the trial. Are you willing to rely on my limited experience? And imagine how he'll feel finding out after fifteen years that he has a grandson. And then there's your father."

"And what exactly do I write to the anonymous email address?"

"Tell them that you invited me to Rome, that we became lovers, but that I'm anxious and unbalanced and crazy, and left early without giving you any useful information. That's what I'm doing by the way. Leaving right now. Tell them you understand you won't get two hundred and fifty thousand, but you've done all you can and expect them to keep Justin's identity secret."

"Then you have to make up the money, Paul."

"I don't have that kind of money, Grace. After paying Liebowitz's bills and the divorce."

"Borrow it."

Paul knew it would come to this. "I'll get what I can."

She eyed him. "What I think is that Louis was working with the police. And they were paying him a reward to help solve the case." He ran both hands through his hair and pulled at his right lobe. "I can see you're thinking about that. Body language."

Paul put down his hands. "I don't think the police work that way."

"I think they do."

Paul exhaled. "You know, I have no idea. But I do know you have to stay tied up till I get back to Toronto. Because if you do go to the police and tell them I tied you up, I'd much rather be fighting that from Canada with Liebowitz. If he's still alive."

"You have to let me go *now*," Grace said, her eyes firing again.

"Sorry. Once I get there, I'll call your mother to release you. I found her phone number on your laptop. She has a key to your apartment?"

"I won't go to the police."

"I'm sorry. I'm not going to take that chance. I'm sure your mother has a key. Can you keep her quiet?"

"Yes."

"So we have a deal?"

Grace hesitated. "Can I trust you, Paul?"

He held his hands in the air. The cuffs of his shirt fell below his wrists, revealing angry cuts and chafing. "You're asking *me*? What about you? Can I trust *you*?"

With a deep breath, she said, "You can, and we have a deal." He didn't believe a word of it, but he thought he'd bought enough time to get rid of the gun. Her eyes shot daggers at him. "Now get a pan or something. I need to pee. This is going to be *so* humiliating."

48

At exactly nine Tuesday morning, in his new suit and with his suitcase and carry-on beside him, Paul rang the buzzer to Di Strata's villa. He needn't have. Signora Tramente stood on the landing, arms folded, her beakish face carrying its dirtiest look yet. The gates unlocked and Paul pushed through with his luggage. Signora Tramente pointed to a black Maserati sedan idling in the driveway. "Please have a seat in the back. The driver will take your bags. Signor Di Strata will be out momentarily." She spun around and returned inside.

A few minutes later, Di Strata emerged from the villa in his usual dark suit and tie, Signora Tramente dragging his luggage behind. The driver shot out of the sedan and scurried up the steps to retrieve the luggage. As Di Strata limped down the stairs, the driver held open a rear door. Like a sack of cement falling from a labourer's shoulders, Di Strata dropped into the back seat next to Paul.

If Di Strata was put out by leaving a day early, he didn't show it. "Ah, Mr. Tews," he said, extending a hand, "so nice to see you again. And so nice of you to take the trouble to escort me to Canada."

Paul shook his hand. "I'm sorry about having to leave today. A small family emergency."

Di Strata scanned Paul's cuts and bruise. "I hope everything is all right."

"I just need to make sure everything is tied up properly."

"You can't be too careful," Di Strata said.

The driver powered the Maserati through morning rush hour traffic onto Via Cristoforo Colombo and the A91 to Fiumicino. Di Strata fell into a long story about the results of an art auction he'd attended Saturday. Despite his lack of sleep, Paul had plenty of adrenalin and was attentive. After Di Strata finished his story, Paul texted Mark that Di Strata and he had connected.

At Fiumicino, the driver parked illegally at departures and disappeared. A minute later he reappeared with a wheelchair and luggage trolley. "This is a bit embarrassing," Di Strata said to Paul as he stepped out of the car into the wheelchair, "but it speeds things up. Would you mind?"

"Of course not," Paul said.

Pushing Di Strata, Paul followed the driver as he manoeuvred the stacked trolley toward the airline counter. An attendant appeared and took over the wheelchair from Paul. The driver gave a polite goodbye and vanished. "A good man, Giulio," Di Strata said. "They all take excellent care of me."

Fifteen minutes later, they had checked in their suitcases and received boarding passes. The attendant pushed Di Strata in the wheelchair to security; Paul followed with their carry-on. As they waited in the priority line, Di Strata said, "I don't know how long I can travel like this. I'm getting old. But I need to clear up these family matters. My older sister will die soon and her husband is a *criminal*." After Di Strata was pushed through the metal detector, he became confused when the alarm went off and security ran a wand over him. Paul understood why Mark had asked him to accompany Di Strata on the flight.

Another fifteen minutes later, Paul had followed the attendant and Di Strata onto the airport train to Terminal 3 and to the departure gate. The P.A. blared that the flight would start boarding in half an hour.

"We'll be eligible for early boarding," Paul suggested.

"Yes, I'm afraid that's what it's come to for me. It's quite warm in here, don't you find?"

Paul went to get espressos. When he returned, Di Strata was shifting back and forth on his seat and looked flushed. "Are you all right?" Paul asked.

"I do find it warm in here. And my chest, it's a bit heavy. Something I ate for breakfast, I think. This will help, though," he said, taking the espresso with a smile. They each snapped back their tiny cup. "And how is Signorina Campbell? Exquisite woman."

"Always surprising me," Paul said. But he was diverted by Di Strata running a finger under the stiff white collar of his shirt. "Are you sure you're all right?"

Di Strata didn't answer right away. With his right hand, he began rubbing his left arm. "I have a bit of a heart condition," he said after a few seconds. "I hope it's not causing problems."

"Let's see if a doctor's available," Paul said. He explained the situation to a gate agent who immediately put out an announcement for a health professional.

A man of about thirty approached Di Strata and Paul. "I'm a resident at St. Mike's Hospital in Toronto. I think there's airport medical staff coming, but is there anything I can do?" As the resident took his pulse, Di Strata explained what was happening, all the time rubbing his arm. Tilting his head to one side, the man said, "I don't have any equipment with me to examine you but those are concerning symptoms. You certainly need to have that looked at."

"Can I fly?" Di Strata asked.

The man's eyebrows shot in the air. "I'd say no. It could be something very serious. In your situation, I would have tests done first."

Moments later, a nurse from the airport medical staff arrived. As Di Strata and she spoke Italian, the announcement for early boarding was made. After several minutes, Di Strata turned to Paul. "They insist I don't fly. What a waste of money. I'll see if I can transfer to another day. I'm sorry, Mr. Tews."

"Don't apologize, Signor Di Strata. You need to see a doctor."

Reaching into his carry-on, Di Strata said, "Can you do me this favour, please?" He pulled out two brown envelopes, thick and sealed. "One is for Mr. Koslovsky and the other is for my sister. Can you make sure they get them today?"

"Of course."

"Today. The latest, first thing tomorrow. The one for my sister, particularly." The nurse turned the wheelchair and began pushing Di Strata. "Goodbye, Mr. Tews," he said with a wave. "Please don't forget."

Boarding for first-class passengers was announced; people formed a line in front of the gate in restless anticipation. Paul curled the first of Di Strata's envelopes into a side pocket of his carry-on. But the second envelope was stiff and had to go inside. He unzipped the carry-on and forced aside contents, but as he pushed the envelope in, one side caught the zipper and tore.

Cursing, Paul pressed the envelope in further. It tore more and a plastic lining emerged. He slipped two fingers inside the envelope and around the lining. Underneath, he felt hard cardboard either side of stiff contents. "These aren't documents," he muttered. The announcement for boarding of his row came across the P.A.

What was in the envelope was none of Paul's business—except that he'd been asked to carry it across international borders. He removed the envelope and stuffed it under his armpit. With the carry-on slung over his other shoulder, he hurried to the men's bathroom around the corner. The hall was emptying fast as the boarding line moved apace.

Paul stepped into a vacant stall, closed its door and sat on the toilet. Pressing his knees together, he placed the envelope on top and slowly withdrew its contents. The plastic lining was folded around the two pieces of cardboard and held together by a short piece of red tape. Gently peeling away one end of the tape, he unfolded the lining.

He reached inside and lifted off the top piece of cardboard. As a musty smell rose, something like a large book appeared, with a dark brown cover, elaborate white geometrical patterns in the middle and a matching border. He withdrew it and opened it at a random page. He choked at what he saw. The page was stiff and cream-coloured. In the centre was a block of Latin writing. It began with large capital letters, the first encased in a colourful picture of a scribe working at a writing table. The rest of the text was in a small neat script. Around all of it was a border with elaborate curlicues in gold, blue and red, interspersed with tiny, detailed illustrations of angels, animals and castles.

Paul turned to the inside of the front cover. Inside was a single sheet of paper entitled "Provenance".

"*This Renaissance illuminated manuscript of Duns Scotus, with 270 stunning folios on the finest vellum and its original binding, was written in Naples in 1481–2 for Ferrante I, the King of Naples (1458–94) by Pietro Hippolyto da Luna. The manuscript has been owned by a private Swiss collector since 1932. It has been kept in climate-controlled conditions and is in excellent condition except for some thumbing at the top right corners of the first folios.*"

"Fucking hell," Paul uttered, shivers coursing through him. He had to get that flight—there was no choice. He reassembled the envelope's contents, threw a book from his carry-on behind the toilet and found room for the envelope inside. Seconds later he bolted out of the bathroom.

All the passengers were through the boarding gate and the agents were immersed in paperwork. Paul rushed up clutching his passport and boarding pass.

"You're very late, sir," the agent said. "I was just about to close." He checked Paul's documents. "Please hurry, before they shut the plane door."

Paul ran down the passageway to the plane. A flight attendant was struggling with the door. "Last one in," she said, waving him through. Breathing hard, he worked his way to his window seat and carefully stored the carry-on.

Once he sat down, Paul went straight for his smartphone. Mark answered, even though it was six thirty in the morning in Toronto.

"Mark, it's Paul. I'm on the plane leaving Rome. Listen, Di Strata took ill and couldn't make the flight. His heart, I think."

"Whoa. He has documents I was supposed—"

Paul cupped his phone from his neighbour. "He gave them to me."

"Okay, that's good."

Paul dropped his voice to a raspy whisper. "Except, Mark, listen to me, one envelope has a manuscript from the Renaissance, or whatever it's called. For his sister. For Christ's sake, what's that about?"

"You opened it?"

"It tore open. Just kind of fell out."

"I don't know anything about that."

Mark's deep voice had gone hollow and weak, and he sounded off firm ground. With a stab of anxiety, Paul wondered if he was joining him in quicksand. A flight attendant came by and asked him to turn off his smartphone.

"Thirty seconds," Paul said. He turned to the plane window and returned to his whisper. "Mark, listen to me. This is *bullshit*. This is not the way people transport this kind of thing. You need export licences and stuff. Remember? Di Strata said so. What am I supposed to do at Canadian customs?"

Mark's voice had recovered. "You're going to keep quiet about it and you're going to get through. There's nothing to declare and nothing to say."

"I'm not even supposed to have someone else's luggage on me."

"You're walking through, buddy. The tough part is over. You're through security."

Like an optometrist shining light in his eyeball, Paul was blinded by the obvious. He'd been set up as a journeyman and Mark, knee deep in financial shit, knew.

"*Sir*, your phone please."

"*What the fuck, Mark?*"

"Honest to god, Paul, I don't want to do this. But if you don't walk through, I've got no choice, even if you are a friend. I'll call your shit about the gun in the file box and take you fucking down. Yes, I've known about that for a long time. Now do as I ask."

Paul's throat felt like he'd eaten gravel for breakfast. "Whatever, Mark," he said and hung up.

TORONTO

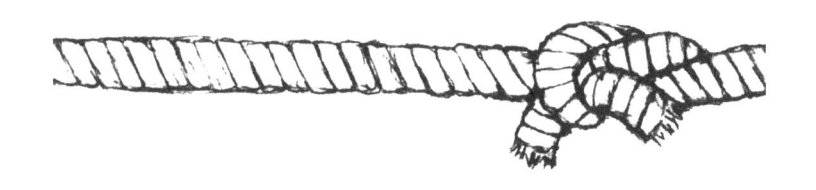

May 21, 2013

49

"Did you get the file box?" Paul asked.

"Yeah, it's here in my office."

Paul was on a landline. He could hardly hear Mark over the persistent drone. "It's a bad line, isn't it?"

"Very bad."

"I'm coming to get that box."

"Feels light," Mark said. "Is that all you had here? Before the arrest?"

"Yes."

"Sneaky putting the file box in storage under my name."

"Sneaky? I was just a summer student with a cloudy future. It had to go under an associate's name."

"Well, you made it after all. Just took two years at trial and third-year law school before articling at the famous Collins, Shaw. By the way, I looked inside."

"What?"

"The file box. I looked inside. It wasn't easy. Your mother was here."

"*My mother?* She's still comatose from the trial. She doesn't even know where Collins, Shaw is."

"Actually, three of her were here in my office, dead likenesses of each other. All crazy as loons. Each one asked to look inside the file box before I give it back to you."

"You're bullshitting me, Mark."

"Don't worry. I didn't let them. I looked myself, though, with my big ass sticking out at them like I was hogging the puck in the corner. I should tell you, I think they know."

"About what?"

"Oh, come on."

"Honestly, what?"

"The black lacquer box?"

Paul paused. "You *saw* that?"

"I always go straight to the bottom of a file box. That's where the good stuff is."

"Did—did you open it?"

"Didn't have to. You told us the story in university enough times. I know what's in there. Little surprised to see it, though. You said you grandfather took it back. You said you have to fill out a declaration form."

"What?"

"About the value of the goods you're bringing in." Mark's voice sounded female.

"What's happening to you, Mark?"

"*Sir.* Your Canadian customs declaration form."

Paul awoke with a start. With her arm across the passenger next to him, a flight attendant waited for Paul to take the form.

50

Paul adjusted his shirt collar and jacket. The key was to focus on something else, some calming topic. But the same thoughts pushed to the surface like a volcano's sulphurous bubbles.

One was that he'd underestimated the importance of his Granddad's gun. Maybe it was more than an inconvenient unregistered firearm. Maybe it even was more than the piece of evidence that could have tilted the jury to convicting him of first degree murder. Maybe the impenetrable Grace had been right to suspect the gun had been used to murder Art. *Why else would Louis care?*

And since only his friends had ever heard about the gun, there was the other thought, the likelihood even, that one of them had murdered Art with the gun … and set him up. Liebowitz had been right. "Look, others had motives," he'd kept saying. "You weren't the only one the victim pissed off. I've got to get that seed growing in the heads of the jury." But one of *his* friends, people he thought he knew so well, letting him suffer an arrest and trial? Paul had always guarded himself from the idea. Yet now, Mark was throwing him under the bus. So was Louis, somehow. And he didn't even want to think about his object of lust, the Foxy Lady.

"Next." Paul approached the Canadian customs officer and handed her his passport and customs declaration form. She swiped the passport's barcode to call up his history then looked at him without smiling, glancing at the mess on his forehead. "Where are you travelling from?"

He thought of saying something like, "From wild Mediterranean parties." But any unnecessary lie seemed gratuitous and dangerous. "Rome," he said trying to look the officer straight in the eye.

"And how many days were you away?"

"I arrived in Rome last Wednesday, so seven."

"What did you purchase?"

"A summer suit. Cost about $500," Paul said. He was sure his voice croaked. "That's it. I was visiting an—an acquaintance."

The agent's eyes held tight on Paul's and she took her measure of veracity. *Don't look away. Don't swallow. Don't crap your pants.* She paused, and Paul imagined the needle on her dial of truth registering low. He grit his teeth so hard, he worried the tautness of his jaw muscles were a giveaway. "Any alcohol or tobacco?"

"No."

Boom came down the stamp on his declaration form followed by the scrawl of a pen. "Have a good day." Ten steps later, another agent checked the scrawl and a third took the form after Paul got his suitcase. Nobody bothered him. Outside the terminal, he released the clamp of his jaw, sure that he'd split a molar.

It was almost five in the afternoon when Paul dropped into the back seat of an ancient black Lincoln. The limo pulled away into the tail end of a lustrous day. He exhaled billows of carbon dioxide and ran both hands through his hair. Thousands of people lied on their customs declaration form every day. But most were bringing in clothing, shoes or booze. Not so often, under threat and without the proper paperwork, a fifteenth-century illuminated manuscript of unknown value and purpose.

Paul shook his head. The lies had to stop—*they'll fucking kill you.* He couldn't remember feeling such outrage. At Grace for tying him down. At Mark for putting him in an impossible position. At Louis for his indecipherable con. At least the anger was liberating, hinting at a belief in himself that his anxiety eviscerated. He went back over the revelations of the last seven days and let the anger well up further. *Piss off with your self-doubt and fight back. Fucking fight.*

The limo crept toward downtown Toronto in rush-hour traffic. Paul reached into his carry-on and felt the envelope with the illuminated manuscript. He remembered Di Strata asking him to drop both envelopes off that day. But it could wait till next morning. Then he would lay into Mark and cancel the friendship. As he imagined the scene, he accessed a side pocket of the carry-on and found his smartphone. It had been off since he spoke to Mark before the flight home departed.

Texts started landing. Only the one from Grace concerned him. "*Left you a voicemail.*"

For Christ's sake. He'd forgotten to call Grace's mother after the plane landed. It was past 11:00 p.m. in Rome. His thumb flew over the touchpad; Grace's was the last voicemail.

"*Paul, you're an asshole. You didn't call. It's a good thing my mother checks in on me. She wants to the call the police. And maybe I won't stop her. You know, you didn't need to treat me that way. I'm starting to trust my other source of two hundred and fifty thousand a lot more."*

He had to reach her. Pulling hard at his left earlobe, he found her number in his contacts then waited for the call to connect. But when it did, it went straight to voicemail. He dabbed his damaged brow waiting for the long Italian message to complete. "*Grace, it's Paul,*" he said. "*Please call me as soon as you can. I'm sorry I didn't call sooner. Honestly, a crazy thing happened. I'm glad you're okay. Like I said, please call.*" After hanging up, he also sent her a text that used "urgent" three times.

His mind raced through facts and uncertainties. If her mother had found Grace two or three hours earlier, she might already have spoken to the police in Rome and they might already have contacted Toronto police. And if Grace was really bitter, she had painful information about the gun to pass onto the police. They would want to talk to him right away. On the one hand, he should stay as far away as possible from his condo. On the other, he had to get the gun.

Paul found the contact for the concierge at his condo. "Hi Hari, it's Paul Tews."

"Oh, Mr. Tews, how are you?" Hari's habit was to metamorphose Paul's last name into "Tooth".

"I'm well. I've been away for a week. Just, ah, just checking that everything's okay at the condo." As soon as he asked the question, Paul realized how unusual it sounded. But Paul was surprised with the answer.

Hari's voice dropped and it sounded like he was cupping the phone so his words wouldn't travel. "Mr. Tews.

How odd you should ask. Two men have just arrived and are waiting in the lobby to talk to you."

It was like a boxer had punched him in the solar plexus. "Did they say who they are?"

"No, sir."

"And what do they look like?"

"I don't really know how to describe them, sir. One middle-aged man and one younger. Both quite large. Not very friendly." Now the boxer was through his ribcage, grabbing at his heart. "Will you be home soon?"

"My plans are up in the air," Paul said, trying to sound casual. "Could you just tell them you don't know—and haven't talked to me?"

"That is what I already told them, Mr. Tews."

"Okay. Then just leave it that way. Thanks."

Paul's plans had a lifespan of no more than three hours. Avoid his visitors by accessing his condo through the parking garage, get the gun and get the fuck out of there. Then make some new plans, whatever the hell they might be. Anything to avoid the surly, sweaty Beecham.

The limo driver knew the way to Niagara Street. When they arrived, Paul leaned in from the back seat and pointed out his condo building. "Up there, turn left, then go into the parking garage. I'd like you to drop me off at my car." Fifty yards later, Paul opened the garage door with a fob on his keychain, and the limousine bounced over the sidewalk toward the inbound lane.

Paul directed the driver along several rows of cars. Five cars from his, where he knew the surveillance cameras wouldn't see him, he told the driver to stop and paid him. After the limo left, Paul approached his car then tucked in behind a concrete pillar and put his suitcase and the two envelopes in the trunk. Keeping the carry-on, he found a baseball cap on the back seat, tugged it on and scooted toward the building's two elevators.

A couple was manoeuvering a large box with an unassembled Scandinavian table into one of the elevators. Half a minute later, the other elevator arrived. Paul stepped in, glancing at himself in the mirrors on three sides. Against his hope it would go directly to his floor, the elevator stopped at ground level and a second couple pushed in a stroller with a young boy. Resorting to the corner with the panel of buttons, Paul kept his head low and thumbed the button to close the door. Out of the corner of his eye, in the mirror behind the couple, he caught a reflection of the lobby.

The two men Hari had mentioned sat on a square-backed black couch across from a glass table centred by a vase of flowers. Each wore a crisp dark suit. The younger one rolled his fingers on the end of the couch and looked around the lobby for something of interest. The other sat forward in his seat, elbows on his knees, flipping through a newspaper. "Look," the boy in the stroller squealed, pointing at Paul's cap and giggling, "Blue Jays." At the same time, the ringtone on Paul's smartphone sounded.

The man holding the newspaper looked up. His face went from casual interest to recognition to alarm. Letting the newspaper drop, he slapped his companion's arm and pointed. As the elevator door closed, they both stood and ran toward Paul.

51

The elevator door inched along; Paul's entire body went stiff as a rail spike. He was sure one of the men would get a hand between the elevator door and frame. But the door slipped shut and everyone in the elevator heard a resounding "shit" from the other side. "That's a *bad* word, isn't it, honey?" the mother said. The boy nodded with a grave face.

Paul got off first at the fifth floor. He prayed the other elevator was still in use at the parking level and that he had enough time. He ran down the hall to his unit, pummelled pockets for the door key and rammed the key in the lock. Once inside, he dropped the carry-on to the floor and bolted to the kitchen.

A stacked washing machine and dryer sat in a closet at one end. Paul grabbed a chair from the dining room and dragged it over to the closet, then opened the door and turned on the light. Standing on the chair, he looked at the back half of the ceiling, which hadn't been dry-walled to allow for the dryer vent. He perched a foot on the edge of the washer and pushed himself up. With one hand he clutched the top of the dryer; with the other, he curled fingers around the open edge of the ceiling drywall. He moved his fingers back and forth but felt nothing. *Where is the goddamn box?* He jerked his fingers farther right and bumped up against something hard, pushing it back. *Crap.* He stretched as far as he could and his fingers found an edge. Pressing hard, he dragged the object toward the lip of the drywall. A second later, amidst falling dust, he saw the edge of the black lacquer box.

After carefully removing the box, Paul stepped down, rushed the chair back to the dining room and closed the closet. Then he ran to the front door, jammed the box into his carry-on and inched open the front door, listening for activity. It was quiet, and he slipped out with the carry-on and locked the door.

Bolting down the hall toward the stairwell, he heard an elevator arrive moments before he reached the door. He blew into the stairwell and shut the door as fast as the graduated closer allowed. Slumping against the back, he waited for several seconds. Then he peered through a narrow window. The older man from the lobby was knocking at his condo while the younger one stood watch behind. Paul dashed down the stairs two steps at a time.

By the time he reached P1, he was out of breath. He put a hand against a cinder-block wall and stopped to grab chunks of air. Then, with one final deep inhalation, he stepped into the parking lot and headed for his car, his head lowered and covered by the baseball cap for surveillance cameras. He opened the trunk and dropped the carry-on alongside his suitcase and the envelopes. Checking his smartphone, he saw it was past six and that Mark had left another voicemail. *He can go fuck himself.*

Paul's best idea was to drive west and get some time alone to figure out what to do. It was the height of rush hour and every route was busy. He decided to take King Street to the Queensway and eventually the Queen Elizabeth Way.

On King, though trying to concentrate on driving, Paul's mind flitted to the Smith and Wesson in the trunk of his car. Maybe *now* he should get rid of it and keep to his old story. If Grace didn't keep her side of the deal, that was the best way to beat a perjury charge. That, and the fact she'd tortured him to extract a confession about the gun. But the gun might also have been used to murder Art. More lies. More trouble. It didn't feel right. He needed time to think. He had the gun—and, temporarily at least, the police didn't. *What was the right thing to do with it?*

Paul reached the end of King Street where it bent north. He was behind several streetcars in the left lane reserved for turning west onto the Queensway, while the right lane continued straight onto Roncesvalles. Grabbing a look in the rear-view mirror, he nearly plastered the windshield with vomit. Two cars back, a black car had pulled a foot into the oncoming lane. Instantly, Paul recognized the driver as the younger man from his condo lobby. In the face of a streetcar, the black car realigned itself with traffic.

Goddamn it, the police were behind him *and the gun was in his possession.* Beecham would savour a charge of perjury and maybe another for possessing an unregistered firearm. There was no way Paul was giving up without a fight.

The pedestrian light at the end of King showed eight seconds before the green traffic light in Paul's favour turned yellow. The streetcar in front inched left onto the Queensway, its steel wheels squealing in the rails in protest. Paul knew the light would be red before he could make the turn. He signalled right and jockeyed his car into the neighbouring lane. Among a sea of horns, the black car lurched out and followed.

The traffic light changed to yellow. Paul thumped the Lexus's gas pedal, flew into the intersection and made a left turn from the right lane. The streetcar to his left banged its warning bell. Out the other side of the intersection, Paul stayed on the right side, driving slow and steady to avoid further attention. He smiled, proud of his evasive action.

Seconds later, more horns. The black car had entered the intersection against a red light and noodled its way left among irate drivers. Clear of the intersection, it accelerated hard toward Paul. The Queensway pitched down, then up and left, and straightened with High Park to the right. As fast as Paul went, the black car bore down on him. It tore up beside him then swerved hard right, forcing Paul to veer into Colborne Lodge Road and stop. The cars sat side by side, a yard apart.

The younger man got out the driver's side and stood with the door pinched against him, looking at Paul. The older man followed out the passenger side. He made sure his jacket sat right then rotated his upper trunk as if correcting a spinal misalignment.

You're done for, you're a goner, you're finished. Paul rammed both hands through his hair several times. Then he gripped the top of his steering wheel and looked straight ahead. *Maybe it's fine. Maybe it's okay to face the lies.* Fatefulness settled on him like a shroud pulled over a dead body, and he put the gearshift in park.

The older man tapped on Paul's window. His clothes had an edge, his grooming a precision, his movements a swagger that didn't match the all-business attitude of detectives. The black car didn't have a computer screen on the front dash or a cage in the back—and it was a Mercedes. Paul let down the window a slice.

"Hey buddy, you got something we're looking for." The man's voice was high-pitched, like it was touched with helium, a mismatch for his stocky build. "A package you brought from Italy, from Mr. Di Strata."

These are not police. "I'm sorry," Paul said. "My instructions are to give it to a colleague of mine."

"Well, there's been a change of plans."

Paul cleared his throat. "Mr. Di Strata is a client of our firm. I can't hand over documents to a stranger. I'm sure you understand."

The older man's ratty eyes flared. "Well, we'll just make a fuckin' phone call," he said. He moved his jacket aside to paw his pants, and Paul caught the stubby handle of a gun peering from the left jacket pocket. "Gino," the older man yelled to the other, "get my fuckin' phone. It's in the glove compartment."

"Just a sec." The younger man returned to the driver's seat of the Mercedes, letting the door fall shut. He opened the glove compartment and found the phone. Then he threw the door open again and began heaving himself out. He hadn't seen the cyclist in the bike lane.

The cyclist screamed. His bike's handlebar caught the younger man in the abdomen while his right shoulder smashed into the man's lower jaw. The cyclist plowed into the door, catapulted over and landed hard on the pavement. Stunned from the impact, the younger man sat slumped against the door frame, clutching his side.

The older man rushed over. *Really, these are not police.* Paul rammed the Lexus's gearshift into reverse and gunned the car backwards. "Hey," the older man yelled, his face flushing deep red. He reached toward his left jacket pocket then thought better of it. Jerking his car around the Mercedes, Paul smashed the gas pedal and shot past drivers slowing to look at the bodies struggling on the pavement.

52

For the next half hour, Paul checked the rear-view mirror every five seconds, but he'd lost the Mercedes. Heading west in dense traffic, he had an idea for his destination. Mark texted twice to call him immediately at work and phoned once more. Paul let the call go to voicemail.

At Winston Churchill Drive, he pulled off the QEW and parked at a coffee shop next to a gas bar. He walked around the back of his car, opened the trunk and studied the label on the envelope with the illuminated manuscript: *Signora Marianna Genovese, 92 Kaymore Gate, Woodbridge, Ontario, Canada.* Signora Genovese had an odd way of taking deliveries.

In the coffee shop, sipping an Americano, Paul was trying to paint a picture of what was going on with the manuscript when Mark called again.

"Well, if it isn't my lying, conniving bastard of a friend," Paul said.

"Jesus, at least you picked up," Mark said. "Where are you?"

Paul grew careful. "Doesn't matter. Half an hour ago, guys with guns tried to force me off the road for that fucking thing you conned me into smuggling."

"Why didn't you just give it to them?"

Paul caught himself raising his voice and took a deep breath. He slumped over his table and turned toward a window, protecting his conversation from nosy neighbours.

"Well, who the hell are they? I was expecting to give it to you. Not fucking gangsters."

"They're not gangsters. They're friends. What the hell, all you had to do was call me and I would have told you what to do. Why do you think I was trying to reach you?"

"Why do I want to talk to *you*? I thought you were a *friend*. Instead, you and Di Strata saw an opportunity for me to transport something illicitly. Isn't that right?"

Mark paused. "You were more of a backup. Di Strata does have a bad heart."

"And then you threatened me. Fuck you, Mark."

Mark paused again. "Sorry, Paul."

Paul sighed and focussed on a young woman gassing up her car. "What in hell's name have you gotten yourself into?"

"I need to get the envelopes," Mark said. "Both of them. Plain and simple."

"It won't be today. You wouldn't believe the other shit that's going on. I'll get them to you as soon as I can."

"I need them *today*, Paul."

"And I said I'll get them to you when I can. Besides, Di Strata said tomorrow morning is fine."

"Listen to me, they're pissed off. That one guy's hurt bad."

"None of my business. Tomorrow—maybe."

"*Paul*, you don't know—"

Paul hung up. He sat back and finished his lukewarm coffee. A wave of fatigue rushed over him; he'd hardly slept the night before and had only napped on the plane. He went through all the recent texts and voicemails on his phone. None was from Grace. It was well after midnight in Rome but not too late for a call, he thought. He had to know if Grace had contacted the police or sent the email to the anonymous address. She didn't pick up.

Forty minutes later, he was parked on Harvest Road, looking up the rise toward Rachel's house. He called her.

"Hello?"

"Rachel, it's Paul."

There was a pause. "Are you calling from Rome?" Her voice was distorted, as if her larynx was covered with mucous.

"I'm back," he said. "Things didn't quite go as planned."

"Sorry to hear that. Not surprised, though. They haven't here, either."

"I heard. I need a favour. I need a place to stay for the night. No questions asked, Rachel. And I'm parked in front of your house."

Paul heard Rachel walking and guessed she'd gone to a window to scan for his car. "It's not a good day, Paul."

He let some seconds pass. "Okay. I'll go to a hotel or something."

She sighed. "Maybe the company will do me good. I see your car. Come on up."

He parked under the same maple as two Sundays before. Other than the light chatter of birds, it was quiet. He walked up the landing to the house. The front door was half ajar and he let himself in.

Rachel emerged from the kitchen at the back. If it was possible, she had aged further, her red hair more matted, her eyes teary and red-rimmed. Her large frame was swallowed by a loose-fitting sweater. "I have an idea," she said, heading toward Paul. "Let's go for a walk."

She stepped out the house and Paul followed. "Do you notice anything different?" she asked as they walked down the lane to Harvest Road. Paul sensed something but couldn't place it. "Dante was run over yesterday."

"Dante? Who's—?" Paul asked, and then guessed. "Your dog?"

Rachel nodded and her eyes instantly welled up. "You're his replacement today," she said, her voice quavering.

"I'm so sorry to hear that. What happened?"

"Some asshole in a pickup driving too fast. Didn't even stop. And I didn't get a licence plate. I was too stunned and worried about Dante. That damn prick. I carried Dante home myself and buried him last night, in the back of the house."

They reached the end of the lane and walked west toward Greensville, their shoes crunching over loose gravel. The sun was low against them, distributed through treetops. Blooms showered off forsythia bushes while odoriferous fruit tree blossoms bulged whole and proud. Rachel spoke of her best friend and of plans for a new retriever. Eventually they crossed Brock Road and walked into Crook's Hollow. It was a narrow road with overhanging ash, butternut and maple trees. Spencer Creek's coppery water meandered through the valley to their left.

"I heard about Cyril leaving rehab," Paul said after some silence.

"I don't even want to talk about that," Rachel said, shaking her head. "He claims he's going back next week." She turned to Paul with a half-smile. "Let's talk about you. So Rome was so bad you couldn't face a night alone in the condo?" When Paul grew thoughtful, she dropped her smile.

"Rachel, it was all a sham."

"What was?"

"Her interest in me. It was an invention. Grace was trying to pump me for information."

Rachel looked straight ahead. "What information?"

Paul chose not to answer the question. "Did you know Louis met with her at the hospital? Just like he met with all of us?"

Rachel walked more quickly. "Yes."

"Pardon me?" Paul asked, trying to keep up.

"I said yes. It was something about Dagger's current production, wasn't it?"

"The information she wanted from me was for Louis," Paul said. "He asked her to have a fling with me to get it. And made it worth her while to carry it through."

Rachel stopped in her tracks. "That fucking brother of mine. He just couldn't leave things alone. He's *dead* and he's still got his hands in everything."

"And she's supposed to email someone with the information."

"I don't even have a laptop. I bet, somehow, it has to do with rejigging our useless, dysfunctional family. I told you Father and Louis had it out in Louis's final days. Deep old secrets, better left alone. Louis was probably trying to make us all look good when we're all deeply flawed. You wouldn't believe the shit I'm facing with his will. Some money to charity here. Some money for a film school there. He wanted his name plastered everywhere, to recreate himself."

"That's not what I'm talking about."

"You're probably talking about Art then, aren't you?"

Paul stopped in his tracks. "In a way I am. I mean, yes. So you know about—"

Rachel had walked ahead. She stopped and whirled around. "The cocaine? Of course I do, Paul."

"The cocaine?"

"That's what you mean, isn't it? Louis saw how close you were to Art and wondered if you knew he fed his habit."

"I had no idea."

"Louis would kill me but I don't care if you know. Louis introduced Art to that dealer, Rivera. And Rivera knew people in L.A. for Art to go to. Once his first movie became successful, Louis *wanted* Art to use cocaine, thinking somehow it meant he could lord it over him and keep him as his lead. And then, later, when Art abandoned him, as revenge. He *despised* Art for doing that to him on—what was it called?"

"*Rot-A-Tot-Tot.*"

"Yes. He even gave money to Art to cover the cocaine when he visited him in L.A."

"I thought that was Lee."

"Art spent a lot. Louis contributed much more than Lee. Maybe the Foxy Lady was supposed to find out if you knew."

"No," Paul said. "Louis could have just asked me that. It was something very different." Paul approached and put a hand on her arm. "Is it possible, Rachel, that Louis murdered Art?"

Rachel's face blanched. "I can't imagine. Not—not that way. And yet, almost nothing would surprise me."

"Imagine for a second, hypothetically," Paul said, "that I had—and have—the weapon used for Art. And imagine that, somehow, Louis knew about that, and wanted Grace to seduce me into telling her its location."

"Did you use the gun, Paul?"

"No."

"Then Louis has yet another crazy plan from the grave." Rachel turned and started walking back to the house. Darkness was throwing a cloak over the trees around them. "How disgusting," Paul heard in the distance. "He would've honoured our family more by just leaving us alone."

53

Not long after their walk and a few silent bites of dinner, Rachel made up a small bed for Paul in the spare room upstairs. Nearly comatose with fatigue, he fell onto the bed in his suit and instantly went to sleep. He slumbered as if making up for all his lost sleep since March in one night.

He finally awoke Wednesday morning at eleven. In the first moments, he felt refreshed and light but his baleful circumstances quickly invaded and agitated him. He went downstairs and discovered he was alone. In the kitchen he made instant coffee then stared out the back window. Intense sunlight had taken hold of the day. Not far from another maple, there was a patch of granola-like, earthy crumbles. He guessed Dante lay there.

Paul found the door to a porch along the back of the house. He sat in a creaking rocking chair, looking through dented bug screens. In the midst of birds hailing the morning, he searched for a new beginning. He wanted to become Catholic and go to confession; to press CTL-ALT-DEL; to wave the magic wand. He wanted to release himself from the vulnerability created by his lies and guilt.

That was a lot to want, he realized, and it seemed unlikely the gift of any would follow. Maybe the lies could be fixed. Sometimes, with the soap and water of amends, lies vanished after one scrub. Other times they needed years of scouring. But guilt—guilt was like an ugly tattoo, removable only by surgery without anaesthetic.

An hour and a half later, Paul was still pondering a way out. Rachel appeared with groceries and asked if he wanted lunch. She made bacon and eggs, her shoulders and heart heavy, tears intermittent. Conversation was sporadic as they ate. She returned only once to their conversation on the walk, to ask if Paul had given Grace the information she wanted. Guessing Rachel was wrestling with the implications for her brother, he pretended he didn't hear. He knew it was time to leave. After sharing a quiet hug, he walked out the front door.

In his car, Paul checked his smartphone. More hyper voicemails and texts from Mark. But what hijacked Paul's attention was a text from Grace. "*My brother Sandy will call you at 3:00 p.m. your time. Please speak to him.*"

He drove east on Harvest Road. The bucolic farm country did nothing to moderate the racing of his heart. He read into Grace's text an open line of communication and that she hadn't called the police. Then he wondered why she needed to speak through her brother and worried what she'd told him.

Close to three, Paul was on the Gardiner Expressway heading into downtown Toronto. He'd decided to banish the torment of Di Strata's envelopes and texted Mark he would drop them off at Collins, Shaw shortly. At exactly three, a call rang on his car's Bluetooth.

Sandy Campbell introduced himself. When Paul encountered anyone named "Sandy", it prompted an image of a surfer on a beach enthusing, "Cool waves, man," in a gooey lilt. This voice was constrained and unwilling.

"Grace asked me to call you. Frankly, I don't know what this is about. But I have something for you."

"What's that?"

"Well, you'll see, I guess. Can you meet me at four thirty? I'm in the west end. There's a Greek restaurant at the southeast corner of the Queensway and East Mall. It's got a yellow roof that you can't miss. At least that's how I remember it."

Paul grew apprehensive that Sandy was a decoy for the police. "I don't know," he said.

"She said you can trust her. She said to tell you that it's really important. That she'd never have involved me if it was crazy." Sandy sighed. "Which is true. I don't do well with stress."

"I actually have something else really important to do."

"Well, I know my sister. And, ah, this sounds *super* important."

Yeah, right. It's about money. "I tell you what," Paul said. "Is this the number I can reach you at?"

"Yes."

"I'm going to pick another place for us to meet. Does this have to be in person, by the way?"

"I think so. Yes. Actually, I'm definite about that."

"That's my best offer then. I'll call you at four thirty and tell you where. And Sandy? If this is a set-up, I'll cripple you."

"Oh, geez. It isn't. Not as far as I know." Sandy sighed again and under his breath added, "Why did I agree to do this?"

"Why indeed?" Paul said and hung up.

He took the Lake Shore exit from the Gardiner, found a U-turn and slipped into heavy westbound traffic. Fifteen minutes later, he was on the Queensway and found the restaurant with the yellow roof. Doubling back two blocks, he spotted the All-Day Diner in front of a mall. He stopped in the back parking lot, noting an entrance on one side and a kitchen exit on the other.

Ten minutes later, standing at the diner's back entrance, Paul had firmed up his plan. He'd parked his car on Algie Avenue, the next street parallel to the mall. If Sandy arrived with the police, he would flee through the kitchen exit and across the back parking lot to Algie. From there it was easy access to the Gardiner. And if Sandy arrived alone, well, it was important to hear what he had to say.

The place was nearly empty and smelled like stale coffee and cheese omelet. Paul took the seat closest to the kitchen and ordered a cappuccino. At four thirty, he called Sandy.

"H—hello?"

"Are you at the restaurant with the yellow roof?" Paul asked after sipping the coffee.

"Yes."

"Two blocks east, on the same side of the Queensway, you'll see the All-Day Diner in front of a mall. Come and find me."

Paul hung up. Moments later, Mark called. "For Christ's sake, not now." Paul let the call go through to voicemail, then texted Mark. "*Will come by your house tonight—probably. Tomorrow for sure. Tell them to relax.*"

Five minutes later, an anaemic-looking man in glasses, shoulder-length hair and fraying jeans came into the restaurant. No police followed. Paul nodded his chin and Sandy came over.

"H—hi," Sandy said after clearing his throat. He took the seat across from Paul. "Like I said, I don't know what this is about."

"Really?" Paul stared at him with the greatest intensity he could muster.

Sandy propelled back and put both hands up in protest. "And I don't want to know. I don't care how much depends on it."

"So what do you have for me?"

"Ah, well—" Sandy said, his face turning colourless. He snapped his head twice to one side. Paul thought he was starting a seizure. Then he realized he was supposed to look toward the back entrance.

Pale and defiant, Grace stood just inside the door.

54

Grace walked toward them. With her eyes on Paul, she said to her brother, "Can you wait in the car? I want to talk to Paul alone."

"Oh, for sure," Sandy said, jumping to his feet. He held out a hand but Paul was too thunderstruck to reciprocate. Like a mouse that had just escaped a trap, Sandy scurried out the diner.

Paul leaned back. "This is a surprise," he said, his body creeping with wariness.

"May I sit down?" Grace asked. Paul turned a hand toward the seat Sandy had vacated. Grace settled in, placing a large purse on the table. "How about a cup of coffee? That was a long flight and I don't remember the last time I slept well. No thanks to you." Paul looked past Grace, scouting the diner and environs. "Are you worried I've led the police here?"

Paul cleared his throat and resisted pulling a lobe. "A little."

"I haven't, Paul," Grace said. "And I also told my mother not to call them. I told her it was a lover's spat." With a small laugh, she added, "Some spat."

Paul ordered Grace's coffee. After it arrived, he settled both elbows on the table and held his hands, fingers interlaced, in front of his face. "Why are you here?" he asked. "Why didn't you just call?"

"There are things I needed to say in person."

"You want the two hundred and fifty thousand?"

Grace cocked an eyebrow and flicked some hair back. "Damn right I do. But right now, I'm trying to fix things between us."

Paul inhaled with incredulity. "You're a woman who literally cut my balls. Who had as much motive for murder in 1998 as I did. More, actually. And you're trying to fix things?"

Grace's face turned almost white. "You don't seriously think—?"

The truth was he didn't. She'd never known about the gun. "What are you fixing?" he asked after a pause.

"I told my mother about you."

"You *what*?"

"Not about the gun or perjury. But I did tell her you were put on trial for Art's murder. And that, though you were acquitted, you feel guilty for not helping him, in the same way you feel you didn't help your brother. And that I actually enjoyed the time with you, before things got out of hand. Which I haven't with someone in a long time."

Paul exhaled hard. He didn't know what to believe anymore. "I don't have a lot of time, Grace."

"I also told her that Art was Justin's father."

"She didn't know? The surprises keep coming."

"She was never able to meet him, of course. So why tell her about him?"

"But she must have wondered. She must have asked."

"When I got to Rome," Grace said, "she accepted that I wanted nothing to do with the father. It was something she could understand, because she'd had the same sentiment toward my father. Did you catch a glimpse of my brother? That's what happens when an overbearing jerk of a father takes away someone's childhood with fear. My mother was completely done with my father, never wanted to see or talk to him again. And she left me alone when I wanted something similar."

"I told you, I don't think Art's father is like that."

"I heard you say that in Rome. As I said, it got me thinking. A lot. That maybe I've been wrong. Even my mother, when she heard how losing men in your family affected you, especially your Granddad, suggested I'd made a mistake."

"Where is this going, Grace? Honestly, I've got a *lot* on my mind."

"I don't know yet. Maybe you can help me figure it out. Maybe you could introduce me to Art's father. My father doesn't deserve time with Justin, but maybe Art's father does."

Paul looked away. He had no interest in dealing with Grace's issues just now. "The last time I saw him was after I was acquitted. It's complicated. He probably hoped that Beecham had found the right guy, and that I'd be convicted."

"The other thing that I'm trying to say, Paul, is that I'm truly sorry for what I did. The threat to Justin, the prospect of a windfall. I lost my way. I'm hoping you can accept my craziness."

Paul snorted. "Accept it?"

"Maybe we can even help each other," she said, her dark brown eyes piercing his skin. "We *all* have our craziness."

Touché, Paul thought. He met her stare. "Two hundred and fifty thousand dollars is a lot of money for me."

"We can work out the money. If I have to continue taking advantage of my father, I will."

Paul read her face for veracity. "If you don't send your email soon, Art's father could find out about Justin, the wrong way."

"Before I get to that, there's another thing. I had a visit from Signor Di Strata before I left."

Paul smirked. "So his heart's not that bad after all."

"His heart? He told me he'd gone to the airport with you and asked you to deliver some envelopes to Mark when he took ill. Does Mark have them?"

"No. I was lying low, trying to figure out what to do. I've created a web of lies I can't get out of. I *have* to find a way out, a way where I can hold my head up high. Plus Di Strata sent a couple of tough guys after me. I had no idea who they were and got scared and ran. I know the envelopes are important. I'll get them to Mark today."

"He was very unpleasant. He said he'd counted on prompt delivery. He tried to make me responsible."

Paul leaned toward Grace. "After Di Strata pretended to get sick at the airport, one envelope split as I put it in the carry-on. There was an illuminated manuscript inside, from 1481. He was using me to smuggle it out of Italy. And Mark, that asshole, is involved in this somehow."

"That could explain why he was so threatening. Can you show it to me?" Paul looked at her doubtfully. "Paul, please, this is important."

"Give me a few minutes," he said.

Paul went to his car on Algie, drove behind the diner and got the envelope from the trunk. After wiping clean their table, he removed the manuscript from the envelope, plastic lining and cardboard. Grace gasped.

"Here's something about the provenance," Paul said, finding the document behind the front cover.

"This is making me nervous," Grace said after reading it. "Do you remember Di Strata talking about the *cordata*?"

"Unfortunately, yes."

"Chains of people who bring illegally excavated artifacts to market for collectors. There's something similar for stolen artworks. Maybe he's part of that. At the very least, Di Strata is exporting something illegally from Italy to sell to another collector."

"Mark said he's raising cash."

"A book like this, it's part of Italy's culture. It shouldn't leave the country at all. This is serious business."

"I bet Mark is a paid mule for Di Strata. I don't want any part of this kind of thing." Paul ran both hands through his hair. "These lies, I can't get rid of them."

"And to make matters worse, Di Strata knows about Justin."

"What do you mean?"

Grace swallowed hard. "He saw him when he visited me. He said, 'Perhaps you should speak to Mr. Tews. Tell him Mr. Koslovsky *must* have the packages *immediately*. By the way, Signorina Campbell, how old is your son? I hope he stays well and grows into a fine young man.'"

"'Stays well?'" Paul repeated. "Is that a threat?"

"I don't know." Grace's eyes went glassy and Paul felt his heart romp. "I need to call my mother," she said.

"And I need to check my messages from Mark."

As Grace dove into her purse for her smartphone, Paul fished his phone from his jacket. He found a new text from Mark and his head spun. "*JESUS, WHERE ARE YOU? THEY'RE GOING TO HURT ME. CALL!!!*"

55

For several seconds, Paul felt a surge of guilt. Grace had begun speaking with her mother and he waved at her to interrupt her call. "Tell her to make sure Justin stays with her," he said. "I have to call Mark. I'll be in my car at the back." It was like Grace had seen a ghost.

Paul repackaged the manuscript and rushed out to his car. Three vehicles over, Sandy looked back and forth between Paul and his car's dashboard. In the driver's seat with the envelope on the passenger seat, Paul tapped his smartphone then held it to his ear.

"Oh, thank god," Mark said. "I'm looking at a fucking gun, Paul."

"Where are you?"

"And he's talking about my good knee."

"*Where are you?*"

"I'm at the firm. My floor. In the Laurier meeting room. When are you fucking getting here?"

"Half an hour, Mark. With traffic, at most forty-five minutes. Tell them half an hour."

As Paul tapped "End Call", Grace knocked on the passenger window. Paul unlocked the door and Grace dove in beside him, putting the envelope on her lap. "Well?" she asked, her eyes wide.

"I have to drop off both envelopes—now." He pointed to her lap. "If that thing's stolen, in theory, I should take it to the police."

"Paul, no," Grace said, her face turning fierce.

He took one look at her. "I said 'in theory'. I have to go, Grace." He started the car, waiting for her to join Sandy.

"Take me along," she said. "I need to know what's going on." Paul lips fluttered as he exhaled violently. "And, if it needs saying, you can trust me."

Paul nearly ripped a lobe off. "Grace, all this shit is mine. My problems—and I keep making new ones—are my own. I got into them myself. Now I've got to get out of them myself."

"*This* one isn't, Paul," Grace said, holding up the manuscript. "This one involves Justin. And I'd simply rather be with you than Sandy. Do you understand?"

Paul revved his car's engine a few times. "Absolutely not. But go get your luggage. I'll open the trunk."

Fifty minutes later, they drove down the ramp to underground parking at the Bay Wellington Tower. Taking the first free spot, Paul grabbed the envelope from Grace's lap then jumped out of the car and retrieved the second from the trunk. They took the parking elevator to the ground floor then a second elevator to Collins, Shaw's main reception on the twenty-ninth floor.

Debbie, the young after-hours receptionist, greeted Paul with a wide smile. "Mr. Tews, so nice to see you. Are you going to your office?" She gave Grace the up-and-down.

"No, I actually have to go to thirty-one and I don't have my pass. And my friend here will wait for me in the small reception area up there."

"I will?" Grace asked.

"You will. Debbie will want you to sign in."

They walked up two flights of open stairs to the thirty-first floor. "I'll find you here," Paul said, pointing to a buttoned black leather couch with a view between other buildings of Lake Ontario. Before she could say anything, he was down the hall with the envelopes.

Paul turned the corner and stopped two doors later in front of the nameplate "Laurier Room". He gave the closed door a hard rap. A few seconds later, it opened a crack and one side of a face appeared. It was the older of the two men who'd forced Paul's car over on the Queensway. The pupil of his eye burned like it had been plucked from a hearth.

"Well, look who's here." Again that silly high-pitched voice attached to the macho body. He opened the door enough for Paul to slip by then closed it again. The air hung heavy with the smell of stale coffee. Mark consumed a leather swivel chair with its back pushed against the floor-to-ceiling glass. His face was ashen and drawn.

Paul stacked the envelopes in the middle of a large table. "Is this what you want?" he asked.

"Grab a chair and sit next to your buddy there," the man said, sporting another well-cut suit. For the first time Paul saw the toy-like black gun in his right hand.

Paul pointed at the gun. "Is that really necessary?"

The man examined the label on the top envelope. When he saw Mark's name, he flicked the envelope with the tip of his gun, sending it skidding along the table's gleaming surface. "It is, asshole. Now get into that chair."

Paul complied. The man ran the tip of the gun along the torn side of the second envelope. "Why has this been fuckin' opened?" he asked, turning to look at Paul.

"It tore after it was given to me. The envelope isn't big enough for the contents." The man pushed out his lower jaw. "For Christ's sake, put the gun away," Paul said. "This is a professional firm."

"Paul, shut up," Mark said.

"If this was professional, you would've gotten this shit here on time, you know? Did you look inside?"

"I didn't, asshole."

"You're very fuckin' brave, you know that?"

"I'm not," Paul said. "I just think stuff is delivered late sometimes and it's not a big deal. What's in there anyway?"

"None of your fuckin' business. Solicitor-client precedent."

"Privilege, asshole."

"What?"

"It's called solicitor-client privilege. And it doesn't apply to *that* envelope."

"Paul, shut the fuck up and leave," Mark hissed.

"No, he doesn't get to leave yet," the man said, waving his gun at Paul. "I have to make a call."

Seething and trembling with fear at the same time, Paul stayed put. As the man spoke on his smartphone, Mark leaned over and whispered, "What's in there is worth a lot of money. *That's* the big deal."

Paul glared back. "I don't care if it's a damn Picasso. You don't treat people like this."

Ending his call, the man whirled toward Paul, thrust his left hand around Paul's throat and slammed his head against the floor-to-ceiling glass.

"Listen, you fuck," he said, his mouth spewing putrid breath onto Paul's face, "you got a big fuckin' mouth, you know that? And you know what else? What happened to my buddy, who's still in hospital by the way, was *your* fuckin' fault."

"Bullshit," Paul squeaked.

"Jesus, Paul," Mark said, his deep voice skipping up an octave.

The man tightened his grip and Paul groaned. "Your face looks like fuckin' shit with all those scratches and stuff. Believe me, I can make it worse. A lot worse. Do you want to try me?" Paul didn't answer. "I said do you want to fuckin' try me?"

"No," Paul hissed.

"Then keep your mouth *shut*."

The man stood and churned his shoulders so his jacket sat to his liking. He grabbed the envelope with the manuscript and walked to the door. "I will see myself out," he said.

Paul rubbed his aching throat. Mark pushed out of his chair and went to a side table to pour a glass of water. His large hand shook so hard, water splashed from the glass.

"Do you want to tell me what this is about?" Paul asked.

Mark looked out the window and followed the path of Lake Ontario's eastern shoreline, tan and sinewy like a length of rope. "Not particularly," he said. He drank half the water. "I want you to know, Paul—I wouldn't have told."

Paul snorted. "I have no way of knowing if that's true."

"I looked in that file box before you picked it up when you came back to the firm. After the trial. What was that, thirteen years ago? I don't know why. I guess because I was surprised you'd stored it under my name."

"I only shot the gun twice, Mark. Before university. And Granddad never registered it."

Mark paused and nodded. "I figured it was some story like that. And that you panicked when the police questioned you. Innocent people do that, too, not just guilty ones."

"Did you know Di Strata was going to set me up?"

"I did. Sorry. I needed the fee."

"The fee? Mark, you're a professional—and part of the *cordata*."

Mark laughed. "I'm not sure what I'm part of. Di Strata can sell stuff for a lot more outside Italy than in. He just has to get it out without anyone knowing. That's one of the ways the fucker got rich."

"And that's why you travel to see him so often."

"I actually do give him a lot of legal advice, too. And there really is a sister in Woodbridge, who's going to inherit a shitload of money one day. Anyway, believe me. I won't tell anyone about the gun."

"I'm done lying, Mark."

"To me, you're a straight-up player, Paul. And a good friend. Just wanted you to know, I won't tell at my end."

56

Paul found Grace in the small reception area. Perched on the leather couch, legs bouncing, she stood as soon as she saw him. He held up a hand, catching her before she said anything.

"Everything's all right, I think," he said, trying to hide his anger and trembling. "They have what they want."

"You think Justin's safe?"

"I do. I really do. I might keep him home from school till you get back—just to be sure."

"That's not making me feel better."

"It's just a precaution, Grace. Call your mother and tell her to relax."

Grace pursed her lips. "Okay."

When she finished her call, they took an elevator to street level and stepped into the warm, windless outside air.

"I need a drink," Grace said above the noise of rush hour's residue. "And some food. It's past seven thirty. I'm starving."

Paul caught her eyes. "These have been three crazy days," he said. "My mind is completely fucked up. I need to be on my own."

"I apologized, Paul."

"I heard you. And I'm telling you, I don't have forgiveness in me right now. And I don't have it for Mark. Or for me."

"I'm not sending the email, Paul, if that's what you want to know. And don't worry about the money, either."

"Honestly?"

"I already told you I don't need to worry about it. But you have to help with Art's father. That's the new deal."

Paul looked away. "What I need to do is escape my past. That's what's important."

"*Come on*," Grace said, tugging Paul west along Wellington Street. "You need a drink as much as I do. You're going to have dinner with me."

They crossed Bay Street and walked up wide granite steps toward the hulking black mass of the TD Bank Tower. Inside its lobby, they went to the elevator bank for the top floor and rode fifty-four ear-popping storeys. They exited into a hardwood foyer; signs pointed to a dimly lit restaurant. Grace asked for a table for two, and they were escorted to one by a south-facing full window.

It was a half hour to sunset. Past a wall of shorter towers and the curl of the Toronto Islands were Lake Ontario's concave grey-blue waters and the faint outline of the opposite shore. The eastern horizon bled red-brown while its western counterpart blistered a fiery yellow.

As they shared a bottle of wine, Paul shrank from his earlier ire and became distant. By the end of the main course, Grace's tolerance had waned. "Are you going to let me in?" she asked, drumming fingers on the table.

Paul stopped scanning the darkening sky and turned his head toward her. "Louis went to a lot of trouble to locate the gun. Why? *After* he's dead."

"I don't know. He didn't—"

"I know he didn't say. But I've had this thought again and again in the last twenty-four hours. Everything circles back to the gun. The burden of my lies. Closure on Art's murder. This pain-in-the-ass guilt. But if I attach the gun to the right person—"

"What?"

"It goes away."

"What does?"

"All of that. Well maybe I can't eliminate the guilt for not helping Art more and for owning the gun that I'm now guessing killed him. But the thing is, I can mitigate it. And then maybe I can live—and be available for others."

Grace eyed Paul. "Where is this going?"

"I think I have a way to draw out Art's murderer," he said. An odd, mild-mannered smile settled on his face.

"But—but if you do that, then—"

"Yes, Beecham might charge me with perjury."

"Exactly," Grace said, putting her hand to her mouth.

Paul looked at her impassively. "I don't care."

"But what will that mean?"

"I don't honestly know. Maybe another arrest and charge. Maybe jail. Perjury's serious. But the thing is, I really don't care. It cleans things up for me."

"Seriously?"

"Honestly, yes. It'll be better than what I have now. It'll be liberating. I won't be vulnerable to people who know my appalling secrets and use them against me. Goodbye, Mark. Goodbye, Louis."

"And goodbye me?" Grace said, her voice strained.

"I don't know."

"And your law career?"

"Maybe finished. Don't care," Paul said, keeping his smile. "I was never meant for it anyway. I was a fraud, really."

"You made a mistake," Grace said, her eyes darting around the restaurant. "Who hasn't?"

Paul snorted. "It feels like much more than that. But I can be released, Grace. And maybe with enough hard work, redeemed."

They stayed quiet until Paul paid for dinner. Tucking the receipt in his wallet, he said, "I'm going home to clean up and plan. Watch your emails. If you like, you can help me with a very interesting dinner tomorrow night."

He kissed her on both cheeks and walked out the restaurant.

57

To: Kate; Rachel; Grace; Cyril; Mark; Lee
Re: Tews Intervention Dinner: May 23

Art had a saying you may remember: "Life is what you make it." I always thought that was easy for him to say. Now I'm finally taking up his suggestion.

It's rare that someone asks for an intervention. But you're my closest friends and you all know, more or less, that the soul and spirit of Paul Tews have been fading. So now I'm eating some humble pie and reaching out for your help.

Tomorrow night (Thursday), let's enjoy each other's company and eat some good food and drink some fine wine together. Then I'm going to confess some past transgressions. There will be consequences but I'm prepared for them. In fact, I'm looking forward to getting them out of the way.

Attendance mandatory. My condo, #502, seven o'clock. There's a spare key on top of the hall light to the right of the front door. Let yourself in.

Paul

58

The kitchen counter of Paul's condo was stacked with dirty dishes and the air was rife with the smell of vinaigrette and salmon. Grace busied herself loading the dishwasher. Bringing the last plates in from the dining room, Paul thought she looked nervous.

"I'm tired of talking about our mayor and city politics," he whispered into her ear. "Let's make coffee and I'm going to see who wants cognac. Then I start." She looked at his eyes, wavy hair and lips. He felt her searching for another way. "I'm resolved," he added.

The living room, kitchen and dining room were one open space. The dark oak dining table had been extended to accommodate the group of seven. A matching buffet sat on the wall opposite the kitchen, and a giant abstract painting, heavy on reds, hung on the back wall.

Paul put cognac glasses at each setting and walked around pouring Remy. Kate covered her glass with a hand. "I've had enough," she said. "I don't want to do anything I'll regret." Grace followed Paul, asking about coffee and tea. Five minutes later, the smell of freshly brewed coffee filled the condo.

Paul resumed sitting at the head of the table beneath the painting and Grace sat at the opposite end. Mark and Kate sat on one side while Cyril, Lee and Rachel were on the other. The apprehension on their faces when they'd arrived had dissipated some. Paul regretted that he was about to revive it.

Lee was doing his best to ease the tension. He flexed his biceps for the table to see. "You can have these, too," he said, looking at Mark, then Cyril.

"No one wants them," Mark said, a little less fraught than the evening before. "Makes you look insecure."

"You're just jealous. Cyril, what do you say?"

"What I say is give me more cognac, Paul." His back rounded in his chair, Cyril shoved his empty glass toward Paul. "Might as well enjoy life before returning to rehab. Lee, ask the ladies what they think of your biceps instead. How about you, Kate?"

"Lee," Kate said, leaning forward, "they make you look *hot*. Those muscles, they just make me *quiver* inside."

Half of the voluminous smile on Lee's face dropped away. "Seriously?"

Kate couldn't suppress a burst of laughter. "*No.* Sorry, Lee."

The rest of Lee's smile fell like a heavy stone through water.

"Oh, he's crestfallen," Rachel said. "*I* like them, Lee." Her hair, freshly curled, looked vital and orderly, and her face smoother. "But I'm too old for you."

"No one's too old for me as long as they want kids," Lee said, putting an arm around Rachel.

She pulled away from him as far as she could. "I'm about to have hot flashes," she said.

As the laughter subsided, Kate's face became quiet and she cleared her throat. "Okay, Paul, I care about you a great deal. So does everyone else here. Tell us what's going on."

Paul put on a rueful smile. "Thanks, everyone, for coming to my self-initiated intervention," he began. He put his forearms on the table and joined his fingers. "You all know I fall into funks from time to time. You know what worries me most about that? It's that, to you, it must seem very self-indulgent. That I *choose* to immerse myself in my own shit, to be inside my own head instead of seeing the important stuff in front of me.

"I *do* see beyond my own face. I take note of who my friends are, for example. And at work, usually I'm on top of files and know the issues. But these funks aren't voluntary. I don't choose them the way I choose shampoo or a movie. They choose *me*."

Paul rotated a hand above his head. "I said to Grace last week, I have feelings of apprehension nearly all the time, like a bird of prey circling above me, always ready to dive down and carve out a chunk of flesh. And that apprehension weighs me down, as if I've got lead instead of blood in my veins. And then I can't move. My legs especially don't want to move. And I have no vitality and I just want to be by myself.

"So that's what it's like. And this thing hanging over me, it's been there since David died. Always there. Sometimes closer, so I can almost touch it, and other times not. Right above me during the trial, circling and circling. In 2002, it led to outright depression. What I've been going through the last three months, I think it was triggered by Louis telling me about his diagnosis. Honestly. Why did I get to live when he didn't? That was my thought. And then the apprehension rose in me again, and I worried a lot about another depression. And when that happens, I just exist, wondering what I'm worth. And I can tell you, the answer is not good."

Paul took a sip of cognac. "They say that the definition of insanity is doing the same thing over and over, expecting a different result. I've gone over and over why I didn't talk to my parents after David spoke to me about the voices that kept rattling his cage. Why I didn't say something when, fresh out of rehab, shortly before he died, he said he doubted that he could go on. I don't get any peace from that. I end up in an empty hole, at a loss why I didn't do *something* to stop David from smashing his car into that truck. The police said he could have stopped. But he didn't. And there were no tread marks."

"Paul, you can't *treat* yourself like this," Kate said. "You weren't responsible. We've talked about this."

"But I do. And worse. I've gone over and over why I didn't offer Art more help. It was the *same* thing. Someone so obviously in desperate need of help. But I came up short."

"He could be an asshole, Paul," Mark said. "And you didn't kill him."

"He was what I aspired to be. Same with David."

"Yeah, yeah. Ease up on yourself," Cyril said. "That's what they told me in rehab, before I flunked out."

"Cyril's right," Lee said. "You're a *good* guy." Lee looked around the table. "Right?" Everyone nodded.

"I appreciate it," Paul said. "I appreciate the support. I really do. Except I can't keep doing things the same way. I made a mistake—it relates to Art—that I've covered up. At first, I convinced myself it was nothing, that it was inconsequential. But part of me always knew that wasn't the case. A part I hid deep inside. And over time, this mistake acquired its own life, never letting me forget it's there, never letting me forget my *real* nature. And with that hanging over me, I'll never get to the point where I can believe that I did the best I could with David and Art." From the corner of his eye, Paul felt the glare of Mark's eyes. "So tonight I'm going to fix the mistake as best I can."

Paul pushed back his chair and walked to the buffet. Two large drawers were below its top. He opened one and removed the black lacquer box. Returning to the head of the table, he pulled off the lid and tilted the box so everyone could see its contents. Then he set the box and lid side by side in the centre of the table. The Smith and Wesson sat snug in the green velvet, its six cartridges to the lower left. To Paul it looked both playful and menacing. Kate gasped, Cyril let out a long low whistle and Lee blurted, "Jesus."

"For those of you who don't know," Paul continued, "this is my Granddad's gun. The .38 Smith and Wesson I bragged about shooting with him and David. The one I told you he gave me shortly before he died and my mother made me give back. But Granddad and I had a little secret—he gave me the gun anyway. And I was glad he did. It was a connection to my past I didn't want to lose."

Paul took another sip of cognac but hardly felt its burn in his throat. "In university, I never told you I had it because I was afraid of what my mother's reaction would be. I also knew it hadn't been registered, and by first-year law school, I knew that an unregistered gun was a serious offence.

"But much more importantly, when Art was murdered and the detectives at 14 Division first interviewed me, I stuck with the lie—under oath. I was still worried what my mother would say and about firearms offences and just didn't see how it was relevant to the case. And then, in the second interview, when I first met Beecham and he and I didn't get along, I thought, well, if I tell Beecham about this gun *now*, I'm going to be convicted for sure.

"And I stuck with the lie after I was arrested and charged. The idea of retracting my statements became harder and harder to imagine because of the damage to my credibility. On and on it went, through the preliminary hearing and eventually at trial, when I testified. Again I was under oath and again I perjured myself.

"I made this god-like decision to manage the future and it seemed to work. For Christ's sake, I was eventually acquitted. And I kept telling myself that it was okay. It wasn't my job to figure out who Art's real murderer was. That was for the police. And I didn't see what difference knowing about the gun made. So I hung on to the lie, and I thought I could live with my lapse in judgment. But like I said, it hangs over me, reminding me I'm frail. Frail and tainted. I can't stand it."

"But if you *were* innocent—" Kate said.

"I did not shoot the bullet that killed Art," Paul said.

"So you lied. But—"

"I committed perjury then went on to become a hot-shot corporate lawyer, basking in the lifestyle and prestige. I was a fraud. But worst of all," Paul said, pointing at the Smith and Wesson, "I now believe I might have accidentally protected Art's real murderer. What I think now is that *that's* the murder weapon. Honestly, I'm a fucking fraud."

He looked around the table. His guests were more transfixed by the gun than his confession.

"So, let me get this straight—" Cyril began, sitting up in his chair.

"Yeah," Lee said, interrupting. "What do you mean? That's the gun that killed Art? There's no bullet missing."

"I'm not a hundred percent sure, but I think that's the gun," Paul said, exhaling deeply. "And I'm pretty sure the cartridge that was shot was replaced. Anyway, tomorrow morning, somehow, the box is going to find its way to my friend, Detective Beecham. He won't be happy with me. I'm bracing myself for a charge of perjury or obstruction of justice or something. And maybe for a firearms offence, too. I accept that. But I'm sure he and the forensics folks can figure out what secrets that gun has. And that's more important to me now."

59

It was just after midnight on Friday morning. Paul sat in his reading chair, tucked in the corner of his living room across from the balcony and beside the front hallway wall. A small table sat left and an unlit lamp overhead. Occasionally he caught a sound: a motorcycle tearing up King Street; a clubber given voice by drink and drugs; a dog in neighbouring Victoria Memorial Square Park barking at imaginings. Otherwise he still heard the ticking of the grandfather clock in Grace's apartment.

For an hour or so, the guests had stared at the black lacquer box and spoken in false confidence about Paul's future. Then they'd developed undue concern about next-day obligations. After they'd left, Grace and Paul had cleaned up cognac glasses and coffee cups in silence. Then she'd corralled his attention and matter-of-factly made an offer. He'd briefly assessed her sincerity but told her it wasn't the time; he needed to be alone in his reading chair. After she slipped away, he'd turned off all the lights and opened the balcony door a few inches to dissolve dinner odours. Then he'd gone to the chair where he'd been for the last two hours.

Swells of air crept past the balcony door, capering with a half-drawn floor-length drape. The dim light from lamps in the park created a play of shadows in the dining room and kitchen. The lacquer box remained in the centre of the dining table, its lid to one side.

It was too early for cathartic relief from Paul's revelation about the gun. There also was no gain in thinking over the reactions of his guests; so many astonished and apprehensive faces couldn't be parsed for insight. And Grace's surprising offer was best left to the next day. Everything now was in the watching and the waiting.

A noise, sharp and hollow, startled Paul. He sat forward in the chair and it repeated. In a flash, his mouth went dry. He drove his eyes and ears to penetrate his surroundings, to zero in on the source. The cord for opening the balcony door drape danced forward from a gust of air, then swung back and slapped against the door's glass. He fell back in his chair, trying to relax.

Saliva reappeared but with an unpleasant tinny taste. Paul circled his tongue inside his mouth then ran it across his lips. The cord was a distraction and he needed to concentrate—for who knew how long. Walking across the living room, he rumbled the balcony door shut. Back in the chair, he smacked his lips. Still that tinny taste.

He forced aside all thoughts. For half an hour there was only the ticking in his head, the taste in his mouth and a growing strain on his patience. Then, as his concentration began to fail, there was another noise, probing and grinding, metal on metal. He went dead still.

It came from only a yard away, in the hallway beyond the thin wall beside him. He imagined the spare front door key from the top of the outside hall light, pushing bit by bit into the cylinder of the door's lock, forcing one internal pin after another out of its path. A few seconds later, he heard the bolt slip into the body of the lock. He gripped the on-off switch of the lamp above the chair.

Silence. But after thirty seconds, against the feeble light through the balcony door, a new shadow appeared, gliding like a skater across the living room floor. At the near end of the dining table, it stopped. A hand curled toward the box. Paul turned on the lamp.

He blinked through the sudden brightness and searched for the shadow. "For Christ's sake," he hissed. "Cyril."

60

Cyril's head shot up and he sent Paul a ferocious glare. Stooped over the dining table, his slight body froze. His right hand, perched over the gun, held a napkin from dinner.

"You should be in rehab," Paul said.

"They told me to let stuff go," Cyril said, so quietly Paul strained to hear. "So I thought I'd let *it* go. As long as I can, anyway. And I would have missed your show. Maybe you should let stuff go, too, Paul."

"That hasn't worked for me, Cyril."

Cyril's face grew calmer and he looked down at the box. His hand moved closer to the gun. "I just came back because, unlike you, I've never held one of these before," he said. "Sorry to intrude."

Paul got up from the chair. "Bullshit. Don't touch it, Cyril." He closed half the distance between them. "The thing is, something about that gun interests you a lot. And Louis was helping you find it, wasn't he?" Cyril turned to look at Paul, devoid of expression. "That's right, Cyril. I know Louis set up all that crap with the Foxy Lady so I'd reveal the location of the gun. And I did. What you weren't prepared for was that I had my own reasons to disclose the gun to the world."

Cyril nodded, looking back and forth between Paul and the gun. "Yeah, yeah, that certainly was melodramatic. You had us all on the edge of our seats."

"I suppose what you want to do is wipe fingerprints from the gun. And the cartridges—especially the one you replaced."

A crooked smile fell onto Cyril's face. "What are you talking about?"

"Fingerprints. From fifteen years ago. That's my suspicion. The police can lift them many years after they're left. I checked. Most will be from me. I suppose some from Granddad, too. But also some from you, I think. And they'll be hard to explain. Am I right?"

Cyril straightened up and dropped his arms to his side. He looked thinner and rattier than ever. "If you're expecting some grand confession from me, Paul, forget it. I just wanted to have a closer look at the gun that took out Art."

"You were never fond of him, were you? Why not?"

"All that 'little man' stuff. Rubbing my nose in shit all the time. Reminding me and the world every second how he had everything going for him and I didn't. That's all I ever heard. Right down to the last days of his life."

"Envy, jealousy, resentment?"

"Yeah, yeah. Let's not get too complicated. You're hardly a rehab counsellor."

"Enough to shoot him? He really ground you down, didn't he?"

"That's enough talk, Paul. I'm going home."

"Come on, Cyril. It's not like Beecham is going to believe me over you. But for my own satisfaction. Why? Why'd you shoot Art?"

"Fuck you. This is a trap."

Cyril leaned toward the dining table. Paul wasn't going to let him get at the gun and smudge prints with the napkin. He rushed at him, but Cyril was spry and dodged him. Then Cyril threw himself across the table, clutching for the box. Paul turned and grabbed him by both ankles, pulling him off the table toward the floor. Cyril had managed to clamp two fingers and a thumb on an edge of the box. As he fell to the floor, he flung the box backwards at Paul's head. The gun flew out, clattering under the buffet, but a corner of the box caught Paul above the left eye and he raised his hands in defence.

Cyril jumped up and lunged for the front door. Throwing himself along the ground, Paul clipped both his feet. With a heavy grunt, Cyril sprawled, and Paul was immediately on top of him, dragging him back into the living room. Then he forced Cyril over and sat across his bony chest, holding both arms down. Cyril thrashed his head back and forth, his face purple with rage, spit frothing from the corners of his mouth.

"Yes, this is a fucking trap," Paul hissed. His left eye's vision was hazy. "Do you have any idea what you cost me?" Cyril continued to fight. "You're not going anywhere." A drop of blood fell onto one of Cyril's cheeks and Paul realized he'd been cut above the eye. "Tell me, you little fuck. How'd you know about the gun?"

His lungs gasping for air, his eyes bulging at Paul, Cyril stopped thrashing and clamped his mouth shut. Paul put a knee on one of his spindly arms and applied pressure. "Jesus, get your knee off my fucking arm," Cyril said.

"*Tell me.*"

"I found the gun under your bed in your old apartment, at the party you had for Art when he got back from L.A."

Paul remembered. "That's right. You were sulking in my bedroom after Louis chewed you out for something. And so you planned to murder Art? With my gun?"

"I'm not saying anything more," Cyril said.

Another drop of blood fell onto his face. Paul increased the force of his knee on Cyril's arm. "Listen, little man, you better talk to me." Cyril's face contorted in pain and anger. "That 'little man' stuff really gets to you, doesn't it? Why don't you be a big man for a change? Just tell me how you planned to murder Art."

"What I'll say is that we all expected the cocaine to take him out, didn't we? And we all got tired of waiting, too. When he left for his dealer that Friday night, *anyone* could have said, 'I have enough time to get the gun as long as Paul stays at Kate's.'"

"You took the gun from my place? To set me up? How'd you get in?"

"You had a spare key under the front doormat anybody could have found and made a copy from, asshole. Enough. *Let me go.*" Paul's anger grew exponentially at the thought of a set-up. He pushed harder on Cyril's arm. "Fuck off," Cyril squealed. "You really will break my arm."

"*More*," Paul yelled back. "When did you get the gun?"

"Theoretically, I had time after the doctor's appointment for my sprained ankle," Cyril said. "No one set you up, Paul. No one would ever do that to you. The great fucking Paul, the nicest guy around. For fuck's sake, someone who wanted to do that would have left one cartridge empty in the box. You took the chance of not telling people about the gun, not me. Now, Jesus, ease off my arm."

"Was that stuff at Art's intervention with the crutches even real?"

"Real. But not all that bad."

"So you had an apartment on Euclid then. Maybe a six-minute walk to where Art was shot. And the same amount of time to return the gun to my place before going home again. So that wasn't a problem. But how did you manage to leave prints?" Cyril started to thrash again and Paul jammed his other knee against the free arm. "Fuck, Cyril, I'll break both arms if I have to."

Cyril settled once more, still gasping for air. "I was in your place, and about to wipe the gun down before putting it back in that stupid fucking box you're so proud of, when I heard you put the key in the front door. I only had time to get the gun back in the box and hide under your bed."

"That's right. I was early because of the headache Beecham didn't believe I had."

"I was patient. I waited until you went to the bathroom."

"And why didn't you come back? Ah, but you did. And you couldn't find the gun because I'd moved it."

Cyril gave a scornful smile. "I thought maybe you'd gotten rid of it after the murder. But I doubted that, since you'd kept it all that time against your mother's wishes. The good part, though, was that you kept insisting you'd given the gun back to your grandfather before university. From the morning after Art died when we got together at Kate's place, to the investigation, to the trial. You didn't know it, but you were protecting me."

"Oh, fuck," Paul said, shaking his head. "So why are you even here? Why didn't you let things alone?"

Cyril had gone limp. He didn't notice when a third drop of blood splashed across his nose. "I just worried—all the time—about this exact thing. I saw your mood swings. I saw the anxiety and depression. I wondered if it was the gun that was eating you up. All I needed to do was wipe it clean. But I couldn't get at it."

"So your cocaine use—"

"You want me to say it helps. It does. It helps a lot of things."

"It helped screw over Art."

"Sure," Cyril said. "It brought the big man down, didn't it? I use it because it keeps me calm and powerful."

"You, powerful?" Cyril spat but Paul continued. "And did you prod Louis to help pay for Art's cocaine when Art was cut off by his old man and Lee? Help Louis feed off his anger toward Art for spurning his second movie, you weak piece of shit?"

"How do you know this?"

"I do. Am I right?"

"I contributed. I'm not saying anything more."

Paul gritted his teeth. "This is where I truly break both your arms unless you finish answering questions." He lifted himself, about to apply more force. "Ready?"

"Oh, Jesus," Cyril hissed. "What the fuck else?"

"So you finally told Louis about the gun—and Art?"

"Let's just say that after his diagnosis, he was at me with all kinds of questions why I couldn't dump the coke and rise to the challenge of running Dagger."

"But when you told him, why didn't he—"

Cyril closed his eyes. "Hand me to the police? Because we share a father. He told me the deep family secret. The French Canadian *au pair* affair, as I call it."

"Oh, the philanderer father," Paul said. "I heard about that. Those damn daddy issues."

"You and your pop psychology. Turned out Louis's mother insisted that the affair—and I—never be revealed outside their family. So I never found out who my father was. My mother kept it that way in exchange for money and a nice place in the same neighbourhood. But Louis was shamed by the whole thing. He kept it a secret, but during high school he searched me out. Made sure I got good marks. Got me to U of T and introduced me at Robert Street. Groomed me into assistant producer. Now *fucking* let me go."

"But when he's diagnosed," Paul said, ignoring Cyril's plea, "he needs you to run his business, but doesn't understand what's wrong with you. So you have a big tell-all session. He tells you about your father and you tell him about Art. And Louis guesses that, with a wiped gun and some rehab, you'll be okay, and he can die with his vision for Dagger intact."

"We talked about lots of things after his diagnosis."

"What does Rachel know?"

"Only that we're related."

"More than that," Paul said. "I told her about the set-up with the Foxy Lady."

Cyril gritted his teeth.

Paul rolled off him. "For Christ's sake, all this started because of your small-man complex. Because you weren't beautiful like Art." Cyril pulled himself off the ground, wiping blood off his face, and returned to his ferocious glare. "Thanks for all the pain and suffering," Paul continued. "Honestly, I used to care. Now I just want you dead."

"Yeah, yeah, very fucking funny," Cyril said, his face streaked with anger. "You know I'm going to deny all this, don't you? I made up everything so you wouldn't fucking break my arms. Who the hell is Beecham going to believe?"

Paul looked at the gun under the buffet. "The prints are still on there."

"Maybe you smudged them over the years."

"Trust me, I haven't touched that gun," Paul said.

"Fuck you," Cyril said, scrambling to his feet. With a final fierce glower, he left.

After the front door slammed shut, Grace stepped out from the bedroom. Her face was white as porcelain, her pouty lips stuck open. She blinked rapidly as Paul grabbed the tip of the gun under the buffet with a kitchen towel and reunited the gun with its box.

"I hope you got all that," he said.

She held up her smartphone. "All on the voice memo," she said, swallowing hard. "By the way, who exactly is the Foxy Lady?"

61

For several hours after Cyril left, Paul learned it was possible to feel manic, exhausted and relieved at the same time. Once Grace went to bed, he needed to speak with someone else, and despite everything, he could only imagine it being Mark. They shared anger and awe until they had a foundation for forgiveness and a path forward for Paul.

At 9:30 a.m., Paul met with Liebowitz, still alive and practicing in his messy office. Close to eleven, feeling calmer and tolerant, Paul picked up Grace at his condo. As rain spat on the windshield, they drove east on Adelaide, then north on Yonge. During the lengthy red light at Bloor, Grace said, "Explain it to me one more time."

"Liebowitz is going to meet with a senior Crown counsel," Paul said. "Someone he really knows well and trusts. He's going to say that we have evidence that could solve a cold case. The thing is, in exchange for the evidence and testifying, he'll ask the Crown to promise not to charge me with perjury or anything else. Or, at the very minimum, not to seek jail time if they think they have to charge me. There's no guarantee he'll be successful but he seemed confident. I guess I'll know in a little while."

"And your life as a lawyer?"

"I don't know the answer to that yet. If I have to leave the profession, I'll make a new start."

As the traffic light turned green, Grace's shoulders rose and fell, and she swept her hair to one side. "My offer still stands," she said. "If you want my help and commitment as a friend, and whatever else, you have it. But—"

"Art's father. I know."

"I was going to suggest something similar from you."

Drawing closer to a woman who'd tortured him, and whom he'd briefly suspected of murder, was an improbable thought. But of all people, it was Liebowitz who said, "In my practice, Paul, I've seen many parents do crazy things for their children. But I think you like her, and as you get older, friends are harder to come by. If you were my son, I'd say, 'Give her the benefit of the doubt.' I really would. Especially if she was called the Foxy Lady."

"You'll visit Toronto more often?" Paul asked.

"Maybe I'll use *your* spare bedroom. I haven't sorted that out yet. But I know what I want. The best for Justin, for me—and for you."

Traffic crossed Davenport. Grace couldn't keep still. "You seem very nervous," Paul said.

"Aren't *you*?"

"I actually feel a bit serene."

"Where does he live?"

"Not far. On Walker Avenue. Justin's ready, right?"

"He's waiting at home on Skype, with my mother."

Paul nodded. At Walker, he turned left, slowing between parked cars on the narrow street.

"What number?" Grace asked.

"Forty-one," Paul said. He strained over the steering wheel to see. "Right up there."

He made a U-turn and parked on the south side. They dashed ten steps in the rain to the pristine red-brick Victorian. Paul rang the doorbell.

Five seconds later, the front door opened. Paul hadn't seen Art's father since the end of the trial, thirteen years before. He was stooped and his eyes were halfway into his skull. Loose skin hung from his cheeks and jaw.

"Mr. Featherstone," Paul said, reaching out a hand. Art's father hesitated then shook Paul's hand. "It's nice to see you again," he added. A stoic smile crossed Art's father's face. "And this is Grace Campbell. As I said on the phone, we have some important news for you."

"I doubt if I'm ready for this," Art's father said, "but it sounds like I have no choice. Come in out of that weather. I've put some coffee on." He returned inside the house.

Paul held out a hand for Grace to follow. She clutched his forearm and took a deep breath. "My god," she said, "I hope he'll forgive me." Then she walked in.

Acknowledgements

Great thanks goes to the following friends and family for their support of *False Guilt*: Peter Armstrong, Simone Davis, Dr. Konrad Eisenbichler, Peter Fischer, Renate Fritze, Hellen Hajikostantinou, Retired Detective Thomas Klatt, Peter Lindsay, Angie and David Littlefield, Lelia McDonald and Dr. Robert Westermann. Special thanks also to Tara Murphy, Allister Thompson, Emma Dolan and Kaleeg Hainsworth.

About the Author

Peter Fritze was a partner in a downtown Toronto law firm and general counsel of a Canadian multinational. He now writes thrillers and blogs about writing. Before *False Guilt*, he wrote *The Case for Killing*.

Visit his website/blog at http://www.peterfritze.com.

If you liked this book, please give it a review.